I0739947

HEARTSTONE

THE DROWNED TOWER

by

NICHOLAS RINTH

Cover Art, Design, and Illustrations by Fabian Rensch
www.fabianrensch.com

ISBN 978-0-9988216-0-3 (Print)
ISBN 978-0-9988216-1-0 (Ebook)

PRINTED IN THE UNITED STATES OF AMERICA
FIRST EDITION

To my father,
*the shaper of my world
and the one I've created.*

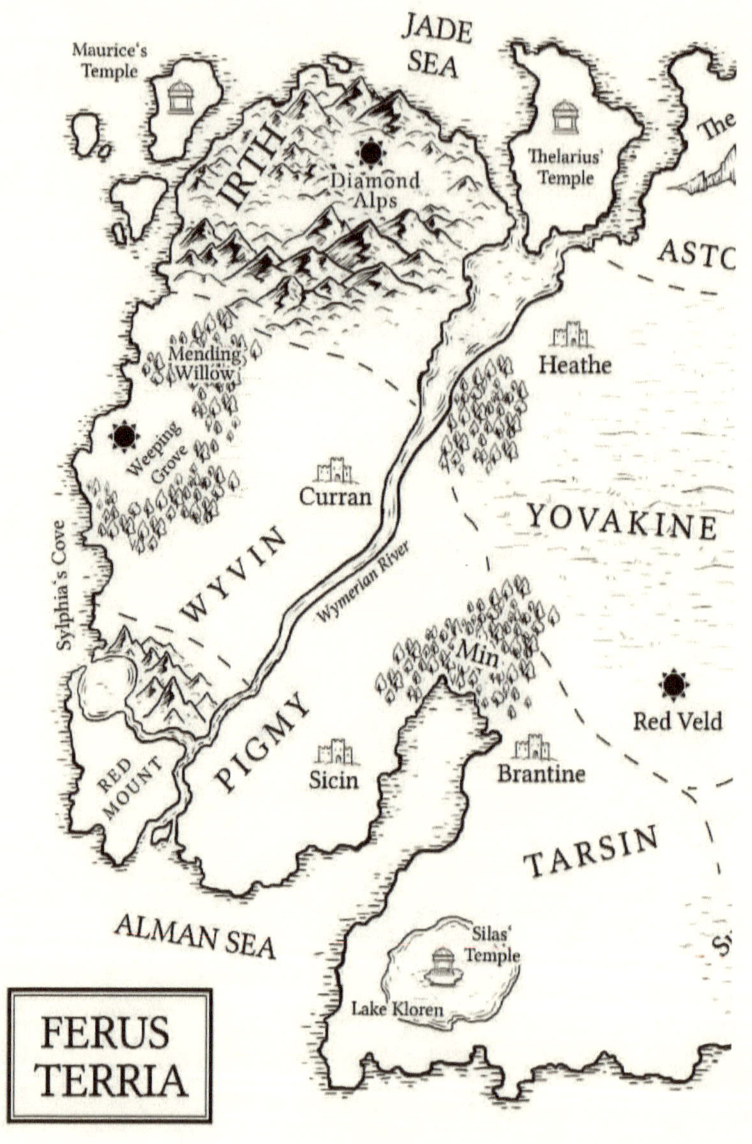

Maurice's Temple
JADE SEA
IRTH
Diamond Alps
Thelarius' Temple
The
ASTO
Mending Willow
Heathe
Weeping Grove
Curran
YOVAKINE
Sylphia's Cove
WYVIN
Wymerian River
Min
Red Veld
PIGMY
RED MOUNT
Sicin
Brantine
TARSIN
S
ALMAN SEA
Silas' Temple
Lake Kloren
FERUS TERRIA

Pit
Tor
Hermit's Hovel
PULKA RUINS
Purine
ON
Narrow Marsh
Rotten Woods
Yorn
Ice Crown Mountains
Spier
Eirinne Mountains
Tearwood
PLAINS
ERIAM
Thyme
Cheryll's Cottage
ZEXIN SEA
Drowned Tower
urbug Mire
Pernelia's Temple
N
W
O
S

May Pernelia's wings guide you,
To where the first Zenith dwell,
Enveloped in the healing light of Maurice,
So shall your soul be purged of all sorrows,
Cleansed of final weary,
And be granted passage through Silas' flame,
Ablaze with the cries of judgment,
Before open arms of divinity,
Where Thelarius awaits.

-Prayer to the Departed-

1

Magic is an existing uncertainty that dwells within the minds of men.

It was a vague description, but it was one Sylvie had been taught. The Masters of the Institute had ingrained the teaching in her mind. They described magic as powerful energy that resided between each fingertip. Its sole purpose was to be brought out, used, and honed. Not necessarily by those with the skill to wield it. But by the higher echelons of power that governed their world.

A system Sylvie had never questioned.

"P—Please don't!" a man begged.

Her hand was planted over his face, fingers prepared to crush his skull. As he pleaded on his knees for his life. He reeked of blood and fresh fear. Too pungent for her to ignore. Sylvie grimaced, coldly watching him tremble beneath her gaze. It was always like this. Though the skies were never so sympathetic. The air was heavy and humid. Clear signs of a downpour. Gray skies overhead cast a shadow above them, rumbling with flashes of thunder that served as sparse illumination against the gloom of their surroundings. Tonight, the world was painted a depressing cerise. A color even the nearby shrubbery wasn't spared from.

The bodies of the nameless man's comrades littered the ground in forced sleep or as well as. Proof of the turmoil that currently dominated Ferus Terria. Sylvie didn't know how many she had killed—if any at all—the enemies were countless. She barely recognized their faces. Only the clothes they wore and the way their screams fizzled into the background, lost to the ringing in her ears. In this battle, and in the many that preceded it, there existed only those that stepped in her way and those that died.

He was going to be part of the latter.

"The Elders send their regards," Sylvie murmured.

His eyes widened.

Above them, electricity cackled, laughing at his plight. As a current of fire coated her bare hand. Her fingers dug into his skull. Fire sizzled against raw flesh until her nails met red, and she clamped her hand shut, scraping burns along his skin. Her chest rippled, as she watched a silent scream escape him. His eyes threatened to pop from their sockets. But before he became anymore unrecognizable, she suddenly stopped, drawing away as if she'd been the one burned.

The man's blood spilled over long before his body hit the ground. Another faceless casualty. Another enemy whose single purpose was to paint the floor an even darker red. Sylvie hated the color, staring at it for too long made something bitter and sopping wet rise in her throat. A rancid taste. One she'd long gotten used to. Not enough to like it. Not yet.

Sylvie ran a hand up her cheek, accidentally smearing it with iron and dirt. Its ascent continued up her brow and through dark tresses that clung to her like a second skin. She was only vaguely aware of the warm blood that stained her form, focusing instead on the scent of her robes. A putrid stench of sweat, rust, and fear. Though she was disinclined to admit that the fear may have been her own.

There was so much blood.

The color made her stomach lurch, so she averted her gaze to the sky. Where there was no explosion of gory confetti. Only static stoicism. Despite the moist air, the skies didn't cry for the lives of those lost below. No. The heavens remained silent in their unloving ways, watching over them with judging eyes that soon gave way to light.

Dark clouds parted around them, shedding grace over her face and the aftermath of the battle. It took all of her will to tear her eyes away from its glow and focus back on the world around her. Where her comrades scrambled about. Their robes billowed behind them as they scurried off to wherever it was they so hurriedly needed to be. Some met with their partners, others assisted in the cleanup of the area. They gathered bodies and prepared to ship them off to some unknown location she wasn't permitted to know. While more than a few had already taken it upon themselves to search for any injured—a ruse, of course—a necessary excuse to loot bodies. And amidst the scattering people and idle chatter, Sylvie could hear the smug ramblings of a few battle hungry men loudly boasting about their skills.

She sighed. The action as exaggerated as their stories.

From the corner of her eye, Sylvie found a small herd of local Snuff. They were small rodents with light brown coats and strong hind legs that could push them ten feet above ground. They had floppy ears that doubled as gliders, which they used to float over low hanging branches.

Snuff were notorious for making themselves scarce, but today, they were poking their noses into a damaged cart that had been forgotten amidst the chaos.

"Hey, Sylvie!" a familiar voice rang out, cutting through the noise. She turned to see messy platinum blond hair and gangling limbs bounding up to her. Blue eyes that were common among Healers stared unwaveringly in her direction.

"Reed," she greeted with a nod. As he skidded to a halt.

"Just look at them all!" Reed cried, looking around in distaste. "I heard they had to send two dozen pairs out just to deal with… all of this. I didn't even know we had that many people on the roster."

"I'm glad they did," Sylvie said, her eyebrows scrunching in displeasure when she saw the blood staining her boot. It was dark and barely noticeable. But it bothered her. Much more than it should have. "The reinforcements were welcome."

"Oh? It's rare to hear you say that."

"These weren't normal circumstances. This wasn't some ragtag mercenary band. They were trained practitioners. Fleeing the north most likely."

Reed's eyes widened.

"They're *all* deserters?" Reed asked, stunned. "This is getting out of hand! The Zenith Council needs to set aside their differences and choose a new leader already. Before more decide to take advantage of their… their…"

"Lack of concern?" Sylvie supplied. "Utter indifference for the rest of the world?"

Reed nodded dramatically. "This is the twelfth time we've been sent out this month! That's two times more than the last two years. Years, Syl! They're lucky the east is so closed off or we would've caved in a long time ago. We house more children than the other branches or does the Zenith Council not understand that?"

Sylvie shrugged. "It's not the Council's blood being spilt. As long as they have their drama and their servants, then they're perfectly content to ignore the rest of us. After all, how do our petty problems compare to those in the Diamond Alps?"

Reed grimaced, his eyes flickering around him in discomfort. This conversation never led anywhere. No matter who he spoke about it to.

"Are you done here?" he asked instead, wanting to change the subject.

Sylvie ignored his question as something else caught her attention. Singing. Soft and sweet. A low hum that danced upon her skin. But the voice sounded drowned. She couldn't make out the words. Sylvie turned, trying to find the source.

"Do you hear that?" she asked.

"Hear what?"

Sylvie saw a flash of light against the gloom. Bright and momentary. A stark contrast against the dimness of their surroundings. With deft feet, she made her way around the blood soaked terrain. Sylvie passed a man who'd been impaled by his own dagger, his mouth opened wide in a silent scream. Another whose entire bottom half sat a distance away from his top. She avoided looking at them, certain their lifeless faces would haunt her dreams. How such brutality happened on the battlefield was a truth better left unsaid.

She finally stopped before a man with dull eyes, half open in disturbed slumber. He'd stopped breathing some time ago, if his ashen skin and blue lips were any indication. She took his satchel and inspected his meager belongings, but when she came up with nothing, she moved on to his body. His flesh chilled her hands, and she hesitated for all of a moment before shoving her feelings aside. His hand was closed over something, as if he were still trying to keep it with him even in death. Sylvie squinted when she saw another flash from the gap between his fingers.

The unintelligible melody rang stronger in her ears. A soft call. A gentle pull. In desperate want of her attention.

And here she was, actually offering it.

Sylvie pried the man's fingers open, claiming her prize. A cheap piece of string with a small stone as its pendant. Despite half of it being coated in blood, it still shone brightly. The stone was smooth and pellucid, pulsing in her hands. Almost as if it were responding to her heat. Perhaps it was a rare gem of sorts? Or maybe even some worthless marble. Whatever it was, the inside was dark and cloudy like trapped mist. Black mist. It reminded her of a crystal ball. And as Sylvie watched her reflection stare curiously back at her, an alluring voice urged her closer.

"Don't steal from the dead," Reed's soft voice snapped her from her stupor.

The music suddenly stopped and the voice reaching out to her faded into silence. Sylvie saw Reed's reflection on the stone. He stood behind her with his arms crossed and a displeased frown marring his lips. The blackness inside the stone disappeared. Replaced by air.

Her eyes hardened.

Did I imagine it? she wondered.

"You'll be cursed," Reed warned.

She scoffed and closed her fingers over the necklace, hiding it from view. "These are post-battle spoils."

"Stop making it sound pretty. It's looting the dead." He averted his gaze from the man's body in disgust, pinching the bridge of his nose. "Are you done? I don't want to stay here. The stench of blood is making me nauseous."

"I'm done," she finished with a nod. Sylvie watched from the corner of her eye as Reed blanched at the sight of all the carnage, his hands visibly trembling in terror. "I told you to wait for me to call you."

"Then I wouldn't be doing my job," Reed said shakily. "They don't pay me to sit around all day."

"They don't pay you."

He shrugged, taking a deep breath to gather his composure. "They might start. You never know."

"Reed." She stared pointedly at him. "Even I'm not paid, and I do all the dirty work."

"Well, that's because you never ask for compensation. If you asked properly then they might start to see reason."

"Yes," Sylvie said sardonically. "I'll be sure to bring it up when the Council Elders announce that they give a damn about the sorry state of our pockets."

Reed frowned.

He pulled out an old, intricately designed grimoire. The size of a large bird. Silver decorated the cover and more lined the pages. Sylvie had no idea where Reed kept it, since his robes were more form fitting than others, but she knew better than to ask the tricks of a practitioner's trade. Reed gestured for her to stand before him, while he continued to run his mouth about trivial matters. It was one of his more noticeable tics.

"Don't even get me started on those Elders!" Reed exclaimed. "Look at all these bodies! Just because they have problems in the north doesn't mean they can just—"

"That's enough, Reed," a voice admonished.

Two pairs of eyes snapped toward the authoritative figure of

Columbus Cephas. His body structure and facial features were an older version of Reed's own. Except his posture was far more poised, his long hair more controlled from where it sat in a neat ponytail behind his neck. A black streak of blood stained the front of his robes. An indication that he'd participated in the slaughter mere minutes ago.

"Master Cephas." Sylvie bowed her head in greeting. "I'm sorry for taking so long."

"Fret not, child," Columbus said. His guttural voice made him seem older than his years. He took a moment to eye her dirty appearance and minor injuries, before shooting Reed a disapproving frown. "I'm afraid my son is also to blame. He's always been the kind to run his mouth when there's work to be done."

Reed's ears burned. "I was just about to heal her!"

Columbus lifted a skeptical brow, tilting his head to indicate the still closed grimoire in Reed's hands. Reed furiously opened the book and hastily went through the delicate pages, searching for the magical incantations that would heal his partner's injuries.

His father didn't wait for him to find them.

"Come along now, we must make haste," Columbus said suddenly, already turning on his heel and briskly heading back in the direction of the Drowned Tower. The other practitioners respectfully bowed their heads as he passed. "There is much to do."

"Master Cephas! Wait!" Sylvie jogged to catch up with him, leaving Reed behind to frantically search his grimoire. "What's going on?"

"A representative of the Zenith Council is on his way to the Tower, child. It may very well be an Elder. Prepare yourself for a Choosing."

Sylvie lurched to a stop.

Her eyes widened with shock, as Columbus continued on his merry way—unaware of her sudden halt. Sylvie clenched her fists, the necklace digging uncomfortably into her skin as if reaffirming her of its presence.

Sylvie had no intention of propositioning herself as a candidate for a Choosing. Why the Masters of the Institute insisted on forcing her away from the east, she would never understand. She was fine where she was. Why couldn't they understand that?

A heavy hand fell on her shoulder, releasing her from her inner turmoil. The soft blue glow it emitted forced her tense muscles to relax.

"You okay?" Reed asked, concerned. "Relax, Syl. Breathe. In and out."

Sylvie closed her eyes and followed his words. She matched her erratic breathing with his steady exhales, slowly returning to herself. She could feel the warmth of his hand spread throughout her body. His magic forced her to unwind, soothing her in a way nothing else could.

"I'm fine," she paused, then added, "but thank you."

"That's what partners are for." Reed grinned. "Someone has to remind all you brawny meatheads to breathe every once in a while. Healers, contrary to popular belief, are great both on the battlefield and off of it."

"You get queasy at the sight of ants, Reed."

"Oh, that was low. I'm not completely useless!" he defended, showing her the open book in his hands and looking immensely pleased with himself. Its pages were filled with numbers and symbols arranged in a complex code that only he seemed to understand. He had horrid penmanship. Hasty scrawls on paper. His writing was blotched in more areas than she could count. There was even an entire paragraph of crossed out words so bunched together that they might as well have been another stain. How he understood that mess, Sylvie didn't know.

All she saw was old paper.

"See?" Reed went on, holding the grimoire like a priceless jewel worthy of song. "Aren't you glad you have me?"

"Don't get cocky." Sylvie smiled, as his own fell from his lips. "Let's head home."

2

Home was a congregation of their kind hailed as, The Practitioners Institute of Magic: Eastern Branch, or colloquially referred to as "the Drowned Tower." It stood as the center of all things magical in the eastern side of Ferus Terria, hence its more formal calling. Home to a countless number of people of all ages, its inhabitants had their every need catered to and every possible expense paid. All in exchange for their service, should it be requested. Though not everyone was allowed within the Drowned Tower's mighty walls. Only those of special blood were permitted within. Those that could harness and bring forth magic. No matter how weak. It was a structure birthed for the sole purpose of honing skills and teaching control over the limitless power sleeping beneath each and every one of its residents. Unauthorized use of those powers were strictly forbidden outside of the Drowned Tower's dismal halls.

The Nebbin, those without magic, made their living on the nearby island of Eriam. Close enough to be given protection at a moment's notice, but far enough so that the citizens wouldn't be bothered by the happenings within.

The Drowned Tower was a triangular edifice that sat in the middle of the Zexin Sea. A massive structure that remained mostly submerged in the sea's salty waters. Lofty towers served as the triangle's points. Footbridges on each of the tower's floors connected these points and made it whole, while high rise walls enclosed it in a nearly impenetrable fortress. A large dome placed just above completely blocked out all traces of sunlight and isolated those within from the outside world.

It was a magically fortified box.

Above the dome stood a statue of the apotheosis, Pernelia Merve, renowned Amorph, and esteemed member of the first Zenith Council. But perhaps what she was most known for was being the wife of Thelarius Merve. The abolisher of slavery.

The man responsible for assembling the First Council and for reforming the Institute. Gifted with the strength of magic in his veins, he was said to have been able to split the heavens themselves with a flick of his wrist. History's first recorded Elementalist. His name was glorified across Ferus Terria, but his worshippers originated from the north. Where it wasn't unusual to find men and women praying before wooden idols carved in his liking.

Pernelia's statue glinted over the waters, shining with untarnished beauty. One arm curved toward the sky, where a motionless falcon perched. Her face was crooked downward, observing all that walked the desolate stretch of stone bridge that led to the Drowned Tower's sole entrance. It was a formidable distance. Long worn from continuous years of neglect. It made land dwellers tremble and gave them a front row view of the Sea's restless waters. At the end of it, stood a spiked iron gate that could be opened and shut in an instant. Beyond the gate was a small enchanted door which served as the pathway to a seemingly endless stairwell that led underwater, and to the top floor of the lower right tower. Not many frequented the top floor of this particular tower. It was dark and cold. With unexplored storerooms mostly filled with nothing but dust.

The floors below were warmer. The sounds of idle chatter and even laughter echoed through the halls, breathing life into the Drowned Tower—and the Zexin abyss.

It was within this tower that practitioners studied, honing their skills to near perfection. Sylvie was no exception. She slouched comfortably in her seat inside Research Archive nineteen. Dozens of bookshelves lined the walls around her, housing books about magic and old lore. Books about herbs, music, philosophy, remembered history, and forgotten spells. Some were written in tongues so ancient that even the older generations couldn't speak them.

A few shelves doubled as dividers, separating the room into three sections. The middle featured its own fireplace, only lit when someone came to read. A rare occurrence. The nineteenth archive was typically empty. Thus, Sylvie had claimed the area as her solitary dwelling. Her happy place. Where she found solace in the stillness of her surroundings and in the silence of undisturbed pages. Here, she forgot all about the torpid passage of time.

So, when Sylvie heard the noisy pitter patter of feet, her head snapped toward the door. Her face morphed into a mighty scowl that would have sent lesser men quivering away with their tails between their legs. The footfalls were followed by a shrill voice that was distinctly familiar to her. A moment later, and she was able to attach it to a face. Master Zelpha Miriam. The aging woman had never been her mentor, but Sylvie had heard enough horror stories and loud reproaches to pick her voice out from the most boisterous of crowds.

"Magic," Miriam began, "a formless object of the past, a controlled commodity of the present, an unseen force driving the future. In these halls, you will be presented with the opportunity to live with others like you. To learn from those that have already experienced your fears. Should their knowledge fall under your jurisdiction of concern, I advise you to take the time to learn from them."

Sylvie shuddered with each word that left Miriam's lips. She didn't know if the walls were just absurdly thin or if her voice was just that utterly cringe worthy, but Sylvie could hear each word as clearly as if they'd been standing side by side. This was a speech she'd heard over a dozen times. The same one each Master gave every batch of newcomers. It happened four times a year. At the same place. At the same time. Sylvie had long tired of this particular pitch.

Miriam clapped twice, gathering the attention of the tenderfoots. "As you all should know, the Drowned Tower is famous for the talented Amorphs that dominate its halls. Three towers make up the Eastern Branch. The residential tower is to your left. While the Assembly's Tower is above. You'll find your Masters there along with various shops which you'll have an adequate amount of time to explore after the tour."

Sylvie pinched the bridge of her nose and let her head fall against the table with a loud thud. She tried to ignore Miriam's raspy voice and focus on something else. But her high pitched screeches completely shattered any and all buds of thought.

"The tower we are in now is purely for education," Miriam went on. "Barring the topmost level, the tower has eleven floors with three research libraries per floor. Floors one through six are for Amorphs. The seventh is for both Conjurers and Elementalists. While the rest are for Healers," a stiff pause, "you may only enter the libraries that correspond to your specialty. Failure to abide will earn you a trip to the Iniquities Chamber."

Sylvie heard the soft, immature voice of a young boy. Proof that the walls of the Tower really were just incredibly thin.

"But Master Miriam," the boy said, confused, "I thought all the Conjurers and Elementalists were in the northern and southern branches."

"We have one or two of our own," Miriam's voice invaded her ears once more. But this time it was accompanied by a flurry of incomprehensible babble.

The newbies had broken out in gossip.

Sylvie groaned. "You're ruining my happy place."

"Quiet!" Miriam yelled, and Sylvie was sorely tempted to throw something at the door just to let them know that they were being a bother. "We'll be visiting the testing facilities next. Don't lag behind."

Miriam's voice was drowned out by more footfalls.

Sylvie sighed in relief. It was short lived, however, as another voice shattered the terse silence.

"Is the banshee gone?"

Sylvie's ears perked up at the familiar tone. She carefully looked around the library, then toward the door. Only to find no one. Had she imagined it? No. She wasn't that tired.

"Up here."

Sylvie's eyes trailed upward, scanning the ceiling. Seated atop a bookshelf was a forest green toad staring at her with large beady eyes. A sense of panic washed over her. Her heart pounded in its cage. Sylvie inched away from the frog until her back came into contact with another shelf. One of the books stuck out and dug uncomfortably into her spine, but she didn't dare move. The toad just continued to sit there. It stared at her with its unnaturally large irises. The abysmal eyes of Amorph's were the only things that differentiated them from the animals they mimicked. But that stark difference didn't make frogs any less terrifying. Neither did the fact that she knew just who this particular Amorph was.

The frog croaked. A translucent bubble rose from its throat. Sylvie yelped at the sight.

"Myrrh! Stop! Turn back!"

She tried to back away in a sorry attempt to blend with the books behind her. She would've gladly suffered the company of Miriam than be around such a revolting creature.

"This isn't funny!" she yelled.

Sylvie shrieked when the amphibian leapt high into the air. Its limbs stretched outward, color shifting, as its tiny extremities transformed into much larger hands and feet. Black beady eyes now peered at her from the face of a girl with short brown hair and pale skin. Myrrh straightened, barely reaching Sylvie's shoulder. Her robes pooled around her feet, swallowing her tiny body whole. She was much too childish for her age. In both personality and appearance.

"Sorry," Myrrh said in a completely unrepentant tone. "I didn't know you were still afraid of frogs."

Her large grin fooled no one.

Sylvie took a deep breath, gathering her wits. She peeled herself away from the books behind her, trying to salvage what was left of her dignity.

"Don't lie to my face," she said.

Myrrh adjusted the amber tinted glasses on her nose. Hiding, but not completely masking the pitch black eyes that all Amorphs shared. Unlike the soft blue orbs of Healers, their eyes were an endless abyss. A dark hole that swallowed those that caught their attention. Big and piercing. They looked like they'd pop out of her head and shift into an entirely separate being.

"This is what I get after coming all the way up to the seventh floor?" Myrrh crossed her arms, affronted. "Accusations thrown in my face?"

"Would you rather I say them behind your back?"

"Don't make me turn into a frog again."

Sylvie's eyes widened. She instinctively took a step back, holding her hands up in surrender. "Don't be rash now."

"That's what I thought." Myrrh pinned her with a stare that reminded Sylvie of slimy skin, long tongues, and croaking. "You haven't left this room for the past three days. Three days, Syl! What have you been studying?"

Sylvie's eyebrows shot up, unaware that she'd been cooped up for so long. "History, mostly. I'm brushing up on northern politics, too. Master Cephas told me to prepare for a Choosing."

Myrrh rolled her eyes and sighed as if tragedy had just occurred. In her mind, it did. "Will there even be one? For all we know an Elder just wanted to check in and say hello. You know, travel the world before he kicks the bucket?"

Sylvie couldn't argue with that. Though she had yet to see the Elder for herself, the title didn't suggest youth.

"Besides," Myrrh went on, "why would Master Cephas want you of all people to be chosen? You'll be taken to the north! You can't go there! You're his primary apprentice, or has he forgotten about that? And hasn't he heard about the power struggle going on in the Alps? Going there isn't like throwing you to the wolves, it *is* throwing you to the wolves!"

"I'm sure he hasn't heard a thing," Sylvie said sardonically. "He's only one of the figureheads of the solitary Eastern Branch. What would he know of the outside world?"

Myrrh scoffed. "Obviously nothing if he thinks you have a chance at being chosen. Everyone already knows who's going to win. Would you like a hint? It isn't you, and his daddy's on the Zenith Council. Oh, wait… that's two hints!"

"Thank you for the vote of confidence." Sylvie glared at the triumphant grin Myrrh wore. "The never-ending support of a friend is truly magnif—"

"Jacques Dace is an Elementalist with connections," Myrrh interrupted, "while you, my dear, Sylvie Sirx, are a lowly Conjurer. Last I remembered, Conjurers had an affinity for only one element. How does that compare to the skills of an Elementalist?"

"Well, when you put it that way you make us Conjurers sound second-rate. At least we fully master ours. Besides, Elementalists are a dying breed. Sooner or later, Conjurers will be the ones to take charge."

"Which makes Jack all the more valuable."

"I do have other skills, Myrrh," Sylvie defended. "I know Embrocology."

"Yes, because making gels and salves parallels the skills of an Elementalist. They can play with fire, freeze things, and do all kinds of wicked stuff! While you can only play with fire." Myrrh finished with a dramatic roll of her eyes and the downward point of a thumb. "Besides, I've heard that some Elementalists actually have the ability to resist magic. Isn't that neat?"

"That's a myth, Myrrh."

"See?" she exclaimed. "They even have myths surrounding them!"

"Have I told you how much I hated you recently?"

"It's been a while."

"What are you doing here, Myrrh?"

Myrrh fiddled with a thin wire she always kept tied around her wrist. It was an old habit. One she did when she was feeling sheepish. "I was on my way topside to grab myself some dinner and realized I had no company."

In the Drowned Tower, every meal was dinner. With no natural light, it was too dark for anyone to call their 8 A.M. meal: breakfast. The lack of light kept everyone on hectic schedules and made most eastern practitioners unable to function properly in the sun kissed lands of Ferus Terria. Not that they needed to. It was rare for a practitioner to permanently leave the Tower. Even rarer for practitioners older than a few years to be sent away. They were raised to adapt to the gloomy environment.

"I do hope you find somebody," Sylvie said, turning back to the pile of books she'd abandoned on the table.

"Come on, Syl!" Myrrh whined, grabbing her by the elbow and forcefully pulling her along. In no time at all, the Amorph dragged her out the door and through the halls lit by infrequent torches placed meters away from each other. They provided just enough light for Sylvie to see the wispy outlines of her peers. But it was a dimness her eyes had long accustomed to.

"Wait, Myrrh!" Sylvie struggled, but Myrrh only tightened her bear-like grip. "Let go!"

"You need fresh air," Myrrh insisted, "and yes, I said fresh. They just purified it."

By the time they made it to the mess hall, Sylvie's voice was hoarse and sweat ran down her brow. She squinted when the artificial brightness of dozens of oil lamps assaulted her sensitive vision. The mess hall was always too bright. Amorphs in the form of birds flew above them, holding large baskets filled with food. As they delivered them to those seated below. The sounds of clinking utensils, flapping wings, and incomprehensible prattle echoed cheerfully throughout the room.

They navigated their way through the throng of people. A colorful bird narrowly missed Sylvie's head. As they found a small table in a shady corner of the room with a magically fortified window that provided a limited view of the clear water and various walkways.

The waters beyond were dark. Small blue crystals floated about, providing faint light in what should've been pitch darkness. Sylvie could just barely make out the stone wall that closed them in. She was, however, able to see a school of fish swim by. They had glowing crystals tied around their fins and bodies.

A class, Sylvie realized, noting how poor and small some of the transformations were. Those with skill would go on to have private mentors, while the rest were free to do what they wished. So long as they abided by the rules of the Tower.

Myrrh rang a bell attached to the base of a small bird stand on the corner of their table. A bulky, jet-black raven immediately swooped down, beating its long wings, and drafting a strong gust of wind that tousled their hair. The raven perched its portly body on the stand, completely overwhelming it with its talons. The Amorph's dark eyes fixed them with an intimidating stare.

"What'll it be?" a distinctly male voice asked.

"Oh." Myrrh scowled at the bird. "It's you."

"That's my line," he squawked. "Don't I see enough of your gag worthy face? Now you're invading my workplace, too?"

"What? I can't eat now?" Myrrh banged her clenched fist on the table in anger. The raven wasn't impressed.

"Not while I'm here."

"I'll have the usual," Myrrh bit out with a sneer.

"I've never taken your order before, genius."

"Sausages, eggs, and bread."

"Lovely," he said snippily, before turning to Sylvie and in a more polite manner, asked, "What will you be having today?"

"Baked blitz with Roco sauce," said Sylvie. She reached out and brushed her fingertips along the fluffy heckles that stood from his puffed chest. He ruffled his wings obediently, letting her touch him until she pulled away.

"Careful," Myrrh warned. "He'll bite your fingers off."

"Please stop involving me in your sick fantasies." He raised his wings and darted back into the air, purposely hitting Myrrh's temple in his ascent.

Myrrh gritted her teeth, but otherwise ignored his jibe. "That was Tiv. Tiv Grovegg. And before you ask, yes… *that* Tiv. We're both under Master Celaris right now. I wish I'd chosen a different mentor this year. I didn't think his primary apprentice would be so insufferable."

Sylvie followed Tiv with her eyes, all the way until he disappeared behind a tunnel in the wall where dozens of other birds flew in and out of. She spotted a small red bird struggling to hold onto a basket of food. All the others seemed too busy to help. She didn't know why the Amorph didn't think to turn into something bigger. Preferably something with larger talons and more raw muscle. Was it some kind of punishment?

She turned back to her dinner companion, realizing that she was still waiting for a response. "You're past the age of mentors and tutors, Myrrh. Life's too short to spend it aggravated. But… I am curious. What exactly did you do to him?"

"Nothing!" Myrrh said too loudly to be believable.

Before Sylvie could say otherwise, Tiv swooped down with a pleasant smelling basket in his talons. He hastily dropped it on the stretch of table between them, before flying off again to help that feeble red bird she saw struggling just a moment ago. Myrrh was quick to claim her dish. Sylvie, on the other hand, took her time peering inside the basket and letting the tantalizing aroma of caffeine cloud her senses. Before she dipped her spoon in a bowl filled with amber syrup, giving herself up to the sweet taste of Roco sauce.

"Look," Myrrh said around a mouthful of sausage. She tilted her head to the doors, and Sylvie couldn't help but notice that the hall had gone completely silent. The others in the room sat frozen in place, their plates abandoned. The birds that had been flying about were unmoving, perched quietly on tables and chairs. Time had stilled. Or it might as well have.

When Sylvie saw the two figures speaking in hushed tones by the hall's doors, she understood why. A badly aging man with a short boxed beard and deep blue eyes stood there. They were kind and crinkled in mirth, as he smiled patiently at the Drowned Tower's resident Elementalist—Jacques Dace.

The Elder, Sylvie guessed.

His towering height and peach-toned skin made him stand out from the ghostly pallor of the Tower's denizens. He completely dwarfed Jack's pale and spindly self. But Jack's height deficiency did nothing to put him off. As he stood with his chin high and his feet spread as wide as his shoulders. An impudent smirk crooked his lips. Confidence personified.

They spoke for a moment longer, before the Elder was called away by one of his servants. Or maybe it was his apprentice? Either way, he left with the boy. With his smile permanently carved into his face, as if he held a secret that only he knew. Perhaps he did. Sylvie wouldn't put it past him. Practitioners from the north weren't known for their guileless natures.

Sylvie hated lies.

Another reason not to participate in the upcoming Choosing. The Diamond Alps was a locus for the ambitious and the greedy. It was an unspoken truth that everyone kept at least two faces there. Sylvie had no intention of leaving the comfort of her home to participate in their intricate games. Where one was forced to assume the role of player or pawn. Most were both. But never anything else.

At that moment, Jack turned. His head swiveled before the rest of his body. Blood red eyes unintentionally met her orange ones in a splash of color only produced by the setting sun.

Jack raised an eyebrow, and Sylvie immediately dropped her gaze back to her plate, chewing her lip uncomfortably. There was something unsettling about being the only one caught and acknowledged as staring. Even though the rest of the room had been as well.

"I told you he'd be chosen," Myrrh suddenly said. As she bit crudely into her bread. "He has that Elder wrapped around his little finger."

Sylvie shrugged. If Jack had already been singled out then it was better for her. She'd even congratulate him on his way out.

"There you are!" a familiar voice exclaimed.

Sylvie turned once more to find Master Cephas entering the hall with an exasperated look in his eyes. He rushed over and sent Myrrh a quizzical glance that she bowed her head at.

"I've been searching everywhere for you, child," Columbus said. "Why aren't you in the study? The Elder is already here. He arrived some time ago. I'll arrange a meeting for you tomorrow. He's asked to see you, you know? Yet here you are idling about when there isn't any time left to waste."

"I was dragged here," Sylvie said.

"This is no time for your excuses, child!" Columbus gestured for her to stand. A silent order that she instinctively obeyed. "You must study! Brush up on your history. Have you practiced?" He didn't give her a chance to answer. His mind was already set on what had to be done. "I shall have food sent up later, but for now you must come back to the study. Hurry now, child! The archives await!"

Columbus walked out, fully expecting her to follow.

The other occupants of the hall turned to Sylvie, who tried to ignore their piercing stares and loud whispers. It was impossible though. Columbus' thundering footsteps always left uncomfortable silence in their wake.

Why bother whispering when your voices are still loud enough to hear? she thought in disdain.

"I'll see you tomorrow, then?" Myrrh turned, but Sylvie was already gone.

Oblivious to the pair of red eyes that followed her.

3

In Research Archive nineteen, Sylvie sat by the hearth. As she quietly read through a sappy ballad. Stacks of books both old and new lay around her, waiting to be opened. A bowlful of gruel sat in an abandoned corner, just outside her fortress of paper.

Sylvie was spent. Her mind was foggy, her movements sluggish. Despite this, she also felt strangely alert. As if her senses had become hypersensitive to every sound. To every flickering shadow. She even heard the furtive romance between two juvenile practitioners in the next room. Judging from the pitch of their voices, they were young. Perhaps too young. Why they were sneaking about though was beyond her.

Relationships weren't forbidden. Though they weren't encouraged either. Especially not at their ages. Their breathy rasps penetrated the thin walls, making it difficult to focus.

She pinched the bridge of her nose, thoroughly annoyed.

Sylvie heard the door creak open, the rustle of clothing, a tired exhale, and the soft sound of lethargic steps coming closer. Her nose scrunched up as it was assaulted by the scent of burning wood, caffeine, and smoke. So much smoke.

Pursing her lips and preparing a half-hearted tirade for the intruder, she looked up, only to find the slender physique of a woman—or perhaps it was a man? It was too dark to tell. The darkness concealed faces and made the scrawny androgynous. But in its cover, she saw a pale neck and the flash of frightening eyes.

Jack Dace stepped from the shadows.

The darkness moved aside as if making way for him. She was

met with shaggy black hair, framing red eyes that popped out of a colorless face. Pale skin was common in the Drowned Tower, but Jack's was especially so. His skin was smothered in paste and ash. The fire cast an eerie glow over his figure, allowing Sylvie a bare peek at blue veins protruding from his temple. Jack looked like a walking corpse. His eye bags did nothing to help his case.

Sylvie had mistaken Jack for a girl once. His lanky limbs and slender build could've fooled anyone, especially since his figure was always hidden under flowing robes—not that she'd ever tell him that.

She watched as he inspected the mess of books around her with the eyes of someone who never missed much and recalled everything. Sylvie couldn't say if all Elementalists shared that peculiar, all-knowing gaze or if Jack was a special case. Because just as she was the only Conjurer in the Tower, Jacques Dace was the only Elementalist. So, she'd never had room to compare.

Three archives and the entire seventh floor of the research tower all to themselves. If special treatment ever existed, that was it. Why Jack was sent to the Eastern Branch though, Sylvie neither knew, nor cared to. Better private training, perhaps? That was common among his class. He was a blue-blood to the core.

Despite being the only pair permitted on the seventh floor, they only spoke occasionally. Not because they despised or disregarded each other, but because it was rare for Jack to drop by her self-proclaimed safe haven. He usually holed himself up in the other two archives or another place altogether. Where that was, again, Sylvie didn't know. They were acquaintances at best.

Nothing more, everything less.

So, Sylvie thought, *what's he doing here?*

"It's you," said Jack. His voice was a lazy drawl. Quiet, but not gentle.

"Were you expecting someone else?"

"No." Short and to the point. "Is Orion's Proposal here?"

She blinked blankly up at him for one long moment, not fully registering the question. Sylvie's mind half-heartedly ran, as she wondered why the title sounded so familiar to her ears. It must have been a book. *Of course it is,* she berated. *What else would it be?*

Jack cleared his throat, snapping her from her stupor. Sylvie instinctively pointed at the empty space on the shelf behind him.

"I believe Master Cephas took it, along with his other works, a few hours ago."

"Where is he?"

"Asleep most likely," she said, scowling at the thought.

Jack lifted an eyebrow at her sudden irritation. "Then what are you still doing here?" he asked. Sighing, when Sylvie mimed his expression, before gesturing to the books around her. "Well, yes, I can see that you're studying."

"Then why are you asking?"

"I meant, why?" Jack clarified, exasperated. "Why are you studying? What's the point? Is it really that interesting?"

"That's something you should be asking Master Cephas. He seems to love studying just as much as he loves subjecting me to long and sleepless nights filled with it."

"You don't have to study." Jack gave her a self-assured smirk that rubbed her in all the wrong ways. Sylvie hated that smirk. Confident and full of mischief. It belonged leagues below the Zexin Sea where beasts birthed from tales as old as time dwelled. The kind used to terrify children and the superstitious.

"Tell that to Master Cephas."

"I'm saying it to you. Just sit back and relax. I'm going to be the one that pompous windbag chooses."

Sylvie scoffed at his impertinence. His mouth had gotten him yelled at for hours by the Masters, but his cheek seemed to know no bounds. That rakish grin he wore didn't help his case.

"If you must know, this is actually personal research," she told him. Her words were laced with the kind of petty animosity one could only have for a stranger. "While I do *adore* Master Cephas and whatever knowledge he may have to impart, my life is my own to run. And I've decided not to get involved in the power struggles of the north. But by all means feel free to go up there and suffer an early death."

Jack swiftly shrugged off her harsh words with all the ease of someone who'd been doing it his entire life.

"What are you researching then?"

Her eyebrows scrunched up at the question. "Why?"

"Humor me," Jack said aloofly. The skeptical look didn't leave Sylvie's face, but nevertheless, she raised the book for him to see. He read the title aloud, *"The Ballad of Dulcet Grays."*

Sylvie blinked owlishly. She looked down at the faded cover. The words were two centimeters big. Blotchy and thick. Nigh unreadable. His sight was something else.

"Poetry, huh?" he commented offhandedly. "I thought you despised poetry."

"How did you know?" she asked, then as an afterthought, "I don't despise it."

He gave her that smirk again. The one from Ferus Terria's deepest hellhole. "I remember that old bag Cephas yelling once because you didn't want to read Lady Eupho's famous poem, *'Tender Billows,'* which if I recall has only four lines."

Sylvie shot him a scathing glance.

Not because he'd remembered something so pointless or because of his unintentional reminder of the Tower's horribly thin walls, but because of his open disrespect. She'd always known his mouth had no filter, but being subject to it was another thing entirely.

"Master Cephas isn't that old," she defended.

"Have you seen his wrinkles?" he asked seriously. His voice dead of all inflection. "You could shelve books on them."

Sylvie's eyes widened and despite herself, she laughed. It was lower and rustier than she remembered, startled out of her. She tried stifling it with a hand. To no avail. Jack seemed to take her mirth as an invitation because he joined her on the floor. His shadow interloped with the overburdened shelves to form an oversized monster with straight lines for a body and half a circle for a head.

A toothy grin adorned Jack's face. As he curiously examined the various books scattered about. He picked each one up and read their titles aloud.

"*Minerals of the South, One-Thousand Gems with Illustrations, Loric Crystals, Slavery and Mining, Zexin Tales and Myths.*" Jack flipped carelessly through the pages of a particularly aged one. Its title was so faded, even he couldn't read it. The paper was yellow and thick with years. Soon, it would no longer be readable.

"Are you interested in that?" Sylvie asked.

Jack only dropped it back with the rest, not even gracing her with a response. Though from the way his eyes lingered on its spine, she already knew the answer.

"What's all of this for?" he asked.

"I told you, personal research."

"And here I am, fully willing to hear you out. Perhaps even offer my help. Are you really not going to take this chance?"

"Are you really this bored?"

"It wouldn't hurt to tell me…" Jack's eyes lit up with barely restrained curiosity. "Or would it?"

"No, it wouldn't. Well, okay… maybe. I'm not entirely sure."

"Eloquent, aren't you?"

"Oh, get out already."

"Let me help you figure out—whatever it is first."

Sylvie mulled over his words. *I suppose it wouldn't hurt,* she thought. *I'm not looking into anything prohibited.*

As if anyone would keep forbidden tomes in public archives anyway. Those were usually kept under lock and key in some far-away vault only select Masters of the Drowned Tower knew the location of. Besides, Jack was known for locking himself up in the archives for weeks on end. He might know something she didn't. Might see something she'd missed.

And if he isn't interested, then the sooner he'll leave me be.

Sylvie reached into her robes and exposed the necklace she'd impenitently taken from the clutches of the dead. Quiet and dull. It didn't look anything like the spectacular stone she'd been so enamored with when she found it. But it did seem much more expensive now, despite its lackluster appearance. Sylvie had exchanged the cheap string for a thin silver chain and scrubbed it free of all traces of blood. It made a nice bobble, if nothing else.

She raised the pendant for him to see. She wanted to search his eyes for any hints of recognition, but she paused when the orb shone in the darkness, producing a brighter light than the curling fire could ever hope to. Sylvie searched it almost desperately. But she still couldn't find the dark haze that had made her so curious in the first place. Had she imagined it? Was it simply a trick of her mind? A hallucination of the battlefield?

"That's it?" Jack slumped, thoroughly unimpressed. He was still taller even when folded in on himself. "I thought you'd be showing me some age old symbol or a fire spell that could evaporate the entire Zexin Sea. Or at the very least, set water aflame." Jack stood and smoothed out his robes, clearly no longer interested. "You're skilled at keeping a man waiting though. I'll give you that."

Sylvie frowned, her eyebrows creasing at his words. "You know what it is?"

"You don't?"

"Can't you just tell me? You're the one that offered to help."

"Fair enough," he muttered, bored. "The people across the Wymeran River call it, *Aethilium greviya,* or, Heartstone. It's a common fashion item, especially in Curran. They were initially created for storage purposes, but women like to use them for jewelry. Sparkly charms. Or whatever else women like to use glittery things for. Why they're so fascinated by shiny rocks is beyond me. I suppose it gives a man something to focus on at least. Who knows? Maybe it's a great conversation starter. Break the ice with a rock. Can't go wrong with that."

"Wait." Sylvie held up a hand, stopping his digression. "Did you say storage? You mean like a satchel of some sort?"

"More like a room." Jack pointed at the stone in her hand. He squinted at the black haze lingering inside. "Though from what I read, you should be able to see right through it. It should have a glossy surface and be completely transparent when empty. Like an extra shiny marble. Maybe it's broken. Or, who knows, maybe there's dirt stuck inside?"

Sylvie immediately looked down, belatedly noticing that the dark haze had, indeed, returned. The lullaby, too. She could hear it better now. Gentle and feminine. Sweet and alluring.

It grew louder, whispering senseless words into her ears. The melancholic hums sent shivers down her spine.

"What's that sound?" Jack asked, narrowing his eyes.

"You…" Sylvie's head snapped up. "You hear it, too?"

They shared an uneasy glance. But by the time they looked back down, the blackness was gone. Along with the voice.

"Where did you find this?" Jack bent to inspect it. Though he tried to hide it, his curiosity had been piqued. Again.

"Outside. Last time we were sent to chase the deserters."

"You took it?"

"No," Sylvie immediately denied. Jack lifted a disbelieving brow, and she tore her gaze away from his smug face.

"Are you sure?"

"I found it."

"I didn't peg you as the looting type," Jack said, grinning slyly. "Don't you know better than to ransack the dead? They'll haunt you."

Sylvie ignored him.

She rolled the Heartstone between her fingers, debating if she should ask a few of the Masters about it. But she didn't exactly want to go through the hassle of explaining just where she'd gotten it from. That might land her in an entirely different kind of mess. She'd never seen anything quite like it, and loathed the idea of someone taking it away, before she figured out all of its dirty secrets. If it had any. She could only hope.

"You mentioned those across the Wymeran River," she said, resting her gaze on him. "Do you know how they open it?"

Jack spared the stone a glance, before his gaze flickered to the ceiling. As he tried to recall the little he'd read about Curran's history. It wasn't a subject he enjoyed, so he'd skimmed through the absurdly lengthy book of their past and culture. He had to hand it to the author though—they'd perfected the art of excruciatingly descriptive detail. But that worked against them. Because Jack had instead opted to take notes of names and events that were of more significant import. Rather than go through every single mishap they'd experienced over the last two ages.

He might've even wrinkled a few supposedly priceless pages just for the sake of keeping himself awake. Not that he'd ever admit that. When asked, he'd fake surprise and nod along. That was always easier.

"Apparently they have some sort of magic words to activate it," Jack said. Not really remembering if the words had even been written in the book he'd looked over. It was likely. "I don't know them though. You might have some luck looking into Curran's history. Or basic books that focus on spells for more mundane situations. A shrinking spell, maybe? You'll need permission to learn such troublesome things though, and I doubt you'll get it. Those pesky Masters of ours do like to keep us focused on our specialties."

Sylvie frowned. "What about mystical rocks?"

"You mean the kind they use for charms?" Jack shrugged, apathetic. "Heartstone is its own miniature space, so it might be worth mentioning in a few enchanting manuals. Though I can't say for certain. I don't find this area of study all that interesting. You'll be better off asking practitioners that study the art."

Sylvie nodded appreciatively. She inspected the Heartstone. Her reflection peered curiously back at her.

"What do they usually keep inside?" Sylvie asked.

"If you're thinking what I think you are, let me just say now that I don't believe shrinking to be a particularly… well, pleasant experience."

Her eyes widened. "I'm not going to put a person inside!"

Jack shot her a skeptical glance that had her hands itching to wipe it off his face. Sylvie's fingers twitched and she knew he saw the slight movement because Jack gave her another one of his infuriating smirks. He reveled in the fact that he was getting under her skin.

"You shouldn't yell," Jack whispered. "You might scare off that couple in the next room."

Sylvie instinctively looked behind her. Petty frustration gone. Only for surprise to take its place. "You heard them too?"

"I *saw* them." Jack grimaced. "I go inside to sleep and what do I find? Mild cannibalism. I would've gone to the other archive had it actually had its own fireplace. It's as cold and dark as the Zexin abyss in there. Whoever made this Institute clearly cut back on our floor's budget. Purposely, too, I bet. Greedy bastards."

Sylvie smiled. "That can't be helped. This isn't exactly a place where Conjurers and Elementalists are known to… congregate."

"That's no excuse."

"You could've gone back to your room."

"Too far."

"Frankly, I'm surprised you didn't curse them out."

"Remind them that they're brainless maggots?" Jack threw his hands up, exasperation creeping into his tone. "I'm not a fan of reiteration."

"With all the lectures you've received, I'd be surprised if you were."

Jack didn't respond.

Instead, he kicked a tall pile of books, making them noisily clatter to the ground. They listened carefully as the sound of two surprised gasps and shaky whispers burst forth. There was a loud crash. Thick tomes hit the floor in rapid succession. Followed by the bang of what could only be an errant appendage meeting wood. They spoke louder now, each blaming the other for making so much noise. Sylvie didn't doubt that their voices could be heard throughout the entire tower.

A few more accusing hisses and hushed insults later, they finally heard the sound of their hasty steps getting farther away.

The loud, conclusive creak of the archive's old doors opened and closed, leaving only silence. Sylvie wondered if they'd heard them as well or if their ears simply deemed them unimportant. Selective hearing affected everyone, so long as it was convenient.

"That's my cue," Jack said, a book tucked under his arm. It was definitely one of hers. Which one though, she couldn't say for certain, but she had an idea. "You should head back as well."

She waved him out. "Leave already."

"You don't even know what time that wrinkly codger will return." The corners of his mouth tilted up into a highly amused grin. "Unless you like waiting around for old men."

Sylvie threw a book at him.

Jack merely lifted his palm, glowing a soothing blue. Before a blast of scorching flames burst forth and sent a wave of heat throughout the room. The fire brightened their surroundings, blinding her for a moment. She felt the flames lick tantalizingly over her skin. Close, but not enough to burn. Sylvie's hand twitched, magic coming to life beneath her fingertips at the sudden threat. By the time the flames died down, only ashes and a thoroughly burnt hard cover remained.

"Damn. That's hot." Jack shook his steaming hand.

"Show-off. You didn't have to go that far." Sylvie stared forlornly at the pile of cinders decorating the floor. He sure knew how to desecrate things. Scholars everywhere would've wailed at the sight. "I don't think we had another copy of that. How am I supposed to explain this to Master Cephas?"

"Can't you act more surprised?" he huffed, indignant. "Yell, faint, or something! You've just seen the flames of the Drowned Tower's only Elementalist."

Sylvie held up her hands, burning the same soft blue. She moved it and heat radiated from her fingertips, blurring the air.

"Did you not know or have you forgotten?" she asked. "I'm a Conjurer with an affinity for fire."

Silence.

Jack stared at her for a seemingly endless moment, before a

roar of laughter escaped him. The sound rang throughout the room. Deep and distinctly virile. The walls stored and kept it, all too happily adding another secret between them. Sylvie grinned at him, reveling in the comfortable atmosphere that settled between them.

"I should've used ice," Jack said between laughs.

"I would've liked to see that."

The image of a book frozen in a block of solid ice came to mind. Would it melt? If so, how long would it take? But if it did melt then the book would be soaked—its words as unreadable as the ash before her—it might even be more of a hassle to clean up than the cinders.

Jack only shrugged, half smiling. "I don't want to hear any noise coming from this room, hear me?"

Sylvie dismissed his words with a wave of her hand, as he turned to leave. *He isn't all bad,* she decided. She liked the smile that lit up her face when he made a smart remark. *Though his personality needs to be toned down.*

But there was no point in dwelling over absent company. She had received enough answers for today—more than she'd hoped to find. So, she departed shortly after.

The ashes on the ground definite proof of their meeting.

***

Everyone collectively griped about the unusual brightness of the Drowned Tower's halls. More torches had been put up to help the visiting Elder see better. All the light, however, unsettled the locals who had all decided to crowd themselves inside the residential tower. Which had been spared from any additional lighting, simply because there existed no room to place them.

The left tower's sole purpose was to accommodate.

It was made up of gargantuan rooms filled with countless smaller ones. All separated by wooden partitions. Each area was relatively large, housing one double decker bed, two cabinets, and two desks. Candles were the only source of light.

A myriad of voices could be heard from all floors of the rarely filled tower. It appeared as if those with nothing better to do than gossip had locked themselves away in their rooms where they wouldn't be bothered by the new found brightness of their surroundings. The extra light left a sense of lingering dread in what should've been cozy halls. A sore reminder that one of the powers of their world was among them and might even choose someone to accompany him back to the north.

Sylvie though was neither reminded of the Elder, nor worried about who he'd be choosing. When she saw everyone, she was only reminded of animals. The kind that kept themselves hidden under the safety that darkness provided. If they ventured too far, they'd be lost. Blinded by the sun.

She grimaced when she realized she was one of them. But, unlike many, she'd happily remain oblivious to the outside world forever. Sylvie didn't mind. She liked where she was. Change was out of the question. Out there, where the Council sent them to do their bidding, the air was cold. But there was no breeze.

"First," Myrrh began, "everyone talks about the last mission, then the Elder, now it's the light! Can't they just be quiet for one moment? Just one measly moment! That's all I ask! That's not too much, right?"

With one last huff, Myrrh fell unceremoniously back onto her bed, inadvertently shaking Sylvie who lounged below.

"You can't blame them for complaining," Reed answered, leaning back into the chair beside them. His soft voice was mostly muted by the boisterous chatter around the room.

"And why not?"

"Well, they've been sending us out more and more for the past month and now an Elder suddenly decides to drop by."

"I hope he at least addresses the deserter problem," Sylvie said.

"It's unfair!" Myrrh sat up and peered upside down at her. "How come I'm never chosen to go outside? I'd like to stretch my wings and use my powers, too!"

Sylvie sighed. "Since you weren't ordered to find a partner. You'll only be considered after finding one for yourself and then proving yourself capable."

"As if it's that easy! I don't get along with any of the available Healers."

"It *is* that easy," Sylvie said dryly. "You don't need to get along. Just choose someone you can tolerate. Your partner doesn't have to be a Healer. They're just my personal preference."

"It would've been easier if you'd just been my partner, Syl." Myrrh shot Reed a scathing glance. "How did you two end up together anyway?"

Sylvie gave a negligent shrug and a small ambiguous tip of her head. "I was told to find a partner. Reed volunteered. There was no reason to object."

"Why do you even want to go out there?" Reed questioned. "Anyone not instructed to find a partner isn't required to do anything. Least of all, the Assembly's bidding. In fact, aren't you already—what? Twenty?"

"Twenty-two," Myrrh chimed.

"That's three years past the age of requirement. You should just relax. Going outside and using your powers gets very old, very fast. Why bother when you weren't chosen?"

"That's why I do! Unlike you two, I wasn't chosen! But if I keep a Master, then I'm just that much closer. Do you two even know how many people further their studies just to be given the privilege you have now?"

"Well the Drowned Tower is known for its Amorphs," Sylvie reasoned. "So, it's only natural that they have a higher standard when it comes to those that are sent out."

"What's that supposed to mean?" Reed asked, affronted. "Are the rest of us non-Amorph's second-rate?"

Sylvie shrugged.

"Hey!" Myrrh called, trying to get them to focus. "I just want to do something. Don't you two understand that? I can't exactly run away."

Sylvie watched Myrrh pause. The Amorph blanched in fear at the thought of running off. Deserting. Those that ran from the Institute were usually tracked down by specialists only referred to as, "Hunters." Ominous in its simplicity. They were hidden in plain sight in every Institute. Whether the runaways intended to use their powers or keep them hidden didn't matter. It was too dangerous to allow a practitioner freedom amongst the Nebbin.

Those that weren't killed during retrieval were forcefully dragged into the dungeons and kept in solitary confinement. Forced to swallow a tonic that zapped the energy from their veins. Those that built resistance to it were never heard from again, and those that hadn't, were set free when they were no longer deemed a threat to themselves and their fellow practitioners. Their freedom usually lasted all of three days, before they tried to escape again. The process always ended with one less life.

"You're better off in here," Sylvie said. "The outside world isn't as interesting as you believe."

"Better off trapped in the walls of this Institute forever?" Myrrh scowled, irritated at the thought. "Amorphs like me need wide open spaces filled with nature."

"Funny then, how the solitary Eastern Branch is the one that specializes in teaching your kind." Sylvie grinned patronizingly up at her. "Are you sure you're not mistaking need with want? It's alright. It happens."

"Not to mention, you can be flaky at times," Reed added.

"Exactly."

"This stuff must confuse you."

"No one's asking you!" Myrrh exclaimed, cheeks reddening.

"Being confined isn't always a bad thing. It's more about how you take it." Sylvie stifled a yawn with the heel of her hand. "It's comfortable here. I don't mind being trapped."

"Only you think like that," Myrrh grumbled.

Sylvie watched as two grinning practitioners walked past the entrance of their room, talking animatedly about trivial things. They were older Amorphs. The kind with little talent for their art, and thus, were never instructed to find partners. But even so, they were allowed to stay in the care of the Institute. No one would throw them out or force them to do the bidding of others. They could live the rest of their lives in torpid comfort.

"I'm not the only one," Sylvie muttered, closing her eyes.

The two disappeared down the hall, oblivious.

Sylvie envied them.

***

Jack dreamt of dripping ink.

Black fell onto never ending white. Pigment smudged, flowing to form the figures of men, women, and children. Every slight shift of his eyes and the ink took it upon itself to fill his view with the portraits of nameless people.

One figure stood out, tilting its blotched head to look at him. It took on the familiar features of an aging woman. One he knew well. But there was something wrong. The figures cheekbones were too protruding, wrinkles too evident, eyes too lifeless. Ink dripped down her face like blood. She flashed a grim smile in his direction, and then she fell.

A haze of black liquid plunged toward him.

Jack lifted his arms, trying to catch the liquid donning the face of familiarity. Only to realize that he was a hundred meters away and lifting his arms toward air as his eyes helplessly watched the blob make contact with stark white, soundlessly painting the world in tar.

"Come to me," a sweet voice whispered.

And Jack was enveloped in tendrils of black.

***

Red eyes snapped open.

Jack's head throbbed in protest, worsened only by the wild pounding of his heart. His vision was filled with white. The salty scent of the sea washed over him, while his eyes darted violently around. He only saw a blur of colors that assaulted his senses, as they tried to make sense of something—a book, a table, his robes, anything—to give him an idea of where he was. But the constant blending of colors made his head spin, and suddenly, he was struck with the fierce urge to vomit.

He took a deep breath, gathering his wits and waiting for the moment to pass. Once the white spots in his vision subsided, he more calmly observed his surroundings. Only to find himself in his room. The sheets were damp and his skin was slick with sweat. From the corner of his eye, he saw a shadow flicker and his head immediately snapped toward the possible threat.

Jack had the uncomfortable, gut-wrenching feeling of someone staring at him. His hands clenched around the sheets that had somehow wound their way around his legs, before he forced his tense muscles to relax.

After a moment, he lit a small fire in his hand.

"Who's there?" Jack called, eyeing the looming darkness.

The familiar shadows of objects slinked away from him in a decidedly creepy manner. While he waited for an answer that never came. Unsurprising, given the lateness of the hour. But he was still alarmed. Still on edge. And he knew enough about sleep to know that it would continue to elude him tonight.

Jack stood, balancing himself on shaky legs. He walked past the rooms and through the halls. The fire in his hand shed light over the faces he passed, as he continued to observe everything around him. The feeling of eyes on the back of his head sent shivers down his spine, and he turned, questioning the silence once again. The quiet held unspoken truth and likewise, unseen lies. But Jack wasn't patient enough to try and figure out the kind hidden within the current stillness.

Though he still couldn't escape the feeling that he was being watched. So, if someone actually was creeping around then he wanted to know. Jack fueled the fire in his hand. He didn't stop until the flames were bright enough to wake even the heaviest of sleepers.

"Come out!" he yelled.

"Jack?"

He whipped around at the sound of the familiar voice.

Sylvie stood there, furrowing her eyebrows. She tilted her head at him in silent contemplation, and Jack let the fire in his hand die down. The flame's flickering light seemed useless against the halls glare. Too many torches were lined up, and he flinched away from them. Now that he noticed the unusual brightness, it made his head pound even more.

Why is there so much light? Jack thought, peeved.

"Have you been in the archives since last night?" Sylvie asked, observing him. He was breathing heavily and his eyes looked bloodshot. There was a thin layer of sweat over his brow, as if he was running from some unknown creature hiding in the relative brightness of the Drowned Tower's halls.

Jack's eyes widened at the question. He quickly glanced around him, seeing the familiar sign that read, '*Research Archive No. Twenty: Conjurers and Elementalists Only,*' on a door to his far left. With his mind so preoccupied, his feet had instinctively brought him back to the seventh floor.

He schooled his expression into neutral.

"No," Jack said, giving no further elaboration. He breathed deeply, trying to gather his wits. As she continued to stare curiously at him. Sylvie opened her mouth to speak, but she was interrupted by two pairs of loud footsteps.

"Sylvie!" Myrrh called, running up to her. "When did you leave? Reed and I have been searching…" her voice trailed off as she caught sight of Jack. "Oh."

"What are you two doing here?" Sylvie asked them. They'd taken it upon themselves to openly gape at Jack, who stared right back. His mind so preoccupied trying to recall their names that he didn't register the sheer disbelief decorating their faces.

"Father asked us to bring you to the Iniquities Chamber," Reed said carefully. His soft voice was an echo in the otherwise silent halls.

Sylvie's eyebrows shot up in an attempt to reach her hairline.

"Did I do something wrong?" she asked.

Jack cleared his throat and laughed mockingly, regaining his usual bearings. Those two proved a good enough distraction from his previous confusion, allowing him a moment to gather his poise. "What? You've never been called there?"

"She isn't like you!" Myrrh defended, turning to Jack with an angry glare. She had the air of someone that hated him. It was clear that she'd heard one or two of the—admittedly—many rumors circling around him. None were particularly good. As the only Elementalist in the Drowned Tower, he garnered all sorts of unwanted attention.

"Like me?" Jack couldn't help but ask.

"Not everyone finds constant punishment fun!"

"You think I like getting lectured?"

"Of course! Why else would you keep—"

"Do you have to yell so much?" Jack interrupted, looking down at Myrrh's tiny frame. "I suppose you do, huh? Squeaks like you are usually overlooked by all us normal folk."

Myrrh snarled furiously, reminding him more of a wild animal than an educated practitioner.

"You're dead!" She pounced, but Jack sidestepped her with ease. He shot her a cocky smirk, further antagonizing the small brunette.

"You're slow," he taunted. "Must be the stubby legs."

"What are you even doing here?" Myrrh roared. "Get lost!"

"I'm an Elementalist, and last I checked only Conjurers and Elementalists were allowed on the seventh floor." Jack raised his eyebrows at her expectantly. "So, the question is, what are *you* doing here? Did you get lost on your way to the privy? Should I call someone to hold your hand?"

Myrrh growled and made another move to grab him. Only to be pulled back by Reed whose palms were coated in a soothing blue that forced her tense muscles to relax and fall limp. But even magic couldn't stop her mouth from spouting out whatever insult came to mind. Most were disturbingly detailed threats of severe bodily harm. Jack took them all with an amused grin lighting his face. There was a gleam in his eyes that spoke of enjoyment. The twisted sort.

"That's enough," Sylvie said with a tone of finality. "Myrrh, relax. And you," she turned to glare at Jack, "stop."

"Scary," Jack mocked, holding his hands up in the universal sign of surrender.

Sylvie ignored him, turning to Reed who still held Myrrh by the arms. "Did Master Cephas mention why I needed to go?"

"No," Reed answered with a shake of his head. "But he did say that as your partner, I needed to go with you."

"He wants both of us?" Sylvie asked, surprised. "Is it another job? Don't tell me we have to deal with more deserters."

"I don't think so," Myrrh chimed in, roughly shoving Reed's hands away. "Others have been called in, too. I don't think it has anything to do with fighting though. I know for a fact that some of them have never even seen the sun."

"And you? Were you called?"

"No," Myrrh grumbled, annoyed. "Apparently I'm not good enough to go to whatever secret meeting this is, but that turkey Tiv is."

"Tiv's there?" Jack asked. "Tiv Grovegg?"

"Of course you know him. Let me guess, you're friends?"

"He's my partner," he muttered venomously. "That busboy never calls me for important matters like this."

"You're partners? That makes sense. Now I know why I hate you both."

"You hate us because we're at a normal, healthy height."

"We're going now," Sylvie intervened, before Myrrh lost the battle for her composure. Getting angry at Jack was useless, he'd only give that galling smirk in response. Sylvie turned without a word and walked away. Reed was at her heels in an instant, while Jack followed leisurely behind.

Jack could see her stiff shoulders and tense gait. She looked uncertain, not knowing what they needed them for or what they were expecting them to do. Jack didn't know either. But if he had to guess, they'd probably be sent out again. Why else would they gather pairs? Unless they had some kind of sick, evil experiment they wanted to conduct.

He wouldn't put it past them. The possibility of this sudden meeting becoming something he'd hate was far more likely than he liked. The Zenith Council always had something up their sleeves, and his recent dream did nothing to appease his worry.

Jack quickened his pace.

Despite his doubts, it was foolish to assume the worst. Jumping to conclusions would get him nowhere.

Might as well get this over with, Jack decided.

No one noticed the distinctively virile figure that stood, peering at them from the shadows.

4

The Iniquities Chamber was located deep in the recesses of the Assembly's tower. In a place past stored treasure and lingering people. It sat before empty dungeons. Dozens of crumbling cells lined the walls leading toward its entrance. Most no longer functioned, having decayed from age. But it was still far more than the Tower's residents would ever need.

The floor was clearly vacant and had been for some time, making their walk a silent one. Their footsteps echoed throughout the long stretch of hall that led to a shut door made of thick, black wood. A thin layer of dust coated the door's surface. Moldy and chipped from unuse. Even the floor wasn't spared from the cover of filth. Reed, with his unsteady constitution, was forced to muffle half a dozen sneezes as they approached. Rarely, was the silence of this area disturbed. And the lack of visitors clearly had a direct relationship with upkeep.

Sylvie found a simple station to the far right.

Just as abandoned as the rest of the floor. It housed a destroyed chair, an unlit lamp, and a large rat. The rodent scurried about, nibbling on the already ruined seat. Either unable to leave or knowing a secret entrance invisible to the naked eye. Sylvie couldn't begin to fathom how Jack could be sent alone down here and still have the gall to stir up trouble after punishment.

The mere walk was frightening.

Through the darkness, Sylvie could just make out the engraving above the door.

It read:

Iniquities Chamber

Home of consequence for sins not yet past,
Punishing deserters of the mass.

Reed tensed at the words. "What's that supposed to mean?"

"Don't let it scare you," Jack said, easily shrugging it off. "It's a sign from another time. Now, this place is just your standard time-out room. They tell you to sit in the dark and reflect."

"Because that's supposed to make it better," Sylvie said, flexing clammy hands.

Jack eyed her sidelong. His eyes caught every one of her movements, filing them away for later. "It should. Why they chose this room though, is beyond me. It's near the old sector of the Tower. Where the previous Potentate Union used to dwell. Even I hate it there."

"Perhaps that's why they chose it," she guessed, giving him her best patronizing grin. He opened his mouth to retort, but she didn't let him. Sylvie firmly grasped the cold handle and gave the door a strong push. It creaked loudly on its hinges, sounding as if it would break apart at any moment. She didn't doubt it. Sylvie crinkled her nose at the scent of dust, moldy wood, and iron that immediately assaulted her senses. There was a twinge of something else as well. Old fear, perhaps? It lingered in the room. Enclosed it. Just as much as the blanket of dust.

The room was humble—in a poor, unfortunate way.

Chipped stools were littered about. While a scarcely lit fireplace in the center served as the sole source of light. There was an aged fresco to the far right. A mix of colors depicting an event Sylvie couldn't quite make out. The paint had long since been ruined by time. Rusty chains decorated the walls, dangling from thick steel hooks embedded into the stone. There were scorch marks around them. For one foolish moment, she debated asking what those chains were for, before thinking better of it.

This was a punishments chamber. Once.

Their entrance was greeted with fierce glares by the chamber's most recent denizens. Tiv was the easiest to identify. He was the only Amorph and stood in the corner with a displeased frown marring his lips. His short hair did nothing to cover the agitated twitch of beady eyes. Occupying the stools were another pair. A man and woman with auburn curls that Sylvie recognized—not enough to know their names, but enough to know that they were famous around the Institute for being a pair of Healers. How they got their jobs done was a mystery. Even to her.

Jack brushed against her as he made his way in first, strolling right up to Tiv and slapping the Amorph over the head.

"What do you think you're doing?" Tiv yelled, staring Jack down with large, black eyes. Tiv was taller and more muscular, but his towering appearance didn't seem to deter Jack. As he spoke in his usual biting tone.

"Why didn't you call me?"

The Amorph shot him a fierce glare. One Jack returned, and after a second of tense silence, the two grinned happily at each other, bumping arms and uttering greetings like the old friends they undoubtedly were. Deciding it best to ignore their antics, Sylvie took a seat on a nearby stool. Reed followed behind her, fiddling with the sleeves of his robes. As he discreetly eyed the Healer duo.

"You know them?" Sylvie asked. Softly, so none could hear.

Reed nodded, his voice was a whisper lower than hers. "The Mane siblings. Ethil and Duward."

Sylvie observed them from the corner of her eye.

Their stoic faces and straight postures surrounded them with an unapproachable air. From their faces, she guessed they were the serious sort that fancied by-the-book affairs. A stark contrast to Jack and Tiv, both of whom had settled into a comfortable rhythm. Tiv's mouth ran, while Jack listened with his eyes closed. The Elementalist was either asleep or just incredibly skilled at tuning out his chatty companion. Probably the latter. They were individually known around the Drowned Tower for their lack of inhibition and proneness to going postal.

Three pairs with completely different methods. Just what did the Elder want from them?

"I can't believe they're making us wait here like this," Tiv complained. "Locking us all up in this abandoned room is be-yond disturbing. Do they think we have nothing better to do than wait on them day and night?"

"Feel like a woman yet?" Jack quipped. Sylvie shot Jack a scathing glance that went ignored, as he kept his focus on Tiv. The Amorph, however, saw her glare and snickered. He turned to include her with a mischievous grin lighting his face.

"If you let him run his mouth," Tiv said, "you'll never hear the end of it."

"The only mouth that I hear running is yours," Ethil spoke up suddenly. All eyes turned to her, as she glowered at Tiv. Her blue eyes glinted dangerously in the gloom. "Is this wait not un-bearable enough without your incessant need to spout unnecess-ary noise?"

Tiv raised a challenging brow. He was never one to back away from a good argument. "So, you do talk. And here I was just about to comment on your utter lack of social skills. But I suppose Healers must be used to staying quiet. In case you distract others with your mindless prattle from the sidelines."

"I just know how to control myself," Ethil said through gritted teeth. "I don't suppose you've ever heard of self-discipline? Filthy Morph."

"With that stick shoved so far up your ass I expected you to be howling more," Tiv said harshly. "In fact, I commend you for your silence. I'd almost forgotten the healing brigade was here. Don't you have somewhere else to be? Like healing one of the new apprentice's itty bitty boo-boos."

Ethil clenched her fist. "Do you think yourself super—"

"Think?" Tiv scoffed. "I know I am. True battle prowess is what's needed on the battlefield. Not wannabe fighters that don't know their place."

"It's thinking like that which has our lands so divided in the first place!" Ethil squeezed the sleeves of her robes. "Healers are at the bottom of the food chain, yet when someone on the battlefield is on the verge of death, who do you all call and plead and *blame*? What's the point of all this useless raving about who's better? Making snap judgments based on your own set of prejudiced standards is ridiculous! Our differences don't make us any less worthy."

"Equality is for the jealous and preached only by the subpar. Your naiveté is offensive and changes nothing."

"This is exactly the problem!" Ethil criticized. "You hear, but you don't listen! Never understanding, never choosing to understand our plight. The plight of the minority! Do you think you'd last even a day on the frontlines without the support of Healers?"

"Watch me."

"Your arrogance is unbelievable!"

Duward abruptly stood. His stool clattered noisily to the floor, garnering everyone's attention. "That's enough, Ethil," he rebuked, with a cold glare. "Don't waste your breath quarreling with mindless barbarians that know nothing of peace."

"Oh?" Tiv mocked. "Is that how it is? You consider me a barbarian for speaking the truth? I'd say I'm quite the upstanding citizen."

"You…" Ethil's cheeks burned. "You small-minded prig!"

"Is that the best you can think of?" Tiv sneered. "If I'm small-minded, it's because of the class I was born in that allowed me to be so. Don't blame me for your pathetic progenitors."

"Tiv," Jack said, interrupting the conversation before it took a turn for the worse. His cool demeanor and harsh tone lacked its usual flare of mockery. "Don't waste your breath arguing in a back room with excessively thin walls. It's the middle of the day. No one wants to hear your voice."

"You're one to talk."

"Their skills on the field will speak for themselves," Jack went on, disregarding his comeback. "That's when we'll know if they deserve to be here with the rest of us."

Tiv huffed, but otherwise didn't respond.

The silence that settled after was heavy, the tension even more so. Reed, wanting to vent the pressure, crossed his arms and turned toward Jack. All forced casualness. He donned a smile that showed too much teeth.

"Have you spoken to one of the Masters, Jack?" Reed asked, putting his best foot forward. "How are you so sure that we'll be heading out to fight?"

Jack shrugged carelessly. "Why else would those old crones gather three of the most sought after pairs on their work roster? That pompous Elder probably has a special little quest for all us elites. Something hard enough to determine who'll get selected in the Choosing."

Interested, Sylvie raised her head, her eyes catching Jack's. "Weren't you so sure that you'd be the one chosen?"

Jack pinned her with an unreadable stare, clicking his tongue in annoyance. "No back-sass from you."

She smiled.

Then the ancient door suddenly banged open, slamming against the wall with a resounding echo. Its hinges creaked in a way that made Sylvie's ears itch. But there was no time to pay attention to the door as a young man strode inside. Sylvie recognized him as the one that had called the Elder away from Jack back in the dining hall. His gait was brusque and filled with confidence, exuding an air of authority that came only with experience.

His eyes were as red as Jack's own. An Elementalist then. A frighteningly large one at that.

Columbus and the Elder followed shortly after, taking their time. As if they weren't already late to this meeting.

"Ah!" A kind smile lit up the Elder's wrinkly face. "What strong looking young men and women we have here. You six are the best, yes? The cream of the crop? The capable and astute? I called in a few other possible candidates, but I believe your Masters dismissed them shortly after. Well, no matter. They know their students best. The six of you are more than enough. It's been so long since I've seen such variety. The Alps has far too many Elementalists. Both young and mature."

"These are our best and brightest," Columbus said. He bowed slightly to the man, before stepping forward to introduce everyone. "The one to your right is—"

"Columbus, my boy, I know who they are," the Elder interrupted. Sylvie heard Tiv snicker under his breath, and she tried to hide her smile. "But they don't seem to know me. Shall we remedy that? My name is Serach, Elder and twenty-seventh head of embrocological research for the Zenith Council. The frightening man behind me is my primary apprentice and aid, Rior Wolden. We have travelled all this way for research."

Everyone's expressions shifted, clouded by varying degrees of confusion. What could possibly be interesting about the Drowned Tower? Or the entire east for that matter? What you saw was what you got. Uninteresting foliage, ruins, and men and women living in solitude, locked away from the rest of the world.

Contact with other capitals was a rare occurrence. Even the most adventurous of the Drowned Tower's practitioners never ventured too far from the eastern border.

Duward was the first to recover. "Research?"

"Why, yes," Serach said patronizingly slow, as if he were speaking to a child. "Spritely I may be, but I am old. I'm afraid my bones can no longer handle the weight they once could. This is why I've gathered all of you! The most talented practitioners of the east! I have a special request."

"A request?" Jack's eye twitched. "You travelled here not for a Choosing, but for research into matters that I could care less about? You should've told me this in the dining hall instead of having me listen to your useless prattle, you saggy geezer."

"Jack!" Columbus called in warning.

Everyone in the room turned to Jack, as he stared unwaveringly at the Elder. His dissent could've been worded differently, but it wasn't without reason. The entire Eastern Branch had been buzzing with false excitement for the past few days, and they'd all worried over what Serach was doing here in one way or another. Jack was no exception. But he'd actually been able to talk with Serach, yet the Elder hadn't bothered to tell him of his intent. And so, Jack currently suffered from the worst type of frustration — petty.

"Jacques Dace," Serach stated. He donned that gentle smile again, kind eyes shining and filling with what seemed to be an endless pool of patience. "You look just like your father. Though that impudent tongue of yours undoubtedly comes from your mother."

"Spare me your unwanted opinion on my genetics," Jack said, crimson eyes hardening as he glared. "Explain to me why this research of yours is so important that you had to personally travel all the way to this backwater hellhole for a few… what? Samples?"

"Maybe," Sylvie interrupted, "if you stopped mouthing off then he'd be able to get a word out."

Jack's glare moved to her.

His fingers twitched as if he were about to bring out the magic that slept beneath. Sylvie had never pegged Jack as a man of patience. She'd always seen him as temperamental and prickly. Oh, he could be serious when he wanted to be, but that sort of disposition only seemed to arise when he saw fit. He was, more often than not, ready and willing to lash out when annoyed. A brat. That's what he was. An extremely intimidating brat with the power, connections, and drive to get whatever he wanted. It was unnerving, being stared at with eyes the color of freshly spilt blood. But Sylvie held his gaze, and despite the thick tension that tainted the air, they continued to stare intently at each other.

"Sylvie Sirx," Serach said, shattering the tense atmosphere. "Youngest of the Sirx family. I had the pleasure of meeting your brother once. But it's your father that I've had the honor of conversing with a great number of times. He's truly an invaluable advisor to the Zenith Council. His zeal for the growth of the north is second to none. Though I'm afraid to say that I don't see much of you in him."

"My father is a fanatic," Sylvie said, breaking her stare down with Jack. Her tone was filled with finality. "The growth of Ferus Terria doesn't interest me. Had it, then I wouldn't be in the east."

Serach sighed. "Children these days all seem to lack the ability to enjoy the simple joys of conversation. Then, as everyone so desperately wants, I will be frank."

Rior brought him an ancient text bound in tattered leather. The Elder flipped carefully through the pages. Yellow with age. He stopped to scrutinize something and nodded to himself, before turning the book to show them the picture within. To the left, was a hanging plant with large leaves and droopy flower heads that were held by twig-like stems. There was another illustration by its side which seemed to be a smaller subspecies. Its roots were completely submerged in water.

"I need this to create a special potion," Serach explained. "It's a unique species of shrub that grows in the topmost floors of the towers. Another form of it grows by the shores of Eriam. I would have the six of you split up and retrieve them."

"If the plant grows on Eriam, then the trip should be a relatively safe one," Sylvie said evasively. Not wanting to participate, but also not outright voicing her displeasure at being given such a mundane task. "Why not send someone else? I'm sure there are many in the Drowned Tower far more skilled at herb collection. It's a rather…" she paused, trying to find a word that masked her opposition, "delicate affair."

They easily saw through her, but Jack was the one to call her out on it. "So, you don't want to do it."

She glared fiercely at him. "I never said that."

"Wait." Tiv held up both of his hands. "So you'll be treating us like embrocologists now?"

"You *are* an embrocologist," Jack muttered.

"In name only!" Tiv defended. "I don't exactly go out of my way to do these types of things. In fact, I'd proudly admit that I even avoid them whenever possible."

"Yes, well," Serach cleared his throat in an attempt to get them to focus. "This is why I called the six of you here today. It is, as Miss Sirx says, a rather delicate affair. You all have embrocologists in your party and have enough skills to fend for yourselves should something out of the ordinary happen."

"Out of the ordinary?" Ethil asked.

Serach looked at her. His face was the embodiment of gentle. "The problems in the north have made the entirety of Ferus Terria unsafe. I'm merely taking all the necessary precautions. The Zenith Council is still in turmoil. More and more deserters have been using this time of disagreement to their advantage."

"Yet here you are collecting samples," Tiv deadpanned.

"Why, my boy, I assure you that these samples are all for the sake of the Council."

Jack made a face. More sour than usual. "I still don't see why I should help an old codger like you."

Serach smiled.

"Because if all goes well then I'll be taking three of you back with me to the north."

5

Sylvie, Reed, Jack, and Tiv walked down the desolate stretch of bridge that led to the shores of Eriam. Duward and Ethil had stayed behind to gather the specimens inside the Tower.

She peered around her, carefully examining their desolate surroundings. The sea was calm tonight, the air humid. Disturbingly so. Her gut churned in unease. Instinct told her that these were telltale signs of a storm. But as she looked overhead, the skies were bright and clear. Falsely promising sun.

Sylvie knew better.

She could see the shores of Eriam and the brooding trees of Tearwood that stretched outward a distance ahead. Eriam was a sequestered piece of uphill land with the Zexin Sea on one side and the Eirinne Mountains on the other. Closed off from the rest of Ferus Terria. The Nebbin dwelt in Thyme, a small town that strove in its isolation. The very definition of provincial. And as they approached, Sylvie saw pointed rooftops peeking out from just above the trees. Smoke rose and polluted the air. She could hear the clang of metal and the loud, repetitive drum of tools meeting dirt—the sounds of the townspeople hard at work.

They weren't too far.

"Anyone up for dropping by Thyme?" Tiv asked. His hands crossed behind his head in a mixture of boredom and relaxation. "I haven't been out for a leisurely stroll in a long time."

Sylvie turned her head to shoot Tiv a quick glance. "They'll know immediately if we veer off course. A trip to town isn't worth an hour long lecture."

Tiv grimaced at the reminder of the tracking spell they were required to submit to whenever they left the Institute. A precautionary spell only taught to Masters with a certain degree of authority, so at least one of them could figure out their last known location should they decide to flee. The spell itself took the form of black letters in ancient tongues that encircled their ankles. Master Cephas had been the one to cast it. He'd done it so quickly that they barely had time to register his hand sparking a cold blue, before the mark appeared on their skin with a pinch.

An unwelcome blemish.

"The Demar spell is an old friend," Jack muttered darkly. Low enough for Sylvie to know that she wasn't supposed to hear. She raised an eyebrow, but otherwise didn't question him.

"There's not much to do in town," Sylvie continued, nodding at Tiv. "And I've got an appointment to keep."

It was a meeting with books. Though she'd sooner bite her own tongue than tell him that. But she knew Jack had understood because he glanced her way. Sylvie was far more interested in searching for the spell that controlled the stone sitting around her neck. If nothing else, it would make for good storage.

"Why am I not surprised?" Tiv frowned. "You don't know how to have fun. We're practically free to do whatever we want. Loosen up, Syl."

The moniker wasn't lost on her. It wasn't unwelcome. But she raised an eyebrow all the same. Had he heard it from Myrrh? "We still have to get those plants for Elder Serach."

"They're just plants. How hard can it be?"

"Have you ever sat in on one of Master Merin's classes? It's a nightmare. He had his apprentice's collect Dragon's Spit. Not an easy feat. Not very pleasant either."

Tiv's face twisted in disgust, as he recalled that horrid affair. It was a class he'd personally participated in—and one he sorely wanted to forget. He'd completely stopped pursuing advanced Embrocology after that, opting instead to focus solely on shape shifting. The slimy muck Master Merin referred to as Dragon's

Spit was nothing short of repulsive. It was more of an ooze rather than an actual plant. And though it was an effective cure for muscle pains, its odor was so pungent that even the mightiest of men would scrunch their noses in dread at the mere sight of it. Its scent was a menace. Tiv had been on the verge of hysterics when he found that so many still used it.

"That thing wasn't a plant," he declared.

"It did look like… mucus," Sylvie said, amused. "But it was definitely a plant. At one point at least."

"It wasn't even green! Plants should have at least a little green in them. That thing was unnatural!"

Everyone turned when they heard Jack let out a loud, irate sigh. "If you two could stop it with the Embrocology talk that would be fantastic."

"What? They're just plants," Tiv said.

Jack raised an eyebrow. "Here I thought it was slime. Glad to know you're just making pointless arguments."

Tiv halted, eyes widening. "You're aggravating!"

"I try."

"Ugh… Why am I even your partner?"

"Funny, I was wondering the same thing."

Sylvie listened to them as they continued to shoot insult after insult like children. Children armed with extensive knowledge and an obscene amount of free time. They got along well. Their banter was amusing and from what she could see, Tiv liked being the center of attention. While Jack was the type that stood out wherever he went. A walking ball of charisma.

As two alpha males, she thought they'd clash in more unpleasant ways, but their contrasting personalities matched each other in a strange, yet agreeable blend. The fact that Jack could get someone as obstinate as Tiv to drift away from his thoughts with a few words spoke volumes.

Before long, even Reed was talking. The two provoked him into speech, as they insulted various renowned Healers with sly grins and disrespectful tones.

"Clercie Borris could outmaneuver any Amorph, any day," Reed said, defending his idol. "He's known as the most brilliant Healer to ever grace Ferus Terria since Maurice, himself!"

"Borris?" Tiv scoffed, affronted. "He's a Healer! He could never beat an Amorph like Rocous."

Reed opened his mouth to protest only for Jack to interrupt. His gaze distant. "Didn't Rocous have a food named after him?"

"Roco sauce!" Sylvie exclaimed, butting in as well. "You like it, Jack?"

Jack raised an eyebrow at her sudden excitement. "I've never tried it."

Sylvie stopped. "What?"

He looked her straight in the eye, making sure to emphasize every word, extra slowly. "I've never—"

"Borris would definitely beat him!" Reed's voice drowned out the rest of Jack's sentence. Along with Sylvie's disbelief.

"I told you," Tiv said, exasperated. "There's no way that a Healer, even the best of them, could beat an Amorph genius."

"Hey, you two," Jack called. His voice filled with authority. "Stop it with the pointless arguments already."

"Says the one quarreling with his partner just a few minutes ago," Sylvie remarked.

Jack immediately whirled around to shoot her a glare. His red eyes narrowed dangerously. "I'm trying to help."

She grinned sardonically. "How kind of you."

Jack clicked his tongue, but otherwise ignored her as they finally stepped off of the bridge and onto the shores. A vast plain of sand and nothing surrounded them. Which meant that the plant must've been in the forest.

Tearwood looked menacing as it sat there—trees taller than houses, light barely seeping in from the cover of the branches. A blanket of mist surrounded the area, not spreading past the trees.

It was far too quiet. Strange for a place that should've been bursting with sounds of nature. Almost as if the trees and all inside were asleep. A deep, undisturbed rest.

Practitioners were warned never to pass through Tearwood unless absolutely necessary. Even during assignments, they were required to take only official routes lit by lamps.

"There's no place for hanging plants to grow on these shores, so I assume he expects us to go in there?" Sylvie poined at the trees. She wasn't even in the forest, yet she felt as if she were suffocating. The mere sight of the mist had her breath catching in her throat. The air was too heavy to breathe.

"Just what kind of research is he doing?" Reed questioned.

"It's no wonder he needed us to do this," Tiv said, "isn't this forest haunted?"

"It is," Reed said, recalling the legends and tall tales he'd heard from the villagers during the rare times he dropped by. "The Nebbin say that the mist surrounding Tearwood is the physical embodiment of all the souls that are lost here, eternally trapped and forced to wander the forest evermore. A limbo of sorts."

"Do you actually believe those fairy tales?" Jack scoffed. "It's senseless babble. Nothing more."

"Looks haunted to me," Tiv said, staring up at the trees.

"Foreboding is more like it," Sylvie said, already walking in.

As soon as she stepped inside the cover of mist, shivers rocked her. Sylvie felt a dozen eyes lock onto her figure, but as she looked around, she only saw her three companions. It felt like ghosts lingered in this mist, crying out their regrets and trying to get her to join them. A company of dead without corpses, all wondering why she had a body.

No wind blew, but she could hear whispers. A soft whistle, sometimes a long howl. The nonexistent winds carried voices into her sensitive ears. Never ending tendrils of gray surrounded them, but not enough to completely render them blind. Though they did realize that the strange fog was slowly getting thicker the further they ventured.

"I don't think our lives are worth a few plants," Sylvie said, shaking nervous hands just for the sake of moving. An attempt to release the tension in her body.

"Just our sleep," Jack said.

"What if they're really nice plants?" Reed asked casually. His soft voice gave him an air of naiveté that made him seem more childlike than he actually was.

"If they look anything like Dragon's Spit then don't count on it," Tiv said, sneering at the mental image of his most abhorred plant.

"I should've volunteered to search the upper floors of the Tower instead," Sylvie said. "Duward and Ethil lucked out."

"They're Healers," Tiv commented dryly. "Of course they'd be given the supporting role."

"Hey!" Reed exclaimed. "Could you stop with the bigotry?"

"Maybe if you all started blaming the Elder instead of focusing on each other, you'd actually reach a consensus," Jack bit out, slapping a leaf away with more force than necessary. "I know for a fact that the lot of you want to call that ancient prune out on his ridiculous abuse of power. If you didn't put those codgers on such high pedestals then perhaps you could speak more like me."

"What? Freely and without restraint?" Sylvie lifted an eyebrow in challenge.

Jack mimicked her expression.

Reed looked worriedly between them. Sylvie and Jack had never spoken much, but they seemed to be bumping heads more often. At least, from what he saw whenever they were together. Which was becoming questionably more frequent as of late. Was he missing something?

"At least I can say it to their faces," said Jack.

"I'd rather not be reprimanded every hour of the day. How many times were you confined to your room for speaking out of turn?"

"And here I thought I was the childish one," Tiv muttered.

"Well, let's just say we're all a little childish," Reed said, feeling a lot like his father at the moment. He stopped for a moment to squint at a clump of shrubbery a few feet away, pointing when he realized they were a patch of hanging plants, dangling from the trunk of a thick tree. Its twig-like stems were a dark brown, while its flowers were a vivid orange that stood out in the greenery around them. Unlike the picture Elder Serach had shown them, there were large bubble like sacs in the flower's center.

"Isn't that what Elder Serach was talking about?" Reed said, catching their attention. They all stopped to move closer, examining the sac and the liquid inside. Reed stepped forward, his hand poised as if to pluck it. "How many do you think he needs?"

"Don't touch it!" Sylvie and Tiv admonished.

"Sorry!" he yelped, snatching his hand back.

"Let the embrocologists do their jobs," Jack told him, noncommittally waving a hand to and fro.

Tiv carefully examined the flower, staring at its petals like he could see what they were made of. He didn't dare try to smell it though. The sac looked as if it might suddenly explode in his face if he got too close. Instead, he settled for squinting and staring up at the large tree it seemed to be living symbiotically with.

Sylvie procured a tiny glass vial from her robes, popping the lid and scrutinizing the stem. It was shriveled up, barely hanging onto the tree's branches. In contrast, the orange petals were full of life.

"This looks like Brimweed," Sylvie said.

"You mean that disgustingly bitter thing the Masters like to use for tea?" Tiv asked sourly. "The flavor of it is murder."

She raised an eyebrow at his words.

"If it's any consolation they also use it for salves," Sylvie clarified. She wasn't a fan of tea. Too flavorless. Too banal. Perhaps she just wasn't drinking it correctly? Not that she cared. Drinking tea made her feel prissy. Though she wouldn't dare say that out loud, lest she get half the Drowned Tower against her. Now, salves. Salves, she liked. "But this looks to be a different species of it. Brimweed is blue and has the same sac. Greasier petals, too. I wonder what this is used for."

"Another slime plant, how wonderful," Tiv said caustically. "Syl, how many of those glass vials do you have?"

"Four." She tossed him two and pointing at the base of the tree. "Let's do the ones on the bottom first."

He nodded.

"Useless duo," Tiv called, turning to shoot Jack and Reed a meaningful glare. "Step back and look away. This is going to look a lot like pus and smell ten times worse."

"How does it work?" Reed asked, backing up.

"We pop this bubble here." Sylvie gestured to one fluid filled sac the color of ripe peaches. "This sac comes from the stems. The fluid gets stored here. It's what makes the flowers droop. Once it gets too heavy, they drop and more flowers grow where they fall. They're spread by birds, so they usually grow at the top of larger trees, but it seems this one got lucky and found itself a batch."

"Its stench is a force to be reckoned with," Tiv warned. "So, I strongly suggest that you two pinch your noses and hope for the best."

They did as commanded, holding their sleeves up to their noses. Sylvie and Tiv nodded at each other before carefully pricking the sacs and squeezing. Yellow translucent goo oozed from the tiny holes and fell into the vials, barely filling a fourth. Small flakes of white were mixed in and they crinkled their noses in disgust at the foul stench that tainted the air. It smelt of dead fish mixed with the strange, pungent scent of dry scalp. Almost like a rotting corpse. The only things missing were blood and festering maggots.

They gagged as they watched the slime pour down their flasks at a sluggish pace. Sylvie shook the container, willing the liquid to flow faster. They repeated that process several times until their hands were coated and the vials were filled.

Once finished, Tiv wildly flicked his hand out to get rid of the leftover gunk. Only for it to fly and land on Reed's grimoire with impeccable precision. Reed shot him a scathing glance. As Tiv turned his head away, feigning ignorance.

"Request complete," Jack said, disinterested. "Shall we head back?"

As if on cue, an ear piercing wail suddenly resounded from deep within the forest. Their head's snapped up at the sound, their ears tingling even as the screech faded back into silence.

"What was that?" Tiv whispered.

"A bird?" Jack guessed, peering into the distance.

"It didn't sound like one."

"Are we really going to stick around long enough to find out?" Reed asked, scrunching his eyebrows.

"We are absolutely going to stick around," Tiv said.

"No," Sylvie denied. She looked around and noticed that the forest hadn't stirred, despite the ear-piercing shriek. As utterly lifeless as it had been since their arrival. "It might be dangerous, we shouldn't linger."

"All the more reason to. That thing sounded huge. We should take care of the problem now. Preferably before it makes a feast of Thyme's residents."

"Maybe it doesn't eat meat," Reed offered.

"Or maybe you'll just end up angering it," Sylvie said. "We came here for plants, not to become animal fodder."

"I'm going," Tiv announced.

Before they could stop him, Tiv jumped up and transformed into a raven. It took all of a second. His form shrunk, skin turned black, and feathers replaced skin. It looked like it hurt. If it did, Tiv didn't show it. His black wings flapped, stirring up a gale, as he soared through the air in the general direction of the sound. His form was quickly swallowed by the mist.

They heard another cry. Closer this time. Near enough that a few branches swayed from the pressure of the shriek.

"And he's gone," Jack commented dryly, already following after his absent partner. This happened far too often for his liking. He took a brief moment to turn to them, pointing a thumb in the direction Tiv had blindly ventured off to.

"Are you two coming?"

They shared a skeptical glance before trailing after him.

***

Ethil and Duward stood at the base of a long staircase which led only upward. Into the outside world. The sole entrance—and likewise exit—of the Drowned Tower. Despite this being the entrance to their grand Institute, there were no guards to speak of. Or any signs of life for that matter. Only a death trap where spikes would fall from holes in the ceiling, skewering anyone that made it past the gate. There weren't many. Most souls fled when they realized an entire house of practitioners lay in the murky depths of the Zexin Sea, their skills unknowable. Only that they weren't ones to be trifled with.

Lighting was minimal on the upper floors. Unduly so. The scant few torches that hadn't already died out were positioned just far enough for them to see their feet. The sorry saps assigned to maintain these halls were at least thorough in their neglect. This area wasn't even officially counted as a floor. Merely referred to as the uppermost level of the tower. As if everyone had just collectively decided to deny its existence. Only coming here when they absolutely had to. Like now.

The top floor was oddly colder than those below. The chill air made their skin crawl and their breaths come out visible, as they breached the undisturbed silence with their steps. They traversed vacant halls and opened creaky doors that led into rooms reeking of unuse and abandon. It was a decidedly dreary place that featured nothing but cobwebs and dust.

"Can a plant even grow in such harsh conditions?" Ethil asked, peering curiously up at the stone walls.

"Apparently, yes," Duward answered. "It shouldn't be that hard to spot. Elder Serach mentioned that it leeched off of even the slightest drop of water. Now the only problem is finding the proper leak."

"And if it's outside?"

Duward grinned. "Good thing you're a fantastic swimmer."

"You're joking," she looked at him, doubtful.

"If only."

Ethil paused, her face blanching in sudden worry. Duward didn't stop to wait for her. He threw open another door, only to be met with dusty floors, moldy crates, and scrambling rats—just more storage. He promptly turned on his heel and threw open another. Then another. And another.

This is getting us nowhere, Duward thought.

His sister lagged behind, rechecking each room with even more vigor. In case he was serious about sending her out to swim. They repeated the process several times until his ears picked up on the faint sound of trickling water falling onto stone.

Tap. Tap. Tap.

"Do you hear that?" Duward asked, walking toward a room near the end of the hall. Following the rhythmic drops.

"Hear what?"

"Water. Dripping water."

"I don't hear anything," Ethil said, cupping her ears and trying to pick up on what he so easily could.

The sound ceased as Duward threw open another door, exposing yet another dry room. His eyes widened in surprise for a moment. So sure that this was where the sound had been coming from. He looked around, searching for any kind of leak or crack in the stones. Only mildly surprised when he found none.

Duward opened his mouth to voice his confusion when the sound began again.

Tap–tap–tap–tap–tap.

Louder this time. Faster. More urgent. It was rushing.

"There it is again," he said, looking around and trying to find the source of the gushing liquid. "Do you hear it?"

Ethil's eyebrows shot up. "I still don't hear anything."

Duward heard fizzing and his head snapped to the left. He took off in the direction of the noise. Ethil hurried after him. Their steps were a loud echo throughout the vacant floor. She yelled something at him. Words his mind didn't care to register, as he came upon a moldy door. Its wood was soggy and worn, as if it would break with the slightest touch. He didn't particularly care if it did. So, without giving it too much thought, Duward kicked the door open, finding it preferable over touching decayed wood. It creaked in protest, slamming against the adjacent wall in a flurry of dust and loose splinters. Bits of it chipped off, falling unceremoniously to the ground at his feet.

His eyes widened and behind him, Ethil gasped, as they were met with the sight of hundreds of orange flowers, growing like vines along the room's floor and walls. A sweet scent poured forth and they crinkled their noses at its intensity.

In the far corner, Duward saw a tiny cave-in where water trickled incessantly. A fissure in the Drowned Tower's stone enchanted walls. He should've considered it fortunate that a clump of thick vines haphazardly clogged the hole, preventing an all-out flood. But he couldn't find it in himself to sigh in relief.

At least this explained the unsteady sound of flowing water he'd heard. They'd have to repair the wall before any lasting damage occurred. How the ones responsible for maintaining this floor could be so careless, Duward hadn't a clue. But he didn't doubt that they'd get a thorough scolding. Such reckless negligence wasn't easily forgiven, and they'd certainly evoke the kind of anger even the most rebellious of practitioners steered clear from.

Maybe those two could give them pointers on how to deal with it, he thought unforgivingly, Jack and Tiv's face coming to mind, before he roughly shook his head to rid himself of them. Thinking of those two gave him migraines.

"I don't have any flasks with me," Duward said, plucking an armful of flowers. "For now, let's just bring down as much as we can. We have to tell someone about this hole here."

His words were met with a loud thump.

"Ethil?" Duward called.

He turned. Only to find her lying on the floor. Face flat against the stone and limbs sticking out in all directions.

Duward's eyes widened. He abandoned the flowers in favor of gathering her in his arms.

"Ethil!" he yelled urgently. "Are you okay? What happened? Hey!" His words were met with another loud thump. Except this time it came from the frantic beat of his own heart. The sound was accompanied by the trickle of water and his erratic breaths. He preferred the previous silence.

Duward attempted to shake Ethil awake out of reflex. When that didn't work, he allowed his hands to glow a bright blue. As he released his magic. With practiced hands, he checked her pulse. While trained eyes searched for any signs of fatal injury.

He found none.

His relief at that was palpable, but not enough to fully free him from the anxiety he felt. Frantic blue eyes searched their surroundings, trying to find the culprit. Only to discover that he was alone. And that the torches had conveniently gone out, shrouding them in darkness.

"Ethil," he tried again. Twice. Three times.

Still, no answer.

He would have to carry her or, at the very least, get rid of the invisible stranger that had done this. Sweat trickled down his brow as panic settled. It made his fingers tremble, but he didn't dare run. That wasn't an option. He'd sooner die than leave his sister here. Duward backed further into the room. Past the flowers and beyond thickets of vines, only vaguely aware that he was stepping all over the flowers. He only stopped once his back was against the wall, hovering protectively over his sister's unconscious form.

Duward produced a small dagger which he kept hidden in his robes. A plain blade with a leather hilt. It glinted in the gloom. As he sat, waiting with bated breath. He did nothing, merely shifted on his knees into a position where he could quickly lunge if the situation called for it. While one hand remained steady on Ethil's neck. Her small breaths reassured him, granting him bravado and composure in a way the gravity of their situation didn't. The repetitive sound calmed him just enough for his breathing to match her own. His mind cleared with each slow exhale and even the pitter patter of water meeting stone became likeable.

It told him he was still alive. That he was alert and able to take on whoever hid in the darkness.

His eyes continued to roam the gloom around him. It was so dark that white spots appeared in his vision, but he ignored them as best he could, convincing himself that he was used to it. That living in the Drowned Tower trained him for this.

I need to carry her back, he thought. That fact alone had him impatient to leave. *Sooner rather than later.*

The world around him was still.

Disturbingly so.

And Duward began to doubt the idea of another person actually being there, as he peered once more into black. He squinted, trying to catch sight of something. Anything to let him know what he was up against. If anything at all. A foot, the glint of a dagger, he didn't care. So long as it told him that he wasn't wasting his time pressed up against the wall like a cornered animal. That he wasn't just needlessly dawdling, keeping both him and his sister in a slowly flooding room for no apparent reason. That there was actually a threat which needed to be dealt with.

Though he sorely wished there wasn't.

Fate, however, seemed to be conspiring against him because not a moment later, Duward shrieked. His grip on his dagger tightened in sudden terror, and though he knew running wasn't an option that didn't stop him from reflexively reeling back with an urgency that made his blood burn.

For the briefest of moments, someone had peered back.

6

Among the four Institutes of Magic across Ferus Terria, the east was the sole branch with no established Potentate Union. A customary assembly where seven Masters—christened Potens—were elected to lead over the entirety of their branch. The head of the Union, the Arch Poten, acted as the exclusive representative during summons by the Zenith Council. Unlike the former's meticulous selection process, the title of Arch Poten was passed from master to apprentice. In most cases, the name belonged to one family for generations. And only left when an Arch Poten chose to mentor an apprentice of no direct relation.

But such occurrences were few and far between. There was pride in being the head of an entire branch. Prestige that not even the most esteemed Elder of the Zenith Council obtained. It was this hubris that caused previous heads to train only their kin. To ensure that the title remained in their line.

The last recorded change had been little over two centuries ago. When the Tower's Potentate Union had been abolished by Maudré Cephas, then apprentice to Arch Poten Eldon Beau.

Maudré was an idealist.

The infuriating sort that possessed the needed charisma to sway others to his side. He spoke of equality amongst all Masters of Lore—senior practitioners, as he liked to call them—and after his rise to Arch Poten, Maudré immediately pushed for the total dissolution of the Union. Unsurprisingly, anarchy ensued. Havoc wrecked the Drowned Tower's halls, as the Zenith Council turned the other way. With bird's eyes, the world watched what went on in the Diamond Alps. While the rest were left to record their own history.

Those that opposed Maudré's beliefs and clung to the old ways were eventually driven out. Thus, leaving the Drowned Tower to dozens of Masters that collectively governed the branch as one body—the Assembly. But as commanded by the Elders, Maudré and all subsequent generations of his primary apprentice were still required to act as the chief representative when called upon by the Zenith Council, providing the illusion of normalcy.

An order Maudré obeyed, albeit reluctantly.

A sentiment that seemed to run in his lineage.

Columbus Cephas grimaced at the small bundle of crisp parchment in his hands. They were letters from the Diamond Alps. Ones he felt disinclined to opening. He shifted from foot to foot just staring at the rising sun embossed upon a red wax seal. The symbol of the Zenith Council. The other simply held his name in flawless script. The writing was all elegance. And though it was distinctly familiar, he couldn't quite put a face to its composer.

Columbus flipped it over, trying to find the sender. Nothing. Why they didn't think to put a name was a mystery for the ages. An act he would never understand and vowed never to do. But it must've been someone of relative import. The parchment was too fine to consider otherwise.

The curious part of him urged him to open it.

What he heeded, however, was the other, more sensible part that told him this was just another impromptu summon that he'd be obligated to attend. So, he stood there, waiting for a distraction that never came.

When the candles around him finally burned into nothing, he found himself left with no excuse for putting it off. Columbus grabbed himself a bottle of *G'orggio*. The finest, most expensive malt he had on hand. It was dry and burned all the way down.

He'd need it.

With a tired sigh, he read:

Arch Poten Cephas,

The time for the Summit is finally upon us. The Zenith Council requires the immediate presence of all Potentate Union representatives in the Diamond Alps. Please see to it that all pending business and upcoming schedules are handled accordingly.

May Thelarius smile upon your journey.
From the office of Sanclen Sibyl,
Zenith Council

From the head ambassador, himself. His signature took up a fourth of the page. With the names of the rest of the Council trailing behind almost sheepishly. Just looking at it made him want to drink more.

He opened the next in preference.

Cephas,

It's been so long. I meant to write sooner, but work has kept my time. All is well, I hope? Little news of the Drowned Tower has reached our ears. As we're currently suffering from one of the coldest blizzards since the Gelid Glacé, and it has yet to show signs of end. The frost has taken it upon itself to rime everything. Even the ink is frozen! Had the Diamond Alps not been home to so many Elementalists then this would truly be a cause for concern. Nevertheless, many are beginning to believe the snow to be some form of magical frost cast by another one of those pesky deserters. There's even talk of divine punishment brought upon us by Thelarius Merve, himself! Foolish notions, I assure you. Everyone is always following a rumor. Though here it is ridiculously so.

Still, no one should be out here. Let alone travelling amidst what the people have begun to fondly style, "our white woes." They do adore their drama.

A good way to keep occupied, no? Leonas intends to write a paper on boredom and its role in these absurdities.

Well, moving on, it behooves me to mention that I do feel somewhat… penitent, so to say, about the horrid timing of this correspondence's accompanying invitation. As well as the abruptness of its directive. If it is any consolation, then might I add that should you wish to engrave the wonders of the north to memory, the local snowdew are in full bloom and are flourishing marvelously, despite the weather. It's quite the sight.

Perhaps even worth a few unwelcome run-ins with some absconders.

On that note, it is my duty to inform you that included here is an updated list of names and information regarding all currently identified deserters not yet within custody. Along with a letter from Leonas to our son, Jacques. The doting sap is unduly concerned about his well-being.

I do hope that Jacques' attitude has bettered since he was sent there. Please take care of him.

Safe travels,

Cheryll Dace, Vanguard Circle

Hunter Captain

Columbus grinned at the closing, silently chastising himself for not recognizing the thin, loopy penmanship sooner. Just as he'd dreaded, he was called to the north. But Cheryll's words had somewhat softened the misfortune.

Fifteen years ago, Cheryll and Leonas Dace sent Jack to the east. The Drowned Tower practically shone with pride at being able to personally tutor the child of two of the most prominent faces in the Diamond Alps. A feeling that had not diminished with time, despite the sheer abrasiveness of Jack's personality. Which to Columbus' belief, had actually improved over the years. Jack barked often, but rarely did he bite. He grew well, though that was only to be expected after having the entire Assembly carefully monitoring his studies.

His sense of entitlement wasn't baseless.

Sooner or later, Jack would be sent back to the Diamond Alps

to replace his father. And the Drowned Tower would be mentioned in each of his future accomplishments.

They'd be innumerable. Of that, Columbus was certain.

But that was still an age and a half away, ergo undeserving
of his attention. Instead, Columbus procured the list of names attached to Cheryll's letter, mindlessly reading through them. One
in particular caught his eye. And he took a step back in surprise,
rereading every stroke of ink.

To his displeasure, he'd read correctly.

"Master Cephas!" He heard a high-pitched call from just
beyond his door. "I'm coming in!"

A young Amorph, whom he recognized as Sylvie's friend,
Myrrh, appeared before him. She was panting and drenched with
sweat. As she spoke hurriedly about something he couldn't quite
decipher.

"What ails you, child?" Columbus asked, trying to calm her
with his voice alone.

Myrrh swallowed, catching her breath. She shifted on the balls of her feet in unease. "Not me. The other Masters are calling
for you," she stuttered, tripping over her own words. "Something
happened to two of the practitioners!"

Columbus' appall was clear. As dozens of horrible scenarios
suddenly came barreling toward the forefront of his mind. He took one more peek at the list of names in his hands. And couldn't
quite help the cold shiver that washed over him.

"Lead the way then," Columbus said, hurriedly walking past
her. "Tell me what you know."

As it turned out, she knew little. Only tidbits. But they were
important tidbits. And they made his thoughts spiral all the same.
If she knew such details, then what did the other practitioners
know?

By the time they made it to the research tower's topmost flo-
or, a crowd of practitioners had already gathered around one of
the rooms. They babbled about what was going on. Some even
attempted to morph into insects to get a closer look. Columbus

weaved his way around them until he stood before a closed door where Master Horren Orpha's burly figure stood menacingly. A scar ran horizontally across his closed eyelids, blinding him to the horrors of the world and trapping him in a far more personal kind of hell.

Orpha silently crossed his arms in a decidedly vanguard-like fashion. He stood like a sentinel, observing those around him. As two other Masters circled him. Both had grim looks on their faces and were desperately trying to restore order.

"I was told that the Mane siblings were involved in an accident," Columbus said, shooing the nosy crowd away. "How's the situation?"

"Dire," Master Pyrne Celaris answered. His wide eyes gave the appearance of constant surprise. The blackness of his pupils only made them seem larger.

Columbus stepped into the room and his nose was immediately assaulted with the pungent scent of blood, sea water, and blooming flowers. But the floral aroma had soured from lingering in a room for so long. His aggravated sense of smell, however, didn't stop his eyes from widening at the sight of all the orange flora. Or the rest of his surroundings for that matter.

Three Healers surrounded Ethil's still form, their hands glowing blue. As they tried to breathe life back into her. There were two older practitioners fixing a large hole to the side, stealing glances at Duward's body that was laid out beside them.

Columbus trembled as he crouched beside Duward, examining his cold skin and blue lips. He was drenched. Filled with wounds invisible to the naked eye. He placed a hand over his lids and bowed low.

"May Pernelia's wings guide you to where the First Zenith dwell."

"Duward drowned," Celaris said once he finished his prayer. "There was no signs of struggle."

"And Ethil?"

"They're doing everything they can. She has a good chance.

Master Everice said there were already traces of healing magic cast upon her when she got here. Duward's work, perhaps?"

The raspy voice of Master Miriam followed his words. "Not since the time of the Mentalists has such a horrid affair occurred within the walls of the Drowned Tower! We teach hundreds of children, what are we to tell them? That it is no longer safe here?"

"For now, it's best to keep this between the Assembly and select practitioners," Celaris said evenly. "There's no need to involve the others."

"They're already involved in this," Miriam argued. "We should properly inform them before panic spreads and they start trying to leave on their own. After they've been informed, then we can safely evacuate them. I'd rather not have an entire horde of panicked practitioners that don't know the full consequences of deserting."

"Evacuate?" Celaris raised an eyebrow. "To where? Eriam is far too small to house an entire Institute and none of the other branches will accept so many new apprentices. Not when they're suffering from worse problems. Will you have our practitioners become homeless refugees?"

"Then what do you suggest we do?"

"I've already voiced my piece! Are those ears just for show?"

"Enough!" Columbus intervened. "This isn't the time to be squabbling amongst ourselves! Gather the Assembly, while I go and speak to Elder Serach. He needs to be informed."

"And we're to what?" Miriam asked, frustration rising. "Sit and talk, while the culprit roams the halls? That's madness! Complete madness! What will we do if another child falls victim to this vile use of magic?!"

"Go confine the younger ones to their rooms and seal the gates." Columbus narrowed his eyes, tired of trying to appease her. "No one gets in or out! Put up a guard rotation schedule on the roster and assign only your primary apprentices and their partners. I want at least six guards per chamber."

"Seal the gates?" Miriam parroted, aghast. "There are still

pairs outside! Are we to leave them to their own devices? They are young! What will you do if they take this time to decide that they want to use their skills to play in the towns?"

"They aren't going to unintentionally hurt anyone, nor will they foolishly use their magic without authorization. They've been trained and know the consequences of such actions. Believe in them. Believe in what you've taught them, Miriam."

She pursed her lips and planted her hands on her hips, trying to appear more intimidating. "How can you be so sure? More and more practitioners desert with each passing day. If none are allowed outside these walls, then catching them will be nigh impossible should they decide to dispel our Demar spells and flee."

Columbus sighed, rubbing his temples in frustration. "Send messages to everyone not patrolling the mountains. Call them back immediately and under no circumstances should you tell them of our current dilemma. I expect each and every one of them inside before sunset. Barring Jack and Sylvie, of course, they must remain on Eriam."

"What? You can't just allow them to stay! What will the others think?"

"Calm down," Columbus said with killing patience. He struggled to keep his tone even. "This little incident will… pique the interest of the Zenith Council. I don't want to attract the full attention of the Vanguard Circle as well. Should something happen to Jack, then we'll undoubtedly garner the notice of a few of their leaders. As for Sylvie, I'd rather my successor be in a position to flee should something happen to myself. Our Potentate Union may have dissolved long ago, but not exclusively. There must still be a representative. The Zenith Council won't have it any other way."

Silence.

"Now," Columbus raised a brow in challenge, "are you quite done questioning my every decision?"

Miriam clamped her mouth shut, settling for crossing her arms in displeasure. Her livid face returned to its usual pallor.

She looked as if she had a lemon in her mouth.

"And your son?" Celaris suddenly asked. "Shall we recall him as well?"

Columbus swallowed, his hands shaking. He may have hated his position, but that didn't change the fact that he was Arch Poten. Exclusively, he was the head of the Eastern Branch's Union and was required to act as such. He had to think this through. Not with emotion but with logic and sound reason. The bond of primary apprentice and master superseded blood. That was fact. Just as the sun was bright and snow was cold. He couldn't plant the seed of doubt by making an excuse to keep his son away, running the risk of suddenly having the other Masters turn on him. They had children as well. Many of which were residents of the Drowned Tower.

He steeled his resolve.

Columbus took a deep breath to clear his mind. "Don't make me repeat myself. What difference does my son being outside make? I said only Jack and Sylvie were to remain. Send them a message should any of you feel your Demar spells dissipate. I trust those two can handle any that choose to run."

"And if there are too many?" Celaris asked. "It doesn't matter if they're two of our prized students or two of our worst, the probability of defeat through sheer numbers is too high for my liking."

"The only escape is over the Eirinne Mountains. Pernelia's final defense. We have dozens of practitioners standing guard. Our patrollers aren't fools. They've been trained to ask questions later."

They nodded reluctantly.

Miriam looked as if she still wanted to protest, but managed to catch herself in lieu of more important matters. When she spoke, her voice was doubtful. "I will gather the Assembly."

The door opened and Orpha walked in.

"And I'll relay the message," Orpha said, shrugging and pointing at his eyes. "Though I may need help writing it."

Celaris grinned at his poor attempt at shattering the tension.

He clasped the larger man's shoulder. "I'll handle the letter, partner. You scare the kids back into their rooms."

They spared each other one final glance, before going their separate ways. Purpose in their steps.

***

Columbus made his way to Elder Serach's private quarters, located deep in the bowels of the Assembly's tower. Nestled between vacant living spaces and unused commons. Normally it was an undisturbed wing that once housed the branch's Potens, but now it served as accommodations for esteemed guests and other visitors of import. There were no torches here. Only engraved words in ancient tongues and thick veins running across the length of the walls, pulsing a cold blue.

Magic. More concentrated here than in the rest of the tower.

"Elder," Columbus greeted.

Serach was leaning over a desk, reading through a stretched scroll. A bottle of spicy wine and a pile of shabby leather-bound journals by his side.

"I hear the Council summoned you for the Summit. I see that they've finally decided to appoint a new head. It's about time. A shame I won't be able to attend. I still have much to do here. So, I'm afraid you'll have to make the trip alone. But do congratulate the new head for me."

Columbus crossed the distance between them in three quick strides and grabbed Serach's elbow. His hold was strong enough to bruise. "I need a moment," he said seriously. "Now, Elder."

Serach whipped around at the urgency laced in his tone. His eyebrows shot up, as Columbus pinned him with an icy stare. And he asked lowly, "What's wrong, my boy?"

"Where is your primary apprentice?" Columbus asked, his grip tightening.

"Rior? Why? Has something happened?"

"Duward is dead," Columbus said bluntly, his eyes hooded

and unyielding. "He was drowned. Not in the Zexin Sea, but by magic. There were no signs of struggle. It was quick and likely unexpected."

Serach gasped, stumbling back in shock. He placed a hand on the table to steady himself. "What?" he asked. "By who? What about the girl—his partner? Is she alright?"

"Ethil is still being tended to, but we're confident that she'll wake given enough time," Columbus said, carefully assessing his reaction. "Never before has such an incident occurred in the Drowned Tower. Not even during the strife that plagued the lands when Pernelia Merve soared through the skies in search of her absent lover. Or when Silas Drayr's fire defied all logic and set the Zexin Sea aflame. We house many children here and someone with the blood of one of our own on his hands is not someone we can have roaming our halls."

"What are you getting at, Columbus?" Serach asked, low.

Columbus' eyes narrowed in distrust. "Duward was killed by magic. The only Conjurer here has an affinity for fire and she's on Eriam searching for the plant you asked for. The only Elementalist is with her," he sneered, "no, that's not right. There is one more Elementalist. He came with you."

"Rior would never do such a thing!" Serach bellowed. His eyes flashed in barely restrained rage. "To commit such a heinous crime, to even suggest he's responsible for such atrocity, do you realize who you're accusing? Rior is my primary apprentice!"

"And I need to know where he is," Columbus said, brooking no barter.

"Then what?" Serach gulped. His throat suddenly dry. "What will you do? Judge him for a crime he may or may not have committed? Have you gone mad?"

"This cannot go unpunished. The price of murder will be repaid with blood."

"Because spilling more blood is always the answer, isn't it?" Serach yelled in disbelief. "There could be other Elementalists or Conjurers hidden here! How are you so sure it was him? How? I won't allow him to be put on trial for a crime you assume he committed!"

"Whether he was involved or not hardly matters. He still needs to be found and dealt with."

"What?"

"All traitors must undergo rehabilitation. Any unauthorized use of magic cast with the intent to harm will call for the immediate elimination of the threat. Any resistance will be met with force. This includes escape. That is the law."

"Traitor? What nonsense are you spouting now?" Serach's fists clenched and in an attempt to release his fury, he knocked over a goblet of wine. The wine took on a disturbing tint of black as it crawled across the floor, illuminated by the blue veins of magic in the room.

Columbus stared at it for a moment, before reaching into his robes. Slowly. So as not to startle Serach. He carefully produced the letters from the Diamond Alps and waved them before him.

"As you mentioned," Columbus began, "I've been called to the north for a meeting with the Zenith Council. This came with the invitation." Columbus handed him one of the papers. "It's a list I received from the Vanguard Circle."

Serach's eyes trailed down the long list of names.

"What is this?" He knew what it was, but it was always different when what you were supposed to know was said to your face. Still, that didn't stop his body from trembling when Columbus told him. Serach barely registered dropping the paper in the puddle of wine.

"You said this was from the Vanguard Circle?" Serach asked in disbelief. "Impossible! What proof do they have? Rior has been here with me during the entire length of our journey! If he wanted to leave then he would have long ago!"

"Then where is he?" Columbus asked.

Silence.

He didn't have the time for this.

"I'll station two of my apprentices outside," Columbus informed, nodding his head toward the door. "The Tower is officially under lockdown. We have an Elementalist on the loose."

****

A figure crept through the Drowned Tower's halls, recoiling slightly at the large crowd. Not two minutes ago, everyone had been going about their business, before a blind Master suddenly appeared and ordered them back to their rooms. They obeyed, of course. Out of fear. He inspired terror with a few gruff words and the crossing of beefy arms. None were exempt from the sense of trepidation.

Not even an outsider.

The faceless figure stood for a moment, staring at the blind Master and shivering at the thought of getting caught. Dodging a group of rowdy Amorphs elbowing all those they passed.

No one seemed to be paying attention to each other. Instead, they all collectively decided to speak at once. Their dragging footsteps and irritating chatter permeated the air. As they simultaneously complained about the sudden command, their empty stomachs, and the sheer amount of people rushing back to their rooms. Others whispered about a commotion on the upper floors. One of the younger practitioners was even dragged along by the crowd of people, hysterically calling out a boy's name. Until someone bothered to help him.

The figure lithely slipped through an empty hall, heading for a guarded room at the very end. It was a rarely used path. There were no crowds here. Not even a wandering straggler. Footsteps echoed and voices from behind bounced along the walls. The only life came from the guard seated at the front of a large door, barely awake. He yawned loudly, his head nodding downward, as he examined his worn leathers in an effort to keep himself awake. He sat on his haunches, elbows on his knees and hands dangling between his legs. Bored and distracted.

Absolutely perfect.

Another step and the figure shrunk into a newt. Slimy and

wet. With quick feet, the Amorph scurried ahead, attaching itself to the wall. By the time the guard looked up, the newt's flat form had already slinked past the crack over the door and onto the bed within. Where the woman he guarded lay, unconscious.

The figure knew enough about the woman to know that her name was Ethil, and that she was a Healer. One that had somehow survived, while her more skilled brother had not. The newt crept over her neck and down her body in an attempt to find any lingering scents or traces of magic. Ethil smelt of blood and seawater and a plethora of other scents coming from all those that had healed her. The Amorph would've explored further had the door not flown open, forcing the newt to hide under the bed.

Two men entered, and the figure dared a peek to find two of the Tower's Masters, donning furrowed brows and prominent frowns. The figure had seen them roaming the halls on numerous occasions, but couldn't attach names to their faces. From their eyes, however, it was easy to tell that they were both Healers.

"She should wake soon," the one holding a large grimoire said. "We should bring her to the Assembly."

The other, who had a lengthy beard decorating his chin, sighed. "It's unlikely that she'll remember anything."

"We have to try."

"Before or after we tell her about her brother?"

Their frowns deepened.

The grimoire holder solemnly shook his head before clasping his fellow Master's shoulder. They both turned, leaving as swiftly as they'd come. The door closed behind them. Soft and final.

The figure lingered under the bed for a long while, blinking black eyes at the shadows under the door. Until they disappeared completely. The guard outside crouched once more before it. He was fully awake now, and humming an off-beat tune under his breath. With quick steps, the intruder crawled back up to Ethil's side, waiting.

It was still too soon.

7

Trekking through Tearwood had been more trying than any of them had expected. The mist thinned out, as they closed in on the loud wails. But the paths had also gotten steeper. The trees denser. They passed garishly colored birds and packs of Snuff that scurried away whenever they drew near. Their sounds of escape were as silent as the rest of what they would've assumed was a lifeless area, had the copious amount of thriving plant life hadn't been around them—continuously being shoved into their faces with every step. Much to their combined frustration.

"How far is Thyme?" Sylvie asked, trying to pick up on the sounds of domesticated livestock or the heavy clang of metal.

"We haven't been walking long," Jack said. "It shouldn't be too far."

"I can't hear them. Or anything for that matter."

"She's right," Reed said, stopping and peering in Thyme's general direction. "I haven't heard anything either. Not since we stepped foot in this cursed forest. The silence is deafening."

Jack clasped Reed's shoulder and thrust his chin forward. A gesture to walk. "We can worry about the lack of noise later. Right now, we need to keep moving. Tiv's close."

"How do you know?"

"I can feel it," Jack said, rolling his eyes.

"Do you think he's alright?" Sylvie asked.

"If something happened then we would've heard a scream or one of those feeble battle cries he's so proud of."

"Unless he was gobbled up," Reed said.

Jack stared at him sidelong, his eyes hardening. "Tiv may not look before he leaps, but we are partners for a reason. As long as you can ignore the issues with his personality, then he's the ideal practitioner."

"The same could be said about you," Sylvie remarked.

Jack outright ignored her. His attention focused solely on Reed. Unable to let the remark go, despite the lighthearted tone in which it was said.

"Tiv is relatively strong compared to most in the Drowned Tower. I've seen him disembowel a man twice his size without transforming. You'd do well to remember that."

"Right," Reed muttered, coughing uncomfortably.

"Well don't scare him." Sylvie shook her head at Jack, who now had an amused grin playing along the corners of his mouth.

"I'm not scared!" Reed huffed, indignant.

Sylvie opened her mouth to respond, but was rendered silent when a long, sopping wet appendage struck out and brushed against her ear. She halted, the scream dying in her throat, as she looked up.

Coiled around the trunk of a tree was a mammoth sized amphibian with clear eyes that stared down at her, silently judging her worth. Its skin was slimy and yellow. Pulsing blue veins were littered along its body, thrumming with each silent step it took closer to her face. It had bent hind legs that were ideal for jumping great distances. And Sylvie could just make out the unmistakable sight of bones protruding from its back. As it sat up to get a better angle of her shivering frame.

It slowly reeled in its tongue, before opening its mouth to blow a cloud of mist in her face.

Sylvie's breath hitched. Her pulse raced furiously under her skin. As her fingers twitched in horror at the sight before her. Sylvie felt her flames come to life. Her palm sparked a cold blue, but she willed her body still. Not wanting to startle the creature.

Jack noticed the sudden spur of magic and turned.

He blinked owlishly, as he followed her line of sight. With hesitant breaths, Sylvie watched as Jack carefully tapped Reed, who wilted at the sight of the large creature. Reed slowly opened his grimoire and took a few cautious steps back. Close enough to heal, but far enough to not be in the direct line of fire. Reed winced when he stepped on a stray branch, only to sigh in relief upon realizing that the beast hadn't noticed the sound.

Jack gestured for both of them to stay put.

Sylvie gulped, as she watched Jack cautiously circle to the opposite side of the tree. She clenched her fists when the amphibian brought its head closer, giving her a clear view of the glowing throb of its veins. It was such a familiar blue—one she'd recognize anywhere. The color of magic. Sylvie mentally debated if the beast actually had magic flowing through its body or if this was a natural trait. A thought she didn't get to dwell on as swirls of pale blue smoke seeped out of its mouth and over her face. It encompassed her form, clouding her vision.

Sylvie fought the fierce urge to retaliate. She didn't dare move. In fear of it suddenly lashing out and ruining whatever plan Jack had conjured. Instead, she blinked rapidly. As if such an action would get her vision to clear faster. It didn't.

Jack took that moment to slam his hand on the tree.

The sound of rapid cracking immediately filled the air. A thick layer of frost quickly spread over the trunk, coating the beast's legs. It released a deafening cry that made them all flinch, as it slammed its tail against the ground in sudden alarm. Patches of dirt flew up, coating Jack, who crouched to avoid the beast's thrashing tail. He covered his head in an attempt to guard against the sudden shower of leaves and filth, hoping that he wouldn't be next. He wasn't all that interested in flying.

"Sylvie!" Jack's yell resounded poorly over the beast's cries. "Fire! Now!"

She didn't need to be told twice.

Sylvie lifted her hands and unleashed a trail of fire straight into the beast's mouth. It cried out once more and she could see its tongue slowly char—from a light pink to a sickening brown. With renewed vigor, the beast tried to break free from Jack's ice, repeatedly banging its tail against the trunk of the tree in a futile attempt to smash it in half.

Jack's hands lit up once more, emitting chilly fumes. A spray of ice leapt from his palms to freeze the hostile extremity. And with a deep breath, he brought his hands up a final time to help Sylvie roast it. The beast cried in agony. But they didn't stop until it fell to the ground. Its skin seared black.

"For Thelarius' sake," Jack grumbled, shaking his hands and blowing the remnants of smoke away. He crouched before the beast's unmoving form and scrunched his nose at the scent of scorched flesh. Its blue veins were still pulsing, albeit faintly. Jack picked up a stick and prodded its side, grimacing at how easily the stick split skin. "It's still alive. Barely."

"What is it?" Reed asked, slowly bounding up to its legs.

"From the legs, I'd say it's a toad. Very large and very deadly. Maybe a practitioner's pet? Look at its veins." Jack poked one for emphasis, unintentionally piercing it. He bent over to inspect its long, pointed tail. He was no expert, but he knew enough about frogs to know that their tails shrunk long before they matured. Had this one not fully matured? Or were tails common among its species? Or was it something else altogether—magic, perhaps?—he didn't discount the possibility.

"Do you think there's a deserter wandering around the area? Or maybe our beloved Masters have been keeping some kind of twisted experiment from us."

"Kill it," Sylvie said, her face blanching in sudden terror.

Jack turned at the sound of her fear laden voice. One eyebrow raised in amusement, as he watched her back away. "Don't tell me you're afraid of frogs."

Sylvie gave him the best glare she could muster. Though it was sullied when she stepped on a plant and squeaked. Jack openly laughed, while Reed's wide eyes worriedly examined her, searching for any signs of injury. Before Sylvie could move her hand and use her magic to destroy what was left of the toad, its voice sac expanded. The sudden bubble made Jack and Reed stumble back in surprise.

Their hands immediately sparked blue in anticipation.

They waited for one tense moment. Then the sac deflated, releasing a cloud of pale blue from the toad's mouth that blended with the mist enveloping them. The toad's veins abruptly stopped glowing, as it sagged against the ground. Finally dead.

They relaxed, letting out a collective sigh of relief at the sight.

"At least we know where this mist came from," Jack said, brushing himself off. He raised his hands and singed the toad's head one last time for good measure. When he was done, he grinned smugly down at his handiwork.

"This is a large forest," Sylvie said, looking off to the side to avoid direct eye contact with the burnt carcass. She didn't understand how Jack could stand to be near it for so long without gagging. "There must be more of these things. A nest deeper in."

"Perhaps someone's breeding them," Reed offered. "This mist doesn't feel natural. It never spreads past the trees, and we haven't heard anything since we stepped inside."

"A practitioner then," Jack decided. "One fairly adept at muting enchantments. Such magic is only taught to those under the direct command of the Vanguard Circle. I believe the Hunting Division uses it to silence their steps during particularly difficult chases. If these frogs are instruments to spread magic, then I have no doubt that we're up against an escaped Hunter. Not even Amorphs have such strong ties with animals of the wild. Most aren't allowed outside long enough to maintain one."

"It must be a Peose then," Sylvie said, scrunching her nose in distaste at the thought of such a creature being a Hunter's scouting animal. "Why would they choose a frog though? There are so many better options. Ones more adept than… *that.*"

Jack grinned. "For once, I agree."

"I didn't know Peose were instilled with magic," Reed said.

"It's done via crystals," Jack explained easily. He was curious about the creatures his mother dealt with on a daily basis and in the crystal itself. It was a topic he'd studied extensively, and returned to often. "They're called *Orivellea,* or simply, Orive. They function as magic circuits, among other things. I believe some even use them for lighting."

"I've never seen them before."

"You'll find many across the Wymeran River. Since they're made by a select division in the Western Branch."

"The Weeping Grove," Reed whispered, thinking of the western Institute. It was every Healer's dream to study there. He was no exception. "I wonder why they don't export them more."

"The Vanguard Circle keeps them under strict regulation. They're used for their beloved Peose after all. A shame. They'd turn up a nice profit, don't you think? But I'm sure there are a few black market traders that deal in them." Jack curiously ran the stick along the toad's veins. Though they no longer pulsed, he could still feel the whispers of something otherworldly within. "Someone once told me Orive could only be created by Healers. Just another secret in those giant books of theirs, I suppose. I wouldn't know. But I do know that these crystals are attached to their bodies." Jack took a step forward, bending once again to inspect the carcass. "Want to extract it?"

"No!" Sylvie cried. Their eyes turned to her — Jack's amused and Reed's filled with concern — and her ears burned with embarrassment. She cleared her throat, reigning in her panic. As she desperately tried to change the subject. "I didn't realize a Hunter could keep more than a single Peose at any given time. We've already killed one pet. Its owner will undoubtedly seek revenge if we decide to add to the tally or… desecrate its body."

Jack lifted an eyebrow at the quick excuse, but conceded nevertheless. "Of that, I have no doubt. Though I know for a fact that having more than one Peose violates the laws of the Vanguard Circle. If you're correct and there's a nest further in, then we're undoubtedly against a deserter. We shouldn't venture too deep. If this truly is a runaway Hunter, then we need to go about this more carefully."

"Runaway Hunter or not, it doesn't change the fact that this person is dangerous," Sylvie said. She looked around, trying to find any clues that could lead them to the toad's nest or, more preferably, the one responsible for this. "To cancel out sound over such a large area, then to engineer frogs to somehow spread it. That doesn't just require great skill, but time. Frogs don't just become this size overnight. If this really is a deserter, then they've been gone for a long while. The fact that the Assembly had us avoid this area means that they must've had their suspicions."

"And if it isn't a deserter?" Reed asked. "What if someone from the Drowned Tower has permission to do this?"

"Permission to play in the forest, you mean?" Jack muttered. His brow furrowed in thought.

"Well, not exactly… but, yes."

"Why though?" Sylvie wondered aloud.

Jack met her eyes with a firm nod, acknowledging and backing her doubt. "Tampering with a creature's genetic makeup isn't exactly run-of-the-mill research. We should've heard of it at least. A passing rumor of some sort. Not everyone's tongues are as quiet or as still when it comes to matters like this. And Thelarius knows how much practiitoners like to gossip."

A loud squawk and flapping wings broke their conversation.

Their heads snapped up, magic licking against their hands once more. A fight or flight reflex they'd picked up from years spent patrolling their borders.

A pitch black raven swooped down to rest upon the branches above them, tilting its head and examining them with beady eyes. They were momentarily blinded by a sudden flash of light, before those same eyes peered at them from the head of a man.

"Tiv!" Jack called harshly. "Pernelia's feathered ass! We've been looking everywhere for you."

"Here I am," Tiv said coolly. He plucked a handful of berries, before jumping down and dusting himself off. Tiv spared the burnt toad a glance, raising his eyebrows in wonder. "You deep-fried a toad? Were you hungry, Jack?"

"Very." Jack sighed in derision. "Care for a taste? Plenty to go around. Oh, wait! That isn't some form of cannibalism, is it?"

Tiv flung a berry at him.

Jack sidestepped, almost as if he'd been expecting it. The bastard probably had. Tiv wouldn't put it past him. "There's a pit up ahead. It's crawling with these ugly fiends. I can say for certain that these things are carnivorous. There were rotting carcasses everywhere. The scent was revolting."

"Next time," Reed began, "refrain from going off on your own. We don't know what we're dealing with."

Tiv glared at him before snorting.

"Look *Healer*, I'm an Amorph, and Amorphs are scouts! Always have been, always will be. Besides, I was able to get some good information." Tiv produced a scroll from his robes, waving it wildly. "This was given to me mid-flight by one of Master Celaris' messenger birds."

Tiv showed them the broken wax seal.

"A dispatch?" Sylvie wondered, squinting at the seal. "Are they giving us new orders?"

"They're calling us back."

"You should've opened with that," Jack told him.

"Not you." Tiv made a face. "You and Syl have been ordered to stay in Thyme and wait for further instruction, while Reed and I bring in the samples we collected for Elder Serach. No one is allowed out of the Tower."

"Yet they're allowed to open the gate?" Jack asked, raising an eyebrow in incredulity. "If they're trying to keep people from going outside, then doesn't that just seem, oh, how to say it... stupid? Risky? Stupidly risky?"

"It'll only be for a second," Tiv said, shrugging off his mutual skepticism.

Jack shook his head. His eyes trailed carefully down the path they'd just come. Somehow, it seemed more foreboding than before. *I should've marked it,* he thought. It was too late now.

"Those old codgers clearly aren't thinking straight," Jack said, turning back to them. "The dementia must've finally settled."

"Wait." Sylvie stepped forward. "We're to remain on Eriam? What exactly happened?"

"I'm not sure. But clearly nothing good." Tiv tossed her the scroll, so she could read the message herself. It was short and direct. Written in such a way that left no room for question and even less for argument. "Master Celaris is skilled in the art of vague explanations and ambiguous orders. But I'm sure something big must be happening for them to not want you and Jack inside. Keeping their prized pupils safe, while the rest of us bite the dust is just good strategy."

"I didn't ask to be Master Cephas' primary apprentice."

"That doesn't change the fact that you are. The next in line for Arch Poten, what a blessing that must be!" Tiv pointed a thumb back at Reed. "I wonder how your partner feels about all this. I'm sure as the current Arch Poten's son, he must hold some resentment at the fact."

Reed sighed, tiredly rubbing his face and accidentally smearing dirt across his forehead. He couldn't be bothered to wipe it off though. "Please don't involve me. You're the only one with the problem, Tiv. I'm not going to take your side in this."

Tiv gaped, surprised and disappointed. Though his feelings were real, his expression was too exaggerated for them to take him seriously.

"Well, I don't exactly care for those old bags. Or the order they want us to croak," Jack said, tilting his head in the general direction of the Institute. "But we should leave now, before whoever's in this cursed forest decides to send their army of oversized toads after us."

Jack didn't bother waiting for them. He trudged forward. His head down and his mouth pressed into a thin line, as he stalked their trail back home.

They shared a glance, before following after him.

Orders were absolute.

***

Any spark of hope Tiv and Reed had about being rewarded for successfully completing Elder Serach's requisition had been forgotten upon their arrival at the Institute. They were greeted by the stench of fear and the nagging suspicion that something was terribly wrong. Their doubt only intensified when they found a group of practitioners desperately huddled together just inside the gates, ardently praying to Pernelia's statue for strength. They knelt there for a full minute, before they were rushed inside by a man, whom they failed to discreetly hand a small pouch to. The sack clinked as it hit the ground, loosening just enough to flash the silver coins within.

"Hey," Tiv called. The man turned with a start, hurriedly pocketing the purse.

"What do you want?" he stuttered, and Tiv rolled his eyes.

"Tiv Grovegg and Reed Cephas reporting for lockdown."

"What?"

"Look, dimwit," Tiv said, extra slow. "I don't care about you earning a little on the side. Just hurry and let us in, yeah?"

The man hesitated for a moment before nodding, calling out to those behind him to open the gate. It took a full fifteen minutes longer than usual, and when the gates of the Institute shut behind them with an ominous screech and typically unused chains were pulled up to lock it back in place, they knew they wouldn't get to see the outside for a long time.

The chains were six inches thick and made of solid steel, requiring the combined strength of twelve burly Amorphs to secure them. As much of an extra security measure as they were propaganda of days past. During a time of rampant bloodshed and duels of supremacy. When the Drowned Tower housed more slaves than it did children. Conducted more live experiments than lectures. Prison cells were the research labs and the people favored sated curiosity over morals.

It spoke of a time when the Drowned Tower was once filled

with animals in human skin, calling themselves Mentalists. An outdated title, as they'd been officially rechristened Masters of Lore by the first Zenith Council. The Mentalists may have been gone, but they certainly weren't forgotten. Never forgotten.

Reminders of them, and of what this place once was remained. They could be found everywhere, covered under years of dust. Those chains weren't to keep people out. They were to ensure that secrets stayed within.

Tiv and Reed were escorted underwater by three of the more distinguished practitioners among their branch. All primary apprentices and all donning the same serious expression. There was a feeling of dread that lingered in the air, tainting the Tower. Strangely, no one traversed through the halls. And the practitioners escorting them anxiously glanced down every corridor they passed. An obvious sign of unease.

Their steps were stiff and their shoulders were knotted, as if they were expecting someone to jump out and attack.

Reed's eyes widened in surprise when they stopped in front of his chamber, explaining to him that all but a few select practitioners were to remain in their quarters until further notice.

His father's orders.

"Wait," Reed called, just barely grabbing the sleeve of the spindliest of the three. He nearly fell over, and Reed had to wonder just how he became a primary apprentice. He was gangly and thin, but unlike himself, he wasn't lean. Just another pile of skin and bones with hooded blue eyes that darted around nervously and a high-pitched voice that served as a testament to his easily startled disposition.

"Yes?" he squeaked, before coughing and righting himself. An attempt to look professional. But he only looked more out of place alongside the towering forms of Tiv and the others.

"Won't you at least tell me what's going on?" Reed asked. He met Tiv's eyes and the Amorph immediately shook his head, silently telling him to stop.

"I'm sorry," the thin man replied, his shoulders sagging in

true remorse. "But we can't."

Reed ran his hands through his hair in exasperation, gesturing wildly to emphasize his desire for answers. Any would do. "If you can't tell me then at least let me see my father. Or a timeframe! Yes! If you do happen to see him, then I'd appreciate it if you'd ask for an estimated timeframe of however long he thinks this," Reed gestured vaguely around them, "will last. It's unsettling to know that I'm here safe and sound, while my partner isn't. I'm sure you can relate?"

The two more muscular practitioners shared a knowing glance. From the way they acted, Reed assumed they were partners. And had been for a long time. Their movements were one fluid motion, constantly complementing the other without realizing it.

"I'll ask," Tiv muttered then, pointing a thumb assuringly at himself. "I'm a primary apprentice, too, remember? I should be allowed to walk around a bit before they order me around again."

Reed's eyebrows lifted in surprise. "If you wouldn't mind."

"I offered, didn't I?" Tiv snorted, cracking his neck. "Wipe the surprise off your face. It's infuriating. Don't be conceited and let it get to your head either! I have my own reasons for doing this. You're not the only one that left a partner behind."

Reed nodded, swallowing the lump in his throat. As the four before him turned to leave. "Thank you, Tiv."

Tiv flicked his hand in acknowledgement.

8

Thyme was an overcrowded community of houses built on top of each other. With no magic and cursed with rocky terrain, the people grew practical and kept their flatlands for farming. Shops were littered between the many rooms that served as their residence, selling everything from trinkets to old meat. Men and women loudly called out to any who would listen, trying to get them to buy their wares with false claims about how they're products differed from all the rest. Many from the Drowned Tower usually fell for such banal scams. The practitioners were just happy to be allowed outside and gladly traded trinkets they'd find lying about the Institute. Things that wouldn't be missed until someone noticed they were gone.

Any sort of foreign good was priceless here. As not many had the will to climb over the mountain ranges, nor did the majority want to.

The lands beyond the Eirinne Mountains were riddled with strife. A burial ground for those without magic. The Drowned Tower's practitioners had to constantly patrol the mountainside, dealing with those that posed a threat. Those that didn't, were allowed passage to the safe haven that was Thyme.

Where clotheslines hung from rooftops, dangling alongside numerous wooden bridges that connected the entire town. The many passages formed a maze of back alleys and winding paths. There were a dozen ways to enter one area, along with an unspoken rule about which ones were for carts and which were for people. The clink of metal was a recurrent ring that echoed in the alleys, and the air had the distinctly overpowering scent of steel.

The residents of Thyme didn't typically receive visits from the Drowned Tower, except when they requested aid. So, when the heat dimmed with the evening and rain began to pour, Sylvie and Jack became walking spectacles as they took cover in the city. Both poorly prepared for such dreary weather. But at least it wasn't cold. It wasn't a depressingly chilling downpour.

Many gathered for the sole purpose of staring at them. While others pickpocketed the sorry fools that did.

Jack and Sylvie each held fire in their palms—a poor source of warmth against the chill—their deathly pale skin and cloth robes were a stark contrast against the leather and wool covering the sun kissed tones of those around them. Many of whom, were caked in dirt. A testament to their long day of labor. But even grime couldn't mask the disbelief in their eyes.

In an effort to ease them, Sylvie extinguished the flame in her hand. They took a collective step back as smoke rose from her fist. Jack admonished her with a glance, but otherwise remained silent. His own flame still burning bright.

"Is there an inn nearby?" Sylvie asked, struggling with her sopping wet robes that had doubled in weight from the rain.

Her words snapped them from their stupor. As an older woman stepped up, silently pointing them in the direction of the town's sole inn. The citizens gave them a wide berth, allowing them to pass through with relative ease. As if they were afraid something terrible shadowed their heels. They didn't blame them.

The inn was a small establishment nestled in a tiny corner beside the forest. It quickly became apparent that they were the first guests in a long while because the hostel had no embellishments to speak of. Nothing to attract travelers and merchants. Just chipped wood and a flickering lamp outside the door that made the shadows of the trees more terrifying. It was the kind of place one would miss if they weren't careful.

Easily dismissed unless needed.

Jack peeked through a cracked window, seeing a woman leaning against the countertop. She spoke to a hidden figure.

A scullery maid, he judged by the outfit she wore.

Jack reckoned that if they still had help, then they were still in business. Foregoing knocking, Jack flung the door wide open and stepped inside, trailing water all over the floor. The woman yelped in surprise, banging her elbow against wood. While the innkeeper—a heavy set man that stood cross-armed behind the counter—looked ready to admonish them. He was immediately silenced by the burning flame in Jack's hand.

"We need a room," Jack said, pinning them with a stare. The woman flinched at the color of his eyes. Her gaze darted between him and Sylvie, trying to make sense of what was happening.

"A room," Jack repeated, slower this time. He made sure to emphasize every word. "We'd like to rent one for the night."

"She isn't a child, Jack," Sylvie scolded.

"Clearly."

They eyed each other sidelong.

The innkeeper coughed, straightened his shoulders, and smiled—too broad to be real—as he registered their garments before their words. He gestured to them with the kind of false enthusiasm only those on the brink of desperation had. He was ready to milk them for all of their worth. As he opened his arms in welcome.

"Yes, of course!" the innkeeper said, flashing them a smile filled with missing teeth. "We'll have it prepared right away. Not much business 'round these parts. Have a seat by the fire, while Laura gets your rooms ready."

Laura jumped to attention. "Right away, sir."

"Room," Jack repeated, before she escaped earshot. They watched as Laura quickly hopped up the stairs, giving no indication that she'd heard.

The innkeeper excused himself to look for towels which they had no doubt they'd have to pay extra for. Jack extinguished the flame in his hand, as they waited patiently for Laura to return. As soon as she did, she glanced up at them nervously, giving them both the feeling that they wouldn't like what was coming.

And they were right.

"Upstairs to your left," Laura muttered, shakily handing Jack two keys and staring fixedly at the wall that had suddenly become incredibly interesting.

Jack's eyes narrowed and Sylvie poked his back, silently telling him to drop it. He bit the inside of his cheek, the vein on his forehead looked dangerously close to popping. He opened his mouth to speak, but conceded to Sylvie's mute demand after another harsh poke. Were her fingers made of steel? He swore she was bruising him.

On their way up, Jack dropped the extra key inside an empty vase in retaliation. And only when they were inside their shared room did he allow himself to fully vent, spewing out curses in an impressive display of his creativity.

"*Filan vahs,*" he damned. A bit too loudly. It was followed by a string of words Sylvie couldn't make out. Spoken too fast and with too thick an accent.

Íarre, Sylvie thought absently, *the native language of the north.* She couldn't understand half of what he said, but she distinctly recognized one word—*glin*—it meant goat. *Just what is he cursing about?*

Jack kicked a nearby nightstand, accidentally making a small statue clatter to the ground. The room they were in had been stripped down to the bare necessities. A chair and bed in the corner, an unbalanced nightstand beside it, and an unlit candle sitting precariously on top. There was a cracked window overlooking the forest, providing an eerie sight. Though it was a welcome difference from the four, creaky walls that made up their room. If it could even be called that.

Given the condition of the inn—which they hadn't even bothered to learn the name of—privacy, at least, was well enough that they didn't need to worry about being overheard. There were no other customers, and the boisterous noise that filtered in from the tavern two houses down covered their softer tones.

Jack sat on the rickety bed with his elbows on his knees and a displeased frown marring his features. He lit a flame to slowly begin the banal task of drying his clothes.

"Couldn't you make some sort of elemental barrier to avoid being pelted by the rain?" Sylvie asked, genuinely curious about the extent of his abilities. "Or perform some other trick that could've prevented yo—us from getting wet?"

Jack's eyes narrowed into slits. He didn't even look at her. Too focused on the flame in his hand.

"I'm an Elementalist," Jack told her. "Not an enchanter and certainly not a deity that controls which way the wind howls. There's a limit to my abilities. Think of me as… an evolved Conjurer." He ignored the way Sylvie bristled at his words, her eyes flashing with offense. He spoke the truth. Even she couldn't deny that. He wouldn't sugarcoat his words for her sake. "I create water and fire and rock. Wind, too. Though just enough for a strong gale. I certainly can't fly, mountains don't move for me, and rain still soaks me. I'm not the almighty Thelarius Merve. But if you'd like, I could always conjure up more water in case you haven't had enough."

"Touchy, aren't you?"

"Only as much as the next Elementalist."

Sylvie decided to leave him be. For the sake of his throbbing veins and her own sanity. She moved to stand by the window, grabbing the fallen statue on her way. It was an idol, carved into the shape of Thelarius Merve. Sylvie ran her thumb down its side, over stone robes and maintained ruffles. Though the carving was small, who it represented was a man larger than life itself. It was a physical affirmation of his legend. More concrete than mere words on paper. On scrolls. On record books. Documents printed out like they meant something. Perhaps they did. But only to the scholars that saw them. Statuettes were far more real. And were widely available.

Her eye's roved over a slender build and a distinctly virile set of shoulders. He had all the features of a brooding man. But this particular version of Thelarius donned a frown so prominent, not even the scar running diagonally across his face could distort it. It was remarkably detailed for something left in a barely used room.

"I didn't think there were statuettes of Thelarius here," Jack said, finally bringing himself to speak. His form remained tense, but his voice was far less irritated. He still didn't meet her eyes.

"He did abolish slavery," Sylvie said. "Who else would the Nebbin pray to?"

"Pernelia?" Jack suggested with a displeased scowl. "Her name is thrown around so much I honestly believe that those dolts in the Drowned Tower have forgotten that there are still three others."

"But this is Eriam. Thelarius saved the mundane."

"Pro-Thelarius are you?"

"He did reform the Institute," she reasoned. "The Liberator and the Redeemer. It's difficult not to like someone when their triumphs are repeatedly shoved down your throat."

"Thelarius was still a man. All men have their failings."

"History doesn't record the flaws of heroes."

"Thelarius tore off the shackles of the Nebbin and clasped them on us." Jack gestured to the marks of the Demar spell on her ankles. His own were carefully hidden away. "Except we get clasped willingly."

"A spell that prevents you from running off whenever you please is a poor comparison to slavery."

"You're right, but that still doesn't make me feel better, nor does it stop deserters from being hunted when they try to leave the Institute." His words were angry and bitter. With a touch of radicalism even he probably wasn't aware of. But then it was gone. Hidden behind a pleased grin, when she tilted her head in contemplation. "Still think we don't have it bad? Why should the Nebbin be the only ones who get to experience real freedom? They're no more deserving than the rest of us."

Sylvie looked at the inscriptions on her ankles. It would be so simple to dispel them. She believed them to be designed that way, so that those that chose to run could do so at any moment. A test of loyalty. As much of a tracking spell as it was a means of purging their ranks of the perfidious. The spell was extremely sensitive to even the slightest touch of magic, sending a signal back to the caster, and leaving a trail of whoever had dispelled it.

A frighteningly effective thing.

The likes of which only the First Zenith could create. Though to her knowledge, the Demar spell was created during a time of relative peace. Sylvie couldn't understand their reason for developing such magic during those quiet times. She didn't want to either. How could she even begin to understand when she wasn't even of the same existence? To try and fully comprehend the thoughts of someone long gone was like asking a predator to never bare its teeth. Absurd. She could speculate, but it was a waste of energy to try to understand something she'd never be sure of.

Sylvie wasn't excessively curious, nor was she striving to obtain knowledge unknown. She was content in her standing. Being in the east kept her away from the grittier side of practitioner life. She was free to linger about in the archives and progress at her leisure.

She shrugged, letting her robes fall back over the marks.

"If these are our chains, then I have no problem with them. They're awfully comfortable. I'll leave changing the world to those with the will to do it. I'm fine where I am."

Jack shook his head. "You've been brainwashed. Lambs shouldn't talk about their views, lest others be persuaded by their lackadaisical way of life. But don't worry, I'm here to fix that."

"You're welcome to try."

Jack grinned and walked up to her. He gestured to the forest below with a conspiratorial look in his eyes. "The frogs. They're watching us."

Sylvie shivered at the thought, looking around in search of the large beasts. She saw a puff of mist from the corner of her eye and found a toad crawling up a tree. "If we really are dealing with a Hunter, then we should leave. Best the Nebbin not get caught in the crossfire should those toads decide to attack. Assuming they can leave the forest, that is."

"Not yet. They told us to stay put."

"I never thought I'd hear that from you."

"I can be patient when the time calls for it."

"You mean when it suits you."

Jack's lips tilted upward into a manic grin. "Doesn't it make you wonder about what's happening in the Tower? I think this is the first time I've ever wanted to go back. My parents would be pleased by my progress."

Sylvie took a step back when she saw another frog, her eyes darting in the direction of the Drowned Tower. Her jaw tightened. As her mind raced with dozens of possible scenarios. None good. Sylvie forced the thoughts away and instead tried to focus on Jack's words.

"Pleased by your progress?" she asked.

"Let's just say, I was sent to the Drowned Tower because I have problems staying put, too. But if all goes well," he coughed when her eyes narrowed in warning, "I mean… if the situation unfortunately worsens, then maybe we'll be ordered to go somewhere safe. Like the Diamond Alps or another place altogether. How's that for staying put?"

Sylvie rolled her eyes. "Quiet, you. How many times must I tell you that I'm fine where I am? I don't want to leave the east."

Jack clearly didn't believe her. He didn't agree either, barely tolerating her words. And Jack had no problem voicing his scorn.

"Don't you want anything more for yourself? Grasp for something! You do realize there's an entire world out there, don't you? Bloodshed may be just a tad too common, I'll give you that. But otherwise, life is good. Good enough. Well, it isn't bad."

"Very convincing."

"You know what I mean."

"Yes," Sylvie said derisively, "it would be small-minded of

me to not know that the outside world was there waiting. I'm not that much of a recluse. But unfortunately for you, I reject it."

"Do you? Do you, really? You can't tell me that you're not even the least bit curious." Jack pointed at her neck where her necklace sat, covered by her robes. "I saw how curious you were when you found that Heartstone. There are so many more unknown things in this world. Wonders both large and small just lying past those mountains. All you have to do is grasp. Well, and dispel this ridiculous tracking spell. Oh, and actually cross the Eirinne Mountains. You get the idea."

"You sound like a deserter."

"Because you've spoken to one? I highly doubt that."

"Those are the notions of someone who seeks to leave the Institute. I don't need to be on speaking terms with a deserter to know that."

"Is leaving so bad?" Jack asked, gesturing to the world beyond the window. "Is it so bad that I tire of the same view every morning?"

Sylvie rolled her eyes. "And deserting is the answer?"

He frowned. "Now, when did I say that? I said I wanted to leave. You're the one that brought up desertion. Maybe it's you that plans on leaving."

She glared at his blatant provocation.

"Look," Jack said, trying to explain himself properly. Why he even bothered to, he couldn't say exactly. Perhaps it was because of her own notions on the topic. Notions he couldn't agree with. And maybe that made him the small-minded one. But he didn't care. He needed to say his piece. Perhaps then she'd change her own mind. "I want my world to change. But if I were to leave, I doubt it would be very fun if I'm chased for the rest of my life by Hunters. Which is why I want to go to the Diamond Alps! I want to change my life from the place where my ideas can actually take shape. I'll change the entire Institute if I have to. So long as I get the freedom I deserve. Why should the Nebbin be the only ones without chains?"

"It's good to know that you're doing this out of your own selfish desire and not for the actual people. If you had been, I would've laughed at such faux nobility."

"Funny, aren't you?" Jack snorted scornfully. She wasn't taking him seriously. At least, he didn't think she was. "Magic isn't a burden, nor is it an excuse. They can't use it to keep us tied. I wasn't asked to be born with these gifts. If others want freedom then they're free to try and change their fate. I'm not going to do it for them. I don't want reform. I just want what I rightfully deserve."

"I wasn't criticizing you," Sylvie said, ignoring the way he rolled his eyes. "Quite the opposite, really. You're doing it for yourself and that makes it all the more believable. Greed and selfishness are good catalysts. If you want to go to the Diamond Alps so badly then I'm sure you'll have the chance to do so. You certainly have the pull. Give my father my regards once you finally make it there."

"Ah, yes, your father, Victor Sirx. Invaluable adviser to the Zenith Council, whose fervor rocked the very foundation of the once immovable society of the Diamond Alps," Jack said, smoothly reciting words he'd heard countless times. He looked at her pointedly, as if to say, *'Why aren't you more like him?'*

Sylvie scoffed, turning away from him in a huff. "And yours is Leonas Dace, youngest and arguably the most valued member of the Zenith Council. Not to mention, one of the three leaders of the Vanguard Circle. The sect responsible for protecting Ferus Terria against any and all threats. Highly trained Hunters and specialists all at their disposal. Your father flicks his wrist and Ferus Terria moves. Is there a point to this?"

He grinned in amusement. "No, I suppose we've lost it, haven't we? I believe we were talking about you."

"No, *you* were talking about me," Sylvie said. "I don't need change. I don't want it."

"That's such a waste." Jack eyed her carefully. He searched her face for any indication of buried interest. He found none.

"There's so much more to the world. How can you be so content? Are you really alive? It's unnerving."

She grinned solemnly.

"Is it so wrong to allow others the reins?"

Jack looked out the window. He didn't want to see that kind of dead grin on her lips. On anyone's lips. "Fate comes for us all. I wonder what she has in store for you."

"Games of sorrow?" Sylvie offered with a grim smile.

He laughed at that. Bitter and withering. He didn't like where this conversation was going. He didn't want to believe that someone could just go through life leaving things to other people. Yet, isn't that what most people did? Then they'd get inexplicably angry when something didn't go their way.

At least she was ready to accept it.

Jack's mouth abruptly set in a thin line without his consent. Why in Thelarius' name was he even backing her? He had to wrestle with his lips until he was able to don his trademark rakish smirk.

"Just admit it," Jack said instead, done with the conversation. "You could learn a thing or two from me."

"I don't doubt it." Sylvie laughed, her voice slowly growing used to the gleeful practice the longer she argued with him. It felt like an age since she'd last disagreed with someone so much. Perhaps the weather was getting to her. She looked outside. The world beyond the glass faded into gray, suffocated by the rain. Until only the room they stood in was left.

And she grinned at him.

Jack's magic sung, his blood howled, and something inside of him coiled uncomfortably at the sight of her smile. Tight, but not unbearable. In fact, he kind of liked it. Call it obstinance or even narrow-mindedness that had him reluctant to accept her views, but when he saw that smile, Jack swore he'd change her mind.

9

Deep within the bowels of the Drowned Tower, a flurry of voices in heated debate could be heard. Shouts of outrage and echoes of fury echoed throughout the otherwise silent halls. The top brass had all gathered to discuss the current dilemma, but they accomplished little more than the rejection of every proposal and a loop of endless arguments. Each pettier than the last. And all deplorably conducted, as they waited for their unofficial head, Columbus Cephas. This was supposed to help them reach a consensus. But instead of attempting to find compromise, they seemed to collectively decide that this was the best time to release their hidden animosity toward each other.

"You propose total evacuation?" Master Fritz sneered at his fellow Masters. His baldness made the lines on his forehead more prominent. "Where would you have them go? To Eriam? Surely, not over the Eirinne Mountains! Only a country torn apart by a leaderless Council awaits us there."

"I agree," Celaris spoke. All eyes landed on him. As he crossed his arms, signifying that his mind was made up and wouldn't be moved anytime soon. "The greed of men is rampant in the south, while those in the west have chosen to live in total seclusion. That leaves the north. But the Diamond Alps has never been a place for such a diverse crowd of practitioners. They accept Elementalists and the chosen. Not refugees. Certainly not ones with little talent for magic. Which we'll have an abundance of should we choose to evacuate."

"We can't just sit and do nothing!" Miriam argued. Her voice was backed by half a dozen others, all exclaiming how others would aid them during their time of need.

Fritz clenched his fists, his cheeks turning red. "And what if the murderer leaves with us? We can't watch everyone. Your optimistic delusions won't get us anywhere!"

"He's here for Elder Serach, isn't he? Then I say hand him over! Hand him over before there are any more casualties!"

"Don't let panic cloud your judgment! One death isn't enough cause to abandon the Tower!"

"Duward was one of the best we had to offer," Miriam said. "Yet he was taken care of so easily. What about the rest of the children? Do you even realize how many we have sitting in their rooms right now? How powerless they'd be should this murderer strike again? Hand Elder Serach over and let us evacuate until the situation has been resolved."

"This tower houses more than just an Elder!" Fritz yelled. "There are secrets of old here. Do you propose we hand those over as well? We don't even know who was responsible for this!"

"Rior Wolden!" she exclaimed. "Who else could it be? He must've been planning to murder the Elder within these very halls and then pinning the blame on one of us. He only stopped when he realized that an updated deserters list had been sent to the branches. Killing one of our own is his solution! Can you not see that?"

"You're jumping to conclusions," Celaris spat. He gestured obscenely to those backing Miriam, his every action laced with venom. "How, pray tell, were you... no, were the entire lot of you ever given the title of Master?"

Outrage followed. Coupled with threats of severe bodily harm. At that point, many of the neutral Masters chose to quietly pray. While others merely closed their eyes and opted to ignore the bedlam spreading throughout the room. It was in this state of disarray that Columbus found them. His entrance went ignored, as they continued to squabble amongst themselves. Their faces long red from shouting.

Columbus moved to stand between the groups that had gathered behind their apparent representatives. They were so easily divided. That didn't bode well for any of them. "Are you quite finished? Or shall I be forced to call a recess because you've all decided to behave like toddlers? I've gone out of my way to bring Ethil here. Surely, we can show her better than this hostile display of discord."

At the mention of Ethil, mouths instantly clamped shut and threats of laceration faded into silence.

Ethil stood by the door with wide eyes and pursed lips. Her hands trembled at the weight of their stares. Columbus led her to the center of the room, as the others immediately dispersed to form a half circle before her. Their heads cocked, scrutinizing her every twitch. There were a few she didn't recognize riddled in amongst them. A woman who sneered, before speaking in hushed whispers to the man by her side. A man that smiled kindly at her in a futile attempt at comfort. Columbus stood a step in front of them all, his arms stretched wide. As he spoke a soft prayer of guidance to Pernelia.

"Ethil Mane," Columbus called, watching her tense. "You've been brought here today to shed light over the incident involving you and your partner, Duward Mane. We understand that the two of you were roaming the upper floor to fulfill Elder Serach's embrocological requisition. Were you or your partner able to find the desired plants?"

"Yes," Ethil stammered. Her eyes darted around the room, feeling as if she were being put on trial for an unsaid crime she had no knowledge of committing.

Columbus stared at her with hard eyes that lacked all of his usual candor. "Did you, at any time separate from your partner?"

"No." Ethil shook her head for emphasis. She tried to recall the moments before she blacked out. "But Duward did say he heard something. It was… water, I believe."

"Water?"

Ethil's eyes widened in sudden realization. "There's a hole! I forgot to mention that we found a hole on the upper floor! It needs to be sealed immediately."

Columbus held up a hand. "Do not fret, child. The hole has been sealed and the walls reinforced. Now, you said something about water?"

She nodded, hesitant. "Duward said he could hear dripping water. We followed the sound into a back room and realized it was coming from a hole. That was where we found the plants."

Whispers erupted among them, and Orpha stepped forward. His eyes shut in constant darkness. "Can you describe Duward's demeanor at the time. Was he panicking? Or was he alarmed in any way? Did he hear or see anything else?"

"He was acting as he usually did, but then he started to hear that sound. He was so sure that it would lead to the plants, so he ran in its direction. I tried to tell him to slow down, but he's never been one to listen to me. I followed him and we found the source of the sound. After that…" Ethil trailed off, vaguely recalling Duward picking up an armful of flowers. He told her something, but she couldn't remember what.

"After?" Orpha urged, snapping her back to attention.

"I remember falling," Ethil said, her eyebrows scrunched in thought. "The next thing I remember was waking up in that room with Master Cephas."

There was a brief moment of silence.

"You have our gratitude for your cooperation. Should you remember anything else, do let us know." Orpha nodded curtly, before turning to Columbus. His movements were quick and square, wound with tension. "Two of my tracking spells have dissipated. I'll send a message out."

Columbus nodded. A grim expression marred his features, before it was carefully hidden behind his usual kind smile. "I didn't want to believe someone would take this chance to flee, but I suppose that was nothing more than foolish optimism. Well, no matter. Who was it? And where are they?"

Orpha's brow furrowed in concentration.

"These are old spells. Weak. They were cast months ago. I believe it was cast on the Amorphs, Darien Gravis and Marian Sind. They dispelled it near the outskirts of the Eirinne Mountains. To think that our own patrollers would do such a thing. It seems there is need to reevaluate those along our border."

Columbus expertly ignored the surprised whispers around him. Ignored, too, their sighs of disapproval.

"Contact the patrol teams," he ordered. "Have them deal with it."

"There is another matter," Orpha went on. Slow and thoughtful. "Not all the practitioners have been accounted for."

"What?" Columbus asked in disbelief. "Haven't the gates already been sealed? I wanted everyone back within these halls before sundown, but I see now that that was too difficult an order to follow. How many are left?"

"One."

"One? What do you mean, one? Who? Why would their partner leave them behind?"

"I believe they may have been under the personal order of one of the Masters," Orpha said carefully, easily ignoring the slighted complaints that erupted around them. "Those registered to leave have all been accounted for, but one of my apprentices reported seeing another leave just a few hours ago. She had an official seal and a tracking spell on her ankle. She was apparently under orders to warn our patrollers to strengthen their defenses."

"On whose authority?" Columbus snarled. As the hall once more erupted into chaos. Shouts of accusation being carelessly thrown around.

"That must have been the murderer!"

"Lock the doors and don't let them back in!"

"What about the people on Eriam? We can't just leave them!"

"That was not the murderer. It was my doing." Elorian stepped up, and a dozen pair of eyes zeroed in on him. He was once a tall man, but now his back was hunched and his eyes were permanently squinting. Elorian was an older Master that had been teaching for more years than others of his rank had lived. Age, however, didn't grant him consideration.

"Explain yourself!" they demanded.

"My pupil, Anora," Elorian said softly. "A Healer. Young. Only ten years of age. Despite her few years, she is my primary apprentice. I see great things in her future. She has the ability to surpass a number of our current practitioners."

Orpha crossed his arms. His voice the epitome of calm. "So, you didn't want her locked inside here with a murderer on the loose."

"Who would?" he yelled. But Orpha was undeterred by his sudden shout. Breathing a heavy sigh, Elorian solemnly hung his head. The usual respect he received as a Master with years of seniority and experience was lost in that moment. In its place was anger and distrust. Fritz was quick to jump in, attempting to appease the others, as they began hurling insults like stones.

"Do you believe your apprentice special? We all have primary apprentices here! Some of us even have children!"

"You aren't exempt from commands obeyed by the majority!"

"The Assembly would crumble with people like you!"

"Elorian," Columbus spoke, blocking his view of the other Masters. "You realize why we recalled the others, yes?"

"You fear desertion," Elorian said calmly, his tone unrepentant. "But is calling them back to their deaths a better alternative?"

Columbus' gaze hardened, his mouth set in a thin line. "You don't know that. There have been no further casualties. But should they have been allowed to stay outside and given the chance to desert, then a murderer would be the least of our worries. We called them back to protect the eastern branch from the claws of the Vanguard Circle. Is that so incomprehensible? If you allow your pupil out, then what was the point of calling the others back? Do you realize what you've done? Do you realize the consequences of your actions should she choose to leave?"

Elorian pointed at the crowd of angry Masters behind him,

his tone biting. "I will not be responsible for the death of my pupil because these fools cannot reach a proper agreement. Instead, they choose to quarrel pettily amongst themselves. I will not sleep with a heavy conscience."

"Pray your pupil doesn't run off, Elorian," Celaris threatened, stepping closer and clasping his shoulder so tightly that Elorian winced. He wasn't one to mince words. Elorian's eyes darted between the two Masters cornering him, their gazes as predatory as a wild beast's. "Deserters are already deemed dead. Should she escape our grasp, she'll experience suffering far worse than any fate she may have had here. Trained Hunters aren't known for their mercy or the cleanliness of their methods. The Vanguard Circle has Hunters everywhere. Once they get wind of these events, the east will crumble under their grasp. And I will personally see to it that a heavy conscience will be the least of your worries."

Elorian felt sweat trickle down his brow, and he recoiled in apprehension.

"Step back, Celaris," Columbus ordered, pushing him away. "The deed is done. The gates have already been sealed and chained shut. Where is your apprentice now, Elorian? We'll send a message and have a group of patrollers watch over her. Eriam is a dangerous place for such a young girl. Even more so for one with only healing spells at her disposal."

"I pointed her in the direction of Thyme," Elorian said. "She should be safe."

"What do you mean safe?" Celaris argued. "She should be among her kind! Surrounded by Nebbin and without a partner, she'll only seem like a deserter. The patrol teams can take care of her. In fact, there's no safer place to be. Where is she, Elorian? Surely, you placed a Demar Spell on her? I want to know her exact location."

Elorian gulped. His throat suddenly dry. "Our connection disappeared an hour ago. It dissipated near the shores, so she must still be close by."

"Wonderful!" Celaris exclaimed, throwing his hands in the air in frustration. "According to Institute laws, we now have an official deserter on our hands. A little girl at that!"

Columbus sighed. "Orpha, send a message to Jack and Sylvie as well. They should be closer than the patrol teams, and I'm sure they'll appreciate having something to do. They've always been testy, and Jack especially, has never been known for his patience. I don't want him running off because of boredom. Or worse, have absurd thoughts about dragging my apprentice along with him."

"No, wait!" Elorian yelled desperately. "There's no need to send anyone! Anora's a good girl. I'm sure she was just frightened by the sight of the gate closing! She must've dispelled it by accident. It's no secret that the Demar spell is extremely sensitive to shifts in magic! Practitioners take days, some even weeks, to properly master using their gifts with it cast."

Columbus took a moment to scrutinize him, examining the terror in his eyes. The unsteady rise and fall of his chest looked more alarming than usual due to his age. "Rest assured, I'm only sending them to investigate. If what you say is true and this was merely an unfortunate accident, then I have no doubts about their ability to protect her. But if you're wrong…" Columbus stepped closer, his voice dropping to a whisper. "Pray that you aren't."

Elorian stiffened at the dark undertone in his words. Was this really the same man he'd been speaking to just moments ago? Impossible. The man that stood before him was a demon. An animal trapped in human flesh, baring its ugly teeth. It was as if he'd suddenly swapped personalities with Celaris. Elorian barely registered nodding his head, before the moment passed and Columbus strolled past him.

Columbus walked straight up to Ethil, who awkwardly stood there with her arms wrapped around herself. Her eyes were wide, as she watched them argue. Men and women that were supposed to guide her through life. It was a sore reminder that despite their authority, even they were still human. They felt fear. Anxiety. Terror. They crumbled just as easily as the rest of them.

"Do reign in your voices," Columbus announced, once more commanding their attention. Despite the decorative title of Arch Poten, he still governed noticeable power which was far more influential than those of supposedly equal rank. His voice boomed louder than the rest, louder than even those backed by years of sagacity. He was their leader. Whether the Assembly admitted it or not. It was just another sign that some things would never change. No matter how much blood was spilt.

Columbus turned to Orpha and gestured toward the door. "Send the messages and check on the practitioners. We don't want them breaking the rules now, do we?"

Orpha nodded.

"I'll assist you," Celaris said, desperate to leave this hall and the infuriating people within. He followed Orpha out. The door echoed as it slammed shut behind them, enveloping the occupants in terse silence.

Which, to everyone's surprise, was broken by Ethil.

Their eyes darted to the young girl, who they'd completely disregarded in favor of far more important pursuits. But now that it was over, they couldn't ignore her any longer.

"Excuse me," Ethil stuttered, her hands trembling. "What's going on? A murderer, you say? Lockdown? Deserters? What happened while I was asleep? Was I attacked?"

They continued to stare at her.

Ethil swallowed the lump in her throat, wanting to shrink away and avoid their steady, almost pitying gazes. Her eyes continued to dart around, just as her throat began to constrict in apprehension. The only sound that could be heard was her ragged breathing. But she swore they could hear the wild pound of her heart. A deafening drum that echoed in her own ears.

"May I see my brother?" she continued. They stepped back, others flinched. And she realized that she'd shouted. "I haven't been able to see Duward since I've awoken. Is he hurt? I'd like to see him."

They were silent. Some even turned their heads away.

Ethil felt panic rise within her. She looked to Columbus, her eyes pleading.

"Please!" she begged.

"Duward has passed," Fritz was the one to speak. His gaze was hard and unforgiving. "He follows Pernelia now."

What? she thought.

For an instant, Ethil was filled with vacancy. Numbness. All was well and nothing hurt. But the moment passed, and all that remained was her, standing in a room filled with sorry looking Masters. Her own private pity party where she was the star, and misery, the guest. Her vision was blurring. She scrunched up her nose in an attempt to stop the tears from falling, but her traitorous body trembled. And Ethil closed in on herself. She let out an ear piercing shriek that had the others in the room wincing.

She heard more than saw them approach. Warm arms folded her into an embrace and soft words were whispered into her ear. A warm hand rubbed her back, carefully trying to relieve her of her grief. Comfort her. Trick her into believing that everything would be all right. Liars. Her brother was dead. His murderer roamed the halls. She clenched her fists in fury, but she could do nothing more than sob.

That day, her heart wept.

And it would never stop.

10

Sylvie wore a mixture of surprise and apprehension when she saw one of Master Celaris' messenger hawks perched outside their window, undeterred by the pelting rain. A small scroll was tied around its ankle, which it allowed her to take before flying off again. Jack was by her side in an instant, their eyes eating through the concise letter.

Orders from the Assembly,
> *We require your assistance. There is a child currently wandering Eriam's shores. She goes by the name, Anora.*
> *Find her.*
> *Signed,*
> *Celaris Pyrne, Eastern Branch*
> *Master of Lore*

"Wonderful," Jack said caustically. He scowled, nicking the letter from her hands and burning it to ashes. "Have I ever told you how much I *adore* child-rearing?"

Sylvie smiled in amusement, but otherwise kept her silence.

No matter how trite the appeal of tracking a lost child was, it was still better than sitting around waiting for something to happen. Sylvie had a sneaking suspicion that Jack would burn the bed out of spite if he was actually forced to spend the night in this shabby hostel. The innkeeper and his maid had been keeping uncomfortably close tabs on them, and Sylvie knew that when they finally made it past the door and back out into the pouring rain, even Jack was happy to just pay and leave. Despite their repeated protests to wait until first light.

Sylvie tried not to think about what awaited them. As they made their way back to Eriam's shores. She tried not to wonder about the letter and what its vagueness entailed. But as they ran with sopping wet clothes and a sudden burst of adrenaline, they lapsed into silence. Which made it far harder to ignore her thoughts. Sylvie wanted to break the impromptu quiet. But there was little to speak about, and even less with the rain falling around them, worsening their already prickly moods.

Sylvie wondered what a child was even doing outside during this time of lockdown. Or at all. How did she get out? Was she a deserter they were expected to deal with or simply another overzealous practitioner that had wandered too far? Children were curious to a fault and had little regard for rules. That was fact. Just as the skies were blue and fire was hot.

Her name seemed familiar, but Anora was a common moniker that many shared. Besides, Sylvie had never been skilled at recalling names. She forgot them in an instant. Her memory was good enough to recall the faces of her peers, but what did their names matter? To assign them names was to make them a part of her world. To expand her circle served little purpose. If any at all. Sylvie wasn't the mingling sort. She didn't need connections. As the primary apprentice of Columbus Cephas, she already had access to areas and records restricted to the average practitioner.

Little good it did her though, as leaving the Drowned Tower had never been high on her agenda.

Jack was luckier in that regard. He utilized the Tower's halls. Bled them for their worth. All for the sake of fulfilling unplanned ambitions that appealed to his odd sense of personal interest. Jack may not have been a primary apprentice, but it certainly wasn't from lack of recognition. Many jumped to personally become his official Master, yet he chose to remain on his own. Seclusion suited him well. Sylvie would admit that there were times when she felt a small pang of jealousy whenever she'd catch him locking himself up in the archives with a manic look in his eyes. How he could feel so passionate about something, she hadn't a clue.

What is it like? Sylvie wondered. *To lose yourself to fervor?*

"She should be nearby," Jack announced, scrutinizing the expanse of flat land. He dropped to a crouch and ran his fingers across the hard sand. "May Silas rid us of this ungodly rain. If she was here then her tracks are long gone."

"A little girl alone by the Zexin Sea," Sylvie muttered. It seemed the start of a good horror story. "The sea is frightening tonight. And I'm sure she must've heard stories about its monsters. It's no wonder she didn't stay by the bridge. But then where would she have gone? To Thyme?"

"No." Jack shook his head. "If she was there, then we would have heard something from the villagers, or hell, even the innkeeper. Practitioners aren't exactly common company."

"Well, I doubt she attempted to return. Look, the bridge is flooded. The sea is restless." Sylvie stared at the rough seas as they pounded against the Drowned Tower. Its large gates were sealed shut. While the chains that bound it creaked so loudly even they could hear them. Pernelia's statue stared down at them almost mockingly. As if denying them entrance into her home.

"Maybe she was swept away by the tide? She *is* a little girl," Jack said. He grinned when Sylvie shot him a reproachful look. "Shall we put ourselves in her robes? If you were a little girl with no knowledge of the general terrain, where would you hide from such horrid weather?"

Sylvie tilted her head in the direction of the surrounding forest. The answer was obvious. "Tearwood."

With impeccable timing, a loud screech tore through the air and made their heads snap toward the line of trees. The screamer was abruptly cut off mid-yell. Only to be replaced by rustling, before a pack of Snuff entered their vision. The Snuff squeaked in horror, as they jumped out to escape whatever monstrosity hid inside the forest.

Jack smirked in twisted delight.

Purring, he said, "I hope you're ready to face your fears."

***

Their trek through Tearwood was a slow one.

They saw clear eyes peering down at them from the trees. Momentarily hidden behind puffs of pale white that continued to blow from the branches. It clouded their vision for an instant, before settling and allowing them sight once more. Sylvie shivered when she caught sight of a webbed foot filled with pulsing blue veins, before it disappeared behind another cloud of fog. The air felt thicker in the forest, and the rain did nothing to lighten it. Claustrophobic and suffocating. There was an obvious tension in the air that silenced them.

They were reluctant to call out to Anora amongst so many possibly hostile creatures. Instead, they kept their eyes peeled and their ears open. Their hands twitched at the slightest sound. Bodies stiff in anticipation for the unknown. Only for them to relax when they realized that the only sound in the forest came from their own feet.

"This silence is deafening," Jack whispered, repeating Reed's words. He looked up at the beasts watching them from their position above the trees. The larger ones were curled around thick trunks that supported their massive size in an impressive display of solidity.

"What are they doing?" Sylvie asked. She avoided averting her gaze from the shrubbery before her. Afraid she'd gag at what she saw.

"Watching us." Jack shrugged. "Their keeper must be close."

"Assuming they have one."

"I'm sure they do. Animals aren't just imbued with magic, then left to fend for themselves. They're weapons. Someone must be watching them. Or at the very least, keeping them within the boundaries of the forest."

"And if this was just some failed experiment? A twisted test gone wrong? For all we know, they remain here because they can't survive anywhere else. If someone was here, I would've expected them to show themselves by now. We did kill one of their precious pets."

"If this forest is as empty as you believe, then why aren't they attacking us?" Jack reasoned. "We did roast one of their friends. Animals are weary by nature. Yet they aren't fleeing or attacking. They're just sitting there. Even I'm starting to get concerned."

"I didn't realize my fear was contagious," Sylvie smirked.

Jack returned it with his own. Far more flippant. She was trying to knock his attitude down a few pegs.

How frustratingly charming.

"Being stared down by frogs large enough to knock me unconscious with a mere swing of their tails isn't exactly nice." Jack locked eyes with one of the toads. He warily lifted a glowing blue hand, curious about what it would do. The creature merely sat there, blinking clear eyes at him. Its gaze was curious and unnerving. And Jack was the first to look away, rubbing the back of his neck in an attempt to release the tension building up in his body. It didn't work. "Now that I think about it… has this mist always been here? When I was first transferred, it was already surrounding the forest. If this area really is controlled by a deserter, I doubt the Vanguard Circle would just leave it be."

"This mist has been here since I was a child," Sylvie said, recalling vague memories from years past. When Master Cephas would bring her and Reed to Thyme for trivial things he always claimed was urgent. "It just… appeared one day. I asked Master Cephas about it once, he told me to drop the subject. I can see why now."

"He knew about this then?"

"Maybe… I don't know."

"Damn Assembly and their secrets."

"Well, in any case, if the Vanguard Circle did send someone, then we can safely assume that they're long gone. But I doubt they're so short on Hunters that they'd just allow this place to remain under deserter control for so long. For all we know, this area belongs to them. A refuge of sorts for the Hunters sent to these parts. Or it might even belong to the Assembly."

"Then why did a toad attack us before?" Jack reminded. "If we're on the same side, why try to kill us? We weren't doing anything wrong. We wouldn't even be here if it wasn't for the Elder's request. I'd expect whoever's in control of these parts to at least remember to tighten the leashes of their guard dogs. Giant frogs living in creepy forests isn't something someone just forgets about. Not easily anyway."

Sylvie's eyebrows furrowed in thought, grasping the validity of his argument. "But if they aren't on our side, then why would the Vanguard Circle not send reinforcements?"

They shared a glance, their minds filled with questions.

Apparently no one thought it necessary to inform them of poss-ible threats, yet they chose to send them out anyway. With little regard for their safety or whatever thoughts they may have had on the matter. As expected of the Institute. It made Jack gnash his teeth together in a sudden fit of irritation. Just what were they expected to do once they found the girl? Their orders were too vague. Perhaps it was purposely written that way, so as to be interpreted according to the situation.

But what situation was that? Jack thought. *Was Anora a deserter? Or did she just panic and accidentally release the tracking spell? Did she even have one cast on her? What was she doing on her own in the first place? Was she alone or did she kill her partner during her attempt to escape? Anora could've easily dragged the body elsewhere. She could've even let the Zexin Sea claim it. No one would notice.*

But despite any abilities Anora may have had, she was still a child. Any talent she had didn't matter. Whatever threat she may have posed, stopped being one when the Assembly sent them to retrieve her. Her chances of escape were slim at best.

Jack clicked his tongue.

He hastened his steps, slapping a large leaf out of his path in the process. If someone actually explained what was going on, then they could've found a better way to approach the situation. That is, unless they were actually tasked with killing the girl. And the Assembly had simply deemed it too crude a thing to write.

Jack wouldn't have accepted it. Orders be damned.

He snuck a glance at Sylvie, who kept her eyes trained on the path before her. If ordered, would Sylvie kill Anora? If they found her only to realize that she was a deserter, would Sylvie finish the job like they'd been ordered to countless times before? But a child's life was different from an adult's. They were little things—naïve and innocent. In a way, children were more human. To rid the world of a child was to purposely blacken the soul. Colors would be darker and waking would never be the same again.

Still, Jack thought, *would she do it?*

"Sylvie," he called, not meeting her gaze. He tried to think of a roundabout way of asking her.

"Jack," she replied evenly.

He opened his mouth to speak, but lost his train of thought when he accidentally stepped in a deep puddle of mud, almost falling over in the process. "Oh, for Thelarius' sake! Frogs, rain, Thyme, and now this! I swear to death and back that some deity cursed this trip."

"Jack," Sylvie repeated. Her voice more urgent.

"What?" he asked, running an irritated hand through his hair. It was tangled and matted to his skin. Like everything else he had on.

"Look." She pointed at a muddy puddle a distance away. An abandoned book sat there. A Healer's grimoire. As much a part of them as an arm or a leg. It wasn't something they just willingly left behind. They knew many Healers that would happily die rather than give up their grimoires.

During wartime, many did.

The grimoire was bound in leather and covered with mud. A distinctly cerise shade coated its bottom and ran along a few diligently hand-written pages. Even a few nearby plants weren't spared from the color. Out of place amidst the brown and green.

How much blood did the owner lose for remnants of it to still be visible during such a downpour?

The vividness of its color was a dead giveaway as to what it was, nonetheless, Jack still bent to inspect it. A decision he instantly regretted. As his nostrils were assaulted by something far more unpleasant than the usual rusty stench of blood—he smelt burning flesh and smoke. Something had just been roasted here. But where was the evidence?

Jack fingered one of the grimoire's pages, examining the intricate formulas and drawings. He'd never understood the purpose of their books. Why keep them? Was there some secret only Healers knew? Well, he supposed every class had their secrets. If not, then why would there be different Institutes that specialized in teaching them? The grimoire was filled with words he couldn't make out. Written in an ancient tongue that he may or may not have known. The writing was too botched to be legible. Chicken scratch. A trait all Healers shared. Perhaps it was deliberate.

Sylvie took the book from his hands, her actions swift and sure. She mindlessly flipped to the front, looking for a name. She had spent enough time with Reed to know the ins and outs of a Healer's grimoire—they were more or less all the same, Reed once told her. Though when she reached the first page, she only frowned at the name written there. She'd expected it, but a part of her wished she was wrong.

"This belongs to Anora," Sylvie said.

That was all they needed to know.

"Let's go," Jack said, following the fading trail of blood. He looked up to see the toads still silently observing them, allowing them to pass without mishap. *What are they up to?*

"Wait!" Sylvie just barely grabbed his robes, yanking him back to her. Jack twisted and tried to elbow her out of instinct. Sheer luck and his bad footing were the only reasons she wasn't nursing a broken nose.

"What are you doing?" Jack glared. "Don't just suddenly grab me like that."

Sylvie dismissed his hostile attitude and gestured to the left, toward a nearby clearing. By the time Jack's eyes caught sight of a small bundle hidden under oversized robes and exposed tree roots, Sylvie was already sprinting toward it.

She moved the robes and jumped back in surprise at the sight exposed before her. A mangled corpse with remnants of flesh still clinging to its face. Tiny insects gathered around its torso, swarming over leftover skin and hastening the peeling process. From the small frame, Sylvie supposed that this was Anora. But even if she brought her body back, Sylvie doubted anyone would be able to recognize her. Her face had been burnt beyond recognition. No doubt the source of that putrid smell still lingering about. The remaining muscle and skin she did have were a sick combination of brown, yellow, and pink. None of the stark paleness that characterized the occupants of the Drowned Tower.

"May Pernelia's wings guide you to where the First Zenith dwell," Sylvie whispered the prayer under her breath, bowing her head in respect. This wasn't the first time she'd seen the remains of someone burned to death. Nor would it be the last. How many times had she done the same thing to deserters near their border? She'd lost count long ago. Sylvie breathed deeply, gathering her composure. As Jack finally caught up to her.

For a moment, Jack's face twisted in horror, before he schooled his expression back to neutral. Back to the unflinching practitioner needed at a time like this. Jack's magic stilled to dormancy, calming himself with the sort of disciplined control Sylvie had never seen him exude before.

"Silas' holy flames… what were you even doing out here?" Jack asked her corpse, as if expecting an answer. His voice was less biting than usual, his eyes softening as he walked up to her. He breathed out the same prayer Sylvie had and muttered apologies, as he lifted her robes to inspect any belongings she may have had. Anything to identify her. He found a silver prayer idol in the shape of Maurice in her hand. It had melted, fusing with her skin. "Maurice… this is definitely our Healer. At least, she used to be."

Sylvie held Anora's grimoire over her body, conjuring a fire to burn it before its owner. To ensure her soul wouldn't linger in search of a useless book. To allow her peace after unjust brutality.

"I pray for your safe return to the first Healer's side, follower of Maurice."

"She was no follower of Maurice!" a voice denied. It boomed from above. They looked up to find a small red bird circling the skies overhead. Its wings were small but sturdy. They flapped strongly, despite the weather. Sylvie squinted, trying to recall why that bird seemed so familiar. "The First Zenith neither tolerates, nor welcomes traitors of the mass."

Jack and Sylvie tensed, as it perched on a nearby branch. Large toads flanked it on all sides. The bird let out a squawk far too thunderous for its size and suddenly all the toads set their sights on them. They reflexively stepped back, their hands glowing pale blue. As the whispers of magic came to life under their skin. They looked warily up at the bird. Only to find the beady eyes of an Amorph staring down at them.

"You've come to this forest, despite explicit orders to keep away." The Amorph's voice was deep and distinctly virile. A startling contrast to its cute appearance. "The Assembly made it a rule to avoid this forest. Yet you disobeyed."

Jack stepped forward, a mighty scowl adorning his face.

"Did you do this?" Jack pointed at the toads for emphasis, so the Amorph would know that he wasn't referring to Anora. Jack had already decided that he was responsible for Anora's death, and whatever defense he may or may not have prepared would never be enough to change his mind. Not anytime soon anyway. "Are you the one breeding these vile creatures and tampering with their forms?"

"Tampering?" The Amorph laughed. A screeching noise that grated on their ears. "Why, I did nothing of the sort. These creatures don't belong to me. These are the Peose of a Hunter. Or have you never seen one?"

Jack's eyes narrowed. As the son of Cheryll Dace, he'd seen

far too many Peose. He had a special hate in his soul for Hunters. They preyed on those that wanted nothing more than to escape the clutches of a restrained life. To break invisible shackles clasped upon them at birth.

"Impudent little thing, aren't you?" Jack said, smirking. "Tell me, do you speak to your superiors with that mouth? Is that why you were sent here, to the solitary east?"

"Don't lump me in with you."

"I wouldn't dream of equating myself with someone so far beneath me."

The Amorph leaned forward in contempt, the frogs followed suit. Sylvie grabbed Jack's elbow and harshly squeezed in a sorry attempt to stop him from provoking the Hunter any more than necessary.

"I've never met a Hunter. At least, not that I know of," Sylvie muttered, examining every inch of his form. Her eyes widened in sudden recognition. "Wait! You're from the Drowned Tower, aren't you? I've seen that form before… in the mess hall!"

The Amorph smiled. His feathered cheeks tilting up in a decidedly creepy manner. "You have good memory. As expected from the daughter of Victor Sirx. The Vanguard Circle has its hands in all of the Institutes across Ferus Terria. The east is no exception. I, myself, don't fancy frogs, but I'm afraid my partner has a weakness for slimy creatures."

"But keeping more than one Peose is unheard of," Jack said. "Does the Vanguard Circle know about this blatant disregard of their rules?"

"The Vanguard Circle is halfway across Ferus Terria. Well, not that it matters. As I said, these creatures don't belong to me. They merely do my bidding. For the moment."

"Your bidding?" Jack gnashed his teeth together, his veins showing. He felt Sylvie's grip on his elbow tighten and his entire body shook. As he tried his hardest to refrain from turning and snarling fiercely at her. "And what exactly does that entail? The uncalled for burning of little girls?"

His gaze narrowed. "Burning deserters."

"Deserters? Hardly!" Jack pointed hotly at Anora's mangled corpse, angered that the Amorph didn't even bother to justify his cruel actions. "Did she look like a deserter to you?"

"Oh?" He tilted his head, blinking blankly at them. "If she wasn't, then why did the Peose attack her?"

"Don't give me that," Jack said, breaking free of Sylvie's grip. "Last we were here, those *things* even attacked us!"

"Blasphemy!" The Amorph denied, vehemently shaking his head. "Peose never attack those with active Demar spells. If anything, they were merely observing you. As they've been doing since you entered the forest. Are you sure you didn't strike first? The entire east knows about your… disposition, Jacques Dace."

Jack sneered.

"So she had no Demar spell," Sylvie said, sparing Anora's still form a glance. "That isn't sufficient reason to kill her. What evidence do you have to assume that she was a deserter?"

"Wandering around during lockdown with neither a partner, nor a tracking spell is reason enough."

"She was a child! For all we know, she may have accidentally dispelled it."

"As if I would risk asking her such a thing!" The Amorph's talons dug into the branch, shredding bark. "You're here, so I assume you were ordered to find her. Tell me then, what would you have done in my place? Question a possible threat? Negotiate with a little girl that could be spouting lies and searching for pity? Or would you have just killed her? Get it over with? Quick and simple. Which is the more efficient way to follow orders?"

Sylvie swallowed, clenching her fists. She'd been wondering the same thing as she and Jack left Thyme. If she'd found Anora alive and well, would she have believed her if Anora said that she'd accidentally dispelled her Demar spell? Or would she just kill her? Like how she'd done with countless other deserters and bands of mercenaries that decided to trespass over their borders. No questions asked.

She could feel Jack's eyes on her—assessing her—as if he could see her inner turmoil, could hear her mentally debating with herself. Jack narrowed his eyes and the sight of his glare had her snapping back to attention. His gaze was fury incarnate. Utterly disarming. She met his look with her own resolute one, as she forced her tense muscles to relax. Jack turned back to the Hunter, his posture loose and his features confident.

Jack couldn't—wouldn't—let this Hunter get to him. That was exactly what he wanted.

"Or you could be the one lying," Jack interjected, trying to turn the tables. "Perhaps you knew she wasn't a deserter. She may have even had a Demar spell. No one but you would know. The word of a lone Amorph isn't exactly reliable. Tell me, did she stumble upon something she shouldn't have? I see that she was burned, yet I don't see the cause of the fire. Are you perhaps hiding something in this forest?"

The Amorph squawked, exasperated. "This particular breed of Peose can project lethal spit. Which becomes highly flammable when it comes into contact with this mist. It allows them to spark flames just as hot as any Conjurer. If they wished you dead then you would have been long ago."

Jack's eyes widened.

"What's the matter, Jack?" The Amorph smiled. Slimy and repulsive. "Do my words sound familiar?"

Jack's jaw locked, as Sylvie looked at him worriedly. She was ready to restrain him if he suddenly attacked. They couldn't make enemies out of Hunters. Not when they didn't know the whole truth. They'd done nothing yet, and thus, the Amorph had no reason to attack. She didn't want to give him one.

"What's the matter?" Sylvie asked.

"Enchanted mist," Jack said. He clenched his fists, his body shaking in fury. "A technique unique to my mother. I realized the frogs may have had some form of muting charm cast on them which was set to seep out when they exhaled the mist, but I didn't realize my dear mother had shared her more... vicious secrets with another practitioner. Please don't tell me you're her primary apprentice."

The Amorph grinned. "Do I seem the part?"

"I never thought she'd choose someone so longwinded," Jack said, scathing. "Or someone who'd have such a problem showing their face. So no, I suppose you don't. Which answers that I suppose."

"You can't bait me with such obvious provocations."

Jack ignored his words. "It's your partner isn't it? Your partner is my mother's apprentice. You're just the babysitter. That would explain the insane number of Peose. Bending the rules is always okay, so long as you're high enough on the proverbial chain."

The Amorph screeched, spreading his wings in a threatening manner. The Peose surrounding him reacted to his sudden change in demeanor, inching closer. Some reared their heads back, as if prepared to launch a few burning projectiles at them. While others bent their legs to pounce.

"You'd know that well, wouldn't you?" the Amorph said.

Jack crouched into a fighting stance. His hands let out a pale glow and Sylvie felt a gust of wind caress her cheek. Before it picked up. Their robes billowed around them.

Sylvie was suddenly pushed back.

"You're irritating," Jack said. Cold and factual. "But you're good enough to be considered a Hunter. I think I might enjoy this. So, make this last for me, okay?"

The rain slapped at their exposed skin.

Jack's senses funneled—he no longer cared for the Peose around him or the tempest he caused—only the black anger spreading across the Amorph's face. His world alight with the hiss of magic coursing through his veins.

Sylvie attempted to conjure fire only for it to die out from the strong blend of wind and rain. The cold nipped at her skin, threatening to freeze her blood. Sylvie covered her face with her arms, but not before catching sight of the Hunter shifting into a much larger bird. As big as the toads by his side. His outstretched wings weren't affected by the sudden gale around them.

"Jack!" Sylvie yelled. "Jack! Stop!"

Jack ignored her calls and rushed forward, shooting a blast of scorching flames. The Amorph screeched, as it flew high into the air. Its feathered tail on fire. The toads were quick to attack in his place. They leaped down, shooting burning projectiles of saliva at them.

"Are you trying to get us killed?" Sylvie shouted, hiding behind a tree and just narrowly dodging a ball of fire aimed at her head. The tree lit up in flames, and she darted away, adrenaline and instinct quickly kicking in. Another Peose spat in her direction, but this time, she could only roll, slamming her knee against an exposed tree root in the process.

"Of course not!" Jack barked in her direction. He hid behind a large tree, dodging fireballs and continuously re-freezing it each time the wood caught fire. In that moment, Sylvie envied his powers. Jack didn't seem to notice her petty resentment. He kept his eyes on the skies, trying to catch sight of the Hunter. Who they could still hear squawking.

"It's him I'm trying to kill!" Jack yelled.

"These toads aren't exactly aiming for non-lethal spots!"

"Well, don't blame me!" he said. She made a face, risking her head out to stare disbelievingly at him. "Why these cursed Peose insist on getting in our faces is beyond me."

Sylvie turned around, only to find one of the oversized beasts crouched before her with its mouth wide open. She froze at the sight of its tongue and the blackness beyond its throat. Blue veins ran along the tunnels of its mouth, pulsing at a rate far faster than what could be considered normal. It blew a cloud of mist in her face and she tensed as she saw a clear substance begin to form in the back of its mouth, realizing a moment too late what it was. She suppressed the urge to gag as she dropped to a crouch, a fireball singing the tip of her robes. Her fingers twitched, and she let out a tunnel of flame aimed at the toad's legs. The beast let out a pained cry that attracted the attention of the other Peose.

Sylvie's eyes widened as she was suddenly surrounded by an army of frogs. Her worst nightmare come to life before her eyes. Though reality was different from the land of dreams. Here, her fears would be present to face her whether she was ready for them or not.

They breathed out a collective haze of mist, blocking her vision. She instinctively closed her eyes. Sylvie was afraid of many things, but as a resident of the Tower, the dark certainly wasn't one of them. During that moment of obstruction, Sylvie was quick to flee. She ran blindly away from them and their volatile saliva, turning her head just in time to see the forest burning and two fireballs coming at her from two different directions with extreme precision. But before the nearer one could make contact, it froze before her eyes.

A sudden pain stung her, erupting from the back of her knees and forcing her face first to the ground.

The second fireball missed, scorching the tree behind her. The flames licked her skin. As she tried to move away before the tree suddenly fell and crushed her. But before she could even stumble in another direction, a rush of cold surrounded her. Her eyes widened as the tree suddenly froze. Completely engulfed in glitters of white.

A pillar of frost against the otherwise burning forest.

"Are you alright?" Jack asked.

Sylvie sighed in relief, realizing a moment too soon that he actually had the audacity to kick the back of her knees in a last minute effort to get her to drop to the ground. Despite the realization, she couldn't find it in herself to berate him at the moment. Pacified by the fact that he was so capable. He may have been infuriating to a fault, but she couldn't deny that—unlike many she'd met—Jack had the power to back his words.

No matter how rashly chosen.

If nothing else, he was good at thinking on his feet.

Jack eyed their surroundings, searching for something. He

kept a hand on the tree, freezing it over and over again every few seconds. His breaths were ragged and uneven. And though his fingers shook from the rain, he still kept his eyes on the sky above them.

"That damned Hunter flew away!" Jack roared, barely noticing that he was shivering down to his bones.

"Why don't we worry about that another time?" Sylvie bit out. Tired from constantly ducking for her life. "I suggest we get out of this forest. Sooner rather than later. I'm not sure if these things will follow, but they haven't stepped outside of Tearwood before. I don't expect them to now."

Jack clicked his tongue, but conceded nevertheless. "There's a lone one to your left on the other side of this tree. Head there. I'll provide cover. Burn it if you can, but don't make it a priority. Just run. Don't look back. I'll be right behind you."

"Do you really expect me to just leave you behind?"

He raised an eyebrow. "What? Don't tell me you think I'd actually die for your sake? Ha! I'd sooner drown you in the Zexin Sea myself than willingly die for you. Nor would I suggest anything, unless I came out of it alive and well and relatively unscathed. You'd do well to remember that."

Sylvie rolled her eyes, unsure why she even bothered to question him or his plan. He was too stubborn to die.

"I'll hold you to those words," she said. "Only because you haven't let me down yet."

Jack shrugged noncommittally in response, as she crept up to the side of the tree. She took a deep breath in preparation, expelling her nervous jitters with each steady exhale. Sylvie lit a flame, watching the rain futilely try to extinguish it. Before she turned to him. Her voice snippy and to the point.

"Don't run off in a different direction, Jack. Changing your world can wait. I doubt the north even wants you back."

Jack smirked. A self-assured gleam in his eyes, despite the slight to his ego. He believed in luck. He was a firm believer in it actually, and for all intents and purposes, Lady Luck never turned her back on him. Jack didn't expect her to now.

"For your sake, I hope that insult wasn't as intentional as it sounded," Jack said. His voice was coated with its usual dose of sarcasm. "Just who do you think you're talking to?"

They shared a grin, before Sylvie leapt out and ran.

She didn't look back.

***

As soon as Sylvie made it past the line of trees, she was panting and out of breath—unaccustomed to running such long distances. Despite this, she immediately whirled around for any signs of her pursuers. Only to stumble back in surprise when she found two Peose staring menacingly at her from the trees. They hissed like caged beasts, rocking on their hind legs. Their mouths opened and closed, as if debating whether or not they should continue their assault.

Sylvie's eyes darted between their forms, knees bent and ready to continue running. Visibly tense in preparation for an attack. It didn't come. They stood there for three eternal moments, before finally retreating. No longer interested. Sylvie dropped her stance and let out a breath she hadn't known she'd been holding. As she watched them slink back into the forest, blending into the mist. If she squinted, she could still see their hazy silhouettes a short distance away.

What are they waiting for? Sylvie thought, her eyes widening at her own idiocy. *Jack!*

She wanted to call out to him, but caught herself. Taking a deep breath to calm her frazzled nerves, she crept to the outskirts of the forest. She watched the two nearby toads twitch. One leapt closer to her, its head tilted, wondering what she was doing.

Sylvie eyed it for a moment, before deeming it harmless and continuing to peer into the dense mist in search of Jack. The toad, however, didn't seem to appreciate being ignored. With a great push from its hind legs, its large body stretched outward through the air and landed in a crouch before her.

She stepped back in surprise, raising her hand to stifle a grisly scream. Its large mouth opened and her first instinct was to release her magic, so without giving it much thought, her free hand shot up and released a poorly conjured blast of fire. The toad jumped, dodging the blast with ease. Sylvie made a move to run, but before she could, a figure roughly knocked into her and forced her to the ground. A glob of something slimy and wet followed, coating her and her assailant in transparent gunk.

"Oh, for the love of Silas!" She heard a familiar voice yell, as Jack attempted to untangle himself from her. He grimaced, looking at the state of his robes. "What in the world were you doing there? You do realize you were just standing by the edge of the forest, don't you?"

"I was looking for you!" Sylvie yelled right back, standing and attempting to clean herself. She was covered in so much muck that even the pouring rain couldn't wash it all away.

"I was just about to roast that Peose alive when it suddenly jumped," Jack grumbled, irritated. It was easier to vent intense emotions through the one passion he was most comfortable with. Thus, he expressed the sheer relief he felt at the fact that he'd made it out alive in the only way he could. Annoyance. Tiv had once dubbed him, *'emotionally constipated,'* though it wasn't until this moment that Jack fully understood what he'd meant.

"Are you alright?" Sylvie asked.

"When did you become so great that you could worry about me?" Jack muttered, his voice reaching a realm beyond mocking. He ignored how her eyes narrowed at him in favor of sniffing his robes. His nose scrunched up at the scent. "I think I preferred their flaming spit. At least it would make me feel less vile."

Sylvie's eyes widened. She looked down at her robes. They were covered in a repulsive combination of dirt, rainwater, and some unknown substance. Sylvie shuddered at the gooey feeling slithering across her skin. The rain did nothing to wash it off.

"Don't tell me..." her voice was a disgusted whisper, "the saliva lost its flame once it left the mist?"

"The mist does ignite it. I wouldn't be surprised if it some-how kept its fire going, too." Jack whirled around, searching for any more signs of the Peose. But they were gone. "I swear I'll burn every damned Peose in this godforsaken forest! Tearwood will be ashes once I'm through with it."

Another transparent blob shot out, splattering over Jack's face with impeccable precision. And despite their predicament, Sylvie couldn't help the laugh that escaped her. Jack lit his hands in fury, hissing under the rain like an angry, wet cat. Sylvie mana-ged to grab his arm, before he could storm off and get himself killed.

"We need to go back," she said, trying to keep her mouth fr-om twitching. To no avail. "We need to tell them about Anora and the Hunter in Tearwood."

"Assuming they don't already know," Jack retorted. The flames in his hands diminished and he was left to grumble as they walked back to the Drowned Tower. Jack turned once more to see if any of the Peose had followed them or to hopefully catch a glimpse of the Hunter they'd met. He found neither.

"What's going on?" Jack muttered, staring out at the trees. Sylvie tilted her head at him, a silent gesture to repeat himself.

"I need answers," he told her instead.

But his words were silenced by the rain.

11

Tiv's ego was slighted.

He'd never been difficult to insult, thus he usually forgot most offenses shortly after they occurred. But this time was different. When he'd gone to visit Master Cephas upon Reed's request, and he was denied access into the Assembly's meeting hall on the charge of being a mere primary apprentice, he'd taken it as a personal affront to all the time and effort he'd expended to achieve his current status. Tiv didn't belong to an influential family, nor was he a genius that had talent handed to him on a silver platter. He'd personally worked to earn his position, to earn the recognition of the Assembly, and to rise above the rest of his class in an Institute where Amorphs were continuously pitted against each other. So, when his position was belittled with little more than a dismissive wave of a hand, he'd nearly snapped.

The Master, whose name he couldn't recall, ushered him away with a frown and a few admonishing words.

Tiv obeyed of course. He clenched his fists and clamped his jaw shut, controlling the postal behavior he was known for displaying during times of aggravation. Restraint had never been his strong suit. It's why he and Jack paired so well. Together, they were a lethal combination of unreserved and uninhibited. It was also why he didn't just drop the matter and go off to conduct his guard duties as ordered.

All primary apprentices and their partners were tending to their responsibilities, and though he was given one, his partner was nowhere to be found. Jack was on Eriam. Like Reed, Tiv simply wanted to know when his partner would be allowed return. Walking around without Jack watching his back unnerved him in ways he didn't think possible.

A partnerless practitioner just wasn't natural.

Never one to dawdle, he went directly to the reason behind his partner's absence. Elder Serach.

The Elder's room was hidden deep in the older sectors of the Assembly's tower. In a place devoid of people and animals alike. Tiv involuntarily tensed when he saw the blue veins of magic along the walls. The magic that fortified the Drowned Tower ran stronger here. Deeper. So raw that Tiv felt a rush of cold pulse through the air, sending shivers down his spine.

Two practitioners were stationed just outside of Serach's quarters. Tiv flashed them the vials of plant liquid the Elder had requested, and they let him pass without complaint.

"Elder Serach," Tiv called through the door, not bothering to wait for permission before entering.

Tiv found Serach standing before a heavy oak table filled with flasks and open tomes. A half-empty glass of wine dangled loosely between his fingers. His forehead sported tired wrinkles that hadn't been there that morning, and the crow's feet around his eyes were pulled downward in fatigue. The candles littered about the room cast a disheartening glow upon Serach's face. He seemed to have aged years during the hours between their first meeting and now.

"Ah, welcome," Serach greeted with a worn smile, ushering Tiv deeper inside. He set his wine aside, deciding it best to forego anything that would loosen his lips. Thelarius only knew what this impromptu visit entailed. "Do you have any news for me?"

"Just a delivery." Tiv showed him the vials. "We met this morning. You sent me out to Eriam to procure these."

Serach's eyes widened. When he spoke, he stuttered, "Yes, I apologize for not recognizing you sooner. Your name was Tiv, correct? Tiv Grovegg? Gravice? Or wait, you're not Columbus' boy, are you? Claire or Rendo, was it?"

"The first was right," Tiv said, his eyebrows raising in disbelief at Serach's failing memory. Was this really one of the men in charge of the north? The thought was disconcerting. He refrained from speaking his mind, however, opting instead for a more diplomatic approach. So, he could ask his questions without being thrown out for insolence.

"Did I?" Serach smiled happily. "Again, I apologize for my poor memory. I'm not usually like this. Rior assists me quite a bit. Needless to say, with him gone and currently being accused of such horrid charges, I've quite a lot on my mind."

Tiv handed him the vials. "I don't suppose I could burden you with one more thought?"

"Oh, by all means. New thoughts sound positively divine."

Tiv suppressed a grin. He never thought he'd hear those words said in such a sincere way. All of his friends spoke fluent sarcasm. It always amused him to find those that couldn't be bothered to speak in such wry tones.

"Do you remember my partner, Jacques Dace?" Tiv asked. "Black hair. Sharp tongue. An Elementalist?"

"Ah, Dace, yes," Serach nodded absently. "I remember him. I'd be ashamed not to. His parents are quite famous."

"Yes, well… he's still on Eriam."

"Oh? I thought everyone was recalled."

"There are always a few exceptions to the rules. Jack's always been one of them."

The Elder nodded, contemplating his words.

"As an Elder," Tiv went on, "a few of us wanted to know if you had any information regarding the more minute details of the Assembly's investigation. I didn't want to ask, but I can't help but be on edge without my partner around. Anything you know would be good. It's strange for paired practitioners to be left amongst strangers, don't you think? Leaves a bad taste and all."

"Why, I understand completely," Serach muttered, solemnly shaking his head. He picked up his wine glass and drained the poison liquid in one swig. This was a personal question. Inquiries delicate in nature demanded a certain lack of sobriety when answered. "My partner passed a few years ago. I must admit, it's been strange not having that one friend you can trust to be by your side. But that's what apprentices are for. You'll realize this as well once you reach my age. Being left behind isn't a pleasant feeling. But you'll find companionship in your apprentices."

Serach clinked the vials together, watching the plant liquid slush around in fascination.

"Though I'm sidestepping your question, aren't I? I'm afraid I don't have any more information than you or the others who seek it. I've been confined to my quarters since Rior was charged. I don't believe I'll be allowed out anytime soon."

"A shame," Tiv said.

"Truly," Serach agreed. "I'm sorry about your partner, but alas, remorse will do neither of us any good. Will you be staying? I'm busying myself with the fine craft of potions. The one I'm working on now is a difficult recipe to follow, but not impossible. Never impossible."

"No, I'm afraid I have my own duties to attend to."

Serach sighed. "Very well. If you see Columbus, do relate to him my woes."

Tiv nodded, leaving without a word of gratitude or farewell. The two guards looked up when they heard the door open and he lifted his hands to show that they were empty. By the time Tiv reached the stone stairwell that led to the upper floors, Celaris was already there waiting for him.

"Did he buy the act?" Celaris asked, eyeing Tiv appraisingly.

Tiv grunted, dropping his tactful tone. "If he did, then he's absolutely clueless. In fact, from his manner I'd say he was just as Jack said—a senile old man. Are you sure we should be bothering with him? He seems flaky."

"He knows far more than he lets on," Celaris said, his gaze hardening.

"If that's true, then I'm sure he saw through me. I wasn't exactly a pillar of respect when we first met. Pissing shame, that."

"That's fine." Celaris dismissed with a wave of his hand.

"Really?"

"Children are always quick to change their tune when you have something they want," he ignored Tiv's scowl, "it wasn't the first time your manners, or lack thereof, have squandered an opportunity. And it certainly won't be the last."

"I'm sure there's a hidden compliment somewhere there."

"Then you've clearly gone deaf," Celaris mocked, his lips quirking in amusement. "Optimism doesn't suit you, Tiv. But youth does. Serach's realization that we're onto him works in our favor."

"How exactly?"

Celaris merely smiled knowingly, evading Tiv's question with his own. "Did you tell him about Jack?"

"I did. He seemed interested. Vaguely. Do you really think he's after Jack? If he was, then why would he send us out? It just doesn't add up."

"I'm not sure. But we've made our move. All we can do now is wait for his. Patience, Tiv. Answers will come to us in time."

"And what am I supposed to do until then?"

"Head back to your post." Celaris patted his shoulder in praise. "Good work, Tiv."

Tiv grinned.

"Good enough to skip my duties?" he asked. "Just to let you know, I'm still sore about Jack. I thought partners were supposed to stick together. Yet he gets to play in Thyme, while I'm trapped here doing your dirty work."

"An apprentice shouldn't complain to his Master." Celaris advised, shaking his head when Tiv snorted. "The night is young. Stay alert. I might need you."

Celaris always did.

***

Reed paced around his room like a caged beast.

It was a relatively small dwelling which he recently began to share with an Amorph twice his height and half his weight. Reed heard a few of his friends refer to him as "the Tinker." Article included. So, he simply followed suit, having never asked him for his real name. They had little in common and spoke only when actions no longer sufficed. Their usual communication consisted of a series of grunts, shrugs, and finger pointing. Which suited Reed just fine. He'd never been one for idle conversations or long talks with new faces.

So, when they were locked away inside their room, partitions separating them from the rest, there was only silence. The tense and uncomfortable kind. The kind that kept him on edge. His thoughts had free reign, and he took to pacing erratically just for the sake of it. The Tinker—bless him—didn't mind his march, expertly ignoring Reed's existence. As he lounged on his side, flipping through a worn book about bird behavior. Reed wasn't sure if he was reading it for pleasure or because it was a required text from his current Master. But he thought it to be the latter.

Who actually reads that junk? Reed thought. *Amorphs have it rough.* No longer able to stand the silence, Reed pushed aside the blanket that functioned as their door to expose the large chamber which housed a good portion of the Tower's older inhabitants. He looked left then right, trying to see if there were any stray guards roaming about. There were none.

"Cephas," the Tinker called, finally speaking. Reed recoiled at the name, and for one foolish moment, he looked around him, wondering if his father was around. But of course he wasn't. The Tinker pinned him with a skeptical glance, clearly questioning his sanity. "You're leaving?

"Obviously."

"There might be primary apprentices wandering about."

"I think they're out patrolling the main halls," Reed said, hopeful. "They'd be spread too thin if they were patrolling inside the chambers as well."

The Tinker's face was doubtful. "Where are you going?"

"Out," Reed whispered. Just before he slipped away, he

caught the Tinker rolling his eyes. His roommate clearly wanted no part of this. *Smart man.*

Reed watched shadows dance upon the walls, coming from candles that continued to flicker in the cold. They provided just enough light for him to see the end of the hall.

He passed dozens of rooms, hearing hushed voices whisper everything from ghost stories to fanatical theories. Some rooms were silent, but most were filled with gossipy murmurs that he couldn't fully make out. Something about a screeching demon in the mess hall. Another about a cursed man near the Iniquities Chamber. And lastly, a woman with a raspy voice that sang in one of the seventh floor's archives.

He found the last one interesting, but Reed doubted it was any of the floor's official dwellers. Sylvie couldn't hold a tune, and Jack wasn't a woman. Unless the Elementalist had a secret high-pitched singing voice no one new about, then someone was most likely sneaking into the archives. Reed couldn't blame the perpetrator for wanting some alone time. But if Jack ever caught her chirping away, then Reed highly doubted her ability to escape with her ego intact.

Reed turned a corner and stumbled in surprise when two shrill squeals erupted from the room beside him. The girls inside spoke animatedly about some nameless man, before dozens of irritated yells from all around the chamber put them in their place. Despite the absence of guards, everyone stayed in their respective quarters. Perhaps it was because their chamber housed older practitioners. Reed had no doubt that the chambers filled with younger children must've been far livelier. The older ones seemed to take lockdown to heart, and Reed felt a bit like a traitor when he caught sight of Sylvie and Myrrh's room.

But not enough to go back.

He quietly stepped inside. Reed expected to be tackled or even yelled at, but he certainly hadn't expected the silence that greeted him. Or the darkness that accompanied it.

"Myrrh?" he called, wondering for one foolish moment if she

was just hiding from him. But of course that wasn't the case.

He surveyed his surroundings—the wrinkles on the bed and the clothes strewn about all suggested occupancy. But the coldness of the sheets and the unlit candles hinted otherwise. There was no one here. And there hadn't been for quite some time. Sylvie was on Eriam, so where was Myrrh?

Was she called away by one of the Masters? Reed thought. *Or did something happen?* She may have even taken this time to sneak out. He wouldn't put it past her.

"Myrrh," Reed called again, as he exited. Fully prepared to traverse the halls in search for her. As soon as he stepped out, he immediately noticed something was wrong. All the candles had gone out, shrouding him in total darkness. But the lack of light didn't bother him so much as the sudden lack of noise. Where had his friends' voices gone?

"Hello?" Reed whispered, afraid to speak too loud. "Is anyone there?"

His hand glowed light blue. It was only enough to see his feet, but Reed was used to scant light. He went to open one of the other rooms when he heard something drop. A loud slam that echoed throughout the chamber. Reed stiffened, eyes darting around in an attempt to locate the sound. To no avail. He saw a flash of yellow light and squinted to get a closer look.

Fire.

Small and dying. It came from a candle that slowly melted over an iron holder. Reed's eyes followed the hand holding it, only to see the hazy silhouette of a person. Dark robes and glowing hands. Another practitioner. Reed raised his arm to wave them over, but stopped himself when the fire abruptly went out. His heart pounded in sudden alarm. And he became increasingly aware of its sound—the only one ringing in his ears.

"Hello?" he whispered. "Why did you put the fire out?"

Reed heard the soft tap of footsteps meeting stone and he instantly took three steps back. Who was that? What did they want from him? He'd done nothing wrong. He made it a point to never step on anyone's toes—not too hard at least. Or was it something else? Were his fellow practitioners merely trying to scare him? No. This went too far.

His breath hitched, as an appalling thought entered his mind. *Was this person the reason for the sudden lockdown?*

"Show yourself!" Reed tried again, his voice more urgent.

His words were met with silence. He heard more footsteps. Followed by the soft trickle of something plopping against stone.

Tap. Tap. Tap.

Water, Reed realized. *From where?*

Reed was suddenly overcome by the intense urge to run. A compulsion he obeyed. As he turned on his heel and fled.

His sprint, however, was short lived.

When he rounded a corner to leave the chamber, he collided with someone's side. Reed pulled back immediately. His first instinct was to yell and use magic to forcibly relax the muscles of the one before him, but he stopped himself when he was pinned with familiar eyes. He recognized them. Except they were different from what he was used to.

They were cold.

Cold, cold eyes.

Reed's hand dimmed, before falling limply by his side. His mouth opened and closed and opened again. Too surprised to form proper words. He saw the brief flash of a crooked smile, and he choked, gasping for air.

What's happening?

His lungs were on fire. He looked down to see smoke rising from a glass flask, before it was forcibly smashed on his head.

Reed collapsed. He barely registered the warm, iron streams that trickled down his face and onto the ground, painting it crimson. *Sylvie,* his mind cried. As the world faded around him. *Don't come back.*

And the darkness claimed him.

12

After Ethil's sudden breakdown, all arguments amongst the Assembly ceased in favor of moving the weeping girl to a more private location. Where she could grieve in peace.

Columbus quickly dismissed the remaining Masters and retreated to the Tower's restricted library. It housed everything from ancient history to old healing brews. An entire row of shelves were dedicated to battles long forgotten and old disputes people were better off forgetting. Fire wasn't allowed in this area, so the only light came from a lamp half filled with pulsing *Orivellea* crystals. They weren't common in the lands past the Wymeran River, thus they were used sparingly. The few he had were a poor substitute to real fire, providing just enough light for him to see his hands.

Columbus poured over dozens of texts detailing the Tower's history. He'd hoped to find some form of instruction, maybe even a few wise words from his predecessors. But that was a fool's wish. There weren't any helpful notes. If there were, they'd long disappeared. Or perhaps he just wasn't focused enough to grasp anything truly concrete. Columbus' mind was filled with thoughts of the Drowned Tower's safety, of those wandering outside, of the murderer that walked their halls. He hardly understood the words before him. The sorry excuse for light he held only added to his lack of focus.

The dimness was beginning to give him a headache.

Columbus rubbed his temples. As he reread the same line four times, still unable to grasp the words.

This is impossible.

"Columbus?" a familiar voice pierced the stillness. "Are you here?"

"Here," he said, turning, immensely grateful for the distraction. He held up his lamp to find Orpha standing a short distance behind him. His frown was eerie in the sparse glow, increasing Columbus' worry tenfold.

"Orpha," he acknowledged with a slight nod of his head, discounting his impaired vision. Orpha saw much for one that wandered in darkness. His blindness was as much a curse as it was a blessing. Some horrors best remained unseen.

Still, Columbus didn't envy him.

"Is something wrong?" he asked.

"The turn is ours."

***

The repetitive tap of rushing footsteps could be heard as Columbus and Orpha sped through the halls, making their way to the residential tower. Their steps brought them to the tower's eighth floor, where half a dozen practitioners were being questioned. Columbus eyed the rooms. One in particular caught his attention—the chamber where Sylvie and Reed were situated.

What happened? Columbus thought, worry creasing his brow.

Sylvie was in Thyme, but Reed wasn't so lucky.

From his standpoint, things looked relatively normal. No shattered locks or unlit torches. If Orpha hadn't called for him, Columbus would've assumed that everything was fine. With that thought in mind, Columbus took a deep breath, reeling in his suspicions. Despite his wishes, he couldn't prioritize his family. He had hundreds more to care for—many younger than his son. The Institute was already in a tense situation. If he were to show favor to his own, then his allies on the Assembly wouldn't hesitate to turn their backs on him. It was a dangerous game.

Columbus couldn't have any more dissatisfied Masters.

They watched his minute decisions like hungry vultures

prepared to swoop down during a moment of fault. The Union may have dissolved long ago, but it was clear that there would always be a form of internal hierarchy. The Assembly was proof of that. As was his authority. But where there was hierarchy, there were coups. And rebellion was the last thing he needed.

Columbus sighed.

Across from him, four older Masters interrogated a group of practitioners with practiced skill. They'd lived long enough to know how to coax answers from the most obstinate of tongues. And they wanted to know how someone was able to slip under the noses of primary apprentices—who were supposedly the best the Tower had to offer.

"This is a disgrace!" Columbus heard them say. They were relentless with their questions. Their voices were laced with that horrid mix of disappointment and poise which reminded him of a parent scolding a child. Perhaps at its base, that's what it was.

Some practitioners were scared, while others—those often sent out to deal with troubles along their borders—relied on the steely composure they so carefully called upon during times of crisis. Their faces were emotionless masks. It was easy to tell the subpar from the true elite. The ones that the east relied on for necessary protection and those that were chosen to fill the gaps. But even the most experienced of practitioners trembled when Orpha walked up to them.

Orpha's gait was slow. He crossed his arms, tilting his head down as if to peer into their faces, despite not being able to. His nose scrunched as it always did when he got a whiff of fear. Their masks slipped for a moment to expose a crack in clearly imperfect armor. It was quite the sight.

"Master Orpha!" one of their interrogators spoke. His voice was old and raspy, grating on Orpha's sensitive ears. "I see you've brought Master Cephas with you."

"So he has," Columbus, himself, answered. He turned to the group of presently disfavored practitioners, hoping to find an answer to what was going on. While Orpha walked up to one of the rooms, placing his hand over it. As if he could sense whatever lay within. "And what happened here?"

"Perhaps you won't want to see."

"I'll be the judge of that."

A young woman stepped forward then, but a few of her more jittery companions accidentally pushed a young boy in front of her in their futile attempt to distance themselves from Columbus' gaze.

The boy stumbled, managing with some semblance of grace to catch himself before he fell. He was familiar. And that only meant one thing—the boy was remarkably talented for his age. The sort the Assembly kept their eye on. But he was far too young for such a job. Nevertheless, he was here. And Columbus knew enough about him to know that he was the partner of a primary apprentice. Which one, however, escaped recall. Why someone would choose such a young boy, Columbus couldn't say. Was he some kind of genius? He certainly looked it. The typical portrayal that one usually associated with the word. Thin and awkward. A waspish mouth. And large blue eyes that bounced out of a too round face. He reminded Columbus of Reed. The bookish sort with a soft voice that wouldn't dare hurt a fly.

A shame that the good ones never lived long.

The boy trembled visibly. So, Columbus plastered on his best smile, encouraging him to speak. "What's your name, child?"

"Roval," he answered, hesitant.

The young woman stepped forward to speak, but Columbus held up a hand, stopping her. "Can you tell me what happened, Roval?"

He faltered, but his doubts soon gave way to rising panic. As words tumbled out. "It was dark," Roval stuttered. "We opened the door and everything was dark. And quiet. Very, very quiet. We opened the rest and found the same thing." Columbus raised an eyebrow. He made a move to walk to one of the doors, but Roval grabbed his robes and jerked him back with an urgency that surprised him. "No! Don't go!"

The woman did step up this time, grabbing Roval's collar and yanking him back. She bowed her head. "I apologize for him, Master Cephas. He just recently passed Master Fritz' evaluation to become an eligible partner. As luck would have it, there are still a few primary apprentices crazy enough to choose a child. But Roval isn't field ready yet. He was on his way to the border to get firsthand healing experience when the order calling all primary apprentices and their partners back to the Institute was given. Roval returned. But his partner, Gren, remained outside to continue his patrol."

"I take it he's in your care then?" Columbus asked.

She hesitated, searching for the proper words. "Gren is… a friend. Roval was supposed to be confined to his room since Gren isn't here. Nor is he a primary apprentice, but I…" she trailed off, lowering her head in shame.

"You've done nothing wrong, child," Columbus said. She looked up in surprise. Columbus eyed the group before him. A collection of young, skilled, and talented. The sort they couldn't lose. "Now, go. You're all dismissed. Check the rooms along the lower floors, gather who you can, and bring them upstairs. Tell them that they'll have to share chambers for a while. And don't let them out of your sight. Get as much help as you need."

The Masters who'd been questioning them look appalled by the order, but the practitioners were quick to bow and take their chance to escape.

"You shouldn't have let them go so easily!" they immediately objected.

"They'll be questioned more later," Columbus assured in a half-hearted effort to appease them. "Right now, we need all the hands we can get. So, please," he jerked his chin forward, urging them to go, "assist them."

A few grumbled, but left without further complaint.

Only inward curses.

Columbus walked up to Orpha, who'd finally removed his hand from the door. Orpha wore a look of wary contemplation, worried about what lay beyond the door. Columbus eyed him a second longer, taking in his reluctance and wondering if he should listen to Orpha's almost animalistic instinct to sense danger. But he'd already made up his mind. Columbus grasped the handle, disregarding Orpha, who immediately shook his head, silently telling him not to open it.

Reed was in this very chamber. If something happened, then he wanted to know. Roval's vague descriptions did nothing to quell his unease. If anything, it only made him more curious.

With his heart pounding, Columbus lightly pushed it open. The door creaked, slowly swinging inward. The first thing he noticed was the rusty stench of iron. Sour and pungent after lingering in a confined room for so long. The sight that awaited him, however, had him forgetting about the smell. It was one he'd never seen, despite living in a place where darkness was an almost permanent companion.

The open door exposed a near impenetrable blackness that lingered within the confines of the chamber. It didn't spread past the door. As though trapped. Isolated. A caged animal. Except the dark didn't howl. It only swallowed. An unknown being.

The light from the hall did nothing to brighten it.

"Reed," Columbus called out of instinct. His eyebrows scrunched together in sudden apprehension. "Reed! Anyone? Hello? Answer me!" Columbus took a step forward and his leg was immediately swallowed by black. His eyes widened. As he stared down at the invisible appendage. He wiggled his toes, sighing in relief when he could feel them.

"Reed!" Columbus called again, prepared to take another step forward when he looked up to find something peering at him. But before he could call out to the mysterious being, dark tendrils latched onto his thigh. Columbus stared at it in morbid fascination, but when one shot out to cover his mouth, his eyes widened and he finally began to panic.

With a sharp tug, the tendrils attempted to reel him in.

"Orpha!" a familiar voice cut through shocked stillness. "On the floor! Grab Cephas!"

Orpha didn't know what they were up against, but he knew enough to trust the urgency in those words. He blindly reached downward, his fingers tightening over loose robes. Orpha didn't think twice about who it may have been and yanked. For a moment, Columbus was the object of a fierce tug-of-war between two powerful forces. But with glowing hands and a sudden burst of strength, Orpha tugged Columbus back with enough force to send him flying toward the opposing wall. The sickening crunch of bone meeting stone rang loudly, before it was silenced by the chamber's door slamming shut. A pained groan followed.

"I came to warn you," Celaris said, panting as he checked the door to make sure it was sealed. He held a hand out to Columbus. "Obviously, I was too late."

"No." Columbus accepted his help with shaky thanks. "You were just in time. For a moment, I thought I'd be taken. I underestimated Orpha's strength."

"As did I," Orpha grunted. "I apologize for throwing you."

Columbus shook his head at the apology, clasping the man's shoulder to let him know that more than anything, he was relieved. Columbus breathed deeply, attempting to calm himself. To no avail. His heart continued its erratic beat. As his mind ran with bloody scenarios. Fueled by the sort of irrepressible worry only a father with a missing child possessed.

"What was that?" Columbus asked. "What's it done to the others?"

"I don't know." Celaris spared the closed door a glance, before looking pointedly back at him. "But Elder Serach might."

The implication wasn't lost on them.

Before Columbus could question him further, they heard footsteps approaching. The sound echoed from around the corner. Slow and deliberate. It hushed them into silence. The stranger repeatedly tapped a book against the walls. A soft pat they'd heard a thousand times before when soft spoken practitioners wanted to get someone's attention without yelling across the hall.

It was accompanied by soft singing. Only loud enough for them to realize that it was a woman. The words were echoed whispers eaten by stone.

"Show yourself," Celaris bit out. "Why aren't you at your post?"

The sounds ceased.

Only to start again, as the footsteps became louder. Heavier. The stranger approached with an insistence that put them all on edge. Their fingers twitched and magic breathed adrenaline into their bodies. Celaris crouched into a fighting stance he hadn't assumed in far too long. As Orpha and Columbus took more defensive positions.

They were prepared to strike.

They didn't call out to the possible threat, instead they watched with weary eyes as a familiar figure emerged. Soaked to the bone.

And the sound of dripping water rang in their ears.

***

The night grew colder by the hour. But as a man that hailed from the north, Serach was used to the cold. To sudden frosts and long nights and endless days of snow piling upon snow. There were times when he'd amuse himself with thoughts of day never breaking, of nothing greeting the morning because the sun feared to show itself. Another loser against the biting winds. But, in the end, those were merely fantasies. Playful illusions he conjured during times of momentary boredom or respite. They weren't real. Once the winds died down and the clouds parted, day would always break. The world would begin anew. The sun would sit there without fail, offering warmth against horripilate skin.

The Drowned Tower, however, brought his fantasies to life.

Despite the inhabitant's claims of morning having arrived, there was no sun to greet him each time he awoke. The lighting in the halls remained the same. As did the darkness of the sea surrounding them. A long, terrible nightmare. The only warmth came from fire and hot beverages. His hunger was a reminder that he was, indeed, alive and not another victim of the Drowned Tower's blackness—as its dwellers had become. The lack of sunlight clearly took its toll. Their skin was so pale, they looked to have drowned long ago, yet they continued to walk and laugh as though there was nothing wrong. Perhaps there wasn't. But from his perspective, life in the Drowned Tower was bizarre. It was far more confined than any of the other branches. The people lived like hermits. Dwellers of the sea.

He was there to change that.

Serach stood over a table, carefully eyeing the glass flask that sat before him. The only sound in the room came from a tube filled with yellow liquid which continuously dripped its contents down into his little concoction. With each drop, the contents of the flask diluted until it was just another clear blend of imitation water. It looked harmless as it sat there. Though, if consumed, the results would be anything but.

His head snapped up when he heard a pained groan. Ever cautious, his gaze immediately flickered to the side where two practitioners lay unconscious on the ground. Their open wounds bled crimson over the stone floor.

His guards. Apprentices of Columbus Cephas. They were nothing more than burly Amorphs with more brawn than brain. But they'd make good hostages, if nothing else—assuming they survived. He felt a smidgeon of regret at having to hurt them when the only crime they were guilty of was following orders. But he was no longer in a position where he could twiddle his thumbs and worry about the sins of every sorry individual he happened across.

The Assembly was onto him.

He'd be damned if all of his hard work went to waste because of something as foolish as morals. It was only when Serach was certain they were still asleep, did he allow himself to turn and search for the true source of the sound.

Not a moment later, and it was thrown before his feet.

It came in the pitiful form of Reed Cephas, who used what little energy he had left to groan in pain. His defiance had gone along with his face. Now, a bloody and disfigured mess even his father wouldn't be able to recognize. Reed's cheeks were filled with blisters and fresh burns, while his hands and feet were tightly bound with rope that chaffed his skin. Serach could see the marks already turning a bloody purple.

And he smiled.

A blood curdling smile that chilled to the bone.

"I see you've been busy," Serach said, kneeling down to heal him. He reached into his robes, his eyes lighting in amusement when Reed's orbs dilated, as he futilely tried to squirm away. Serach produced his personal tome. A heavy thing that's cover was crafted from black wood that sported an intricate design impressed with magic. It pulsed with power, emitting a soft blue glow that whispered promises of illness and misfortune. Serach turned to the beginning pages, his hands glowing. As he repeated the scribbled incantation he'd all but forgotten.

It was a rudimentary healing spell used to mend superficial wounds. A spell taught to children during their first years. But when employed by those with experience, even the simplest of spells could become powerful.

Reed's whimpers ceased. His skin mended back together. The burns on his face disappeared to make way for untouched flesh. And he could finally open his eyes without feeling a sting of pain. Reed saw the tome in Serach's hands as soon as he did. It pulsed. Quick and fleeting. Filled with magic that enhanced his powers. Reed had never seen anything quite like it, and he loath-ed to admit that it held his attention longer than it should have because Serach's face morphed into an ugly grimace.

"To ignore me," Serach's voice was an angry murmur, "you really are his blood, aren't you?"

When Reed's eyes finally met Serach's, he trembled under the weight of his gaze. Violent and filled with unconcealed mal-ice. Where had the kind man he'd met gone? Was he killed and replaced by this fake? No. That was impossible. They looked too alike. Down to the wrinkles and the boxed beard.

A mask? Reed immediately shook his head to rid himself of the thought. Wearing another's face was gruesome and something he'd rather not think about. This was undoubtedly the Elder. But Reed found himself struggling to accept the fact, struggling to accept this man who donned the face of familiarity.

"No matter." Serach stood, turning to face his apprentice. "Have you placed them?"

Rior nodded. His face gave away nothing. As he handed Serach an old text covered with tattered leather and dust. It had a solid gold trim which revealed its true value.

"Good, good." Serach bobbed his head approvingly. He traded the tome for a flask filled with amber liquid and a dark haze at its center. One solid crystal floated wantonly within. "Here you are."

Rior squinted, examining it.

"Will this really work?" Rior asked. His voice was low and hoarse from unuse. "The archives you took this from are two ages old. For all we know, this could be the wrong formula. Maybe even an entirely different recipe."

"You won't know until you try," Serach said, uncaring. "But you shouldn't doubt the knowledge of books, Rior. I went to a lot of trouble to get that recipe. What, with the entire north in disarray and watching my every move, moving wasn't exactly easy. Neither was finding that. The book it was written in was hidden all the way down in the catacombs, you know? Beneath a large pile of useless tonics!" Serach sighed exasperatedly, choosing to ignore Rior's continuous skepticism. He dismissed him with a careless wave of his hand. "Be on your way now, Rior. I wouldn't be a very good Master if I let you get caught up in my affairs, whilst you have your own to attend to. I thank you for the book though. You did well."

"I'll be going then." Rior bowed, before turning to leave. His face like stone. Except twice as cold. But his eyes betrayed him, unveiling his underlying suspicion. As he kept subtly inspecting the flask.

"Rior," Serach called, stopping him before he could make his exit. "That Grovegg boy came to visit me. As I suspected, Jacques is still outside. It should be easy to find him. So long as you drink that brew."

"And if it doesn't lead me to him? What if someone else has it? I don't want to risk having to kill someone inside the Tower. Hunters linger. I can feel them. They're waiting for me to reveal as much information as possible before they strike."

"Jacques has the stone," Serach said with such certainty that Reed, whom had no clue as to what they were speaking of didn't doubt his words. "He's an Elementalist. He has part of the crystal already. There's a reason we've been having the east target all those pesky deserters, while we were on our way. And unless one of the First Zenith's descendants were nearby, that *thing* inside the stone only had one choice. Call out to Jacques. I doubt anyone else would risk getting into trouble for grabbing a useless rock."

Reed's eyes widened.

His breath hitched when he realized that Serach noticed the involuntary action. Reed immediately tried to recover, pretending to tremble under Serach's gaze. It wasn't hard. He actually flinched.

"And if one of their descendants picked it up?" Rior asked.

"Their progeny died out long ago," Serach said, scoffing. "The only remaining descendants of the First Zenith are the Drakone family. Useless prigs, the lot of them. They believe being the sprog of Maurice somehow makes them superior. What advantage is there to not being able to use the privy without the entire Diamond Alps knowing about it? I highly doubt any of them would attempt to leave. Let alone succeed! The north would erupt into a stalking frenzy."

"But..." Rior stopped and shook his head ever so slightly, silently reprimanding himself. "Okay, I'll be going then."

"Yes, yes." Serach shooed him out. "Watch yourself, Rior.

The Zexin Sea is restless. Clearly, Pernelia doesn't approve of our actions within her home."

Rior walked out without another word, leaving his Master to his work. Serach turned to Reed once the door closed, isolating them from the rest of the Tower. He smiled. That kind smile Reed once thought to be genuine. Now, Reed could see it for what it was. Condescending.

"Now," Serach's smile widened, "where were we?"

Reed gulped.

This isn't the time to falter, Reed mentally berated. His thoughts were as unforgiving as the one before him. Even as his lips quivered in terror. *Whenever push came to shove, Sylvie never did. Neither did father. Compose yourself, you damned coward!*

Reed smiled in an effort to hide his growing apprehension. He hoped there wasn't any blood on his teeth. Despite his mental reassurances, however, his body betrayed him. As soon as Serach stepped forward, Reed visibly trembled and his gaze wavered in uncertainty. When he could no longer handle the pressure and turned away, he was only met with the still forms of his father's apprentices.

"Ah, I remember," Serach muttered, looking disapprovingly at him. "You were ignoring me, weren't you?"

Another smile. But this one made Reed recoil in fear.

Reed was scared.

And Serach knew it.

13

When Ethil awoke in an unfamiliar room, she immediately closed her eyes again, willing the strange ceiling away. But of course that didn't happen. And when she reopened them, bright spots invaded her vision. As if to spite her. Her body shook from exhaustion, the dull pangs of a sleepy headache assaulting her with it suddenness. Her throat was scratchy and her eyes were sore. Puffy from tears. She'd cried herself into a fitful slumber, plagued with nightmares that escaped recall, but still terrified her body into anxiety. She continued to lay there, panting and frightened with no sense of how much time had passed. As an image of Duward came to the forefront of her mind, her heart squeezing without warning.

Pain defied time, she realized. As one of the Drowned Tower's more capable practitioners that was something Ethil had always known. She'd seen loss before. She'd felt it with the loss of her parents. She'd taken part in its creation on their borders. She'd stood more than once in blood soaked battlefields with only corpses around her for company. Where the scent of blood wasn't a mere taint on the ground—it was the ground. It embodied it. So much so that the only word she could use to accurately describe her surroundings then was 'bloody.'

Ethil knew loss. And she knew pain—both physical and mental—but right now, the mere idea of things she thought she knew made her tremble. Her mind knew, but her heart couldn't seem to catch up. She hated it. The blasted thing. Did she really need it? Ethil shook her head, forcing her eyes away from the ceiling. It mocked her with fixed indifference. And made her think of things she never wanted to.

Where am I? Ethil thought. As she surveyed the room. It was bare, save for the bed she occupied and a torch beside the door. The room was quiet, and in the silence, thoughts of Duward surfaced. They invaded her mind. Plagued her thoughts and demanded her attention. Ethil didn't give it. She wiped the traitorous tears welling in her eyes away and hurriedly crossed the room. Her legs shook so badly that she almost stumbled, but she didn't let that stop her. She didn't want to spend any more time with grief. Her invisible companion, slowly asphyxiating her in a tight embrace of clingy longing.

It's all in your head, she recalled in Duward's voice. In that scolding tone that never failed to annoy her. *Now stop fumbling around like an untrained monkey. We have work to do. Follow me.*

Just the memory of his voice was enough to make her desperate to see him. Ethil covered her ears to drown it out.

It didn't help.

Enough, Ethil thought, desperate. *I've had enough.*

When Ethil opened the door, she was pleasantly surprised to find her guard half-asleep. Before he could react, she placed her hands on him, running them up his arms and forcibly soothing his spent muscles until he became another dweller of the land of dreams.

She wasn't going to stop. Not until she was far away from that room—and her thoughts. Ethil walked down the halls with an almost stone sort of calm. Her face was impartial, her mind, however, was anything but. The Tower was strangely quiet. The guards were either slacking off or wandering about without a care for her presence. Did they think she was assigned some sort of position? Did no one tell them of what was happening? Or of Duward? Or did they know and were currently looking for the perpetrator? They didn't look it. And their indifference to her presence left her to her thoughts. The same ones she tried to escape.

It seemed fleeing was harder than simply running in another

direction. But Ethil didn't dare start a conversation. Mindless chatter might have alleviated some of her worries, but she was afraid they'd force her back into her room. Maybe even call one of the Masters. Their pitying faces were the last thing she wanted to see.

Her feet instinctively brought her back to the tower's upper floor. Where she'd last seen Duward. He was taken so quickly. So easily. One word, one glance at his body, and he was officially gone. Her only family. The only one she could truly count on, despite her occasional frustration with his faulty personality. What was she to do now that he was gone? She'd always followed his back. But somewhere along the way, Duward took a different turn without her knowledge.

He'd gone to a place without worry. One filled with light and peace. By the First Zenith's side. A path she wanted to take, but one she wouldn't dare follow.

She wasn't a fool.

Duward saved her. At least, that's what she was told by the Assembly. And though she was grateful, it was drowned out by self-loathing and misplaced fury. How selfish of him to leave her behind like this. With this unbroken silence and memories of the past. Stained with blood. Soon, those, too would fade.

Ethil was afraid of that.

She feared her memories becoming little more than distant figments she'd only recall when nostalgia knocked on her door. Some would be dreary and gray, while others would be jagged and blurry—forgotten over time. And all she'd have to show for her experiences would be a few yearly accolades. Wrinkles, laugh lines, popping joints, calloused hands. Physical displays of her sagacity. They'd show how she was able to survive, despite being alone. How easy it would be to laugh, despite fate conspiring against her.

Ethil didn't want any of it.

She didn't need a reminder of just how well she could do on her own or how she didn't need anyone to live. She already knew that. She just wanted her brother back.

Is that so much to ask?

Ethil recalled the moments before her sudden blackout. To think that only moments prior she'd been smiling with him. Was death really so eager for more company? Why couldn't it be someone else? Ethil knew plenty of people with far more faults and a plethora of unspeakable crimes under their belts.

Murderer. Avenger. Butcher.

She didn't care about their titles, or the ones they'd use to christen her. Ethil would be more than happy to send a few extra souls to death's side if it meant they'd return his.

Ethil rounded a corner, before jumping right back where she came. A Master and half a dozen practitioners stood at the base of a long flight of steps that led to the Drowned Tower's entrance. The Assembly must've been short on manpower because Ethil hardly recognized any of the practitioners. She'd seen one or two of them in passing during roster handout meetings, but never beside her protecting the borders. What were they doing there? Were they making certain no one left? They lacked the experience necessary to stop any real threat.

What is the Assembly thinking? Ethil thought in disdain. *They might as well give the people a free pass outside.*

Ethil watched them until the Master and who she assumed were her apprentices were called away by a wheezing man with a terrible cough. He babbled incessantly about a problem in the residential tower.

Those left heaved a collective sigh of relief at their exit.

"It's about time," the one with a protruding jaw said. He stretched his back before unceremoniously dropping to the ground. "Guarding with Master Enelle and her two lapdogs around is way too tiring. She needs to ease up on us a bit. We've been here for hours. We could all use a break."

A young woman sauntered up to him, shifting the grimoire in her hands. And without warning, kicked his shin. "Don't you dare talk about Master Enelle that way!"

Protruding Jaw glowered at her, before another man with a

mole under his eye stepped between them. "Now, now, that's enough you two." His smile was placating, but his voice held an edge that warned them of the consequences of continuing.

"He needs to learn a lesson in respect," Grimoire Holder said. "He thinks he's a big shot now just because he passed the evaluation. You haven't even been sent outside yet!"

Protruding Jaw flipped her off. His smile was taunting. "What? And you have?"

"I said," Mole Man scowled at them, "enough!"

As the remaining practitioner turned his back to poke fun at them, Ethil took that chance to quietly slip past their sight. But as she was about to cross to the other side, Protruding Jaw turned. His eyes awkwardly met her own.

"Hey!" Protruding Jaw called, gathering himself. "What are you doing?"

Ethil froze.

And when their eyes zeroed in on her, she did what her instincts told her to. Run. Ethil darted up the stairs, hearing them shout below. Two had already begun chasing after her and when she saw a bat dart upward only to suddenly stop to screech in her face, she screamed. Her hand pulsed with magic and Ethil slapped the bat away, forcing its muscles to relax before it collided with the wall.

As she continued to run, Ethil heard thunder rumbling outside. It was followed by shouting and the sound of waves crashing against the Drowned Tower's iron gates. But before she could throw open the door, she was yanked back.

Ethil's eyes widened.

A glowing hand came down to roughly punch her in the face. She reflexively brought up her own to seize her captor's wrist in a display of strength he clearly hadn't expected. It was wrenched back a moment later, but that was all the time she needed. Her captor's aggressive hand fell uselessly to his side, and he let her go out of shock.

She'd used her magic on him. Why would he be surprised at

that? Ethil turned, placing both of her hands on the stranger's face.

"I'm sorry," she mumbled. As her captor crumpled to the floor, rolling a good way down. Ethil sighed in relief, wiping the sweat off her brow. She could no longer hear the voices below. Instead, they came from above. Petty arguments coupled with the occasional infuriated shout. The voices asked for entrance into the Tower. Curious, Ethil crept up the remaining steps and threw open the door. The wind almost blew her straight into the sea — which looked dangerously close as it thrashed against the gates and flooded inside. The water stopped just before the door, unable to get past the enchantments.

Rain poured and thunder continued to rumble overhead.

The outside world spiraled into chaos, but amidst it all stood two unyielding figures sneering at each other. They looked familiar, as they stood, uncaring for the rest of the world around them. Their gazes focused solely on the other. Vibrant and angry. A clash of red and orange. The rain did nothing to drown their ire.

They're fighting, Ethil realized, mouth gaping in disbelief.

Idiots.

***

"Where is everyone?" Sylvie exclaimed, infuriated.

They'd almost been swept clean off the bridge by the roaring waves. Twice. Jack's constant remarks during the ordeal did nothing to quell her rising annoyance. And when they'd finally made it to the entrance, there was no gatekeeper present. Although Sylvie had been yelling for quite some time, there were still no signs of anyone coming up to open it. It was only then that they realized the Drowned Tower truly was under lockdown. But that didn't excuse the lack of security. Or the lack of waterproofing enchantments along the Tower's bridge.

Although violent, the clash of earth and sky did nothing to deter them as they spoke. The bad weather only fueled Sylvie's already foul mood. Her eyes narrowed when she caught sight of that flippant bow of a mouth adorning her companion's face. It was the only thing spared by the rain. Jack's rakish grin had the ability to press all of her buttons in all of the wrong ways.

And Jack knew it.

"Your little disciple won't come," Jack said. As he rubbed his temples in irritation. Sylvie's pleas to invisible strangers were beginning to give him a headache. "I'm sure Cephas' brat has more important things to do than listen for your cries."

"I called for help. Not Reed."

"The implication is the same. Your gallant knight can't hear us from inside."

"He's my partner, and it's not like that between us."

"Oh, please." Jack scoffed. "He's completely smitten with you."

Sylvie's eyes narrowed. "I hate lies."

Jack looked affronted.

"I don't lie!" His voice came out louder than he'd intended, but he still didn't back away from her gaze. Even as she raised an eyebrow in silent question. His mouth was set in a thin line, daring her to say otherwise.

Before she could retort, however, Jack stiffened.

And then his jaw dropped.

Jack's face morphed into a combination of surprise and dread. As if he'd just learnt of a beloved friend's death. The abrupt change in his expression brought Sylvie to a halt. Jack's mood swings were as infuriatingly unpredictable as they were common. They were familiar enough that she could take them in stride. But she'd never seen a look of utter surprise on his face before, so she couldn't help but stare at the rare sight.

Jack always looked as if he knew a secret only he was privy to. His smirk was all-knowing. His eyes sagacious.

But right now, he was anything but.

Jack grabbed her arm with one hand, while his other scrambled to hold onto the iron gate. Before a large wave mercilessly crashed over them. Jack held on for dear life. As the water attempted to take them.

Sylvie barely had time to inhale. Before the current tried to sweep her away in a half-botched attempt at drowning. By the time the last remnants of water returned to the sea, she was doubled over, wheezing and coughing her lungs out.

Jack was quick to let her go.

Sylvie fell to her knees. She spat out a mouthful of liquid salt. As she tried to inhale as much air as her lungs would allow. It wasn't much. Even simply breathing was a chore. The mouthfuls of oxygen only made her chest ache. She wanted to go back inside the Institute. Back to her room. Where it was safe and warm and comfort was a constant companion.

"Man, you're a handful," Jack muttered, rubbing the back of his neck. He held out a hand to help her. And Sylvie looked up to find him looking no worse for wear. He was as soaked as her. His robes swallowed him in a way that made him seem more like a ratty street urchin than a trained practitioner.

The weather didn't do his image any favors.

Sylvie stared at the proffered appendage with hesitance. As if he would suddenly light a flame and burn her should she actually decide to grab it. Jack, realizing her reluctance, wiggled his fingers in impatience. A silent urge to take it, before he dropp-ed the niceties and left her gasping on the floor. A harsh retort danced along the tip of her tongue. Her pride and her shaky legs battled in her mind. Sylvie's legs emerged the victor. As she grabbed his hand in acquiesce.

Jack scoffed at her bull-headedness, but he didn't comment further. Instead, he whispered, "We've got company."

They turned to see Ethil Mane staring at them with wide eyes and an open mouth. Her emotions spilled over her face. Surprise. Confusion. Shock. Had she seen them almost get swept away by the waves? The Zexin Sea was frighteningly volatile today. Yet she stood in safety. A step behind the entrance's enchanted thres-hold where water bounced back, repelled by magic. It was enou-gh to make even the best of hearts resentful.

They were far from the best.

"If you're done gawking, then open the gate," Jack said, irate. "You do remember who we are, don't you?"

Ethil's eyes narrowed in suspicion. "The Drowned Tower is under lockdown. What are you doing outside?"

"You'd think they'd send someone with actual knowledge of the situation. But I suppose that was just too much to ask for. Those old codgers really need to step down and let the new generation lead."

"Jack," Sylvie warned. He was digressing. Again.

"I know." Jack waved her off with a dismissive flick of his wrist. He produced the letter from Master Celaris, waving them around without a care. The water ruined the parchment, but the official wax seal was unmistakable. "We were doing a job."

"Where are your original partners?" Ethil asked.

"Inside."

She looked skeptical. "So, why the special pairing? Did the Assembly really order such a thing?"

"Yes, they did," Jack said with trying patience. "As I said, we were off doing a job on Master Celaris' reque—order. Work. You are familiar with the word, aren't you?"

Ethil scowled. "That's unheard of."

Jack ran a hand through his hair in frustration. He dropped to a crouch, elbows on his knees and hands dangling between his legs. Jack lit a small fire. It was the only thing he could maintain in such wet weather. The flame provided little warmth, but it helped with the shivers. He didn't want to deal with this anymore. Why he so readily agreed to come back eluded him.

Answers, Jack's mind supplied. Forever helpful. But with Ethil guarding the entrance like a mule, answers were a far-off dream.

"That's it for me," Jack said, drained. "Your turn, Syl."

"And just what do you expect me to do about this?" Sylvie muttered. Her voice was low and not for his ears, yet he heard it all the same. Despite her breath of complaint, Sylvie turned to

Ethil with her hands raised in placation. "We mean you no harm. We *are* residents of the Tower after all. We just want to return. Is that so much to ask?"

"The Tower is under lockdown," Ethil said.

"But we need to see Master Cephas," Sylvie pleaded. "It's urgent."

"What's so urgent that you'd blatantly disregard an order from the Assembly?"

"A dead apprentice."

"What?" she asked numbly. Her jaw slackened when Sylvie repeated herself.

"So," Sylvie went on, "will you let us in now?"

Ethil hesitated. She took a deep breath, gathering her wits, before she shook her head at them in denial. "No exceptions."

"You're aggravating!" Jack yelled, glaring. His usual smirk was replaced by an irate grimace. But Ethil wasn't deterred.

"Said the pot."

"Where's that brother of yours?" Jack asked, peeking around her. "He looked sensible enough. It won't be as bad as talking to you at least. You straitlaced types are all the same. Every time you open your mouths, I end up with another person I want to torch to death."

Ethil's fists clenched. As she saw red. She ignored his direct jab and focused on the little her mind decided to grasp. "Don't talk as if you knew him! Duward was far stricter in his principles than even me!"

"Knew?"

Ethil clamped her mouth shut.

Jack gave her a cold stare. As if he were looking at something unworthy of his attention. His mind ran with dozens of scenarios that all had something to do with the sudden lockdown. Before Jack could digress any further, Sylvie spoke.

"Are you done?" she asked roughly. "I told you that we're on urgent business. Open the gate. Now."

Ethil's eyebrows shot up in an attempt to reach her hairline, caught completely flat-footed by the uncompromising tone of command. She expected that kind of belligerent tone from Jack, but not from the woman before her. From Jack's expression, it was clear that he hadn't either. His usual lopsided grin had an edge to it that betrayed his secretive gaze. Jack enjoyed every second of Sylvie's sudden uptightness. As if he knew what was about to happen. Ethil wouldn't put it past him. Jack saw much for one that cared so little.

Sylvie sighed, exasperated. With Ethil. With the gate. With the weather. With everything. Life in general. She just wanted to be left alone within the confines of the Drowned Tower. Was that so much to ask?

Apparently it was.

"I just told you," Ethil said, "no exceptions!"

"Oh?" Sylvie glared. "Perhaps I wasn't making myself clear. That wasn't a request. As Columbus Cephas' primary apprentice, I command you to open the gate, grant us entrance, and allow us an audience with my Master."

Ethil paused, doubtful. "I can't."

Jack clapped to catch her attention. He had a wild grin on his face that promised only mischief. "Don't tell me you're going to disobey a direct order from the Arch Poten's apprentice?"

"That title holds no value here. The Union dissolved long ago."

"Dissolved?" Jack scoffed. "More like renamed. Do you truly believe the Assembly has no head? Or that Columbus Cephas has just as much pull as the rest of the Masters in the Tower? If you do, you need to open your eyes. Like the rest of those witless fools that actually believe they're on equal footing. That they have some iota of control, of power. It's no more than what they held two centuries ago."

Ethil's face wavered in uncertainty. Her gaze swept over them, and she found herself unintentionally inching away from the threatening looks in their eyes.

"The gate," Sylvie interrupted. Low and serious. Enough to

snap Jack back to attention and send shivers down Ethil's spine. "I won't repeat myself a third time."

Ethil strengthened her resolve and met Sylvie's glare head on. Sylvie's eyes were bright and livid, but Ethil didn't relent. Changing her mind this late in the game was cowardly. Healer, she may be, but she wouldn't yield in the face of those she strived to stand beside.

"Neither will I," Ethil said.

Another wave suddenly crashed over them.

So abrupt that neither Jack, nor Sylvie had time to hold onto the gate. Jack's legs gave out and he was immediately pulled by the current, his side roughly colliding with the bridge's stone rail. Sylvie followed. Her back hitting him in a way that had him expelling whatever air he had left in his lungs. As a shot of pain ran up his torso, making him tremble at the burst of agony that washed over him. His side throbbed. His head prickled with the pain of a thousand needles piercing his skull.

But he could breathe.

Jack's eyes widened. He ignored the pain and tried to focus on his surroundings. He'd been shoved against the stone rail with Sylvie slumped against him, but a hazy bubble sheathed them from the rest of the wave. Hot liquid ran over one eye and he smelt the metallic scent of blood. A jolt of pain from his ribs had him reluctant to move, but he still willed his body to do so. Jack leaned forward, mindful of the black bubble around them. He grabbed Sylvie's unmoving form. The moment he touched her, his entire body shivered.

Jack heard singing. A tantalizingly familiar lullaby.

Where had he heard that again?

The Heartstone, he thought.

Jack immediately looked down. Sylvie was awake. Barely. He watched as she tried to fight a losing battle with sleep, before he loosened her collar. The stone was glowing. Dark and dim, but still somehow shining. The blackness was present once again, lingering inside.

The singing rang clearer now. Clearer than ever before. Jack was enraptured by the melody. It danced upon his skin, calling to him with the urgency of a thousand tortured men begging for death. Frightening and morbidly enticing all at once.

> *My child, come to me,*
> *I'll guide you, can't you see?*
> *I'll see you past the binds,*
> *Past the shores as black as night,*
>
> *My child, come to me,*
> *The dark is gone, can't you see?*
> *Open your eyes and I'll —*
> *Straighten you into line,*
>
> *My child, come to me,*
> *You're here now, can't you see?*
> *Light fades with time,*
> *But you shall live and never die,*
>
> *My child, come to me,*
> *Your eyes open, but do you see?*
> *Or do your cries never stop,*
> *Do your tears leave you blind?*
> *I've brought you past the shores,*
> *Where brightness is abhorred,*
> *To the light of day, where you will breathe,*
> *And I shall sing,*
>
> *My child, come to me,*
> *I'll comfort you, can't you see?*
> *In my arms, you'll be safe,*
> *Lie and rest as you wait,*
>
> *My child, go to sleep,*

My child, go to sleep,
I'll wake you when the end has begun.

Come, the voice of a woman coaxed, donning an undertone of raw malevolence. **You're mine.**

Jack reached, entranced by the seductive voice. His eyes were dazed, his mind was clouded, but he felt as though he'd finally found the answer to every problem he'd ever had.

Everything and anything he would ever want to know lay in that stone. All he had to do was grasp.

Without warning, Sylvie clasped her hand around the Heartstone, blocking it from his view. The singing stopped. The black tendrils around them faded into nothing. And Jack's head snapped up in fury at the sudden obtrusion. He was about to yell, but his voice died in his throat when he saw the state she was in.

Sylvie writhed in pain.

She gasped and struggled for breath. Her free hand clawed at her neck. Where Jack saw blackness creep up and strangle her.

It made her veins bulge. Out of instinct, Jack reached down to help her. His hand glowed a bright blue, and as soon as he touched her skin, the tendrils receded. Her erratic breaths evened out and she collapsed against him. Her eyelids were heavy, and though the rain continued its cold assault, it didn't make the urge to sleep any less powerful.

Jack saw his reflection mirrored in her eyes. He saw fear. It encompassed them both. What was happening?

"Are you alright?" Jack choked out. His voice had, for once, completely lost its taunting edge. He dribbled two fingers against her cheek, forcing her to attention.

Sylvie gasped in response. Her eyes were glassy with pain. She looked ready to cry.

"What just happened?" Jack wondered aloud, looking down at her closed fist where the Heartstone sat—away from his sight.

For reasons beyond reason, Jack could see it pulsing beneath her skin. It momentarily lit up her flesh, before dying down just as quickly.

Once. Twice. Three times.

It didn't stop.

Jack tapped her hand. He might not have known what was going on, but it definitely had something to do with the stone.

What else could it be? Jack thought.

"Don't you dare let go of this," he said. Jack waited for her to nod. "And don't show it to me or to anyone else for that matter. Can you stand?"

Sylvie coughed, but managed another nod.

She reached up and brushed away some of the blood still falling down his face. He cursed the useless rain for not washing everything away. He'd completely forgotten about the injury. But now that it was brought back to his attention, it throbbed with renewed vigor. Along with his side. Jack winced as he shifted. He'd shattered a rib. Perhaps two. He knew his body well enough to tell that much.

When Sylvie spoke, her voice was hoarse. "Can you?"

The grin Jack gave her then was razor sharp, daring her to ask that again. "Don't underestimate me."

They helped each other up, lurching to the side and almost toppling over more than once, until they managed to stand. Amidst the horrid weather, they stood like defiant children as they faced the Drowned Tower's spiked gate. Far more injured than either of them liked and in far more pain than they cared to admit.

And once again, Ethil stood there. Her mouth wide open. Had she seen the black bubble that surrounded them?

"How did you two survive that?" Ethil stuttered.

She hadn't.

That's what I'd like to know, Jack thought in relief.

"You should've drowned," Ethil said, shakily pointing at the rail where they'd been flung against. A long trail of blood was left in their place. Jack's blood. It was slowly washed away by the downpour. Diluting itself until it disappeared completely.

Jack grimaced at the sight.

His injury was far worse than he had initially thought. Jack didn't want to see it. He didn't want to dwell on it.

So, he turned back to Ethil. Despite their common paleness, she was a noticeable shade darker than Sylvie and himself. Her cheeks were redder. It made her look healthier—more alive. So, what did that say about them? With the rain still mercilessly beating down upon them, did they give the appearance of two people near death? Jack had seen death enough times to paint an accurate description of how he looked right now. Blue lips, trembling limbs, pasty skin, and bloody robes. Luck had apparently turned her back on him—already tired of his face—not that he cared. He didn't need a faceless woman like that anyway.

His body was becoming numb, his hands barely moved, and his legs were shaking. It was far too cold.

Jack looked down at Sylvie to see her in the same condition. Even simply breathing was a struggle. But he wasn't about to give up. He wasn't about to sit here and die quietly. He was going to change his world. He'd be damned if a few cracked bones and a concussion stopped him.

"Well..." Jack said, trying to ease back into his usual persona. It was ruined when he coughed a mouthful of blood. "Are you going to let us in? Or will you wait for us to die here?"

Ethil was stunned into silence, but the sight of Sylvie lighting a flame far brighter than anything Jack had conjured had her snapping back to attention. "It isn't that simple," Ethil denied again. "I don't know how to open this gate. Even if I could, I doubt I could do it on my own."

Jack cursed under his breath.

She couldn't have said that before?

Together, they looked up at the large chains holding the gate in place. It was far too big for any one person to move. Too big for even three.

"Get help," Sylvie said.

Ethil tentatively peered back inside. She heard a few shouts from below, but didn't dare mention it. "That isn't possible."

"Why not?"

"It doesn't matter," Jack dismissed. "Can you heal us?"

"What?" Ethil asked, flabbergasted.

Jack didn't care to repeat himself, and opted to continue staring at her. If she didn't believe that they just wanted to go back inside even after all of this, then he truly had nothing more to say. Ethil, unnerved by the weight of his gaze finally conceded.

"Yes," Ethil nodded. "I can heal you. Both of you."

"Get ready then," Jack said, tearing his gaze away. Finally content with her answer. "Stay there and watch. Don't you dare step past those enchantments. If you get swept away by the Zexin Sea, then you'll only have yourself to blame. I'm not going to dive in and help you."

Ethil's eyes widened. *What does he plan to do? Force his way inside?*

"Sylvie," Jack turned to her, his eyes on the fire in her hands. "How big can you make that?"

"Bigger." The light in her hand flickered before roaring to life. It doubled in size, the flames licking at his skin with heat that chased away his shivers and blurred their surroundings. It didn't come without a price. Jack could see the toll it had on her body, sapping what little energy she had left.

Impressive, Jack mentally complimented. During one of his more lengthy research sessions in the archives, he'd once read that Conjurers trained all of their lives to master their powers to a point beyond perfection. All of their focus put into one element to ensure that they had full control over it. While he didn't doubt what he'd read, it was still an extraordinary sight to behold.

Jack was snapped from his thoughts when Sylvie turned. She grinned slyly up at him. "You want me to melt part of the gate, don't you?"

Jack smirked. "Am I that transparent?"

"Your mouth says it all."

"Should I be flattered that you're paying such close attention to me?"

"Hardly."

"You're stubborn and like being inside the Institute. It's irritating," Jack told her. For the first time in his life, he was able to look up at the Drowned Tower's dark gates and not feel contempt at the sight of Pernelia's statue peering down at him. There was a charm to it. To coming home. Jack blamed his newly realized—and incredibly sappy—sentiments on being forced to spend what was possibly the longest day of his life with Sylvie. She had an unhealthy infatuation with this place.

"But I think I'm growing to like it. That desire might even work in our favor this time."

"Desire?" Sylvie questioned. "Me?" All her life she'd heard and rightfully believed that greed was detrimental. For Jack to say such a thing was disconcerting. Sylvie detested being tied to such a word. "What brought you to that conclusion?"

"What?" Jack lifted an eyebrow at her tone. "Isn't it obvious? Don't tell me you hate the word? Or worse, you've never heard of it? No, of course you have. Then... then what? Never heard desire and your name in the same sentence before?" He peered down at her, willing her to speak. But from the way she tilted her head in childlike perplexion, he already knew the answer. "That explains why you're so unnervingly content. Did your parents never buy you anything as a child? It's strange not to want things. Or do you not know that as well?"

"It's always insults with you." Sylvie shook her head. "If we're forced to be with each other, the least you could do is stop for an hour or two. I don't care how cleverly disguised they are, I don't like hearing them."

"Get used to it," Jack said. He paused for a moment, before repeating the words he'd told her back in Thyme. "Don't you want anything in life? Grasp for something."

"Of course I want things," she admitted with a frown. "Just not the exaggerated, life-changing sort you constantly think of."

"You're boring."

"Disappointed?"

Jack shrugged. "Not particularly."

He flexed his fingers and summoned a gust of wind, fueling the flame in her hand. It was so sudden and, for a brief instant, the spark was so intense that she lost control of her powers. Her magic fluctuated. Sylvie felt her Demar spell dissipate. She was sure Master Cephas was alerted of the lost connection.

"My Demar spell," Sylvie muttered, unsettled. "It's gone."

"Absolutely liberating, isn't it?" Jack smiled roguishly. "I dispelled mine some time ago."

Sylvie looked down, trying to peek at his ankles. But the marks were still present on his skin. Paler than they should've been, but she blamed her impaired sight on the cold.

"What are you talking about? They're still there."

His smile widened. And she got a glimpse of the secret behind his grin. It was cold. Cold and angry and sad. But then it disappeared behind a flurry of unmasked conceit.

"Don't stray too far, Sylvie."

The wind picked up. And she knew it was Jack's doing.

Despite the pouring rain, the fire in her hand burned largely. Intensely. As they rushed to hold it against the iron gate, praying to whoever was listening that it wasn't enchanted to ward off a Conjurer's flames. Sylvie grinned in delight when connected with the iron bars, brightening along with her mood. Not even the weather could dampen her spirit.

In that moment, with her magic enhanced by Jack's own, she'd never felt more alive.

14

Tiv was bored.

Despite his boredom and despite the admittedly deplorable things he was known for around the Tower, Tiv was never one to leave his position unattended. Not for too long at least. And never without a gullible stand-in to take his place. Tiv would gladly admit that he was, more often than not, indulgent to a fault. He was reckless and brash when it came to orders, always jumping ahead and looking back too late.

But he wasn't negligent. Dereliction of duty was where he drew the line. Tiv always got the job done. His methods may not have always been according to protocol, but from scouting to eradication, he finished it to the best of his abilities.

Guard duty, however, was a different matter entirely. A constant rotation of keeping his eyes peeled was the sort of trite task he'd usually hand off to an unsuspecting bystander. So, when Tiv realized that Master Celaris had decided that instead of securing the halls, he was to watch over his fellow primary apprentices and make sure they did their jobs—Tiv almost jumped for joy. Almost. Had he been alone, he would have.

But people were watching, and he wasn't about to shed his dignity before them. The job was only a cover, Tiv knew. Master Celaris wanted him to run around and eavesdrop under the guise of checking up on his fellow practitioners. But he enjoyed it all the same.

As Tiv traversed through the Tower's halls, going out of his way to shock those he knew were prone to slacking off, he heard shouting. It came from above. And by the time he'd followed it to the upper floor of the research tower, the sight that awaited him had his blood boiling.

At the base of the stairs that led to the Drowned Tower's entrance, stood three practitioners. Fledglings who'd just passed the partner evaluation exam. Tiv knew, simply because he'd never seen them patrol the east's borders, and had there been one or two primary apprentices among them, then Tiv would've singled them out. Contrary to popular belief, he did pay attention to the minute details. Though he usually left such tasks to Jack. Tiv remembered faces and names as easily as the scars littered across his body. What these new recruits were doing guarding such a crucial area, however, eluded him.

Their nervous faces did nothing to quell his rising confusion. *Stupid, stupid, stupid Assembly.* Tiv thought in disdain. *Leaving them here without a Master or even a primary apprentice... it's like they're begging for crisis!*

"Why are you three just standing there?" Tiv asked, raising his eyebrows. As they turned to him with a start. Tiv narrowed his eyes in suspicion when they shared a nervous glance, before collectively taking a step back. "And why are there only three of you? Everyone is required to be with their partner."

The man with a protruding jaw and the female grimoire holder stared anxiously up at him. Tiv stared back, committing their features to memory. If something were to happen here, then at least he'd know who to blame. Their names were irrelevant. Tiv didn't bother with their kind. Obnoxious newbies. They were a loud and overconfident bunch. The weak ones always were.

Being a primary apprentice usually assured Tiv the company of those like him. Or those with renowned relatives. Rarely, did Tiv bother with anyone outside of his circle. He wasn't going to start now.

"Don't scare us like that," Protruding Jaw said. He sported an impressive bruise on his left cheek that had yet to fully blossom. He'd obviously been slapped around recently. Perhaps that was why he was so skittish. "C'mon, we're all practitioners here. Loosen up."

Tiv's eyes narrowed in fury. Protruding Jaw's ease rivalled Jack's. Though it was far less biting and far less suspicious. He had the nervous jitters only novices held. *Did he think I was from the Assembly? But why would he be scared of a Master? Unless...*

"Were you slacking off?" Tiv crossed his arms, watching them tense. "For your sake, I hope you weren't. If so, then silently make your peace with Thelarius now. From here on out, I'll be making your every waking moment a very personal kind of hell."

"What?" Protruding Jaw sputtered in disbelief. "What do you mean personal hell? Wait, no. I mean—you can't just decide something like this!"

"Watch me."

"Have a heart," he pleaded when he saw the serious look in Tiv's eyes. "I swear we weren't slacking off!"

"What were you doing then?"

"Quiet down, Wyatt," Grimoire Holder barked. Her upper lip curled in a sneer. "Why should we tell you anything when you're obviously disobeying the rules? Where's your partner?"

Tiv flashed her a derisive smile. His glare rivalled a snarling beast's in both ferocity and anger. "He's out."

"You're mad if you think we're going to answer to some nameless practitioner wandering around without a partner."

Tiv sighed in contempt. "This is why I despise new recruits."

"What did you say?" Her fists clenched. Mole Man finally stepped up, catching Grimoire Holder before she could make a swipe for Tiv. An action she'd sorely regret. "Let me go, Levin!"

"Stop it, Dallia!" Levin tightened his hold. "That's Master Celaris' primary apprentice, Tiv Grovegg. His partner is the Elementalist, Jacques Dace."

Tiv sneered. The power of titles were amazing. But throw around a few famous names? Suddenly it was legendary.

Dallia's eyes widened and she took an immediate step back. She shuffled her feet in embarrassment, ducking, as sudden shame washed over her. It colored her cheeks and ears. Dallia muttered a soft apology that Tiv barely caught. But the loudness of it didn't matter—it was quickly dismissed. Tiv neither sought, not wanted her words of remorse. The walls could have them.

A door banged shut.

Their heads snapped toward the stairs. Rushed footsteps were headed their way. Followed by unintelligible echoes from different voices. If Tiv listened closely, he could even hear the sound of exhausted pants and the squelching rustle of wet clothes.

Someone's there, Tiv narrowed his eyes, trying to peer into the darkness. *Two, maybe three? What were they doing topside? Are they friends or…?*

"Liam!" Dallia called.

Friends, Tiv concluded, holding up a hand to stop Dallia, before she could rush up. "How many are up there? Why were they outside?"

"One." Wyatt let out a shaky breath. "There was only one."

Silence.

Tiv stepped up, calling the magic resting under his fingertips. His hands were a cold blue. As he prepared to jump up and shift. Before he could, his eyes caught sight of something headed toward him at an alarmingly fast rate. It was too dark to see. But he knew better than to stand around and let it hit him. Tiv sidestepped just in time, sparing the projectile a glance. Only for his eyes to widen at the sight of familiar robes.

It was a practitioner.

"Liam!" Dallia yelled in despair. She shook his shoulders. So distraught that she hadn't thought to check his pulse or even use her magic.

"He's not dead," Tiv assessed. He could tell just by looking at him. His hearing was attuned to listen for the slightest of sounds, the smallest of gasps. Tiv heard him breathe. Slow and shaky. This was why he didn't bother with new recruits. They were too emotional. Trapped in this tower of comfort, they didn't know any better. Most greenhorns died before they could learn.

Who evaluated them? Tiv wondered. *They aren't ready.*

"Looks like I missed," said a familiar voice. They turned to see three figures step from the darkness. Two were sopping wet and visibly exhausted. As the other stood off to the side with an open book in her hands, muttering healing incantations. "You were just standing around with a glare on your face and those brats behind you like some sort of custodian. It was irritating. Are you really my partner? Defense doesn't suit you."

Tiv could recognize that voice anywhere.

"Jack!" Tiv appeared annoyed, but the upward tilt of his lips gave him away. "What are you doing here? You should've stayed in Thyme. We've got big problems going on right now."

Jack shrugged, squeezing the water from his robes. He reeked of blood and the sea, but his injuries were nothing more than dull aches now. Jack wasn't fond of Healers, though even he couldn't deny their usefulness. Especially skilled ones.

"It was raining," Jack said coolly. "We needed shelter."

Tiv lifted his eyebrows in disbelief.

"What did you do to Liam?" Dallia demanded. Wyatt held her by the arms. As she snarled furiously at Jack, who simply disregarded her anger. Before he could respond, her eyes drifted toward Ethil. "You!" Dallia screeched. To Ethil's credit, she didn't even acknowledge her. Only continued to mutter her healing spells. "What were you doing darting up there like an escaped convict? If you'd told us there were practitioners, then we would've helped. Now, look! Liam's hurt!"

Ethil didn't try to defend herself. She'd left her quarters without permission and even assaulted her fellow practitioners. They had every right to be angry at her. But astoundingly, Jack came to her aid. His words and tone were harsh and needlessly blunt. As always.

"Ethil Mane outranks you in experience and importance," Jack said, dismissing her with a flick of his wrist. "She doesn't need to explain her actions. She ran to help us upon our request. Leave it at that."

Their eyes widened. Even Sylvie snapped her head back, her mouth dropping in comical disbelief. Jack met her gaze. *I can be nice,* his eyes told her. Even if his retort was anything but.

Levin shook his head, trying to take his seniors' attitudes in stride. An increasingly difficult task. He'd heard of Jack and Tiv. Their hostile natures and aggressiveness on the field were famous around the Drowned Tower. But hearing about it and seeing it first-hand were two entirely different things. To meet two of the most problematic practitioners with obvious superiority issues was just their luck. Each time they opened their mouths Levin had the urge to yell back. An impulse he didn't dare act on. Instead, he wrestled with his expression until a pliant smile graced his lips.

"We rookies really have it rough," Levin commented.

"Oh, don't you worry." Tiv grinned, showing off sharp teeth. "We don't fraternize with novices often."

"I suppose I should be glad for this chance then?"

"Glad? You should consider it an honor."

Their smiles were tight. The tension in the air was so thick, it was a wonder Tiv didn't explode. As he was known to. Tiv was obviously in an agreeable disposition. For the moment at least. No one knew how long his good mood would last.

"Please stop talking," Sylvie muttered, rubbing her temples in agitation. Her throat was still sore and her thoughts continued to race—aftereffects of being strangled. The feeling of her life being sucked away from her lingered in the back of her mind. "I didn't go through all the trouble of melting that ridiculous gate to stand around playing *'who–can–irritate–who–more.'* Take me to Master Cephas." Sylvie glanced around, then as an afterthought added, "Where's Reed?"

"Cephas first," Jack rebutted. "You can worry about your partner later."

"You say that because yours is here," Sylvie said, angry.

"Wait!" Tiv stopped them, before they could get into a petty argument. "Please tell me I didn't hear that correctly. Did you say you… melted the gate?"

Jack grinned. Proud and completely unrepentant. "Sorry."

"You are *not* sorry," Tiv boldly called him out on his lie. In a way that only he could. Had it been anyone else, Jack would've dismissed them entirely.

"We didn't melt it completely," Jack explained. "It was just a small hole. Small enough to crawl through."

"That's not the point!"

"Then what is?"

"You melted the gate!"

"Sylvie melted it." Jack looked away, carelessly shrugging bony shoulders in an attempt to appear nonchalant. He didn't fool anyone. "Her flames melted those bars. Not mine."

Sylvie gasped in shock. "Don't you dare pin this on me! You fueled that fire. You're just as responsible."

"Really?" Jack turned to hide his growing grin. "I don't recall doing such a thing."

"Have you two gone completely insane?" Tiv interjected. His face was red, his shoulders tense with fury. "How could you do something so stupid?"

They shrugged.

Tiv turned to the three novice practitioners. "You three," he barked, "go outside and protect the damned gate!"

"What do you expect us to do?" Wyatt asked, stumped.

"Make a blockade?" Tiv suggested, his arms crossed in expectance. "You're supposed to be the best, aren't you? Don't tell me only seniors know how to get anything done around here."

They shared a glance.

"Go! Now!" Tiv huffed in exasperation. "And for Thelarius' sake, one of you call a Master or a primary apprentice or anyone else to accompany you. That sorry foursome you call a group is distressing."

They scrambled, taking a moment to split up jobs before darting off. Jack clapped twice, both impressed and amused by the situation.

"Now that the baggage is out of the way," Jack's voice dropped, his eyes took on a more serious turn, "what's the situation, Tiv?"

Tiv scowled, as he looked over their exhausted faces. "You shouldn't have returned. Master Celaris and I have reason to believe Elder Serach is after you."

Their eyes widened.

"Elder Serach?" Ethil muttered, her voice barely above a whisper. But the silence that descended around them made even dropping feathers ring clear. "Do you think he was also responsible for… Duward?"

"What happened to Duward?" Sylvie asked.

"He's dead," Tiv said as calmly as possible. Their eyes naturally drifted to Ethil, who confirmed his words with a solemn nod. "Though I doubt it was Serach's doing. Not directly at least. Duward drowned. From what Master Celaris told me, the water was conjured. The murderer was likely Serach's apprentice. The Assembly held a meeting regarding the matter. But talking did little more than divide them. Half demand we evacuate, the rest want to stay and protect what's ours."

"Who else knows of this?" Sylvie asked, looking up at the steps where Levin and Dallia had disappeared.

"The Assembly and about half of the primary apprentices." Tiv followed her gaze, worry creasing his brow. "Though I'm not sure who ordered those novices away from their rooms. Only primary apprentices and a few select practitioners should be out. Yet I've seen the inexperienced walking alongside them. Their mettle hasn't been tested. And there are far too many for my liking."

Others are walking about? Sylvie thought. As she looked around. *It's quiet. Far too quiet.* They were the only practitioners in sight. The familiar darkness of the Tower soothed her. Sylvie was used to this floor being empty, but this situation wasn't the kind where they could afford to be lax with security. The lack of guards near the Tower's entrance was disarming in its own right.

Where is everybody?

"It could be those that want to evacuate," Jack said, snapping her from her thoughts. "The Masters that want to leave may be ordering them to walk around as assurance. I doubt many of the older practitioners, if any at all, would side with them. They—no, we risk our lives to protect these borders. It wouldn't make sense to abandon it now."

Tiv nodded in affirmation. "Master Celaris thought so, too."

"Does he have any leads?" Jack asked. "Whoever's doing this obviously has some pull amongst the younger apprentices."

"Zelpha Miriam." Tiv grunted, unsure. "Master Celaris is convinced that she's planning some kind of mutiny. She wants to get the practitioners far away from here."

Jack nodded. "We'll begin with her."

"I'd like to find Reed first," Sylvie said. "Then I'll speak to Master Cephas about what we found in Tearwood. You three go after Master Miriam."

"Reed isn't a priority," Jack denied. "If you need a Healer, take Ethil. Walking alone is only going to arouse suspicion. If you see someone from the Assembly, keep your head low. They don't know we're inside. Well, most of them anyway. That old bag, Cephas, should be easy enough to find. You accidentally dispeled your Demar spell after all and right outside the Tower, too. I'm sure he's searching for you. You're his primary apprentice. He'd be a fool not to."

Ethil and Sylvie shared a glance.

Sylvie pursed her lips in irritation at the order, but she conceded nevertheless. "Fine."

Ethil looked up the stairs. They decided on a plan of action so quickly. As if they'd expected such a dire situation. She knew that if Duward were around, he would've easily joined them. But he wasn't around. And Ethil couldn't help but feel that they were moving too quickly. Sylvie and Jack had just returned from an order they claimed to have accomplished. They knew even less than her about the situation—and she knew next to nothing. It was hard to put her faith into people that jumped before they looked. She'd never worked with them before. She didn't think she'd ever have to. But now, Ethil regretted not taking the chance to work closer with the other practitioners of her grade.

"What about those three?" Ethil asked, gesturing up the long staircase. "They know you two are here. One even went to find another primary apprentice. He might even bring back someone from the Assembly."

Jack scoffed. "I doubt a primary apprentice would actually follow him. He'll be looking for a long time. And the Assembly has more important things to do than listen to a skittish novice's ramblings. As for the two on guard, no one will find them so long as they remain up there. They're all too afraid to disobey the Assembly."

"And if they decide to come back inside?" Ethil asked.

"They'll be blamed for making a hole." Jack grinned in triumph. Sylvie shot him a scathing glance, but otherwise kept her silence. Neither of them were looking forward to explaining that.

"We should see Master Celaris first," Tiv said, stretching to prepare himself for the undoubtedly long night ahead of them. "Miriam can wait. Master Celaris is terrifying when he's upset. You're not the one that suffers if we act behind his back."

Jack rolled his eyes at his partner's dramatics, but was quick to comply. "It's decided then," Jack said, walking ahead. He wasn't the type to work with others except Tiv, but he'd have to make an exception. Just this once. He could trust Sylvie well enough. And Ethil had already proved her skills as a Healer.

So, he'd cooperate. For now.

"Jack." Sylvie grabbed his arm before he could walk off. "We need to talk."

Jack spared her a glance, ignoring the look Tiv gave him when he followed her a short distance away. Sylvie worriedly massaged her neck, as if she could still feel the tendrils crawling over her.

"Does it hurt?" he asked.

Her hand ceased. "No."

Jack hummed. Not sure if he could trust that denial. She said it a bit too fast for his liking. "Are you going to tell that old bag about the Heartstone?"

Sylvie looked down, weighing her options. What would Master Cephas do if she told him about the stone? Would he take it away from her? Was it that important? Would he have her locked up for taking it? No, none of that mattered. She didn't care if it was important or if she'd be questioned about where she'd found it. She was curious. More so than she'd ever been before. She felt a clawing need to know more about something so obviously special. If she told Master Cephas then he'd definitely take it from her and never mention it again. That would be unfair.

It fell into her hands.

Surely, that must've counted for something. Nothing in this world happened without just cause and proper reason. Miracles and coincidences were for the ignorant. And Sylvie held onto that belief. It's what she told herself to justify keeping it. For a day, a minute, even a second longer. She'd hold onto the Heartstone. Because there was something undoubtedly interesting at the end of this road.

When was it? Sylvie wondered. *When did I become so greedy?*

Knowledge was a dangerous thing. The desire for it, even more so. But Sylvie didn't care. No. She no longer cared.

"No," Sylvie finally said. It was quickly becoming her favorite answer. "I won't tell him."

It'll be our secret, Sylvie thought, *our very dangerous secret.*

Jack grinned in satisfied delight. He looked at her neck, where the stone sat beneath her robes. Jack couldn't see it, but he could see its pulse. It lit up her skin. A noticeable glow that he was sure was only visible to Sylvie and himself, seeing as how none had yet to comment on the strange light. If Jack listened close enough, he might have been able to hear that gentle lullaby again. But he wasn't foolish enough to try. He didn't want to tempt fate any more than he already had today.

Not unless it was absolutely necessary.

Jack walked back to Tiv's side, turning only to shoot Sylvie a confident grin. "It's time we clean the Assembly's mess."

"I'm surprised you actually want to help," Sylvie remarked.

"Of course I do." Jack's grin widened. "This is going to be my ticket to the Diamond Alps."

Sylvie returned his smile and followed after him.

Jack laughed with exhausted relief at her expression. He finally felt back in his element. As he walked down the familiar halls. The day might not have turned out as he'd expected, but he recalled his thoughts at the hostel in Thyme and reveled in the fact that he at least saw progress in one promise to himself—he swore he'd change her mind about the world. A few more pushes, and he'd wear her down eventually. It wouldn't be too hard. Rather, he was confident in his ability to persuade her.

Because at long last, luck had finally returned to his side.

15

Their walk was a quiet one.

Sylvie and Ethil had little in common. Even less to speak about. They'd just split with Jack and Tiv—the loud ones of their hastily formed entourage. The reunited duo announced their intent to scour the research tower for Master Celaris, before taking off without another look back. Leaving Sylvie with a rigid Ethil, whose face was pulled into a permanent frown that creased her brows and darkened her eyes. Something was clearly bothering her. Sylvie could make an assumption as to what that was, and she was fairly certain that she'd be right. At this point, anyone could figure out the source of Ethil's troubles. It wasn't hard.

But Sylvie didn't want to think about such horrid things happening within the confines of her home. Even though Ethil's thoughts had her unintentionally lagging behind, Sylvie didn't have the heart to question her about them.

So, the silence continued.

Their pace was slow, almost lethargic. It made the silence stretch on for longer than necessary. Practitioners ducked as they passed. Others whispered greetings. But none voiced their wonder about why she wasn't with her usual partner. They didn't seem to know that she'd been outside a mere half hour ago either.

Sylvie quickly decided that those with backbone were either off doing more important tasks or left patrolling the borders. With no knowledge of what was going on in the Drowned Tower.

No one stopped them, no one spoke to them, and no one stood in their way. They refused to question what business the primary apprentice of Columbus Cephas had in the residential tower. It was almost laughable how not a soul amongst them were ballsy enough to stop their gait. As soon as they saw Sylvie, they hesitated. Compelled into biting their own tongues by some unknown force. Even Ethil was taken by it. Ethil followed obediently behind with her, mouth clamped shut and eyes glazed over. Entranced. Stuck in yesterday. Ethil stared straight ahead, yet she saw nothing. She didn't even bother questioning why Sylvie led them to the residential tower.

It was to find Reed.

Contrary to Sylvie's agreement with Jack, she didn't think it necessary to speak to Master Cephas. Not yet. That could come later. She wanted to find Reed. So, that's what she did. It was second nature for her to seek him out after a long day. They'd been partners for years and would continue to be so. And when Sylvie saw Jack reunite with Tiv, the urge to find Reed only grew.

Spending an entire day with Jack was something she didn't think she'd ever live through. She almost hadn't. Sylvie smiled wistfully at the thought.

Jack.

A haughty, hot-blooded, insufferable hell-raiser by nature. Give him an inch, and he'd burn the clothes off your back as well. A complete contrast to Reed, who'd always been overly protective, very kind, and just a little too shy. Even their powers paralleled. Sylvie never had the patience to deal with someone like Jack, whose personality practically bordered on fanaticism.

But Jack is passionate, Sylvie's mind defended, speaking out without her consent. *A bit too selfish, yes. But he's the naturally zealous sort. That kind of drive can't be faked.*

Sylvie shook her head to rid herself of those thoughts.

Silas help me. Sylvie rubbed her temples. *Something must be desperately wrong with me if I'm allowing Jack of all people to invade my thoughts.* She looked down. Only to find the Heartstone erratically pulsing through her robes, as if warning her of upcoming dangers. She scoffed, recalling her close encounter with asphyxiation along the Drowned Tower's bridge. *If anything, this stone is far more dangerous than anything I might encounter here.*

"It's quiet," Ethil suddenly said, snapping Sylvie from her reverie. She was right. Sylvie stopped, allowing Ethil to catch up with her. As she surveyed their surroundings. They'd made it to the residential tower, but security had thinned out.

The lower they ventured, the less people there seemed to be. *Are they in their rooms?* Sylvie wondered.

She chanced opening one of the chambers, wincing as the door creaked loudly. Sylvie peered inside. But only silence and darkness greeted her. The chamber was a mess. Random objects littered the floor and a few partitions had been knocked down in haste. From the corner of her eye, she saw something sink into the shadows. But when she squinted, it was gone.

What happened? Where is everyone?

"Perhaps they were fit into the chambers along the upper floors," Ethil said. As if reading her thoughts.

"No," Sylvie immediately denied. Ethil tilted her head in a silent gesture for her to elaborate. *The Drowned Tower's walls are absurdly thin. If there were more practitioners cramped inside the upper chambers then we would've heard. They're always complaining about something. Talking doesn't just cease, especially not gossip.*

But Sylvie didn't dare voice those thoughts.

Ethil was already on edge. She didn't want to needlessly worry her. Not when she could've been wrong. Perhaps the missing practitioners really were brought to the upper chambers. Perhaps they were just excessively quiet. The Institute was, after all, in a state of lockdown. Or perhaps she'd just drowned out their voices with her overly active thoughts.

It didn't matter.

Sylvie wasn't going to head back to the upper floors to check. Her only option was to head deeper. To the chamber that housed her room.

And Reed's, Sylvie thought.

Ethil caught her sleeve, before she could carry on. "I don't think we have enough practitioners capable of guarding such large chambers. Not unless they were in larger groups. Do you think that's why Master Miriam ordered the fresh blood out?"

"No," Sylvie echoed. "If Master Miriam called them simply for more manpower, then what would be the point of squeezing them all into the upper rooms? I'm sure all those extra hands would be able to guard them well enough in their respective chambers." Sylvie shrugged off her hand, straightening her robes with a frown. "Let's keep going."

"Wait!" Ethil protested. "Shouldn't we return? You're looking for your partner, aren't you? The Healer? The past two floors have been completely empty. I'm sure the lower ones are just the same."

So, she did know, Sylvie thought.

She shook her head.

"You're free to stay," Sylvie said. Reed may have left, but she knew him well enough to know that he wouldn't do so without first leaving her a note telling her of the current situation. Or, at the very least, a clue as to where he was headed. Reed was a terrible worrywart.

And I doubt Myrrh just quietly ran off to some cramped chamber, Sylvie thought, smiling to herself. *Surely, she's scurrying about somewhere. Ready to surprise me.* Sylvie walked ahead, sparing Ethil a glance as she passed.

"Are you coming?"

Ethil hesitated for a moment before quickly running after her with eyes narrowed in doubt. "I'm not going to let you walk around alone. It's suspicious. And I'm still not convinced I can trust you. You said a practitioner died. But you haven't given me even the slightest hint of who did it or who that practitioner was."

"Do you suspect me?" Sylvie stopped. "I didn't do it."

"Then who did?"

Sylvie eyed her sidelong. Ethil stared at her with eyes filled with a mixture of determination and curiosity. Blue, wide, and piercing. As if to further emphasize how interested she was. If

Ethil was concerned because she thought the killer may have had something to do with Duward, Sylvie couldn't say. She couldn't read Ethil well enough. Not yet. But Sylvie didn't rule out the possibility of Ethil seeking revenge or of Hunter involvement in this entire incident.

Perhaps a Hunter really did kill Duward. From what she'd seen, they didn't need much reason. Or provocation.

I best keep the Hunter's presence secret, Sylvie decided. The less people who knew, the better. She doubted Jack would open his mouth. He wanted to personally deal with the Amorph Hunter himself. And Sylvie had to speak with Master Cephas before revealing what could very well be eastern branch secrets.

Without answering, Sylvie turned and continued the trek back to her quarters. Ethil followed. Their footsteps were soft taps stored by the walls. There was nothing more to say. Neither had any answers to give. So, they were once more enveloped by the cold embrace of silence.

It was deafening.

***

Jack and Tiv sprinted down the halls, rounding corners and narrowly dodging startled practitioners. As they shouted curses for them to move. They donned contagious smiles, barreling onward all the while. Their actions were as much for fun as they were necessary. Jack would openly admit that they could've finished their job without the excess noise, but this was far better than keeping his head down and avoiding the Assembly. He'd instead opted to reestablish his initial status of troublemaker, assuming their failing eyes could even keep up with their pace.

They can reprimand me after I save their sorry hides. Jack smirked at the thought. *Or while they send me off to the Diamond Alps.*

You can't escape what you don't want to.

Jack skidded to a halt.

What in th—who said that? Jack whipped around, cautiously observing his surroundings in search of the owner of that haunting voice. Jack easily recognized that siren tone. He was almost pulled in by it once after all. He didn't plan to be lulled into another trance. Never again.

But Sylvie wasn't nearby, likewise the stone wasn't as well. And Jack refused to believe he was hearing things.

I can't be hearing voices. That's impossible and creepy. Very, very creepy. Jack peered above, below, and side to side. But as expected, he found no one.

"Hurry up!" Tiv called, already a good ten meters away.

Jack shook his head. He was exhausted. He'd had a long day. Perhaps this was his body's way of telling him to rest. Jack didn't listen. And in retaliation, he quickly crossed the long stretch of hall that separated him from Tiv, further pushing his already spent limbs.

Jack tried his best to focus on the task at hand. He had more important things to do than worry over cursed pendants and his failing body.

"What's wrong?" Tiv asked when Jack finally reached him. "You look pale."

"I'm naturally pale," Jack deadpanned.

"You know what I meant."

"It's nothing," Jack dismissed, brushing off his concern with a nonchalant tilt of his head. "Let's keep going."

Tiv eyed him in unmasked skepticism. His expression showed he didn't believe a word Jack said. And Jack's avoidance of the issue only made his problems more apparent.

"You've been acting strange ever since you returned. Secretly talking to Sylvie, not even being surprised about everything that's happened so far. Just what happened out there? What did you see? Was it so horrid that you'd come running back to the very place you've always wanted to escape?"

"If you have something to say," Jack said harshly, "then say it."

Tiv met Jack's glare head on, undeterred by his tone. "What are you doing here, Jack?"

There were many answers to that.

Because there's a mentally unstable Hunter with an army of fire-spitting Peose in Tearwood, just sitting on his haunches and waiting for a reason to unleash those animals. There's also a dead apprentice rotting just past the shores of Eriam. Did I mention that Sylvie has a cursed stone that first saves our lives and then tries to kill her? Oh, and I'm dreadfully tired. All I want to do right now is sleep. But, of course, I can't do that. There's always something wrong with the world.

Jack could've vented his problems. He could've ranted like a child. Jack wasn't a child though, and he wasn't one to complain about a past he could no longer change. Wasting time talking instead of actually doing something was pointless.

So, Jack kept his silence. But silence was another kind of answer. One that Tiv interpreted in his own way.

"Are you with them?" Tiv asked, clenching his fists. "Are you aiding the ones responsible for this..." he gestured around them with a grand sweep of his hand, "this mess?"

Jack stiffened. He silently reminded himself to retain his composure. "I'm *no* traitor."

Tiv grinned, visibly relaxing at his denial.

Jack doesn't lie, he thought. Jack hated lies. A trait born from his time in the Diamond Alps. Where everyone wore masks of half-truths. In the north, to be without a façade was to be faceless. Unknown. Anonymous. A doormat for the higher participants that spoke fluently in the complicated language of clever riddles and sarcastic wordplay.

Jack was different.

He strove—even prided himself on—never telling lies. Those he did utter were always done so jokingly.

When they'd first met, that trait had gotten them into trouble. But it was also why Tiv respected him so. Jack was a special brand of jerk. With his own moral compass. He was up front about his opinions. Jack didn't speak ill of others behind their backs, he did it right to their faces. Smirking all the while. To go through life without uttering a single lie was an incredibly daunting principle. As well as extremely stupid. But it was the sort of foolish notion that sat well with Tiv.

"I believe you."

"As you should." Jack shrugged him off. Along with the overly sappy atmosphere that settled around them. An invisible blanket of rainbows and trust and sunshine. It made him want to vomit. "I don't lie."

"I know."

With renewed vigor, they threw open doors until they'd successfully checked every archive in the research tower. There was no sign of Master Celaris. The practitioners they asked were either just as clueless or stuttered incoherently. Some were both. So, now they were torn between which keep to inspect next. They shffled their feet, standing in the middle of a triangular intersection.

Left would lead them to the residential tower, right to the Assembly's tower. Separating was out of the question.

"Great." Tiv crossed his arms. "Now what?"

"You're his apprentice," Jack said, exasperated. "Think, Tiv. Or is that head of yours just for show? The cub should know his mother's den."

"This entire tower is a den!"

You want answers. I can give you what you seek.

Jack jumped back in shock, making Tiv cock his head at him in bewilderment. Tiv voiced a concern Jack's ears didn't deem important enough to register. As he narrowed his eyes at the convenience of it all. Jack could no longer ignore that voice. Not when it so blatantly whispered in his ears. What was it? Why was it speaking to him? Was it even real or had he actually become delusional? He'd certainly done enough horrible things to warrant having a few screws loose—assuming they weren't already. Jack wasn't a good person. Nor did he claim to be. His slumber was plagued by nightmares of death and violence. Tainted red with blood. Like most border patrollers.

But this wasn't a dream. His eyes were open. He was awake. And he was living a nightmare of the highest grade. Where snippets and blurs were nonexistent. And the world around him was the sort of physical perfection only reality could pull. A top tier hallucination. The demon in his head, however, had yet to show itself.

Tell me what you desire, the voice said, *and it shall be yours.*

That voice was the same one from Sylvie's Heartstone. Jack was sure of it. But the Heartstone sat safely around her neck. Buried under layers of robes. Far away from him, and other prying eyes. He'd only ever heard that voice while the stone was in sight, so why now? What changed?

That song! Jack's eyes widened. On the bridge, he'd actually heard it—he'd registered the words—it was no longer an incomprehensible tune. No longer a drowned out melody.

It was a call.

And, here it was, calling him again.

Come to me, the voice beckoned.

Jack's eyes burned. He clutched his face and groaned in pain.

"What's wrong?" Tiv asked, appearing by his side in an instant. Jack tried to respond, but the words died in his throat. They were replaced by a scream that had Tiv dropping down to his haunches and shaking Jack in worry. Jack fell to his knees, doubling over at the sensation of heat erupting from his sockets. His eyes didn't melt. But they might as well have.

He gnashed his teeth together and muffled a scream. Hot tears trailed down his cheeks. They clouded his vision and only made his pain worse.

Jack's blood boiled. It was too hot.

He heard voices. Men, women, children. They echoed in his mind, bouncing around as if they belonged there. He heard the clank of chains and burning fire. Children's screams thrown into the mix like muffled background noise. They cried out to him. Their voices were pitiful whines. But what could he do? What did they want from him? Why were they subjecting him to this kind of torture? Was he responsible for their misfortune?

Certainly not.

Stop it! Jack dug his palms into his eyes, sorely wishing that he was a Healer. *Go away! Leave me alone. I can't help you!*

This was his body. His. They had no right to play in his head. They could cripple him from pain, but he wouldn't allow them to invade his mind. His thoughts were his own. They were his to control. Jack wouldn't yield. He'd sooner die than relinquish the reins that governed him.

"Enough!" Jack bit out, clawing at his throat. His magic burst forth out of instinct. His hands radiated a pale blue, before he conjured fire. The blaze encircled his form, spreading warmth over worn limbs and encasing him in a ball of scorching heat that distorted the air.

Tiv stepped back in alarm, his black eyes were filled with confusion. He'd almost been burned. "Jack! What's going on?"

"I said, enough!"

And as if listening to him, the pain ceased.

Jack clutched his head for a moment longer. He kept his eyes squeezed shut. As the sparks of his magic died down. His head pounded with a vengeance that matched the erratic beat of his heart.

For fuck's sake, was Jack's first thought, *what just happened?*

Jack stood slowly. His eyes were still sealed shut, and his mouth was clenched in frustrated silence. The tears left wet trails down his cheeks. They stung. But he made no move to wipe them.

Tiv squirmed a distance away, unsure. He took a cautious step forward. Close enough to assist him, but still far enough to run should Jack decide to sheathe himself in another circle of fire.

"Jack," Tiv called, hesitant. "Are you alright?"

"Do I look alri—" Jack recoiled, just as Tiv flinched.

Black clouded Jack's vision. He frantically looked around, trying to shake off the hazy tendrils obstructing his periphery. Despite the added darkness, his vision was clearer than ever before. Colors were enhanced. Lines were more pronounced. The world flowed. Seamless. A harmony of utter perfection.

It was almost too bright. But it was tainted.

Jack saw a trail. Black wisps that he followed with his eyes. The path led left—to the residential tower. *What I seek,* Jack thought. He heard a dozen voices whisper in his ear. They were quieter now. More controlled. They danced upon his skin and urged him to move forward. *Is it there?*

Jack heard a gasp and turned to see Tiv shakily point a trembling finger at him. "Your eyes…" Tiv stepped back in sudden fear. "What happened to your eyes?"

Jack tilted his head. *My eyes?*

He looked at a mirror mounted on the nearby wall, his jaw dropping. His eyes had always been a startling red. They were the orbs of an Elementalist. But wisps of darkness had never circled his irises. They didn't continuously move like tiny parasites that scared even him. For the first time in his life, Jack was frightened of his own reflection. He staggered, not liking what he saw. He felt like a stranger in his own skin, wearing the mask of another. It was his face, but it lacked the proper features. A faulty clone. With all the wrong blueprints. As though his fine print had been altered without his consent.

Do you see it now? the voice murmured. *The path of truth. Follow it. And the world will be within your reach. Whatever you desire will be yours for the taking. Men and women. Children and slaves. Scholars and fools. They will kneel before you.*

Jack didn't care.

He'd change his world, not by borrowing power, but by using his own. He'd had enough of this voice. This invisible seductress that lured the faint of heart. It made him sick. He wasn't weak, nor did he like to be thought of as such. He detested being underestimated. Jack would sooner die than succumb to a formless woman trying to appeal to one of humanity's greatest faults—greed. Petty greed. The sort of voracity that characterized the pathetic and needy. Jack was neither. He wasn't like the power hungry practitioners of the Diamond Alps.

He'd already tired of its whispers of grandeur. They were

false promises. Loans always had a price.

He wasn't willing to give one.

"Shut up," Jack muttered darkly. He ignored the puzzled look Tiv shot him. As he focused on the voice only he seemed to hear. Jack tried to control the rage that threated to paint his vision red. He failed. "I neither need, nor want your help. It's my life. How dare you attempt to lead me? How dare you hurt me in your attempt to make me see what I don't want? When I get my hands on you, I'm going to watch you burn. Slowly. Bit by bit. Until you get on your hands and knees and beg me for death. For an ounce of mercy that doesn't exist."

Like many, the voice heard but didn't listen. A strangely human trait. Perhaps it was human. Perhaps this was the doing of a bored practitioner. He'd just assumed it was something otherworldly. Jack blamed its lack of physical form. Could the voice even hear him? It had no ears. But Jack believed it could. His pain had stopped as soon as he willed it after all.

So, who was he speaking to? Or had he finally gone insane?

The fate of Ferrus Terria is at your fingertips.

No, he hadn't.

Twitch, and you'll spark tremors. Wave, and you'll create ripples. The land is your home. The ocean, your court. That, and so much more. My power is yours for the taking.

It wasn't listening. He loathed being ignored.

All you have to do is grasp.

Jack finally snapped.

16

Columbus fancied himself a man of composure.

Many things eluded him, but balance wasn't one of them. He could handle all sorts of situations, expertly defuse any amount of tension, and stalwartly control his emotions. And during times of circumstance, Columbus used his experience to his advantage.

He'd grasped the art of expecting. He took life in stride and pushed back when the opportunity presented itself. Because fate was quick to let her guard down. Columbus had realized that long ago. When he'd decided that it wasn't blasphemous to refer to human made apparitions as people themselves. Lady Luck, Madam Temperance, Ser Justice. They weren't apotheosis like the First Zenith, but that didn't make them any less real. Nor any less condemned for the disasters that fell upon the world.

Many cursed them. He did as well. It was easy to blame an invisible presence for man's shortcomings.

That was also the day he realized Madam Fate hated losing.

Because every once in a while, she came back to surprise him with a new game. Where he didn't know the rules. And his world spiraled out of control. Just long enough until she had her fun, before she left in a flurry of misery and blood. Then the world returned to normal. But with each visit, he'd be a little older, and a little less capable than he'd once been. Columbus feared the day when his life would once more become a turbulent ride where he could fall off at any minute, not knowing what to expect. Where those he trusted abandoned him and even his lifelong wisdom failed his aging body.

Like now.

"Miriam," Columbus said in wary disbelief. "What's going on?"

Miriam's smile was so wide it made her eyes disappear. They were crinkled in absolute mirth. As she spread her arms above her head in wild abandon. She held the sort of manic enthusiasm only associated with hyper children and the mentally ill. And seeing her now, they could safely assume she wasn't too far off from the latter.

Miriam was soaked to the bone. Diluted trickles of brown were mixed in with the liquid that continuously ran down her form, leaving a trail of dirty water with each step. They realized a moment too soon that her robes weren't just blackened with water, but with blood. The garments clung to her in dark heaps that emphasized the blueness of her lips and the deep bags under her eyes.

"I knew it!" Miriam laughed. Shrill and earsplitting. Miriam placed her hands over her cheeks and smiled in glee. She whispered to herself, "I knew those voices sounded familiar, so I ran to see who it could be… and I was right! It was them. Them! What are they doing here though? Have they come to see you?" She tilted her head and gasped. "What… you don't know? Well then, who does? Right, I should ask. Yes, let me ask." Her head snapped up, and they instinctively took a step back at the crazed look in her eyes. "Have you also come to see *her?*"

"Her?" Orpha asked.

"*Her!*" Miriam repeated, uncharacteristically childlike. She placed a hand over her heart. "Can't you hear *her*? *She's* calling us. Calling me. *She* wants me to come save *her*. Take *her* away from this awful place. *She* doesn't know how she got here. *She* just wants to go back. Back into the arms of the Zenith, so he can fulfill his promise."

"What?" Columbus all but stuttered. "Do you have any idea what you're saying? Have you gone mad? She? The Zenith? What's going on, Miriam?"

"They aren't listening!" Miriam whined, closing in on herself and whispering to her imaginary companion. "Am I not enough to release you from this place?" She shook her head in dread, before pointing at them. "Well then what about them? But if they can't hear you then why are they here? I don't understand. You told me there was another. Where? Tell me what I need to do to find them."

"What is *wrong* with you?" Celaris barked.

Miriam didn't listen. "I will… try. But I'll need more. Enough to get them away from your rooms. Enough to call him here. Just a little more, please, I beg of you."

Celaris sighed. He was at his limit. He'd had enough of her idiosyncratic babble. Celaris could barely tolerate her usual neuroticism, but he could at least respect it. Miriam's stringency was the sort of trait birthed from years of discipline. But what she displayed now was just absurd. He had no qualms about the way his shoulders tightened. His magic prepared to lash out.

"She finally lost it," Celaris said, only half surprised. "It was just a matter of time. Still, even this is a bit much."

"This is no time for tasteless jokes," Columbus reprimanded, ignoring the way Celaris' mouth twitched in amusement. It was easy to see where Tiv got his attitude from. "We need to question her."

"First, we need to actually get her to pay attention. How do you propose we do that?"

"Do what you do best." Columbus shrugged, securing his grimoire. "And I'll support you."

Celaris sighed. He shook his head in a way that told Columbus he'd expected this. "When civility fails, resort to rudimentary methods. It's always the same. I thought we were past the age of savagery."

"Barbarism doesn't disappear, Celaris. It just becomes more sophisticated."

"I see no class in seizing the demented. If a limb is infected, remove it. Look at her eyes. She's clearly beyond reprieve. Isn't it about time we rid ourselves of her? I'm quite skilled in the art of amateur amputation."

Columbus' gaze hardened. "You complain about the method, then turn and speak lightly of murder. What you propose is far more beastly. Who's the one stuck in the past, Celaris?"

Celaris' mouth twitched to form a half-smile. "Still not me," he concluded.

"Just get on with it already."

Celaris stepped aside, quirking his eyebrow at Orpha, who crossed his arms in silent contemplation of the situation. Orpha's eyes remained closed, unsure of what they so easily saw in Miriam's mien. Celaris was quick to quiet his worries.

"Are you ready, partner?"

Orpha stepped up in answer. He trusted Celaris enough to follow first and ask questions later. They were partners. And had been for a long time. Celaris wouldn't steer him in the wrong direction. If nothing else, he believed that.

So, without warning, he charged.

Orpha transformed mid-step and suddenly he was flying. Arms shifted into wings that spanned the entire length of the hall. As he donned deadly claws and a large, piercing beak.

Columbus gasped in shock. "Is that a… griffin? How did he learn that?"

The response to his question was a loud caw.

A part of Orpha counted on the rarity of his form to somehow derail Miriam's train of thought. As it did Columbus. Even for just a moment. Orpha swooped down, ready to rip Miriam apart with his talons. But, not a moment later, he was drenched. His feathers lay flat against his large body and his wings suddenly seemed twice as heavy.

"Orpha!" Celaris yelled in alarm.

Orpha didn't need to see, to know that water pushed him back. A tidal wave that threatened to drown him. He could feel it all clearly enough. He felt his back meet the adjacent stone wall. And he let out a strangled gasp at the sickening crunch of his spine. The coldness of the liquid numbed his pain. Though only somewhat. He heard Miriam's manic laughter drizzling off to the side. Columbus whispered an incantation beside him, as he healed his wounds. But it was Celaris' harsh voice that noticeably pierced the air, penetrating his muddled mind.

"Miriam," Celaris called lowly. An unspoken threat.

He didn't back down, despite his wariness at the suddenly conjured element. Many Elementalists and Conjurers alike had difficulty pushing back Orpha, yet she did so with a simple flick of her wrist. But that wasn't his main concern. Because he knew for a fact that Miriam was a Healer. A renowned one with years of experience under her belt.

He'd seen her in action many times before.

So, then how? Celaris thought. *How was she able to conjure an element?*

"You're gawking, Celaris," Miriam mocked. "Whatever for, I wonder?"

Celaris' fingers twitched. As he dropped into a defensive crouch. It was engage or retreat. And Celaris was no coward.

"How did you get those eyes, Miriam?"

She smiled at him once more, her eyes crinkling in laughter.

The red hue made his blood burn.

***

Tiv walked behind Jack, who followed an invisible path only he could see. Tiv didn't know what to make of it. And the tension between them was far too thick for him to break with mere words. He didn't question Jack's sudden pain, the wisps of black in his eyes, or the nonexistent deity he occasionally whispered to — without a care for how utterly bizarre it looked. Tiv didn't even mention how exactly Jack was sure that whatever path they followed would lead them in the right direction. He had tried of course. In the beginning. Before they'd started down the halls of the residential tower. But Jack's answers were disturbing, and he'd occasionally stop mid-sentence to curse at an unseen guest.

Better to stay quiet, Tiv decided. *Hold my tongue and wait to see what this idiot plans on doing.*

To their chagrin, they didn't make it very far.

A loud crash echoed from the long flight of steps below. They halted for a moment, taking in the noise and the echoes that followed. It sounded suspiciously like furniture toppling over. That, or a body. They could name quite a few Amorphs heavy enough to crack stone. But they ruled that out, on the charge of not wanting to think about such a thing happening in the Tower. Again. One death within their walls was enough. Like clockwork, however, the moment took a decidedly creepier turn when the thud was followed by a pained scream.

Tiv recognized the voice instantly. It was one he heard often. One he grew up hearing.

"Master Celaris!" he yelled.

Tiv made to run down the stairs, but he was stopped by Jack, who caught him by the elbow with a grip tight enough to bruise. Jack yanked him back, and Tiv jerked in the opposite direction out of instinct. But Jack was scrawnier and weaker and he wasn't able to stop himself from toppling over. His sudden weight coupled with Tiv's bad footing forced them both down the long flight of steps in a heap of limbs and shouted curses. They didn't stop until they reached the landing that led to the next floor.

Jack, whose fall was cushioned by Tiv's much larger frame, was quick to stand and kick Tiv's side with fresh malice.

"Don't just run wherever you damn well please!" Jack berated in a level somewhere between a shout and a whisper. Not from fear of being caught, but in an attempt to ease the burst of aggravation he felt. The black in his periphery seemed to completely cloud his vision when angered. He found that out the hard way when he almost lost his sanity on the upper floors. As he yelled at the voice in his head.

"What..." Tiv muttered, disoriented.

"We can't just run down without knowing what's waiting for us. Are you trying to get us killed?"

Tiv groaned. He rubbed his aching head. As he slowly sat up. Much calmer now that his skull pounded with the intense pain only a face plant to stone could provide.

"And what do you propose we do?" Tiv asked, once the world finally stopped spinning. "Find an apprentice and throw him in front of us as bait? That's my Master down there. Not some faceless practitioner."

"I have a plan."

"Of course you do." Tiv rolled his eyes. "And what does this one entail? Destroying the walls? Or how about dispelling the magic around the Tower? Really, Jack. Your plans always end with extra problems. They always have."

"They always get the *initial* job done," Jack defended. "We have the highest success rate in the Institute. Have a little faith."

"In you?" Tiv scoffed. "You burnt a hole through the front gate! The front gate, Jack! What if some curious Nebbin stumbles inside?"

"For the ten thousandth time, that wasn't me," Jack stressed, using juvenile hand gestures as if that would get his point across better. "Sylvie burned it. Sylvie!"

Tiv raised an unconvinced brow. It spoke volumes.

Jack turned away, irritated by Tiv's lack of trust. He played with fire in an effort to distract himself, and his eyes widened at the difference from his usual flames. It was larger and far less controlled, featuring a dark center. He looked up at Tiv, but there was no emotion in the Amorph's expression other than his previous well-founded skepticism.

Tiv couldn't see it.

Again? Jack thought in disbelief. *I'm sure Sylvie would've been able to. Is this limited to Conjurers and Elementalists?*

Jack shook his head, brushing the darkness from his mind. The whispers grew louder as soon as he did, demanding his attention. Jack ignored them. He was getting better at that. Just as he was slowly getting used to the tendrils in his enhanced vision, showing the path to an unknown destination. Jack swallowed down each new surprise, along with every angry retort that danced along the tip of his tongue.

It tasted of timidity and cowardice. Absolutely vile.

But Jack didn't want to acknowledge the voice any more than he already had. So, he focused on his hands. Ablaze with one of nature's most primal elements. The power felt good. His magic pulsed with newfound intensity. Jack had to consciously keep himself from shaking in excitement. The power was exhilarating. The flames were just a little out of his control. Enough to provoke. Enough to get his blood pumping. Enough to make his mouth unconsciously tilt up into a smirk.

He overlooked the enthralling voice whispering in his ear.

Invigorating, isn't it?

Jack tried to.

17

Rior strolled through empty corridors, purposely slowing his pace, so he could revel in the pleasure solitude had to offer. He enjoyed the quiet. Where no one could stare. The north was always filled with life. The south and west were worse. Even unclaimed lands always had a few unwelcome noises on stage— the cicadas, for one. Blasted things, they were. They irritated him and made him sleepy all at once.

But the east was different. While the rest of the world bustled about, rising with the sun and resting with the stars, the Drowned Tower remained undisturbed. The practitioners within moved at their own pace. As though time had stopped everything but their age. Rior didn't mind. He wanted many things, but eternal youth wasn't one of them. He enjoyed the tranquility of his current surroundings.

In stillness, existed peace. But peace was a fantasy.

A lie created by children and idealistic fools. A delusion of the sheltered. So long as there was life, there would never be peace. Like holding the wind and pleasing grief, it was just another unattainable dream.

War was inevitable. Violence, a must. Change, a certainty.

The calm was always devastated by a storm. Because people were fickle by nature. That was a lesson he'd learned long ago, when books taught him that even the revered apotheosis, Thelarius Merve, didn't wish for something so foolhardy. And with this knowledge, came the realization that people were warmongers. Who turned their backs on trust and disregarded bone deep principles at their convenience. Though he was in no position to judge. Rior was the same—to an extent. He did whatever his goals required of him.

His conscience came later. Always later. Lest his future evaporate before his eyes. Those that were inherently good never made it very far. Not in his world. And certainly not in any others.

Rior flicked open the flask Serach had given him, peering inside and silently debating if he should drink it or not. There was a time when he didn't care what he put in his mouth, so long as it nourished his starved constitution. During a time when all he had to worry about was his next meal. The poverty stricken plains of the south were truly a sight to behold—worse to experience. Ravished by famine and merchants of death, it was no place for a child. How Rior survived, he could no longer recall. But being raised amongst the Nebbin, who didn't know what to do with an orphan was perhaps the reason why Serach had chosen him.

Serach needed a tool clouded by desperation.

One that would never let power go. For Rior knew, he knew what life without it was. It wasn't pleasant.

But he was digressing, Rior realized, as he furiously shook his head in an attempt to clear it. The past was lonely. And so it chased. But he'd be damned if he allowed ghosts to catch him. Mistakes were a wildfire. If he repeated history enough, he'd get burned. Again. Rior didn't want that.

He scoffed at his own uncertainty.

This isn't the sort of situation where I can hesitate. I need that stone.

Without another thought, he downed the tonic, swallowing it before the taste could settle. Too slow. Rior underestimated its potency. A fatal mistake that ended with him coughing his lungs out in disgust. It was rancid.

The flavor left a burning sensation down his throat. And he suppressed the urge to gag. He'd tasted many brews, dozens of remedies, and even the occasional strangely tinted swill blended through questionable means. But this tonic was a taint. It crippled his insides and left him gasping for air. Rior scratched his neck, smoothing his thumb over his stinging throat. He could still feel the crystal lodged somewhere in his esophagus, but he was breathing fine. Perfectly, even. Each inhale was stronger than the last.

Rior paused, leaning against the wall. He felt neither pain, nor suffering. As he waited for the tonic to take effect.

If it had side effects, they didn't show. Not yet.

The longer he waited for a pull or a sudden change inside of him, the more he felt as if the tonic had no effect at all. Nothing happened. A failed brew, he decided. And could only hope the next one tasted better—something sweeter—anything would be an improvement. But then he found himself smiling at nothing, his lips simply twitched upward without his consent. Until he could no longer contain the all too sudden urge to show his teeth. And he smiled unabashedly from ear to ear.

All he felt was bliss. A chill ran up his spine and made its way to his brain—where it settled. A numb brain freeze of personal enjoyment.

It tickled his nerves and filled him with adrenaline.

Rior felt good. When he reopened his eyes, he saw a trail of black guiding him to his destination. His insides pulsed with excitement. They burned. An incomprehensible burst of anticipation, exhilaration, and a dozen other nameless emotions swept through him at a pace just quick enough to leave him breathless.

But the elation wasn't his.

And he gasped in confusion.

The euphoria he felt didn't belong to him. None of those emotions did. He knew that. As much as the lines that marred his skin. Rior stumbled at the strange sensation of another's passion welling up inside his core— spreading and tainting his body in a wheel of raging madness—until he keeled over.

"What's happening?" he wondered aloud, his voice throaty from unuse. The walls ate his words and answered back with silence. An outcome he only half expected. The other half of him expected to hear the owner of those foreign emotions call out. Order him. Tell him to do something he'd undoubtedly regret.

"Did I imagine it? How absurd." Rior laughed humorlessly. "I've been spending far too much time around Master B—"

Another wave of excitement washed over him. Rior shivered in delight. Unconsciously, he began following the dark trail now visible to his eyes. He rushed with the sort of unrestrained enthusiasm he didn't believe himself capable of exuding.

He was close.

***

Sylvie's jaw clenched in worry.

The stone's pulse had become even more erratic. But it didn't sing. The black haze wasn't present. It just glowed. Incessant and nauseatingly bright. Sylvie would've turned it into a makeshift lamp, had it not been for the questioning glances Ethil kept shooting her way. Every time Sylvie's eyes drifted down to her glowing robes, Ethil would eye her sidelong. As if she would do something incriminating if she didn't keep her eyes forward at all times. Perhaps she would. If Ethil kept looking at her like that then she didn't doubt it.

Sylvie had the nagging suspicion that perhaps Ethil was doing it on purpose for the sake of annoying her. But that couldn't be. Ethil wasn't Jack or Myrrh. She wasn't the sort to purposely infuriate—she hoped not.

"You keep looking at your robes," Ethil observed, finally speaking her mind. "Is something wrong?"

"They're wet and uncomfortable." Sylvie shrugged coolly.

She snapped her fingers, sparking fire, but not fully allowing it to emerge. The action sent a wave of heat throughout her body, courtesy of her magic. She felt weaker now that the adrenaline from melting the gate had been drained from her system. Her movements were sluggish. And she wanted nothing more than to curl up and take a nap. A shame her ethos wouldn't allow her such selfish reprieve. At least not during crisis. If the situation could be called that. Sylvie usually associated disasters with helpless screams and more bloodshed.

The Drowned Tower had neither.

Only a dearth of misfortune and a surplus of emptiness. And rats. Fattening rats. A squeaking plague that festered, as they scurried throughout empty corridors and cracks in the walls. With no practitioners around, the rodents took it upon themselves to roam the halls in their place. Nasty little things.

Sylvie bent to inspect one. It had deep black eyes, but not as wide as an Amorph's. "Not abysmal enough."

"What?" Ethil asked.

"Don't you think an Amorph could be hiding amongst these rats?" Sylvie asked. Ethil stiffened, her face blanching in sudden fear. As Sylvie watched the rat dash away with disinterest. "The move of an apprentice practitioner, no doubt. There may be many of them, but an intruder wouldn't be so foolish as to choose such an obvious tactic. Though if simplicity were their strategy, then this is certainly the best way to disguise themselves."

Ethil blinked in numb surprise, warily scrutinizing her surroundings and hoping someone wasn't watching them. "That's reckless. For both an intruder and an apprentice."

"I agree."

"But why would a practitioner do such a thing? What's the point? If they're curious, it would be safer to ask someone from the Assembly about what's happening."

"The higher the risk, the more thrilling the turns." Sylvie regarded her for a moment before walking up to another rat. She quietly crept up to it, but the rodent scurried away before she could examine its face. "I doubt many Masters would say anything to nameless practitioners or even their own primary apprentices for that matter. Their lips are sealed tight. For all we know, they could be hiding amongst the rats to keep themselves safe rather than fulfill some desire for answers. Desperation beguiles cowardice."

"Did you hear that from someone?"

"No." Sylvie grinned. "But Master Cephas tells me I should keep a broad array of advice laced with riddles ready for when I become a Master."

Ethil stifled a laugh, turning because she failed to fully hide her amusement behind her hand. "Here I thought they just spouted wisdom."

"Improvisation is for Elders," Sylvie said sagely.

"And the rule followers?"

"Conformists are just lazy."

Ethil frowned, a silent indication that she wasn't impressed by that particular quote. "That's not very clever."

"Really?" Sylvie asked, tilting her head. "If you have a way to make it more confusing, then do tell."

Ethil caught herself, before she could voice her thoughts on the matter. *What am I doing?* Ethil thought, willing her expression back to neutral. Nothing good could come from fraternizing with a possible enemy. *She's hiding something. I can't get caught up in her pace.*

As Ethil lost herself to her thoughts, Sylvie stretched her back, working the kinks out and watching as the rats kept their distance now that they knew she'd bother them if they got too close. Sylvie listlessly noted that they were close to her room. Two more floors. But there was no rush. She took her time scrutinizing the large rodents. Some had fabrics and tiny valuables in their mouths, having taken it from the empty chambers.

"Myrrh," Sylvie called loudly, ignoring how Ethil suddenly leered at her. "Myrrh, are you here?"

The response to her question was a loud crash.

Their heads snapped up toward the sound. It came from down the hall. From the echo, it was a few floors below. The noise was followed by unintelligible cries and a pained shout.

What's happening? Sylvie thought. She barely registered running across the hall and down the stairs. Ethil was at her heels, frantically trying to match her pace. The shouts were louder now. They were clear enough for Sylvie to make them out.

"Back away, fiend!" a familiar voice shouted from below. Deep and masculine. Sylvie's mind failed to attach it to a face.

Tap. Tap. Tap.

The sound of dripping water rang louder than the screams. Sylvie abruptly halted. Ethil complained as she bumped into her back, almost sending them both down the long flight of stairs.

"Don't just stop!" Ethil rebuked, but immediately clamped her mouth shut at the sound of trickling liquid. A soft lull that quickly turned into a heavy gush. They took a mutual step back as a wave of water flooded the lower floor.

Their mouths dropped in silent shock.

The screams were gone now. Only footsteps remained.

Sylvie heard a low laugh, as someone waded their way through the water, creating ripples that showed just how close they were to the one responsible for this. Every muscle in Sylvie's body urged her to move, but her feet wouldn't cooperate. Even as Ethil grabbed her arm, forcing her to get back up the stairs.

Sylvie's ears strained to hear more of that shrill laughter.

"Foolish," a woman screeched, her voice didn't pierce the silence—it completely shattered it. It was a voice Sylvie had heard many times before. "How utterly foolish."

Master Miriam? she thought. As the water slowly receded. *No, it can't be. The water's being controlled.* Sylvie unconsciously stepped forward. Her hand radiated a cold blue. As she prepared herself for the oncoming threat. *By who, then? A Conjurer or an Elementalist?*

Sylvie caught sight of sopping wet robes, but before she could lift a hand to release a tunnel of flame, a large chunk of what she assumed was the ceiling crashed somewhere on the floor above her. It was enough to make the stranger below stop and take off in the opposite direction. Sylvie made a move to chase the culprit, but the sound of clapping behind her had her hastily turning back around.

A man stood there with a feral smile on his lips.

His smile alone put her on edge and from the corner of her

eye, she saw Ethil take a step back in a brief display of her inner terror. Before she hid it behind a cold face of indifference and a defensive crouch. Sylvie didn't blame her. Even her magic spurred under her skin, begging to be released. The hairs on her arm stood up in sudden alarm. Sylvie might've copied the move, had she not already been at the edge of a very tall flight of solid stone.

"You're not Jack," he said. As he stepped from the shadows.

Rior Wolden, Sylvie's mind supplied. He was as tall and frighteningly well-built as she remembered. His eyes were the same violent red shared by all Elementalists, but there was something different about them. They sported a frightening darkness that hadn't been present during their first meeting. Literal darkness. Sylvie could clearly make out the black tendrils dancing along the corners of his face, stemming from his eyes.

What is that?

"Jack?" Sylvie questioned instead, raising her eyebrows and shrugging in forced nonchalance. "What do you want with Jack?"

Rior didn't speak. Only eyed her. His gaze settled on her collar. Where the Heartstone lay hidden beneath her robes.

He can see it, Sylvie realized, turning to subtly block it from view. Ethil eyed her sidelong, accusation in her eyes. Accusation for not telling her what she was hiding when they first returned.

But Ethil didn't understand. She didn't know how hard it was for them to explain something they knew nothing about. How difficult it was to describe soft songs and bright pulses only they could see. Ethil would think them insane.

And Sylvie wouldn't blame her. But it was harder to deal with someone who believed her psychotic over someone suspicious of her motives.

"Jack isn't here," Sylvie said, choosing her words carefully. "Shall I pass along a message?"

"No," Rior finally spoke. He pointed at her collar. "It would seem that you have what I seek. Why is that, I wonder? Did *she* call to you, as well? But you're a Conjurer. Conjurers shouldn't be able to hear *her* song. It's a song only for the privileged. Or can you see the trail *she* leaves? Did you drink a tonic, too?" Rior frantically shook his head, dismissing his own guess. "Of course not. That's impossible. That was a special brew. I assume then that you found the stone by chance, yes? How unfortunate."

"Unfortunate? Stone? Song?" Ethil asked, irritated by her own lack of knowledge. "What are you talking about?"

Rior ignored her, and instead voiced out his ramblings. He spoke fast. As if he couldn't get the thoughts out quick enough. If he were to allow them to settle, then they'd be replaced in an instant.

"No," he rejected himself again, "there are no coincidences. That would be too convenient. Which means either you're disguising yourself as a Conjurer or…" His head snapped up, exposing the manic look in his eyes that betrayed their initial stoic impression of him. "You're a descendant of the First Zenith."

Their eyes widened at the sudden conclusion.

"No, no, no," Rior continuously repeated. He shook his head, emphasizing his denial. "That can't be. They died out. Master said so. He has no reason to lie. Or… did *she* corrupt him?"

Sylvie's eyes narrowed. "She?"

Rior stiffened.

His head snapped up. As the haze that surrounded his pupil completely consumed him. And then he was screaming, but even that was muffled. Tendrils latched onto his jaw and sewed his mouth shut.

He tried to light a fire, to summon wind, call upon water, but it was for naught. Nothing listened. His magic had chosen to go on temporary hiatus. Or were the wisps responsible? Rior didn't know. He had no time to ponder over the answer.

Sylvie and Ethil reeled back in alarm, stumbling over the steps and plunging head first into conjured water. They knew better than to stay in such a confined space.

Rior became a faceless mask before their eyes.

And then only darkness remained.

18

The smile on Reed's lips felt unbearably hollow today.

His eyes were vacant, but the same couldn't be said about his mind. At this point, even he wished to be taken by the blankness oblivion had to offer. Reed, however, thought only of the past. He thought of the shameful, aggravating times. Those were always the most prominent. They reared their ugly little heads and made him feel pathetic.

As a child, Reed had always been told that he needed to stand up for himself more often. As if it was that easy. Many had the ability to assert their feelings and get their opinions across with confidence. But little had the skill to not enforce their own gregarious personality onto others. They didn't know what it felt like to have their hands tremble before a group—large or otherwise—to have their mind question every second action they took, to sit before someone and only be able to offer an awkward smile.

And so they pushed.

They told him to do more. To be more. Reed hated it. And each time, he'd think the same thing. *Like hell.*

Why wasn't he enough? What was so wrong with his personality that others always urged him to change? Why did he have to adjust to the world's demands? It was frustrating how society catered to a select few. And despite whatever nonsense others had to say against it, that was the truth. That was his truth.

Others could excel with charisma alone.

But then he'd met Sylvie, and he felt giddy with relief at finding someone as opposed to change as himself.

As if fate had thrown him a bone.

Right now, however, Reed thought that perhaps those push-ers were right. Maybe he needed to break out of his shell. Even for a second. Because right now, he was huddled on the ground. Bound and bloody. His face was long numb from pain, but his side blossomed with it.

Serach measured the room in long, restless strides.

His pacing was a frantic lull that Reed tried to focus on. He wanted a distraction. Anything to root him to his surroundings and prevent him from receding into the corners of his subconsc-ious. Reed needed to concentrate on the here and now. Not fig-ments conjured by his imagine. That was a hole. Where the only thing that awaited him was the snapping of his own sanity.

I… I need to get away from here. Reed's eyes darted around, searching for an escape. It was hard to see when his face was so bruised. But he couldn't stay here. He only had two real options: continue picking at his bindings until his skin was marred by scars or attempt to crawl to the door and scream.

It wasn't much of a choice.

Reed doubted Serach would let him live very long, but if he was lucky enough, then someone might hear his cry. Reed was rarely lucky. But… *He'll kill me either way.*

So, he watched, and he waited for the moment when Serach let his guard down. It wouldn't be long now. Serach was already irritated.

His patience long near its end.

"Where has that fool gone?" Serach grumbled, vehemently running his hands through his thinning locks. As he paced the length of the room. Everyone in the Drowned Tower heard the disturbing noise of stone meeting stone. As if one of the floors had collapsed. Perhaps one did. The sound was far too loud to ig-nore, and though it came from some far off distance, the echoes alone were enough to stir concern. Especially since Serach could still feel Rior nearby through his Demar Spell.

His apprentice was still in the Tower, of that he was certain.

"Why is he still here?" Serach stressed. His eyes widened as realization dawned upon him. *The Heartstone!*

Serach ran to his table, carelessly throwing aside papers and vials. They shattered on the floor, spreading strange liquids that reeked of medicine and antiseptic. He didn't seem to mind how dangerously close the unknown concoctions were to the fireplace, as he searched for his prize. A round glass flask. It had been polished to a shine. Black wisps stemmed from an even blacker center, erratically moving within like a living being. Words in a forgotten tongue were written along the flask's neck to form an ancient sealing spell. It looked like the one he'd given Rior, except far more concentrated.

Serach smiled. Just as the door flew open without warning.

Reed's eyes widened at the sight of the screeching intruder. The world stopped for half a second, along with his heart. As Miriam fully entered, talking hurriedly about someone. Her eyes rested on Reed and he recoiled in fear. Not at the malice behind her gaze, but at the color that greeted him. Bright red. Thoughts of escape left him. Along with his voice. As if she'd wrenched his mouth open, held him by the tongue, and squeezed.

Serach turned, hurriedly hiding both his glee and the flask. "Oh, Miriam," he said, tacking on a dubious expression. All false pretenses. "Back so soon?"

"Serach!" Miriam roared, stalking up to him. She didn't make it. Miriam stumbled, clutching her pounding head. It swelled with pain. "What's happening to me?"

Her eyes felt as if they were slowly being squeezed from their sockets, even as fresh tears clung to them. Clumps of hair fell out with each swipe of her hands and she screamed. A blood curdling scream filled with terror. The fallen strands left Miriam's scalp exposed for all to see. And Reed turned his head away to avoid hurling. A blue crystal had been embedded to the side of her scalp. It pulsed with soft intensity.

Pale blue and haunting.

Magic. Reed shivered at the thought. The crystal was familiar to him and he instantly recalled Jack's words in Tearwood. *Are those Orivellea crystals? Who would think to brand someone like this? Like... a Peose.* His eyes widened in stunted realization. *Who's the master?*

"Answer me!" Miriam yelled.

Serach grinned mischievously, waving his hand in a dismissive fashion. As if her state was of no importance. In his eyes, it wasn't. "Did you lust for more power, Miriam? I certainly hope not. We all know what avarice does to the soul."

Miriam flinched.

"Well, no matter." Serach shrugged, uncaring. "Did you happen to see Rior? I still feel him nearby. He's not with Jacques, is he? After all his complaints about not wanting to attract the attention of Hunters, he still goes after his prey within these very halls. If he doesn't leave soon, he'll be caught."

"Who cares if your apprentice is caught?" Miriam exclaimed. Her shrill voice made Reed wince. He'd always hated her voice. As did the rest of the Drowned Tower. But right now, Reed silently hoped that someone would hear her screams and come investigating. "What's happe—"

"Why, I care," Serach interrupted her tirade before it could even begin, replacing it with his own. "I care very much. I didn't spend all this time grooming Rior into a man only to have him die because he hadn't enough common sense to leave the Tower before I made my move." Serach raised his eyebrows expectantly. As if she were supposed to know all of this. "He's my apprentice, and while I'm ultimately responsible for when he lives and dies, I don't want to be the cause of it. Not the direct cause anyway."

Miriam glared. A silent warning not to interrupt her again. "I've had enough of your prattle, you antiquated dunce. Tell me what's happening to me."

Serach could understand the fossil insults from the younger apprentices, but he didn't think Miriam had any right to call him that. She wasn't exactly easy on the eyes. Especially now.

"Your mask is cracking, Miriam. You best invest in a better

one. If I've learned anything from my years in the Alps, it's that a flawed façade is intolerable, and will be exploited." Miriam looked as if she wanted to retort, but he spoke again with a weary sigh. "Let me make myself plain, Miriam. You've hastened the process with your wanton desire for power that wasn't meant for your… kind. It was simply too much for you. Though I commend you for still being able to hold a conversation at this stage. Your mind still seems to be intact. Luck has saved you. For now. Or perhaps it was *her* doing. Either way, consider yourself fortunate. There are worse things in life than losing a few gray locks."

"Too much?" Miriam repeated, deliberately pronouncing every syllable. "What do you mean too much?"

"Why too much for your magic circuit to handle, of course," Serach said, speaking slowly and carefully. As if she were a child, and he, her master. "The same circuit that separates us from those pesky Nebbin. The very same one that fuels us with magic. It's enhanced by the Orive crystal. An extra conduit, if you will. I suppose you can think of yourself as a human Peose."

"A Peose?" Miriam screeched. "How dare you compare me to those… those vile creatures?"

"Vile?" Serach raised an eyebrow, amusing himself with the knowledge that his tone infuriated her. "Now that isn't fair. Peose have many talents. They can use the elements, some even have the ability to take different shapes, and others even have healing skills. You would've never been able to summon water without the Orive crystal's enhancements. But fret not, Miriam. Soon, even pain will no longer be a concern. These crystals aren't meant for the greedy. You already have a circuit. Two is one too many."

"Just what did you do to me?" Miriam stuttered.

"Me?" Serach asked, dubiously pointing at himself. "Why, I simply offered you the crystal. Nothing more. I don't recall forcing you to take it."

"Liar!" Miriam yelled, trying to stand. To no avail. She couldn't hope to stand when simply craning her neck proved to be a challenge. Her head pounded with renewed vigor, and she was once more reacquainted with pain. Fresh, haunting pain. "You fucking liar!"

A haunted look clouded her expression.

Miriam clutched her head with more fervor, as memories of Serach's predatory smile and Rior's violent hands around her neck flitted across her mind. The feeling of her life being choked away was still fresh. As fresh as Duward's corpse. They'd given her a beating of reassurance. Enough to strike fear in her. Enough to ensure her loyalty. But they miscalculated. It wasn't enough for Miriam to lose sight of her goals. They should've killed her that day. She'd come close, but before she could be swept away by the alluring hands of death, coldness washed over her. It trickled over her skin. Inched its way down her body and settled inside of her head.

A soft pulse that throbbed with pain.

And then *she* reached out. *She* healed Miriam's body.

Miriam did nothing. She was too delirious to move at that point. But she knew enough to know that she hadn't done a thing to accept *her*. Not even when *her* memories flooded her brain. An unwanted, terribly vivid memoir. Miriam gained knowledge of things long forgotten, but with it came the burden of fixing all that was—and still is—broken.

This is his fault, she seethed.

"I merely wanted to help *her*!" Miriam exclaimed. "Gain enough power to help *her* out of the Tower. If *she* left, then the Tower would return to normal. But you don't care about *her*, do you?" Miriam's eyes widened in sudden realization. Her breath hitched, and for a moment, she forgot about the stinging pain of the *Orivellea* crystal in her head. "You want the Drowned Tower! That's why you had me distract them by killing Duward. All the while, dangling the promise of safety before my eyes. Are you the reason *she* wants to leave? What did you do to *her*, you heartless beast?"

Serach sighed, exasperated. "You just don't understand, do you? *She* doesn't want to leave. We brought *her* here. We've brought *her* closer to *her* dream, to fulfilling a contract left unsatisfied for far too long."

"You brought *her* here?" Miriam yelled in disbelief. "How could you? Do you realize what *she's* capable of doing to this place? To those *she* gets her hands on?"

"Controlling *her* does seem to be proving rather… difficult. Look at what *she's* done to you. Needless brutality. As soon as the host falters, *she* overreacts."

"How dare you use me in your convoluted schemes?"

"Use you? Heavens, no," Serach said, appalled. "I merely hastened the process. Had you skip a few steps, but use you? What, pray tell, would I use you for? I choose my tools carefully, and I can assure you that you aren't one of them. You don't even make the cut. You were convenient, but I swear on Silas' flame that you were entirely unnecessary to my plan. You were simply in the wrong place at the wrong time. *She* happened to take a liking to you, but it must be obvious by now that that is no longer the case."

Miriam didn't know when she'd started crying, but sometime during his bombast, tears spilled from her eyes. And they wouldn't stop. No matter how much she willed them to.

"Oh, wipe your tears, Miriam," Serach said, not unkindly. He crouched before her, brushing away her tears and running his fingers along the *Orivellea* entrenched in her skull. He was undeterred by the way she tried to inch away from his hand. Instead, Serach grinned manically. And Miriam flinched. As he dropped his voice to a whisper—a secret only between them. "Magic isn't infinite. Sooner or later, we all return to crystals and dust."

Miriam suddenly stopped.

She let out an ear-piercing scream. Her body was wracked by sobs, as she held her shaking head in mad frenzy. "No, stop! Please. I've had enough! I don't need any more."

A crack shook the air.

Followed by ten more.

Miriam gasped in horror when the crystal spread down her

neck and to her shoulders. She tried to summon water, to yell healing incantations, even kick and turn. But it was for naught. Her futile efforts only made the process feel slower than it was. She was torn from an infinite number of lacerations and she could feel each and every one, as they cut gradually through centimeters of flesh, muscle, and bone.

She was an open wound. Gaping and bloody.

Miriam looked up, her gaze passed over a shocked Reed, who stifled his sobs at the sight of her. Serach, however, was indifferent to the ordeal. As if it was just another everyday occurence. Boring. Trite. Decidedly mundane. Even as Miriam pleaded with her eyes, trying to call upon the sympathy of the compassionate man the entirety of Ferus Terria once regarded as an Elder.

But he was gone.

In his place was an unfeeling monster. Serach flashed her a smile. Kind and manic. And Miriam felt as thought she'd just been doused by a pale of ice cold water. She trembled. The light faded from her eyes. Hope was quick to follow. The crystal encompassed Miriam's form, rapidly deteriorating her body from within. Until only a large *Orivellea* remained.

And the secret was Serach's once again.

"May Pernelia's wings guide you to where the First Zenith dwell," Serach mumbled. His mouth was twisted up into a sardonic smile.

An unwelcomed sob shook the silence. Just loud enough to catch Serach's attention. He turned to find Reed biting his wrist to keep from screaming. As he swallowed his anxiety in unhealthy spoonfuls. All in an attempt to stand his ground.

He'd broken his thumb to release himself from his bindings. The shattered appendage was already slowly mending. While he shakily whispered a soft incantation under his breath.

"Can't you just sit and wait until I need you?" Serach sighed when Reed crouched into a defensive stance, lips quivering in fright. "No? Must you force my hand? Look, you're shaking."

Reed tried to steady his fingers. A useless endeavor. When

he procured his grimoire, it shook all the more. Even more visible now that he had something physical to grasp. He looked down at the torn pages. They were caked with his blood.

"Come then," Serach urged, readying himself. Reed was a coward. But cowards killed. "You best not miss."

19

Jack snuffed the magic from his hands.

As he free fell down the hole he'd just made through four floors of solid stone. Courtesy of a quaking combination of his ice and Tiv's bear like strength. Jack landed in a crouch inside familiar halls flooded with water and swimming rats.

Books and countless objects floated randomly about, polluting it. Jack immediately scanned the area, searching for holes in the outer wall. He found none.

What happened here? he thought, mindlessly sweeping the water away in an effort to turn the rats around. They were getting too close for comfort. But it didn't help. The rats were everywhere. He'd turn, and there they were, swimming or floating or even drowning. Jack squinted when he saw one seated atop a stray piece of wood that suspiciously looked like the table from his quarters.

My table! he lamented, their squeaks grating on his ears. *I already have one voice in my head. I don't need a chorus of mice.*

"Damn, gnawers!" Jack sneered, as a dozen frightened rats tried their best to scurry away from him. They didn't get very far. He looked back up to see Tiv peering through the hole. "You reckon they heard that blast?"

Tiv shrugged. "Only one way to find out."

And the Amorph was off. Ready to do his part in another one of his mastermind partners' sloppy plans. While Jack continued to look around, wading his way through water. He followed the black trail clouding his vision.

It was hard to focus on the path. The blast left him slightly dazed. It was loud. Too loud. They'd made sure of it. The enemy would have to be deaf not to have heard an explosion that jarring. Even if they were, Jack was certain they would have at least felt it. It shook half of the Institute. Which meant that the intruders were either running toward the sound or away from it.

The Drowned Tower was nigh inescapable. Away had only two options: up and down. They'd be ready on both fronts. With different battle plans prepared for each.

No holes, Jack thought, apprehensively eyeing the walls. The only opening in sight was the one he'd made. But that was an internal problem. One he'd be forced to deal with later. Right now, it was unimportant. *Where did all this water come from? Our mysterious murderer? A Hunter? Is it a Conjurer or an Elementalist?*

It comes from the one you seek, Jack's personal entity whispered in his mind. Unsolicited as usual. It was just his luck that this particular deity seemed to know nothing of boundaries. Even less of personal space. Once he got his hands on its physical form, he'd strangle it. Magic be damned.

Oh? Are you still… Jack's eyes widened in shock. *Wonderful! Now I'm talking to the damned thing.*

Neither Thelarius, nor Silas, the voice said, strangely monotone. Finally listening. Finally answering. Yet still in riddles. **Merely a host. Incompatible. Incompetent. A false savior. The contract can only be repaid by blood. By his kin. Thus was the nature of our bond.**

Thelarius? Silas? Wha—no, who are you? Those were names Jack never expected to hear from an unknown being. He'd expected godly beings from far off lands and distant times, but not names from his own history. The paramount of Ferrus Terria's past. *What do you mean a host? A contract? Explain things properly. The way of riddles is obsolete.*

Honesty was more blatant now. As transparent as deceit.

Follow the path and answers will be yours, the voice promised. Jack wasn't foolish enough to believe it.

Get out of my head! Jack mentally shouted. He'd had enough of this voice. Its tone was conceited, as it dangled answers it wasn't willing to truly give. The fact that he was actually entertaining it, just irritated him all the more. *You ruined my eyes. Planted yourself in me like some sick plague. Get out! I don't need you.*

I am your power.

"That wasn't a request!"

You must fulfill that which your predecessors promised. Until your time rightfully comes, you are mine.

"Fuck this," Jack decided. He quickened his pace, frantically searching for any signs of life. Jack did his best to ignore the voice. But it was difficult. Its choice of words begged him to ask questions. Jack wasn't having any of it.

"I won't fall for your tricks."

The scum of Maurice shall never again take you away.

"I won't."

I shall have my fill.

"I won't. I won't. I won—"

Look.

Jack stopped.

Down the hall, lay three battered practitioners piled on top of each other. Each bloodier than the last. Well, one practitioner and two animals. Amorphs, he guessed. How else could a large black bear make it this deep into the Drowned Tower? But what gave Jack pause was the griffin under it. Its body was four times as big as his own. With talons the size of his head. He could only speculate the length of its wings when unfurled. Jack quickly shook his head, putting his amazement on the back burner. This was no time to be impressed by the forms some practitioners could take. No matter how fascinating.

No, they weren't ordinary practitioners, they were Masters. Jack could tell from the light gray robes on their Healer. He rushed over, dropping to his knees and moving the only human figure amongst them.

Familiar features greeted him.

"Cephas," he breathed out in shock. Jack looked around in alarm. "What happened here?"

Jack shook him, while simultaneously searching for any fatal injuries on the three. He found none. He let out a shaky breath when he also found that the griffin—whoever he or she was—had no pulse against his fingertips. *There goes one great Amorph. Hopefully they taught their primary apprentice the secrets of this form, assuming they had one. It would be a shame for it to go to waste.*

Jack recalled Tiv's words, before they made the hole. Tiv was certain he'd heard Master Celaris' voice. So he rushed down to find the man they'd been looking for in the first place. It was a stroke of luck to actually find him here. No, not luck. The black wisps that led Jack forward ended at his feet. Celaris was here. But which one was he? The griffin or the bear?

Jack shook his head. He had more important things to do than worry about his partner's Master. Because the darkness re-formed, creating another trail. He hadn't asked any questions though. And he certainly wasn't looking for anyone.

So, where did this path lead?

For the briefest of instants, Jack entertained the notion of following it, before ultimately deciding against the idea. He could find answers here. Jack snapped his fingers, sparking flames and letting them lick dangerously close to Cephas' face. It usually woke his comrades up, but sleeping and being knocked out seemed to be two different levels of unconscious.

Wonderful, Jack thought, extinguishing the fire. *Now, how did three Masters get their faces shoved into stone?*

Victims.

Of who?

The host.

Filan vahs, Jack swore. He rapped his knuckles against his temple, as if that would silence it. *If you can't give me solid information, then keep your mouth shut.*

But his thoughts were abruptly quieted by the faint sound of someone screaming, and as he focused, it became clearer.

A woman was evidently attempting to rupture her voice box. It was followed by shouts of outrage and a loud curse. But it was from a different voice this time. Another woman. She was yelling for support.

Sylvie, Jack guessed easily. Her voice was familiar enough, and so was her tone. *She's nervous.*

He'd been in enough unfavorable situations with her to realize that much. And before he knew it, he was running.

Away from the path before him.

You mustn't stray, the voice warned, ***answers lie beyond. Here, only more questions await. Deceptive mirrors. They seek your downfall.***

Jack disregarded it. Come what may, he wasn't going to ignore cries of danger. Not when they were so close. Certainly not when he knew something could still be done. He didn't even know what answers it spoke of. Nor did he want to.

Not yet anyway.

As Jack bolted inside a narrow corner, he came face-to-face with a pillar of black. He muffled a scream when it moved. Alive and terrifying. A faceless entity with the body of a man. Whose smooth mask cracked open at the mouth, just enough for the man within to curl his lips. It was a difficult task, Jack judged, from the way dark tendrils tried to sew his mouth closed again.

The man screeched, desperately clawing at the remaining hairs on his head. His eyes were next. They flew open to reveal bright red irises that made Jack's blood boil. Familiarity washed over him. Jack knew those eyes. So similar to his own. He only knew of one other Elementalist in the Drowned Tower.

Rior Wolden.

Despite the blurriness of both their visions, Jack knew Rior recognized him as well. Because recognition flashed across his gaze. Before it was lost to the sudden tremors that wracked his body.

Rior gasped for breath.

He felt his sanity slowly come undone under the constant

thrashes of pain, and he tried his best to separate himself from the blackness across his form. To no avail. The tendrils reached over once more, threading Rior back in darkness.

No, Jack realized. As he bent his knees, magic thrumming. The extra surge of power that coursed through his veins was, for once, a welcome feeling.

That isn't him.

***

"Hurry!" Sylvie demanded, shaking her freshly injured limb around like a rag-doll.

Sylvie nursed a cut running the entire length of her arm. She swallowed back a scream at the sight of her own fat, and instead focused on rapidly blinking her eyes to hold back the tears threatening to spill over. Ethil was behind her, hurriedly murmuring an incantation to help ease her pain. As she flipped through her grimoire in search of what Sylvie could only assume was a proper mending spell. Sylvie gnashed her teeth, clamping her jaw shut. As they continued to sprint after Rior.

What happened? Sylvie thought.

Before Rior could deliver another slice to her arm, he'd suddenly stood stock straight, disappearing down the hall in a flurry of wisps. As if he'd sensed something was amiss.

Where is he going? Sylvie wondered, as she and Ethil rounded a corner in search of the dark unknown that encased Rior. To her surprise, Jack was there, engaging the thing. *What in Thelarius' name is he doing here?*

Sylvie narrowly dodged a stray blast of fire. It set a shelf ablaze, but to her dismay, it didn't stop there. The shelf was pushed back into a wall, where it shattered into dozens of tiny wooden projectiles. At that point, Jack finally found it prudent to change his fighting style. If it was in an effort to prevent any more damage within the Tower or simply because fire wasn't working, Sylvie neither knew, nor cared to—though she believed it to be the latter. She was grateful, so long as he stopped his reckless tactics, before he blew a hole in the wall.

Jack's hands emitted frosty smoke, patiently waiting for an opening.

"Jack!" Sylvie called, catching his attention, as he dropped to his haunches, narrowly avoiding a clean swipe to the face. Courtesy of the razor sharp claws formed around what was once Rior's arm. "What are you doing here?"

"Can't we talk about that later?" Jack yelled back, propelling himself against stone to jump past and behind Rior. Jack tried to touch his body with his icy hands, but he was forced back when Rior turned, almost slashing his fingers off.

"Take this," Jack submerged his fingers underwater and let his magic loose.

Ethil and Sylvie jumped on the arm of a leather chair protruding precariously above the water. Just as an innumerable number of cracks broke the air. Along with the water's surface. The water turned icy cool, hardening enough to drop the temperature just past the brink of acceptable.

Jack's ice, however, didn't last.

His eyes widened when Rior chipped the frost with simple slashes to the floor. He backed away, moving just past Rior's reach. Jack wasted no time and brought his hands up, blasting Rior with fire before he could escape. After what felt like hours, Jack finally stopped. Only to realize that the darkness around Rior remained unscathed by the touch of his power.

"You're joking," he said, stunned.

Jack dove, as Rior slashed at him.

"Sylvie! Ethil!" Jack called, dodging another strike that came dangerously close to chopping his head off. "Do I really need to ask for help?"

"Just a bit longer," Sylvie assured, looking around and trying to piece together a plan. While Ethil continued to heal her arm. Words Sylvie didn't know spilled like lightning from her mouth, even as her breathing turned erratic from being in such close proximity to the enemy. Ethil was used to supporting roles. But outside, where the frontline was everywhere, she'd certainly learned a thing or two about keeping herself in check.

Sylvie was impressed.

As a partner, Ethil was more than ideal. *Perhaps even more so than Reed,* she thought. Though she'd never tell Ethil that—or Reed for that matter.

Jack huffed, rolling his neck and shoulders. Determination in his eyes. "You have ten seconds, Syl."

He stood his ground, already tired of running.

Why is he only after me? Jack thought in disdain. Along with all of the ways he could effectively eviscerate the man before him. But first he needed to rip off his layer of magic resistant gloom.

Tiv could hold him down, he thought wistfully. *Where is he when I need him?* Jack looked up, cursing himself. *Following my plan, right… If he's lazing around, then I'm going to give that backwards turkey an extra nostril.*

Jack dodged another blow. Too late. A claw sliced his robes and slid over the flesh of his collarbone. Jack jumped back, wincing, as he tried to brush off the metallic scent of blood that assaulted his nostrils. His blood. Fresh and pungent. The cut stung, and Jack had the sneaking suspicion that it would leave a long grotesque scar if he didn't have it treated soon. Preferably by a Healer.

Speaking of Healers, Jack thought, looking over at the two women huddled together. They were whispering a strategy he couldn't hear. *Time's up.*

"Done," Ethil announced like clockwork. She held her hands up. A sign that her job was, indeed, complete.

And Sylvie was off. She ran to the narrow intersection Jack had initially come from and grabbed random objects from the water—all of them were either ruined or cut from glass. Their sharp ends, their only common feature. Ethil ran off as well, presumably to heal the Masters further down the hall.

At least, Jack hoped so.

"Jack!" Sylvie yelled, frantically waving her arms in an attempt to catch his eye. She did. "Bring him here."

"She says that…" Jack eyed his opponent up and down. He'd never feared for his life as much as he did now. And his hands trembled at the sensation. Rior wasn't susceptible to magic. None of his usual tricks would work. "But it's not that easy, is it?"

Jack cracked a grim smile. He was never one to back down from a challenge. Especially from one that scared him witless. He'd never realize his dream if he allowed fear to conquer his spirit. So, he stood his ground, and with renewed vigor, he fisted his hands so tightly they drew blood. The pain stopped the tremors, giving him something physical to fret over.

Tried and tested be damned. He'd tempt fate again. Happily, even. Magic coursed through his veins. It was even stronger than before. The cause was undoubtedly the faceless whispers ringing in his ears. And that, more than anything, was what truly scared him. But showing such a disgraceful face was simply out of the question. So, Jack stepped closer to his current bane. Only to be forced back as Rior made another swipe for him.

Rior's talons pierced the air, whistling with each attempt to dismember him. Jack frantically searched his surroundings for a weapon. Sharp, blunt, long, short—anything would do. So long as it was wieldable.

The Assembly needs to put weapons on display, Jack thought fleetingly. A wistful expression marred his lips. As he focused on Rior. *Why isn't he using magic?*

"Jack, I need you to freeze the ceiling!" Sylvie yelled, pointing above her. "Here! I need you to freeze here!"

"Oh, for the love of—and how do you expect me to do that?" Jack grimaced. He glanced up at the ceiling, wondering just how long it would take for his ice to reach her. A minute at least.

I have my hands full. I'm not a damn miracle worker.

Jack glanced at Sylvie, who was staring at him expectantly. This was a poorly conjured plan. But he had no other ideas at the moment. So, he ran to the nearest wall.

I shall aid you.

His personal deity was back. Wonderful.

Jack hated it.

I don't need your help, he mentally bit back. But as he placed his hands upon the wall, freezing it, his magic poured out in waves. Ice swept over stone blocks and chamber doors, covering everything in white gloss half a second after his hands touched the wall. He scowled at the sheer amount of power he exuded. Power he knew himself incapable of producing. Jack knew his limits. They were what kept him grounded in fights and sleepless patrols. Talent had its limits, and though desperation was a good catalyst, it certainly wasn't this strong.

And Jack didn't believe in miracles.

But he didn't dwell on it for too long. Because although he realized the power wasn't his own, Jack only had one thought at the moment. *Please don't let there be people behind those doors,* he prayed. Trapping hundreds of innocent practitioners wasn't exactly a golden mark—in anyone's book—but he took the lack of panicked screams as a good sign.

Rior closed in on him again. As Sylvie urged him to come to her, all the while throwing random objects at a chandelier on the ceiling.

She plans to drop it on him? Jack realized, and immediately wished he hadn't. *Like he'd fall for something so damn simple!* But this wasn't the time to argue. So, Jack shook his head and focused on Rior. It wasn't hard.

Rior attacked.

Jack frantically reached for the nearest weapon. A frozen torch. A useless thing that made for a poor shield. But that didn't keep his jaw from dropping when it split in two. Jack didn't allow himself to dwell on the loss.

Everything after happened in an instant.

The awful parry gave him just enough time to duck under Rior's arm and run toward Sylvie. For once, he was glad for his lithe figure. As he slipped past, running with a demon on his heels. Literally.

"Please work, please work," Jack mumbled under his breath.

He let out a string of curses when he almost tripped over a broken chair.

Sylvie continued to throw chipped wood, vases, and even soggy books at the chandelier above her. She unintentionally lit a few of them on fire as she did—signs of her frustration—but her work paid off. The ice over the metal chains slowly cracked under the pressure until only two remained. Just enough to hold it up.

Jack rushed past her then. His shoulder collided with the wall, before he could stop himself. He'd been running too fast to properly turn. And Rior wasn't far behind. But Rior continued to ignore her. His attention focused solely on Jack.

A fatal mistake.

Sylvie broke another chain on the chandelier.

It dropped down, snapping the other in its descent. By the time Rior looked up to notice the sharp piece of metal about to fall on him, it was already too late. It creaked as it hit his eye, cracking the black veneer and piercing his skull. Tendrils reached out in an attempt to wrap around the chandelier, but the metal had already taken its toll. The darkness around Rior responded to his fading life. They weakened with each second Rior spent stabbed by the pointed piece of metal.

It truly was a splendid decoration—and apparently a splendid weapon as well.

The tendrils wavered, unwrapping themselves from both the chandelier and Rior's body. As they receded back to another place. Somewhere deep inside of him.

With a sickening crunch, Rior's bones were crushed and his legs gave out. As he was completely flattened by the chandelier. Blood spilled over, creating a crimson pool at his feet that dirtied the rest of the water.

Jack slumped against the wall. He breathed out a sigh of relief, uncaring for the blood around him.

Sylvie inhaled deeply, gathering her composure. Before she glanced at Rior, who may as well have been just another splatter of blood for all the bone and red he was currently showing. The darkness was gone. It left him barely recognizable. Or was that their fault? Sylvie didn't dwell on the thought.

"A chandelier," Jack muttered in disbelief, staring at it with wide, exasperated eyes. "A *chandelier*. He's immune to magic, but a pointy piece of cheap metal does the trick. How'd you know?"

Sylvie shrugged. "I didn't."

He gave her a sour look. "Of course you didn't. I could've died, you know?"

"You would've thought of something."

"Oh, Silas' flames! Could you be any more—never mind." Jack shook his trembling hands in an attempt to reduce the tension coiled inside of him. He needed to move. "What's going on here? What happened to Rior? I even saw Cephas unconscious on my way here."

She didn't answer.

"Jack," Sylvie called in alarm.

He swiveled at the terror in her voice.

Was that strange darkness still around? He didn't want to deal with anymore fear inducing blobs that had the power to make men invincible to magic. He prepared to defend himself. Only to find that they were alone.

Jack gave her a look between stumped and irritated, lifting a brow when Sylvie stepped back in apprehension. Not even Rior prompted that sort of fear in her—and Rior was a loon. What did she see? Was there something wrong? Had she been injured? He eyed her, but found her perfectly intact, albeit a bit shaken. But that was only to be expected.

"What?" Jack asked.

Sylvie grimaced, holding her hands up. Fire appeared in her hands. And Jack sneered when she crouched into a defensive position.

"What's wrong with your eyes?" Sylvie asked.

He staggered in response. Jack found his reflection in the tainted water. The tendrils lingered. Little parasites that moved wildly about. The same ones that had encompassed Rior. Though his were smaller, remaining only in his eyes. More tamed. Under his control—he hoped. Jack held his hands up, trying to show her that he wasn't a threat.

"I almost died following your ridiculous plan," he told her, trying to be civil. But his voice came out more biting than he'd intended. "I'm on your side, Syl."

She visibly relaxed.

But her gaze remained alert. Her fingers still had the blue glow of magic. Jack could see the question in her gaze without her having to voice it.

Is he lying?

I'm no liar, Jack thought, chuckling. No humor to be found. *Whatever happened to Rior, won't happen to me. I'm not that desperate. I won't lose to a damn voice.*

But he didn't bother voicing his thoughts, because even he didn't fully believe them.

***

They filled each other in on what they knew. It wasn't much. By the time they reached Ethil, they'd already finished talking about the minute happenings during their brief time apart and were now drying their robes. Though Jack skipped the details of the voice in his head, deciding it best to keep that to himself. For now.

He had time.

The Heartstone wasn't going anywhere. Jack could see it beneath Sylvie's robes. It pulsed, fiercely and erratically. Far brighter than before. The song, however, was gone. That tantalizing voice had disappeared, and Sylvie was only left to wonder.

It's in my head, Jack thought in contempt.

He'd happily return it.

Ethil sat a distance away, holding a healing aid in her hands that strengthened the potency of her spells. As she busied herself with healing the large bear, who'd suffered incredible damage, judging by how long Ethil was taking. It reminded Jack of his own wound, and he wiped the dried blood from the scratch along his collar. His eyes widened at the lack of pain.

It had healed. Only a white line remained—not even jagged.

The only proof that he'd actually been injured. But Jack had a feeling that even that would fade. He didn't know how his wound closed, but he blamed the voice in his head. It seemed like a valid assumption.

Sylvie eyed him warily. She opened her mouth to speak, only to close it again, as Ethil walked up to them.

"I did what I could for Master Cephas and the bear," Ethil said. "They should wake soon."

"This is a waste of time," Jack muttered, glaring at the ceiling. His mind whirred with thoughts about who exactly could put three Masters in such a state.

Ethil plopped down between them with a drained sigh. They both leaned back, innocently looking away when Ethil pinned them with a demanding glare. "In the meantime, I demand to know what's happening. I let you two in and suddenly more blood is spilt! What was Rior talking about? A stone? She? And what in the world happened to him? I've never seen that sort of transformation before."

Sylvie abruptly stood. "I need to find Reed."

"Let me guess," Jack began, his mind easily piecing together the meaning behind those words. His eyes were filled with accusation. "You weren't here with Cephas, were you? You were looking for your partner. I thought we agreed that speaking to Cephas was the bigger priority."

"Don't ignore me!" Ethil huffed, indignant. "I have a right to know. You two aren't the only ones involved in this mess!"

Ethil remained unheard, as Sylvie turned to shoot Jack a careful glance. "I found Master Cephas, isn't that enough? Now, leave me be. I have to find Reed. We can't continue without Master Cephas' guidance anyway. I'll be back before he wakes."

"We can continue," Jack contended. He ignored the look they shot him, in favor of looking off to the side, where the dark trail still remained. Invisible to even Sylvie. He hadn't counted on that. "We just need to follow the path."

"What path?" Ethil and Sylvie asked simultaneously.

Jack pointed at the wisps. They coerced him forward, leading down the hall.

"I don't see anything." Ethil squinted. "Don't tell me this is just a gut feeling. Because I'm not going anywhere until you two tell me what's going on."

Jack sighed in frustration. "Look, even I don't fully understand what's happening right now. But I know enough to go down there." He pointed again for emphasis. "Isn't it better than waiting for these two codgers to wake?"

"No, it isn't," Ethil argued, poking an offensive finger in his chest. "We need a plan. They're there, and can help us make one. They *outrank* us."

"Well, I want to find Reed," Sylvie said petulantly, pointing at the hall behind her. "I'm not going to waste time sitting here. His room is right around the corner."

"Well, you can't go alone," Jack said, ignoring Sylvie's glare. "Haven't you learned anything from what just happened? Walking alone isn't the best idea."

"You were alone," Sylvie noted.

"For a few minutes!" Jack defended hotly. "And look how well that turned out. I had no idea that something immune to magic was walking around — or even existed for that matter. Had I, then I would've thought of a better plan."

"You mean you willingly separated from Tiv?"

"It was in the best interest of the entire Tower."

"I somehow doubt that," Ethil interrupted, ignoring Jack's scowl.

"So, we should all just separate then?" he asked, incredulous. His eyebrows lifted in pure disbelief. "Are the two of you really so stubborn? Splitting up will only get us killed."

"What do you propose we do then?" Sylvie asked. "I want to find Reed. Ethil wants to stay. And I have no idea where you want to go. Arguing amongst ourselves is an even greater waste of ti—"

He rests in the arms of his kin.

Sylvie stopped. Her jaw slackened, and in that moment, Jack knew with absolute certainty that she'd heard that voice.

He grinned, despite himself.

Why can she hear it? he wondered. *Why is it answering her? Because she's a Conjurer? Or is it because she has the Heartstone? What's so special about it? What makes it so different from the rest of the ones in Curran?*

"You hear it, too," Jack said. It wasn't a question.

Ethil looked between them, tilting her head in wonder. While Sylvie nodded. Her eyes stared unwaveringly into his own. No longer afraid of the tendrils that danced along his irises. Only a vague sort of understanding remained. But ambiguity was easily remedied. It was better than her thinking him insane.

Unconsciously, Sylvie gripped the Heartstone hidden under her robes. It still continued to pulse at an alarming rate—a glow only they could see. It illuminated the paleness of her skin and gave her veins a purple tint.

"His kin?" Sylvie asked, aloud. She was skeptical. Yet far more accepting of its ability to speak. "Who? Where?"

There was a moment of silence. Jack didn't think the voice would answer. But it did. And its rage made them both shudder.

In the forsaken arms of the traitor, Maurice!

Maurice? Jack thought. *A traitor?*

No.

He'd heard it refer to Conjurers and Elementalists as Thelarius and Silas once before. *A Healer then?* Jack concluded. Ten dozen people came to mind, but the one that stood out was a certain visitor from the Diamond Alps. Elder Serach.

Jack couldn't suppress the smirk that graced his lips. Finally, he was getting real answers. From riddles easily solved.

The voice laughed. A pulse shook the path before him.

Jack flinched as his vision was momentarily covered by the

colorless wisps in his eyes, before hundreds of grisly murmurs sliced through the silence. They convened into one and suddenly they were singing that familiar lullaby again.

> *My child, come to me,*
> *I'll guide you, can't you see?*
> *I'll see you past the binds,*
> *Past the shores as black as night.*

Sylvie looked toward the chorus of voices. They echoed against the walls, but they undoubtedly stemmed from the hall Jack had pointed down. They silenced everything. Even the whining mice. Sylvie wasn't able to see what Jack so easily could. But she could hear them. As clearly as she could the furtive whispers that blanketed the Drowned Tower's halls during the late hours before dawn broke.

And that was more than enough.

Amidst the haunting melody, the voice continued to laugh. A giggling monster. Its mirth was a warning that hinted at the daunting trials yet to come.

Avoidance, however, wasn't an option. They could only prepare themselves. But even preparation had its limits. And from the way Jack stumbled in distress, as he turned to hide his pain-stricken face, Sylvie knew that this was only the beginning.

20

Tiv whistled sharply, calling to attention the hundreds of practitioners currently squeezing themselves into one of the residential tower's loftier common rooms. They were a surprisingly rowdy bunch. Made up of older apprentices, though very few had mastered the art of respectable silence.

He should've known better than to gather undisciplined practitioners with little talent for magic. Most were passed along from master to master or had taken up another craft altogether—like rockwork or potions—but Tiv had little choice at the moment. He needed numbers, and the mystically unskilled outweighed the talented by a grand margin. The few primary apprentices he did have were brash, reckless, and foul-mouthed. But they made formidable allies, and more importantly, they were willing to follow him. Not completely, but enough to provide ample assurance. And in times of crisis, that's all he could really ask for.

Tiv did a quick headcount.

Seven, he noted. Tiv knew them well enough to know that three were missing their partners. *Where are they? Are they on patrol or did they just have a disagreement over the plan?*

From the corner of his eye, Tiv recognized a few from the Assembly blending in with the crowd. They covered their heads, but the way they walked spoke volumes. They could never fully blend into a horde of learners. But the Amorphs certainly had an easier time. Though that didn't stop Tiv's trained eyes from noticing a few insects with eyes too much like his own.

Why the Assembly didn't stop him, he hadn't a clue.

He could only assume that some were with Miriam, while the rest were neutral about the situation. They were so divided that none dared move in fear of inciting further madness.

But Tiv wasn't like them. Jack wasn't like them. And that, ultimately, was why they were here. Along with the rest of this merry parade of rebels. He didn't dwell on the Assembly's presence. Tiv needed to do his part, so his partner could do his.

You'd better be right about this Jack. If this fails, coercive tongues won't save us.

Tiv breathed in deeply.

"This is quite the turn-up," Tiv bellowed, impressed. A wave of silence washed over them. They settled down, giving Tiv their full attention. It was unnerving. But Tiv wasn't one to shy away from a crowd. He spread his arms and gave them a boyish grin. It had too much teeth, he realized, toning it down a tad.

"I suppose you're wondering why I called you all here."

The primary apprentices by his side scoffed in amusement. They knocked elbows and grinned mischievously at him.

Pom, an Amorph that was far too short for his age, stepped up. His small stature beguiled the unparalleled ferocity he showed in combat. Pom fiddled with a dagger. The blade had been polished to a shine, but the handle was worn. His fingers had left a depressed imprint over the tattered grip. It cast a glimpse of who he was underneath his toothy smile.

"You mean, why you had *us* call them here," Pom said.

"He's right, he's right," Khale, Pom's partner, agreed. He had unnatural red hair and a thick Astonian accent that was difficult to decipher. Thankfully, he'd been around long enough for most to get the gist of his words—so long as he spoke slowly. "Ain't like ya ta keep secrets, Tiv. Jack tell ya off again, eh? This another one of his crazy plans?"

"Of course it is!" Pom exclaimed, scoffing. "There's no good reason for this separatist to bother with these pups. They're still wet behind the ears! Jack can't possibly be serious about using them."

"Jack's fierce, but he seems ta be lackin' a few screws where it counts, yea? Hard ta follow ya when yer' usin' twats like these as actual support."

"God awful amateurs is what they are. I respect you and your partner's ideas, but even I know that you'd be better off getting a few of the older prigs amongst us. At least their skills are tested. Jack's plans work, but crazy has its limits."

That was putting it mildly.

"Kid's a maroon," Khale insulted with an easy smile. "Damn shame, that. Optimism n' strategically daffy ain't the best combination. But this is Jack we're talkin' about, yea? I'm sure he's got somethin' ultra up his sleeve."

"Shut it," Tiv chided. He glared, but considered their words all the same. They voiced his doubts. And he wondered for the hundredth time if this could actually work. Never mind that most of the practitioners on their side were untested, but even the primary apprentices had their problems. Excessive pride. Hubris that even he wasn't exempt from. Their ability to not be embarrassed by their blatant animosity wasn't helping either.

It was uncanny how many traits practitioners of the same rank shared. Tiv felt like he was dealing with another version of Jack and himself. The Institute was just a confined space filled with people that hated each other. Few were likable. Some were tolerable—barely. And the rest were just Snuffs in fancy robes blessed with the ability to speak.

There were plenty of classes and societies where practitioners could find like-minded individuals. But those never lasted long. Favoritism was key to climbing the Institute's ladder of excess. So long as one of the higher-ups liked you, others were a thing of fiction. People no longer mattered. It wasn't as obvious in the Tower, but hint at cooperation, and hatred was quick to rear its ugly head. As if the world had fallen apart in that instant.

"Can we get on with it?" Olivia asked, impatient. She was a Healer that had the skills of a rogue. Along with the personality to go with it. Olivia had a reputation of being a high-strung tempest. As volatile as she was violent. 'Quick temper, quicker kick,' was a phrase her peers birthed and associated with her. The moment she spoke, both Khale and Pom stilled their lips. "If this is just another one of your terrible pranks, Tiv, then say so. I came because I thought we'd be doing something other than standing around and watching over spoiled curs that lack promise."

The crowd erupted with shouts of angry fury.

"How dare you!" An unknown practitioner yelled.

"I didn't come here to be insulted!"

"I should've known better than to expect anything from self-important bastards."

"*Amila kariv!*" someone shouted in a tongue none of them understood. But the tone was hostile enough for them to know that it wasn't anything pleasant.

Tiv groaned in frustration.

What's wrong with these people? Tiv thought, watching dozens of practitioners make for the exit. He may have had a stubborn streak, but even he played nice when the situation called for it.

Why do I always get stuck with the hard jobs?

Pom childishly stuck his tongue out, egging them on.

"Enough!" Tiv yelled, seizing their attention once again. He turned on both parties. Both stepped back from his glare. Irritation radiated off of him in waves, and Tiv struggled to tame it. He succeeded. Though his hands still shook with barely restrained fury. He needed to hit something. Preferably hard and breakable. Tiv settled for a deep breath instead. Slow and steady. Enough to calm his nerves. A tentative finger reached out and touched his elbow. Tiv looked down to see a young boy with blue eyes using his magic to soothe his tense muscles.

A child? Tiv wondered.

"Roval!" a young woman stepped up, pulling the boy back.

Tiv nodded in gratitude, making Roval grin, before he was dragged out of sight.

Everyone waited for Tiv to gather his bearings. All traces of anger and jest were gone from their eyes, replaced by curiosity.

As Tiv donned a mask of seriousness.

"This isn't a game," Tiv said, pointedly looking at his peers. They recoiled when his lips thinned. "It's not a laughing matter. It's not a joke. And it isn't some ridiculous prank. We have a problem! Don't you feel it? A *real* problem that we can't deal with alone. It's not on our borders. It's at our doorstep—no, it's inside the Tower. The Assembly is in on it as well. They're fighting amongst themselves. Don't you see that? Don't any of you see that? Why else would only certain practitioners amongst you be allowed to patrol with the primary apprentices? They're wheedling their way into our ranks. Splitting us up from the inside. They want us to leave the Institute! They want to take it from us!"

Tiv ignored their gasps.

"And how do you know this?" someone asked, hidden within the startled masses.

"Because I've heard it," Tiv told them. "I've seen it. There's an intruder. Here, inside this very tower. Where we sleep for Pernelia's sake!"

"Do you mean Rior?" another faceless person called out. A chorus of agreement followed. "Or the Elder? Things have been going wrong ever since they arrived. What did they do?"

Tiv shook his head. "Not them."

"Then who?"

He shuddered, thinking about the haunting wisps in Jack's eyes. The way Jack spoke to an invisible force, as if he'd gone mad, was enough to put anyone on edge. But not enough to make him lose sight of his latest goal. Tiv needed to unite his peers. So, that they could assist those like them—the ones that had no part in this. That was the beautified reason.

The truth was simpler. Less noble. More despicable.

Jack wanted them to make noise. Sprinkle chaos. Become distractions. Anything to make the traitors riddled in amongst them nervous. All for the sake of luring the Masters that called for evacuation out. While Jack ran off to find the reason behind all of this.

It was a good plan. Albeit, exceedingly selfish. But not in a terribly noticeable way.

It was, for lack of a better word, very Jack.

Besides, Tiv thought, *causing chaos won't be too hard.*

Men were savages by nature. They just needed a reason to run around. The only thing that gave him pause was Master Celaris. But he supposed he'd just have to apologize to him later. Tiv was against moving without properly informing his mentor first, but the situation had changed.

His personal code no longer mattered. Not in the face of strange deities that had the power to enhance magic.

"Who?" Tiv repeated, arbitrarily grinning.

He had no idea.

"They killed Duward," Tiv revealed. The crowd gasped, but from the corner of his eye, he saw his fellow primary apprentices scowl at the revelation. Some had been told, while others merely speculated. But at least they all agreed that something was wrong. That was more than enough.

"One of our own was killed in these very halls," Tiv exclaimmed. "And the murderer and his comrades are still walking around, and you ask, *'who?'* Does it really matter?"

Someone from the Assembly finally stepped up to stop Tiv's tirade. He'd revealed too much. No one had expected him to stir such madness.

But it was already too late. The words were said. The damage dealt. The crowd erupted into a frenzied throng of angered shouts and excitement. Many wanted the chance to prove themselves to the little that remained of the *true* Assembly. They already fabricated stories in their minds, filling in the blanks on their own. Tiv let them. He didn't have the truth. Not yet anyway.

As soon as the nameless Master stepped out, a hundred eyes locked onto him. The gears of betrayal spun.

And there was no stopping them.

***

Sylvie looked up in alarm when she heard a stampede of footfalls echo above her. Heavy and urgent. There were far too many to be a simple intruder. Which could only mean that her fellow practitioners were running about. She heard their shouts in the distance. Their words were garbled, but still discernable amidst the accompanying silence.

"It's starting," Jack said vaguely. He stopped to look up, before he dismissed the sounds and continued on his way. "We need to hurry."

"What's going on?" Sylvie asked.

"My brilliant plan, of course." He gave her a rascal's smile, featuring an excess dollop of pride. Too smug for his own good. "We're forcing the mastermind to make a move. Well, him and his comrades. Though they aren't comrades per se. I suppose you could call them the cowards of the Assembly. I like that word. *Cowards.* Not deserters. Not traitors. But cowards. It has a pleasant ring to it. The truth always does. When it's not blowing up in your face at least."

"Charming," Sylvie said sardonically.

"Don't give me that. Play along, will you? This plan will succeed. I can feel it. I've attempted rasher things, and in shoddier conditions at that. But my instincts rarely fail me. The fact that I'm still here is proof of that."

She looked skeptical. "I'm sure they won't now."

"You don't sound it." He frowned. "Nor do you look it."

"You planned on forcing the mastermind to move by mobilizing an army of practitioners, but won't they just get in our way? They're untrained. Wild cards are unreliable. Their numbers might allow them to catch a few cowards, but when it comes down to it, they might just cause more problems for us. What if they suspect us as well? Dealing with them will be troublesome."

"Tiv gathered them, so that rules me out."

Sylvie sneered unattractively. "Selfless, aren't you?"

Jack shrugged. "I try. But I'm sure you'll be exempt as well. So long as you stay by my side."

"And Ethil?" Sylvie asked, peering behind her to where Ethil sat by Master Cephas' side. They were already a good distance a-way. Soon, Ethil would be little more than another unrecogniz-able speck.

"What about her?" Jack asked, silently debating whether or not Ethil would follow them. It was likely. Curiosity was difficult to quell. "She's busy watching over three masters. One may be dead, but her innocence is sealed. Traces of her mending spells are all over Cephas."

"They had a taste of freedom from the Assembly. Who's to say they won't just get rid of Master Cephas? And Ethil along with him? It would be the perfect opportunity."

"Unless the Hunters finally make their move."

Sylvie's eyes narrowed in suspicion. "Careful, Jack. Some might think you actually want them to leave the shadows. They might even find out about the run-in we had with that Amorph in Tearwood. The one who taunted and got away. Don't tell me you're doing this to lure him out?"

"The thought had crossed my mind," he said honestly. "But no. I'm not that selfish. I want to know why they haven't done anything, and I'd like to see how many are hidden here."

"So you are trying to lure them out."

"Well, don't just say it. The walls have ears, Sylvie."

"You don't have to go through all this trouble, you know? You could always ask that voice," Sylvie commented off-handed-ly. But her tone held an edge to it that told him she wanted answ-ers as well. As much as he could give. It took two to make a secret, and the Heartstone—along with matters directly related to it—was, for the moment, theirs. And theirs alone. The only other who'd been able to see it was Rior. But he was dead.

"Who… what is that thing, Jack? What did it do to you?"

Jack stopped. He knew this was coming. But that didn't ma-ke him dread it any less. Some magical entity was speaking to him and enhancing his magic like an extra circuit. How could he tell her something so farfetched? Would she even believe him?

There was only one way to find out.

***

Ethil had no intention of following them. Not after they'd continuously dodged her questions with practiced ease. Avoidance was a talent many possessed, but Jack and Sylvie were exceptional at it.

She'd suspected they'd be. They were the only ones of their kind within the Drowned Tower, ergo giving them almost instantaneous fame. And the popular were a constant topic of interest in any society—especially closed ones. Gossip spread like wildfire. With each new batch of practitioners that entered their halls, the names, Jacques Dace and Sylvie Sirx, were always tossed into social chatter. So, it was no surprise that they'd honed a few extra skills over the years. Even mastered ones some had yet to grasp the basics of. They simply had more incentive to do so.

It still annoyed her all the same.

Ethil loathed to admit that she didn't have the power to force them to answer her questions. Which is why she'd petulantly decided to remain with their unconscious Masters.

As far away from them as possible.

But that didn't stop her from watching, as they walked further and further away. They didn't stop, uncaring for whether or not she remained. And that, more than anything, irked her. They didn't ask her to come. They didn't force her. Didn't even entice her with sweet smiles and half-baked promises. Yet she felt compelled to follow. Her instincts told her to. Even as the more rational part of her urged her to stay behind.

They need a Healer, Ethil told herself. She spared Columbus a glance. *So does he.*

Then, as if forcing her to decide, dozens of practitioner's shouted through a large hole in the ceiling. Their voices echoed across the floor, disturbing the mice. Unrecognizable and distant. The footsteps heading her way, however, told her they wouldn't be for long. Ethil didn't think as she waded her way through the water, tracing their steps.

Ethil wanted answers.

And they undoubtedly left with Jack and Sylvie.

They knew things the Assembly didn't.

About Duward. About Rior. About what was happening in the Drowned Tower. They may have even been the cause of some of it. Of that, she was certain. Because Jack and Sylvie had never been close. Had they been, then surely, more baseless prattle about their relationship would've existed. They rarely spoke. But even then, many still questioned their connection, simply unwelling to accept that no such rapport existed in the first place. If they were at least friends, then Ethil had no doubt that she would've heard of their affability toward each other.

Gossip was bothersome that way.

Ethil didn't believe in hearsay. Only ignorant fools would, but she did believe in people and their ability to stalk.

Jack and Sylvie weren't friends. That was the truth. And from the way she remembered them glaring hotly at each other in the Iniquities Chamber—what seemed like a lifetime ago—they were hardly even acquaintances. Certainly not amicable ones. So, to suddenly become so familiar in such a short time was nigh impossible. Not unless they were forcefully bound by an adhesive spell, but the chances of that happening were slim to none. There was, however, another more believable affix.

Far simpler, yet just as strong.

What better way to bind two people together than a secret? Ethil thought, feeling quite proud of herself. *But what is it? Confidential information, surely. Of the highest degree! They're definitely plotting something.*

So, she followed them.

She hid behind broken furniture and ducked into corridors when they turned their heads. Ethil knew they noticed her, but she didn't care. If she snuck around long enough, then perhaps they'd slip up. And she'd overhear a thing or two about the secret they kept so close to their hearts.

From the way Sylvie kept grasping at an unknown object hidden just beneath her robes, and how Jack glanced at her whenever she did, perhaps that was a literal description.

As Ethil lost herself to her suspicions, she remained oblivious to the soft paces crawling along her robes. Another stalker. Like her. But far more discreet in its patterns—only moving when it was time to. The head of a newt curiously peered out from the hem of Ethil's mantle. Its black eyes were too great for its tiny head.

And suddenly, without her knowledge, Ethil was once again part of a pair.

21

Reed was trapped in a delirious haze of his own making.

His head felt as though it had been pommeled by the thickest of tomes. Perhaps it had. Reed's mind was too cloudy to recall anything of real substance. His thoughts consisted of little more than the ache that seized his body and the silence. The horrid silence. Even his own breathing sounded muffled to his ears. The flaming things. They had one job.

The world was still—or so he believed—his vision was lost to blurs. He could hardly move his fingers; they ached for his grimoire. He felt naked without it. But at least he was alive to realize its absence. Even his thoughts became more lucid as the seconds passed. Though he still had yet to regain control of his senses.

Perhaps a few more minutes would do.

His instincts, however, urged him to move. An impulse he couldn't quite follow. Nor did he fully want to. And though Reed felt as if a thousand stones weighed him down, his strained mind did manage one thing.

"Sleep a little longer," a voice whispered.

The blow that struck him left him little choice.

***

Serach gasped in momentary panic.

Not because of the angry shouts he heard hollow against the stone. Not because of the mouthful of blood he was forced to spit out, as he healed the letter cutter wound on his arm. And it certainly wasn't because of Reed's blood that unintentionally soiled

his shoes, as the gaping wound on the back of his head bled across the floor. Serach's surprise stemmed from a simpler cause.
One far more base. It affected all Masters of Lore at least once in
their lifetime. A cause so banal that he would've laughed had it
happened anywhere—or to anyone—else.

But this was the Drowned Tower.

Enemies were everywhere. The slightest mishap yielded rad-
ical concern, and when Serach felt another jolt course through
him, his worry only intensified.

The Demar Spell he casted on Rior had dissipated.

Serach knew his apprentice well enough to rightfully conclude that he'd never do such a brash thing on purpose. Nothing
inspired loyalty like debt. Either someone had killed him or he
was forced to fight without constraint, and accidentally dispelled
their connection. Serach believed it to be the former. Rior was
skilled—Serach prided himself on that fact—mere fluctuations in
his magic weren't good enough reasons for him to accidentally
break their bond.

But a fatal injury was.

And the erratic footsteps Serach heard did nothing to ease
his troubled mind.

Have they discovered my plan? he thought, but quickly shook
his head in denial. *Impossible. It's too soon. Someone's gathering them
for something. Someone from the Assembly, perhaps? Or have those
pesky Hunters finally decided to make their move?*

Serach glanced at the vials thrown about the nearby counter.
Only one flask held his eye. It contained the same tonic he'd given
Rior. Except a larger *Orivellea* crystal lay inside, floating along the
outer rims of the dark haze at its center. Far more potent than any
before it. It made him recall the bone chilling sensation he felt
whenever he was near an *Orivellea* crystal. Raw magic that whispered against the bumps of his skin. He didn't miss the feeling, but
this was different. The dark haze completely overshadowed any
effects the unexposed magic circuits had on him—and the rest of
the world for that matter. It negated it. All the while absorbing

the crystal's energy to fuel its own.

Just as it did with Miriam.

When she'd served her purpose, all that was left was to become food for the darkness within. The same haze that gave her power betrayed her in the end. What those tendrils could do once consumed by an incompatible host was frightening, indeed.

"Is this your doing?" Serach asked, knowing he wouldn't receive a response. This was a diluted piece of the whole. Only useable—and only a threat—once consumed. It couldn't speak to him. Even if it could, he wouldn't be able to hear it. And that was perfectly fine. From what his past experiments had told him, it wasn't the most pleasant of experiences. "I've brought you away from the Diamond Alps just as you wanted. Yes, we had a few mishaps along the way. That pesky deserter running off with you for one. But in the end, I still successfully brought you to the east. And isn't that better than remaining locked away in the north? Where you were left to die a slow and meaningless death? I could have left you there, you know, or I could have buried you in the ground. Who would find you then? Surely, not the one you seek. If you want me to continue hauling you around, you must do as I say."

The darkness remained unresponsive.

As expected. But it didn't stop the rush of fury he felt from a dam long crumbling. He didn't come all this way to hear the echoes of his own voice.

"Shall I take your silence as consent?" Serach continued, looking at it appraisingly. He didn't mind speaking to it. Because he didn't want to dwell on the fact that he may have actually lost something he considered important.

"I wonder then why my plans continue to fail me."

No. They didn't fail.

Serach rejected that word. His plans were merely suffering from a few setbacks. Awry disarray could always be straightened out. He'd adjust. He always did.

With or without his primary apprentice.

Even if he wanted to, it was too late to turn back now. Serach was close. He could feel it. And though Rior's whereabouts remained unknown, he knew there could only be one reason for that.

Jacques, Serach thought, snorting contemptuously. The Dace spawn proved to be more trouble than he was worth, but he should've figured that considering his parents. *He's definitely here. Rior wouldn't have disobeyed otherwise. Which means…*

Serach spared the flask another glance.

The brain is here as well.

He beamed in anticipation. All of his adversaries were in one place. The only thing left was decide which to deal with first.

"I suppose that impostor comes first," he said, pocketing the flask. Along with the tome Rior had acquired for him. He double checked his surroundings, making sure to kick his two unconscious guards for good measure. Haste bred incompetence, and he couldn't afford any more mistakes.

It was a good thing he had Rior prepare everything beforehand. Serach made a mental note to find evidence of his primary apprentice's death before proceeding with the final step of his plan. But that was if—and only if—he had the necessary time. If not, then he'd just have to count his losses.

Apprentices were replaceable. Everyone was.

Serach bent down just long enough to heal Reed's head with a rudimentary healing spell. Only strong enough to stop the bleeding. Serach grabbed Reed by the ankle and dragged him along, apathetic to his plight. So long as Reed didn't die, then that was enough. Reed was, after all, an important bargaining chip in his scheme. His death would just complicate matters when he found Columbus. As he passed, Serach's fingers grazed an aged book mounted on a wooden stand. His personal volume. Silver lined its pages. His name was engraved in fine script over the cover.

Serach Beau.

"I shall return for you," he muttered. A personal promise. "When I restore this branch to its former glory. Even if that means taking it with me to the First Zenith's side."

The stage was set. History would record this day. When the skies cleared and dawn finally peaked, he'd reclaim his rightful place as Arch Poten of the Drowned Tower.

It was only a matter of time.

***

Columbus woke to a noisy crowd of chattering practitioners. Just loud enough to be bothersome. They were huddled around Orpha's still form. The Amorph Master was either asleep or as well as. Columbus believed it to be the latter, judging from the melancholy looks on his audience's faces. Some, though, had awe filled eyes that not even sadness could hide. They were stricken by the sight of Orpha's griffin transformation. He didn't blame them. It wasn't everyday they saw a creature of legend. Even if it was just another Amorph. Most could hardly assume a proper lion, never mind a hybrid.

But no expression could compare to the utter blankness that clouded Celaris' gaze. He was a despondent shell. A stranger cloaked in familiar features that stared straight ahead, blind to the world around him. Columbus tried to stand and comfort him, but he immediately crumpled under his own weight, garnering the attention of the gawking practitioners.

"You're awake!" they said in unified excitement.

"So I am," Columbus mumbled, his throat scratchy. He slowly fell back into a seat, momentarily scrutinizing Celaris, before he gave the gathering crowd his undivided attention.

Columbus hardly recognized them. He'd seen one or two in passing. Some had even interrupted his classes on more than one occasion, but he didn't know them well enough to ascribe names. He did, however, know that they weren't primary apprentices. They weren't even on the roster of those skilled enough to do the Zenith Council's bidding. Had they been, then surely they wouldn't be shaking so noticeably.

"Who allowed you out of your chambers?" Columbus asked. As hurriedly as his pounding head allowed. "Or did something happen? Is everyone alright? Where are your Masters? Where are the primary apprentices I assigned to watch over everyone?"

They hesitated for a moment, before one was brave enough to step forward. His head bowed in uncertainty.

"Tiv gathered us," he said.

"Tiv?"

"We're here to rescue you!"

"Pardon?"

"Don't worry, Master Cephas! Tiv explained everything, and we're here to offer our support to the true Assembly!"

"The what?"

"The true Assembly!"

Columbus groaned. He didn't know the details, but he had a good gist. One thing, however, was clear—

Tiv had obviously lost his mind.

What is that boy thinking? Columbus stressed, looking at his broken team. Orpha was dead. Celaris mourned him. He had a handful of inadequately trained practitioners staring at him in awe. As they spouted nonsense about the "true Assembly." And Tiv was running around doing whatever he pleased. With other troublemakers of his grade no doubt.

Where is my primary apprentice when I need her?

Columbus' eyes widened in horrid realization. The Demar spell he'd cast over Sylvie was gone.

When? he panicked, attempting to sort through his blurry memories during his fight with Miriam. *While I was asleep?*

Columbus shook his head. It didn't matter. All that mattered now was the Institute. He could find her later.

Assuming Jacques didn't convince her to leave the Tower with him. He shook his head once more. Noticing, but not really caring about the way some of the apprentices eyed him with wariness. *She wouldn't do that. She must've encountered something. But, what?*

"Master Cephas!" a boy called, picking up a drenched pouch from behind a cushion. It had been half sunken in a shallow part of water. The boy had keen eyes. "Do these belong to you?"

"They're rocks," an apprentice he couldn't pinpoint scolded. "What could he possibly do with rocks?"

"But look." The boy held up one for emphasis. "They glow when you touch them!"

Columbus tore open the pouch, hurriedly examining its contents. It was filled with healing aids. They were only given to select Healers—mostly those who frequently left the Tower. He turned the sack over, searching for a name. Columbus found one stitched carefully to the side in intricate script. Done by either a trained hand or by someone with far too much time than they knew what to do with. Perhaps both.

Ethil Mane, Columbus read. His eyes widened. *Did she come here?*

Columbus staggered over to Celaris, who was still lost to the world. He placed a hand on his forehead, trying to find any traces of foreign magic. Celaris didn't even seem to notice. There were a lot of external pathways around his body—too many to not be concerned about Celaris' health. Columbus checked himself next. Only to find the same thing. Except they were centered around his head.

"Ethil truly was here," Columbus said, his mind whirring. As he rechecked his surroundings. "Was she on her own?" His gaze settled on the crowd of apprentices. If they were ready and willing, then he might as well put them to use. "Who here knows how to search for traces of magic around objects?"

Half a dozen tentatively raised their hands.

"And who among you has taken one of Master Gllaren's tracking lessons?"

Another three joined them.

"Good enough," Columbus muttered, nodding at them. "I want the nine of you to survey the hall for any signs of other practitioners, and try to find from this mess of furniture which way they could've gone. It's a long shot, but any information you find could be worthwhile. Have an Amorph report your findings back to me. And no one, under any circumstances, is allowed to enter any of the rooms. Is that clear?"

They shared a hesitant glance, before nodding in resolution at the order. Columbus waited until they were out of earshot to point at a few of the more burly Amorphs amongst them.

"Two of you bring Celaris and Orpha somewhere safe. You four stay with the others here. In case they need extra manpower. Those left, follow me."

Columbus turned, not even waiting for them to acknowledge the order. As he strode down the hall. He staggered a bit, but quickly cured his own light headedness with a quick spell. His magic circuit was being dangerously overused and he'd need to do something to get his stamina up, before he passed out. He knew where he needed to go—Serach's quarters.

All this started when he came to the Tower. Even if Serach wasn't there, it was still the best place to start searching for clues. Not even an overworked magic circuit could stop him from getting there. His health be damned.

He lifted an eyebrow, as he rounded a muddy corner.

It reeked of blood.

There's blood in the water, Columbus realized when he saw a grotesque body squashed under the weight of an iron chandelier. He reigned in his panic with a long, shaky inhale. *Who is that?*

A few of the apprentices stumbled back in sudden terror. One even hurled. Another did out of sympathy. And Columbus stepped toward the body, finding it just a little more preferable. He moved what he could of the large piece of metal. Only to cringe at the sight that lay beneath.

What was once a face had been inhumanely crushed beyond all recognition, leaving only a mass of exposed ligaments and shattered bone. *A man*, he assumed from the rough contours peeking through clinging robes and the crippled broadness of broken shoulders, still unable to fully mask what must have once been a tall, commanding figure.

Columbus inspected the faceless man's robes to find a small patch that spelled his name and branch in tattered stitching.

Rior Wolden, he read, his eyes widening. *Northern Branch.*

"Master Cephas," one of the practitioners called, shakily pointing behind him. "Look."

As Columbus turned, he saw a thin coat of ice along the wall. It sealed the door of a large chamber, and he was momentarily gladdened by the fact that he ordered a complete evacuation of this level—and those below it.

Columbus pressed a hand against the frost. And a dark aura suddenly appeared before him, taking the form of a monster to bare jagged teeth. Columbus yelped, jolting back in surprise. He was sorely reminded of when he was pulled into the darkness of Reed's chamber. The apprentices immediately threw questions of confusion and concern, but he ignored them.

He merely waved a hand, telling them to step away from the ice. From the unknown assailant's magic that had the disturbing ability to conjure monsters to lash out and scare others witless. Despite not being present.

Rior's? Columbus speculated. *No. Then it should've dispelled the moment he died. Miriam's, perhaps? But then why is Rior dead? Are they not on the same side?*

He didn't know, and he wasn't sure he wanted to find out.

Another practitioner, maybe? Jack?

He shook his head in utter denial.

Columbus didn't even want to entertain that particular notion. If Jack was back inside the Institute, then they could have even bigger problems on their hands should something happen to him. The offspring of the influential were frustrating that way.

The ice trail ended in an odd place—right in the middle of the hall—as if the caster had planned to lure Rior to the end. Perhaps they had. From the state Rior was in, it was likely.

Could someone do this on their own? Columbus wondered. One person must've had to distract Rior, while the other broke the chandelier. Or perhaps the chandelier broke on its own. It was certainly possible. *Or is this Jack and Sylvie's doing? Perhaps Reed is with them,* he hoped.

A father's hope. One he couldn't afford to have now.

First, I need to find Serach.

Columbus eyed his companions. No. They were students.

During battles between the mystic, one tended to recognize the eyes of his comrades. He certainly did. They all had the same cold and unyielding eyes that greeted him in the mirror every day. But theirs were unhardened, slightly hesitant, and a little too zealous. The sort he didn't want to see alongside him. Not now. But he had little choice at the moment.

They'd prove their worth soon enough.

Columbus just hoped they wouldn't die in the process.

22

It astonished him how much could happen in the span of a few hours. Tiv frowned at the brutal display of aggression a number of practitioners displayed toward the Masters they caught. Some were more timid in their actions, while others wore their anger—or was it excitement?—on their sleeves. As if they'd actually done something to protect their borders. Or perhaps this was just their way of proving themselves capable of doing so.

Either way, it was unnerving.

And though Tiv was troubled by the thought, he wasn't surprised by it. In their eyes, they were helping by stopping a rebellion. A coup d'état from within the very halls of the Drowned Tower. Perhaps that was true. Perhaps there really was a planned revolt to overthrow those in power. A secret rebellion that could rock the very foundation of the Eastern Branch. Tiv didn't know. But he didn't say anything against it either.

They'd seize him with a noose if they found out their instigator wasn't sure of his facts. Still, people believed what they wanted to believe. In this case, that worked in his favor.

Many of the Assembly that voted for evacuation came quietly, not wanting to stir the other practitioners into action. Some fought back, succeeding in hurting the very people they were supposed to protect. This only sparked outrage, causing more practitioners to aid them in their plight. While other Masters chose to hide, running for a time until they were inevitably caught.

They had numbers on their side. Properly trained or not, so long as they were led by a skilled leader, then they made a nigh infallible hunting party.

It helped that the Tower was full of skilled Amorphs. It was a wonder why the supposed Hunters hidden amongst every branch had yet to make their move.

Tiv didn't know what to make of it.

Is it just a rumor? he thought. *Or are they waiting for something? More practitioners to choose sides, perhaps?*

Because though they had many, more than half of the practitioners still didn't agree with what was happening. They were easily detained, however. Knocked out and lugged into their rooms like the deadweight they were. Their doors were heavily enchanted to prevent them from leaving and guards roamed the halls of the chamber they stayed in. Those that were able to escape were treated the same as the 'betrayers' of the Assembly.

It was almost surreal how swiftly it all happened.

Tiv took a deep breath to calm his frazzled nerves. He couldn't afford to lose his composure. Not now.

From the corner of his eye, he saw a few of the practitioners dragging an injured Master to a crudely made prison cell. It was carved into the wall. Tiv hadn't a clue as to how they were able to do such a thing in such a short amount of time. But it seemed that some practitioners had taken up a rather strange—and disturbing—hobby of using bombs to mold stone. It was an ugly thing, but the glowing rocks around it suggested it had only the best of enchantments keeping it upright and impenetrable.

To the side, Tiv found a group of women crying, lamenting over something unintelligible. Even as they were cast inside one of the stone cells. A little boy stumbled along, calling for a girl— his sister? Another trailed after him, only to stagger and hurl all over his shoes. A group of younger practitioners saw this and snickered. As if this was just another everyday occurrence.

But, of course, it wasn't.

The ringing screams were a clear sign of that. The Drowned Tower looked like the southern side of Ferus Terria, and his eyebrows creased grimly at the thought.

The Southern Branch, or what many called "the Red Veld" wasn't well off. Its surrounding area was wracked by poverty and riots. Over the years, slavery had once again become common in those parts. Though not legal. Not yet.

The one thing Thelarius tried so hard to abolish was once again a reality. Man never seemed to learn from his transgressions. Only letting their mistakes go when their lives were on the line and a fistful of conjured fire was held to their wretched faces.

Well, Jack wanted chaos.

Tiv could say with certainty that he'd done his job well.

Perhaps too well, he thought.

His pride was boosted at the fact that he could cause such ruin from a few properly placed words, but the guilt in his chest gnawed at him. But not enough for him to cease their plan. He was prepared to protect the Tower. Even if that meant hurting its inhabitants. Perhaps that made him a monster. Maybe his morals were as twisted as the many he'd since rid of this world in the name of the Institute's beloved Eastern Branch. Or was it just because he could care less about most of the people around him? Again, Tiv didn't know. He wasn't one to sympathize with their suffering. In that way, he and Jack differed. Though Jack rarely showed his sympathy anyway, so perhaps there wasn't much difference after all.

Because results were key. Minor details could always wait.

If the needs were met, what did the process of its achievement matter?

What's change without a little sacrifice?

It was time for the next step.

The intruders had undoubtedly moved. Some of the Masters might have even hidden themselves amongst the practitioners. There was no sure way to tell. Though that didn't matter now. So long as they found the mastermind behind all of this then that was enough—for them and the Zenith Council.

Time to seal the floors.

***

Tiv jumped down the hole he and Jack made, cursing when he landed in a sea of drowned rats and soggy furniture. The smell was horrid and his nose scrunched in distaste. As he resisted the urge to hurl the little food left inside of him. He could only assume that the entire floor was drenched, thus only more sourness awaited him. The lack of fresh air clearly had its drawbacks. Tiv heard noises further ahead, and he moved forward to investigate, ignoring his sensitive nose in favor of more worthwhile things. He barely acknowledged Pom and Khale, who trailed behind him, mimicking his expression when the scent of dead rodents assaulted their senses.

"Are you sure it's alright to leave Olivia in charge up there?" Pom asked, lifting a skeptical eyebrow.

Khale agreed with an emphatic nod. "Olive's a bit rickety. Like she'll tippy off at any moment, yea? That ain't a sight I'd like ta see. Damn woman can make grown men cry. It ain't right, I say! It just ain't right!"

"Which is why," Tiv said sagely, "she's the perfect person to run that mess we made upstairs. They're all too scared to do something stupid."

"I still don't like it," Pom grumbled.

Tiv ignored them, focusing on the task at hand. He led them forward. Until they stumbled across one lone apprentice touching the walls and other random objects with a disgusted sneer on his face. His eyes were shut tight, as he picked up a rat. Only to immediately throw it back down when he didn't seem to find whatever it was he was looking for.

"Hey, kid!" Tiv called.

The boy snapped to attention. His back straightened, and his eyes swept the area. As if he'd just been caught doing something he shouldn't have.

"Over here, ratsy!" Pom shouted, waving frantically.

He saw Pom, promptly ignored him, and then cried, "Tiv!"

His eyes brightened, as he ran over, uncaring for the splashes he made with each step. He was drenched long before he reached them. "I heard about the meeting you held upstairs. I didn't get to attend, but some of my friends told me about it and we all decided to help. I was hoping to meet you!"

Khale scoffed from behind them. "An' what are we? Dirty underthings? We're here, too. Treatin' us like sons of ten–penny whores ain't exactly good manners."

"What's your name, kid?" Tiv asked, ignoring Khale's remarks. For both their sakes.

Pom blocked the boy's path, before he could come any closer to Tiv's bulky frame. Pom knew from a rather unfortunate experience that if he were to accidentally trip—he looked like the type that would—then direct contact with Tiv would result in a horrid head injury. Maybe even some memory loss. The likes of which they, as a group of Amorphs, wouldn't be able to heal.

Tiv had a tendency to roughly push away whatever fell on top of him. Acting first and thinking later.

"Who cares?" Pom interrupted the boy with a shrug. He pushed the kid back, disinterestedly watching him stumble. "Let's just call him 'Ratsy.' You can't expect us to learn the names of every single practitioner in this place."

"Yer tiny head might explode, yea?" Khale snickered in amusement when Pom gaped at the traitorous remark.

Tiv quieted them with a wave of his hand, allowing the boy time to answer. He despised greenhorns as much as the next primary apprentice, but if he didn't control himself while these two were around then he'd undoubtedly get caught in their pace.

"My name is Flask," the boy introduced.

They stilled.

Tiv knew he'd never forget the stunned silence that settled over them in that one instant of combined pity. When sheer shock stifled their urge to wildly laugh and made them forget their mutual animosity.

"Like," Khale began, shedding his accent and trying his best to carefully pronounce every letter, "the bottle?"

Pom was the first to break.

"Are you kidding me?" Pom sputtered, previous disbelief forgotten. As he held his stomach for dear life. "Flask? C'mon! That's just cruel. I bet you *hated* Beginner's Embrocology."

Flask's ears burned and he turned his head down to hide his embarrassment.

"Oh, plug it, Pom," Khale said, suffocating him in the crook of his elbow to end his laughing fit. Khale didn't stop. Not even when Pom turned a shade pinker and violently slapped his arm away. "Yer' name ain't that great either, scamp."

"It. Is. Amazing!" Pom choked out between breaths.

Tiv cleared his throat, suppressing the urge to grin. "Enough, you two. We have serious things to do. If you're going to be a bother, then go back topside and help Olivia."

Khale held his hands up in surrender, finally allowing Pom his freedom.

"So, *Flask*," Tiv stressed, glaring when Pom snickered again. Khale clamped a hand over his partner's mouth in an effort to silence his wild laughter. To no avail. It was as irrepressible as the rest of his personality. "What exactly are you doing here?"

"And why, oh *why*, would you willingly touch a dead rat?" Pom tacked on.

Flask grimaced. He discreetly wiped his hand on his robes, as if he could still feel its damp fur. "Master Cephas ordered us to check for any signs of lingering magic."

That shut Pom up instantly.

"Master Cephas?" Tiv repeated. "He was here?"

Flask nodded, hesitant at his sudden interest, and their collective solemnity. "We found him, Master Celaris, and Master Orpha a ways down the hall. They were patched up pretty well. By Ethil Mane apparently."

Ethil and Sylvie were here? Tiv wondered, shocked. *Did they meet with Master Cephas already? No, it doesn't matter. They must've seen Jack. Maybe even ran off with him. The problem now is figuring out where they've gone.* But first, he needed to find Master Cephas and ask what his orders were. Tiv doubted they'd move without guidance. Especially with rule abiders like Ethil and Sylvie there. But a flash of Jack speaking to an invisible deity entered his mind and Tiv grimaced. *Those two wouldn't actually believe nonsense like that without proof, would they? I know Jack definitely has none of that. But would they follow him, regardless?*

Tiv frowned at the possibility.

"And where are they now?" Tiv asked.

"Well…" Flask paused. "Master Celaris was brought to the upper floors. He's suffered heavy injuries. But he'll live."

"And Master Orpha?"

"Dead."

They quieted.

Pom abruptly grabbed Flask by the collar, shaking him and demanding he tell the truth. His eyes flashed with fury. Before Khale stilled his hand. And Pom directed his anger to the walls, vigorously punching and leaving cracks in the stone. Orpha was a highly regarded mentor amongst many of the primary apprentices. His skills were known far and wide, instilling as much fear as they did awe. But Pom was his primary apprentice—Orpha, his secoond father, assuming he even had a first. Though from the way Pom cried out in dread, Tiv concluded otherwise. Such horror could neither be faked, nor repeated.

Khale tried to get Pom to focus, yanking him back and speaking over his anger. But Pom wasn't listening. He viciously lashed out at everything and anything. While Flask stood a safe distance away, his eyes wide and puzzled.

He reminded Tiv of a startled duck.

Tiv watched them for a moment. It was as if time had slowed for this brief moment of sorrow, but he knew that wasn't true. They weren't special. Neither was their grief. There was just too much happening within the stretch of every second. And Tiv felt suffocated by it. He averted his gaze to the ceiling, silently looking up to where his own Master undoubtedly sat in a bubble of his own inconsolable sadness.

Orpha had been his partner for decades. So, his sorrow was as understandable as Pom's own. Perhaps even more so.

"And Master Cephas?" Tiv asked.

Flask looked at him. His eyes hesitant. "Last we saw, he was headed toward the Assembly's Tower. He split us up. Took only a few. Mostly Healers. The rest were left here to examine the wreckage."

"And what have you found?"

"Not much." Flask shrugged. "Just a hall of ice. Looks like the work of either a Conjurer or an Elementalist. But Master Cephas ordered us not to touch it, so I couldn't tell you who. Other than that, there were no other signs of magic. Except for the water. But we suspect it came from a leak since there are no traces of magic in it either. Oh, I also heard they found a body, but they wouldn't let me see it. I could smell it though. Unpleasant, I tell you. I'm not sure if—"

As soon as he veered off topic, Tiv sidestepped him. He had no time for nervous rambling. He'd see for himself.

A decision he instantly regretted when he came face to face with Rior's ghastly corpse. It lay in a pool of water and blood, pruning from the inside. A bulky rat latched onto his broken legs, using it as a temporary raft. And Tiv wondered just what kind of horrible things he'd done to warrant such a death.

Shooing away the rodent, Tiv inspected Rior's robes.

They were as sopping wet as the rest of him and he held his breath at the stench that radiated from underneath.

Pom and Khale poked around—both too jaded to speak. The other practitioners were considerate enough to give them a wide berth. While they searched for any clues those before them may have missed. They had little luck.

The only thing Tiv was able to ascertain was that Rior was, for all intents and purposes, dead. Anyone with eyes could see that. There was no more information to be found from his corpse. If the killer had taken it or if there was nothing to begin with, he couldn't say for certain.

"Find anything?" Tiv asked Pom and Khale, hoping they had more to work with.

They shook their heads.

Pom motioned for one of the practitioners. Calmer now, after walking and focusing on something other than death. But he still looked as if he'd been struck in the face with a shovel. A girl their age quickly stepped up, as Pom pointed to an ice covered door.

"How did the practitioners leave that room?"

"Leave?" she questioned, puzzled. "I'm not sure."

"Take your best guess," Pom said intimidatingly. The other practitioners took a collective step back at the sudden hostility in his voice, and she was left to sputter for an answer.

"I assume before the fight broke out," she stammered. "That chamb—the entire floor is deserted. We knocked on each of the doors. Not a soul. Same goes for the floors below and even the two above this one."

"Deserted?" Tiv asked, trying to recall if the last few floors had been abandoned or not. There were too many practitioners running around for him to tell. And he hadn't bothered to check inside the rooms. "Where did they go?"

"To the upper chambers?" she guessed.

They shared an uneasy glance.

There weren't enough practitioners along the upper floors. Not the older ones at least. And that's exactly what the lower floors housed—practitioner's long past the age of requirement. They lived their lives in comfort, uncalled by the Assembly.

Many established practitioners had shown when Tiv rallied them, but certainly not entire floors worth. There wasn't even that many running around at the moment. Of that, they were all certain. Tiv had initially pegged the lack of response from the lower floors on the fact that they were far too deep to properly connect with. But he saw now that he couldn't be more wrong.

"So, you mean... what?" Pom asked in disbelief. "An odd hundred or so of us just disappeared? Into thin air?"

"Either they're all hiding somewhere," Tiv speculated, "or we've gone completely blind."

"An' I don't think it's the last one," Khale said. "But if they're hidin' then where'd they run off to? Amorphs, I get. Transform into a tiny an' hide in some crack in the wall, yea? But what about the blue-eyes? They just stuff themselves in a chamber and pray no one sees 'em?"

"Actually," the girl interrupted, tentatively raising her hand. "We didn't open the doors. Master Cephas ordered us not to."

"Oh, for Pernelia's sake!" Tiv grumbled, throwing his hands in the air. "Why would he order something like that?"

"We don't know. He just told us not to—"

"Please tell me you're joking."

"—so we didn't."

"How did you find out there were no people inside then?"

"Well, some doors were already open," she revealed, not meeting his eyes, "and empty. Definitely empty. Dark, too. We tried knocking on the ones that weren't. Knocked and listened."

He'd heard enough.

Tiv stomped to the nearest chamber, ignoring the protests from the crowd. As he threw open the door. Water rushed inside and he was greeted by an eye full of darkness. He could make out the slight shape of furniture and stone, but the darkness was otherwise impenetrable. Even by the light of the hall.

"Hello?" Tiv called. He didn't dare step past the threshold, feeling as though the darkness might swallow him whole if he did. "Is anyone there?"

A tendril reached out. Slow and unsure. Afraid of the world beyond the door. Tiv took a step back, one hand grasping for the door, so he could trap whatever monster it was back inside. Just as another tendril flew out, grabbing him. Pom was by his side in an instant, slashing the length in half with his dagger. Only for another to latch onto the hilt.

Pom pulled away.

It pulled back.

23

Tiv tugged Pom back with an urgency that put desperation to shame. Pom cried out in agony. As he was trapped in a fierce tug-of-war between Tiv and the unknown, unwilling to let his dagger go. Despite Tiv's frantic screams ordering otherwise.

The rest stood in panicked shock, watching in frightened stillness as they struggled with the darkness—very much alive and very hostile—until a shrill cry pierced the air. High enough for them to know it was a woman, close enough for them to realize it belonged to one of the practitioners in the crowd behind them, but little else. Still, the sound was startling enough to snap them from their combin-ed reverie, and suddenly, they all sprang into action.

The practitioners filed into a long line, grabbing Tiv by the shoulders and pulling. As Khale, nearest to the door, slammed it shut, imprisoning the last vestiges of black.

A moment passed, where only the rough panting of exertion and frightened gasps filled the air. Before silence descended around them. Thick with tension and unspoken questions.

Pom, as usual, was the first to recover.

"What in Silas' holy flames was *that*?" Pom exclaimed, still slightly trembling. He scooted away from the door by his palms, not yet prepared to stand. "Did you see that thing? Everyone saw that, right? I'm not the only one? I'm not going crazy? There was really some kind of creature, and i—it…" Pom threw his hands up, exasperation ringing clear in his voice. "Snuff muffins!"

"Snuff muffins?" Tiv asked, his mind unwilling to let the

remark go, despite the situation.

"Oh, shut it." Pom sneered. "I was the one that almost got pulled in saving your ugly mug!"

Well, Tiv couldn't argue with that. So, he didn't. Instead, he dusted his clothes off and stood warily before the door. It looked normal. Disappointingly so. Chipped wood, an iron handle worn from age, and a poor lock. As if something hadn't just crawled out and tried to swallow them whole. As if it wasn't still there, lingering behind the easily breakable door for reasons beyond comprehension.

Behind him, the other practitioners clattered about the monster—what was it? Where did it come from? What happened to the others in the room? They were already thinking of names for Thelarius sake!—the shock and terror had evidently worn off, giving way to only excitement and mindless gossip. Just another story. Another scary legend of the Drowned Tower. But this was far more real. Tiv didn't know if they realized that. He certainly didn't want to be here when they did. Some already had. They were frighteningly silent, as the thought of death settled.

Pom and Khale's argument was much louder, and much more familiar. They quarreled in playful relief at Pom's safety, jokingly wishing otherwise. It was almost enough to drown out the thrilled ramblings of the crowd. Almost.

Tiv heard them, even as he cautiously placed a hand over the door's surface, silently wondering if whatever was inside could haul him in through the wood. He'd expected to feel movement from the other side, but was only disappointed when the door beneath his fingertips stood still. Even more so to find that when he placed his ear upon the wood, no sound greeted him.

What was that thing? Tiv thought.

"I see why Master Cephas didn't want anyone opening these doors now," Pom suddenly said, and Tiv turned to him with a start, realization dawning upon him.

"Master Cephas knew then," Tiv decided, his eyes shifting between the door and the hall. Where the others allegedly watched Master Cephas disappear down.

"Reckon he knows what happened ta the others, too?" Khale asked. "Maybe he brought 'em with him."

"It's likely, but," Tiv gestured to the door, shrugging as nonchalantly as his tense muscles would allow, "I think they're still inside. It's too dark to tell."

They stilled.

Behind them, the other practitioners stepped back in unison. Alarm once more making its way into their eyes. The three ignored their collective mood swings as best they could, trying to focus on the situation at hand. It seemed to be worsening the further they went. Made even more so, by the fact that they were trapped with a decision that would lead to even more problems.

They didn't know where to go. Above them, practitioners scurried about in revolt, sparked by none other than them. Below, they had no clue as to what sort of creatures lurked in the dark. And in the halls leading to the other towers, they knew nothing about the happenings within—or even where to go.

The one thing they did know was that unparalleled danger hid in plain sight, traversing the halls in the form of faceless intruders. Those that could shed light on their unwanted ignorance were either missing or off on some venture to stop all this. And all were too tight lipped to say anything of real value.

"I think we should find Master Cephas," Pom proposed. "Ask about this and tell him about what's happening topside. I don't know about you, but I don't want to get anywhere near that thing without knowing what it is and what it can do. It's clearly dangerous. More so than what we can handle."

"I don't know about that," Tiv said, looking pointedly back at the door. "Sure, it's dangerous. But so are we. And it might be holding the other practitioners inside. We should kill it, before it decides to come out."

"This isn't the time to be reckless," Pom told him, irritated and painfully aware of how hypocritical those words made him sound. But he was scared—it was showing—and he just wanted to leave this place. "What if they're dead? Then we'd be wasting our own lives. I doubt that thing just drags people in and leaves them be. Is it even killable?"

Tiv shrugged, clearly unconcerned. "It's alive, isn't it?"

"But," Pom paused, warily eyeing the door and fiddling with his dagger, as if he could still feel its pull, "what if we annoy it?"

"Or we can split," Khale proporsed. They turned to him with a start, belatedly noticing that the crowd behind them had gone silent with uncertainty. Their morale relying solely on their next decision and whether or not they got along. "We run around n' find Master Cephas, while you take these gomer—rookies," he coughed uncomfortably, "and go find Jack. We'll all seal floors as we go. That's why we came here, yea?"

"Well, yes," Tiv answered. "But Jack? Why?"

"He put ya up ta this, didn't he? Insane little twat. Too intense. But he's always got a few extra tricks stuffed up his arse. I'll bet my robes that he knows what that thing is. Maybe even knows why it's there."

"Assuming he'll tell us," Tiv muttered, peeved. He thought of Jack and the strange voice he claimed to hear. Tiv trusted him, but dodged explanations and unanswered questions tended to ruin that fairly quickly. "Jack isn't exactly the pinnacle of stability right now."

"So the rest of us are?" Khale challenged, lifting an eyebrow. Tiv wasn't quite sure how to respond. The man was insulting himself. "Y'know I don't pretend, Tiv. I know we ain't exactly the sharpest of people." Khale ignored Pom's loud protest. "That's okay though. Jack's blunted, too. The crazy sort of blunted. But I trust 'em. Enough to get us… well, me n' Pom really, out of this in one piece."

"That was disgustingly sappy." Pom blanched in distaste.

"What?" Khale asked, affronted. He locked Pom in a sleeper hold. "Care ta repeat that?"

Tiv sighed, watching them fool around. Again. As he mulled Khale's words over.

Well, Tiv thought, *he's not wrong.*

He only needed a moment to decide.

"Fine," he said, looking back up at the few practitioners eyeing him and wondering how to best put them to use. "Let's split."

***

Tiv visited Celaris first.

More concerned about his master's well-being, than going after Jack. His worry only increased when Flask told him about the injuries he'd sustained in more detail—highly descriptive for a novice Healer—also mentioning that Celaris had been utterly unresponsive when they'd found him.

Celaris had been brought a floor above them. To an open room with a dozen practitioners crowding the entrance.

Tiv didn't recognize any of them. But they apparently knew him—or of him—because they greeted him as he passed. He gave them a terse nod in acknowledgement, before shooing them away with a threatening tilt of his head. They were quick to oblige. A bit too quickly. Perhaps they just didn't want to care for an impassive Master or perhaps they were smart enough to read the stone cold expression on his face. Not that he cared for the reason. So long as they left. Only Flask remained—by Tiv's request. He lingered just outside the door as a lookout, ensuring that none of the more curious practitioners came around in search of something new to gossip about.

Because when Tiv saw Celaris, grief-stricken, and seated on an unused crate, drinking heavily from a bottle—swallowing, rather than drinking—as he stared blankly into nothing, Tiv stilled in stunned disbelief for what was probably the thousandth time that day.

And then a shower of disappointment washed over him.

Celaris was only human, Tiv knew. And though he didn't know the difficulties of losing a partner he'd had for decades, he did know the mind-numbing sting of loss. It wasn't pleasant. It wasn't comparable. It had no one defining term. Still, he was disappointed, and that quickly gave way to fury.

Hot, burning fury.

"What are you doing?" Tiv whispered. The threat in his voice shattered the stillness around them, piercing mournful air and dreary thoughts. Celaris turned his head just enough to pin Tiv with a listless gaze. He sneered in distaste. "What," he repeated, slower this time, "are you doing?"

Outside, Flask jumped at the harshness of his tone. He peered through the door, waving his hands around, and mouthing, 'Sympathy.'

Tiv scoffed. He held none for those so quick to lose their composure when so many others needed him. When *he* needed him. Pom was able to maintain his, Celaris should have as well.

Tiv grabbed a nearby trinket and threw it at the door. Flask shut it with a startled yelp, letting out a girlish scream that would have had him laughing had his anger been of lesser import.

"*Master*," Tiv bit out. "Answer me."

Celaris merely sighed. Drained. Weary. And oh, so tired.

"I am grieving," Celaris said rigidly. Too calm for someone in such obvious pain. He looked at Tiv in an obtuse way. As if it should've been obvious. "Many tend to do that when their friends are lost."

"Is this really the time to be doing so?" he shouted, anger consuming him. Something pettier rose along with it. Right up to the surface where his unspoken love for the Institute resided. "We have bigger problems on our hands than Master Orpha's death! We need you outside and giving orders. We're already short on leaders, yet here you are, nursing a bottle and stripping the Drowned Tower of another."

"Not everyone shares your moral compass, Tiv."

"But you do!" he screamed, throwing his hands up in fury. At his state. At the situation he knew less and less about. At everything. "You're going to get up. You're going to go outside. And you're going to be the annoyingly insightful Master that I know you to be." Tiv leaned down, a hair's breadth away from him, as he mumbled threateningly, "Or I'll make you."

"And how will you, I wonder?" Celaris glared. He was as stubborn as he was uncompromising. "Are you prepared to bind me and gag me? Because that's the only way you'll see me leave this room."

"If that's what it takes."

"You talk big, Tiv. You always have. But you cannot best me. You don't have the necessary skill."

Tiv slapped the bottle from his grasp. It shattered against the door, startling Flask who stood on the other side. As it spilled crimson over wood and stone. Like blood. With a far nicer scent. "It's leave this room or die. I'll happily do both."

"So quick to threaten," Celaris muttered, shaking his head, knowing that his tone only aggravated him further. "You're still a child. You want me to leave this room and command a tower full of practitioners that, from what I've heard from their incessant gossip, have already gathered under you. What would you have me do out there that you haven't done already? Enemies lie in plain sight. Is Orpha's death not evidence of such?"

"So you choose to hide," Tiv spat.

"I choose to remain here until I can be of proper use."

"Why?" Tiv asked, nostrils flaring. As he crouched before Celaris. His Master was smiling now. Lines formed around the corners of his mouth and eyes. A bitter smile that exposed the heaviness of his heart. And then it was gone, hidden under a mask of careful tranquility.

"Practitioners are only measured by their usefulness," said Celaris. With a dark look in his eye. "Remember that, Tiv."

He already knew.

Still, it was a bitter pill to swallow.

Tiv swore. He stood, pacing around the room, moving for the sake of unwinding the tension coiled in his stomach, threatening to bind his body with pure stiffness.

"You hesitate, but you won't even admit that!" Tiv yelled. "Are you really that intimidated by these intruders?"

"They're more dangerous than you believe. You were right to rally the practitioners against the Assembly."

Tiv stilled. His hands were fisted so tightly, the knuckles had gone completely white. "What do you mean?"

"Miriam..." Celaris said quietly, a haunted look in his eyes. "She had someone... *something* on her side. It spoke to her. Gave her power. Enough to fatally wound Columbus and myself. Enough to kill Orpha."

"Single-handedly?" Tiv sputtered in disbelief. His eyes widened even more when Celaris nodded. What he described sounded unnervingly familiar, and his mind drifted to Jack. To the voice he claimed to hear, to the blackness in his eyes, and to the overwhelming power he felt emanate from his form. "Did it have anything to do with the darkness in the rooms?"

Celaris shook his head, uncertain.

"We weren't able to ascertain what exactly that darkness was. But Miriam certainly knew the answer. Perhaps Ethil did as well."

"Ethil?"

"She was with Jack and Sylvie," he revealed, watching Tiv settle down enough to drink in his words.

"How do you know?"

"She healed me." Celaris shrugged. "Her magic lingers on my skin even now. She talks while she works. Likes to mumble. Running mouths are dangerous. She mentioned something about Jack and Sylvie, and a secret they weren't telling her. I'm sure she can tell you more. Someone must've chased Miriam off while she healed us. It was probably those two. Perhaps she received those answers she was so desperately complaining about."

"Where's Ethil now?"

"She was gone by the time we awoke. Or, in my case, by the time I was lucid."

"They took her with them then," Tiv concluded, sighing. In the end, he'd still have to find Jack. Hopefully he'd be more open with his secrets. "Are you really going to stay here?"

Celaris nodded.

And Tiv resisted the urge to bang his head against the wall in frustration.

"What will it take?" he asked, eyes darting between him and the coil of rope thrown haphazardly to the corner of the room, unneeded. Until now. "For you to leave this place?"

Celaris smiled. A shit-eating grin that told Tiv he wouldn't be able to make good on his threats. When it came to his Master, he rarely could. Celaris' grin grew just a little bit wider, as the realization of hopelessness dawned on Tiv's face.

But Tiv couldn't revel in the fact that he got his Master somewhat out of his self-induced rut, as Celaris spoke, "More time than you have to waste."

Even now, Celaris was right.

Tiv hated it.

***

"Isn't this fun?" Pom muttered sarcastically.

He pushed a bookshelf four times his size into the middle of the hall, blocking the way for any practitioners crazy enough to traverse this deep.

They'd taken a turn into the Assembly's Tower and headed downward until they reached the Iniquities Chamber. All in search of Columbus, who they still hadn't even seen a sign of. But instead of travelling deeper, they decided upon a much needed break. And what better place was there than the miserable hall leading to the Iniquities Chamber? Where the mere sight of the walls lined with prison cells and old torture mechanisms were a thing to fear? It was a rarely seen sight of the Tower's dark side.

For all the trouble they caused, they were rarely sent down here. The two times it did happen involved a botched escape to Thyme and the burning of an entire archive. They could only guess the kind of mischief Jack and Tiv started to always be sent to such a dreary place.

"That sure as sin ain't enough, Pom," Khale said, eyeing the bookshelf appraisingly. It was, in a word, unremarkable. And he was far from impressed. "Tiv said ta seal the floors, yea? One block shelf in the middle of such a huge place ain't gonna cut it."

"Well, what do you want me to do?" Pom asked, stretching his arms out wide. Nothingness and dust greeted him on both sides. "Line up the dust bunnies?"

"Let's grab some things from the upper floors."

"No," Pom immediately denied, furiously shaking his head. "I'm not dragging furniture down here just for some kind of wall. Why do we even need it anyway?"

Khale shrugged. "Tiv didn't say."

"Of course he didn't." Pom rolled his eyes. "Let's just go."

The bookshelf craned forward suddenly. Pom barely had time to sidestep it, as it came crashing down with a resounding bang. Dust shot up, making them cough and close their eyes at the abrupt assault to their senses.

"What th—oh, damn you, Pom!" Khale blamed. He coughed again, rubbing his eyes in a vain attempt to clean them. "This is why ya shouldn't be prancin' around insultin' nature."

"Dust isn't nature!" Pom yelled, falling gracelessly to the ground. His heart pounded in his chest at such a close call. Another brush with death or something close to it anyway. Still, once was enough. He just wanted to crawl back to the residential tower, or more preferably, flex his muscles out along the east's borders.

Where he could fight a few deserters. Maybe even a band of mercenaries, if he was lucky. Because that was familiar. It was comforting. He was in his element.

Here, he was simply—not.

When they saw the shelf rumble from where it lay on the ground, they stood up in alarm. Their shoulders tensed with anxiety only a nearby enemy could bring. But when they felt the ground shake softly beneath their feet, forcing them forward in unbalanced surprise, they realized that there was no enemy.

Whatever it was, came from below.

And it made the entire tower tremble.

24

The trail led Jack and Sylvie deep into the older sectors of the Assembly's Tower. Silent and unoccupied, the area was a haven for ghosts. Not even the mob of practitioners they heard cajoling on the floors above traversed this deep.

"Did you feel that?" Jack suddenly asked, steadying himself against the nearby wall. It was faint, but he was sure he'd felt something akin to tremors. A soft rumble beneath his feet. Not enough to make him lose his balance. But the thought alone was worrisome enough.

Sylvie looked at him strangely. "Feel what?"

He eyed her, trying to assess if she was lying. When he realized that she had no reason to, he shook his head, and mumbled, "No, perhaps it was my imagination."

They continued onward, stopping every few moments to peer up at the blue veins that lined the stone. Old magic throbbed here. Just as strongly as the Heartstone around her neck. Whispers danced upon their skin, sending cold shivers down their spines that disrupted the steady beat of their hearts. Age hadn't weathered the enchantments of the Drowned Tower, but every so often, they'd come across a newer spell. With words and markings they could more easily recognize. Written in fresher tongues, but still old enough to no longer be spoken. Some spells were minor—improvements to the lighting, slight reinforcement of older barrier enchantments that had been enhanced over the ages—while others were different altercations altogether. Such as fireproofing of certain rooms. And Sylvie found herself wondering about the stories behind them.

They stopped when they found an interesting marking that they didn't recognize. It differed from the rest. For it was crudely clawed into the wall, disrupting the long lines of ancient verses. Only to replace them with words even they could decipher. And though it pulsed like the other veins of magic, its hue was a distinct shade of red and brown. Like copper. Like rust. Almost like blood—it was certainly dark enough to be mistaken for such. It was a stark contrast against the blue and gray tones of the halls.

"Isn't this *Yövín?*" Jack wondered aloud, bending to inspect the strange mark. His hand brushed along the words, as he uncertainly read, *"The Union."*

"I didn't know you spoke *Yövín* as well," Sylvie said, surprised. Few in the Assembly spoke the ancient language—and she knew of only one that taught it. "Did Master Cephas teach you?"

"No, he didn't," Jack paused, "and I don't." He ignored her questioning glance, as his fingers smoothed along the words. "Do you?"

"I do."

"I have no use for a dead language. But I know some. I was forced to learn a few of the more common phrases to survive certain misfor—lectures."

"The Red Veld's history, you mean?" she asked, already knowing the answer. If poetry was her bane, history was Jack's. Hers, at least, she could still escape. Unlike the years of history lectures they were required to attend.

"I'm only interested in a few stories," Jack said quietly. "New ones and those rare, minor ones that give more insight."

"And?"

"What do you mean, '*and*'—what more do you want? That's all. Dates fade. Facts are forgotten. And after a while, even the larger legends get old. Despite the grandeur of their telling."

Sylvie couldn't fully suppress the smile that threatened to split her face at his confession. He bored too easily and wasn't amused easily enough. The sliver of a grin formed along the edge of her lips.

Jack simply shrugged, rolling his eyes at her expression.

"The Union," he repeated, returning them both to the matter at hand. "Isn't that a title? What kind of spell has a title?"

Sylvie lit a fire, hovering it over the verses. The words were small, but not illegible.

With practiced ease, she translated:

The dead walk beyond our reach,
And with every breath,
They remain past our keep,
I shall follow them then,
To the Dawn,
Where love awaits,
All but gone,

But how can I?
For I breathe,
The sea stops me,
While you wander each,
Alone, I wandered, wondering how and why?
To reach your plain,
To cease this lie,

But the answer is quite clear now,
I am certain,
I've learned the secret,
And I am ready to draw the curtain,
I shall leave, not on my own,
But I'll bring them with me, to their true homes,

So, wait for me now, my love,
Soon we, too, shall join you,
In your walk above.

"A poem?" Sylvie grimaced. "I'm not one for poetry."

"Clearly."

"Watch it."

Jack hummed. "I wonder who wrote it, and why. Look, they even disrupted the other spells, though they seem to be holding well enough."

"If it was scraped any bigger, we'd have a real problem on our hands."

"Barring our present one."

"Oh, shut it." Sylvie sighed, upset and amused all at once. "Should we claw the older spells back in?"

"I don't want to desecrate it," Jack said, shaking his head. "This isn't just a poem, Syl. It's—"

"Why, hello there," a foreign voice greeted, startling them. A figure, clad in black robes that looked as if they'd just been thrown on or slept in, stepped from the darkness, greeting them with a familiar smile.

"—a letter." Jack finished, his voice trailing off into nothing.

"I found you," Serach said, grinning from ear to ear. He dropped a lump to the ground and Sylvie gasped in horror when she recognized the familiar platinum blond hair. It was Reed. Still and bloody. "I had hoped you weren't here. I'd also hoped to find Columbus first, but things never seem to go as planned. It makes me wonder if *she's* toying with me. Well, no matter. Since you're here, I may as well get our business over with. Do you know where Rior is? I assume you encountered him, yes?"

I've brought you the answers you seek.

Jack and Sylvie snapped to attention at the voice.

Answers, Jack thought, as he met Serach's eyes. Cold blue eyes. They held a manic glint he'd never seen before. Jack had expected to find him, but he still couldn't quite believe it. But when he saw the wisps encircle Serach's form before fading, he realized that this was, indeed, what he sought.

The path led to him.

Despite this, Jack took a step back in alarm.

Dangerous, his mind screamed. *He's dangerous.*

"My, my," Serach said, stretching his arms out wide. "Why do you all look so defensive? I merely asked a question. I'm not going to hurt you."

Like we're foolish enough to believe that.

"What did you do to Reed?" Sylvie shouted, horrified.

"He's not dead if that's what you mean." Serach looked down at Reed's bloody form. "Though it's certainly not from a lack of trying, I assure you. Not on my part, but his! Can you believe that? He kept attacking me without a care for his own well-being. He's lucky that I'm so adept at restraint."

They stared at Serach in silent shock.

Was this really the same man they'd met in the Iniquities Chamber? Was this really the same smiling Elder that was too kind and too patient for his own good? Impossible. The man that stood before them was a stranger. A demon cloaked in familiar skin. As he borrowed the voice of his victim.

"Oh, don't look at me like that," Serach continued, rolling his eyes at their expressions. "I admit that I have changed a tad, but it's still me. This is me shedding my mask. An exceptional feat, I assure you. Live in the Diamond Alps long enough and you'll understand what I mean. I see now why you both love it here. No masks. No Council. No fakeness. It gets quite boring, really."

Jack took a deep breath, mustering his courage. The voice in his mind was silent, disappearing at the worst of times. Jack sought the bonus assurance he felt whenever his magic spiked at its words. "You do like to hear yourself talk, don't you?"

"And he speaks!" Serach exclaimed. "Good, good. I almost believed you'd gone mute."

They had a brief stare down. It was broken by Sylvie, who stepped up, swallowing the lump in her throat.

"Give Reed back," she told him.

Serach turned to her. "I can't do that. Not yet anyway. There are still goals to reach. Steps to take. Schemes to cackle about. You'll find that age hasn't halted my schedule. I still have much to do, and your beloved partner is an invaluable piece to my plans."

"And, what?" Jack asked, sneering. As his hands lit up with flames. "Do you think we'll just allow you free reign?"

"I had hoped so."

"An absurd notion."

"Truly," he agreed easily. "But I'm merely here to take back what is rightfully mine. You cannot fault me for that."

"Then take it and leave. Why cause all this trouble?"

"It is not so simple, you see," Serach gestured around them with a grand sweep of his hand, "this tower is mine by birthright. It belongs to my family. Not to fools that squander its glory."

"By birthright?" Sylvie questioned. "Impossible. Reed has no uncles. Master Cephas had little competition for the place of primary apprentice to his late father."

"So quick you are to forget that the Cephas line hasn't always ruled the Drowned Tower."

"Eldon Beau…" Jack said, his eyes narrowing in realization. "You do realize that he happily handed over his position as Arch Poten to Maudré, don't you?"

"And what a foolish move that was!" Serach exclaimed. "To hand over all that power to a stranger he had no blood ties with! Can you believe that? Thankfully, I'm here to fix that mistake he made all those years ago. To take back the Drowned Tower and restore it to its former glory. But first, I must restore the Potentate Union. To do that, I need to regain my status as head. Had a single person had the power to hand complete control over to me then this would be have been far easier. But I need not only the consent of that false Arch Poten, but also the Zenith Council. Neither is so easily obtained."

"And so you're going to force Cephas to hand over his position by using Reed as incentive," Jack finished. The answers clicked together in his mind. As he spared Reed's still form a glance. He looked dead, but the slight pinch of his brow proved otherwise. Sylvie was impatient, as she shifted on the balls of her feet by his side. Her jaw clenched tight in fury, holding back shouts of outrage, and he saw her fists trembling in all too obvious restraint. Jack wanted to tell her to stop. To cease her superfluous movements and silence her thoughts. They only served to poison her mind. But he knew it would be for naught. He had no comforting platitudes to offer. He could never ease such blatant worry. Jack knew his strengths—consoling women wasn't one of them. He settled, instead, on Serach's aged smile. At least him, he could deal with.

"Do you really think it'll be so simple?" Jack asked. "Say, for a moment, that this convoluted ploy of yours does somehow— against all odds—work, and you obtain Cephas' consent, or his signature, or his word, or whatever it is you need. How will you convince the Zenith Council to formally decree such an abrupt change in power? You'll spark the embers of chaos. Don't you know that the Alps hates not being the center of attention?"

"All too well," Serach mused. "I have my ways. And contrary to what you seem to believe, I'm not alone in this endeavor. *She* will be there to aid me. So long as I get *her* what *she* wants. Little does *she* know that he has already passed from this world. But—"

He has not, the voice intervened, startling Jack and Sylvie.

"—that is a discussion for another time. When *she* is present and you are not."

"*She?*" Sylvie breathed in deeply, enunciating every letter. Her voice was tight and filled with the echoes of slowly slipping control. "And just who is this enigmatic *she* I keep hearing about? Have both you and your apprentice gone mad?"

"Perhaps we have," Serach answered, shrugging. "For *she* is but darkness with a voice. Pure and transcendent. Not just a shadow cast by the light. But perhaps the truly mad ones are the Elementalists that hear her call," he looked pointedly at Jack, "and are ensnared by it."

He assumes much for one with such scarce knowledge. They are my children. Extensions of myself. To ensnare is to trap. And

to trap is to go against Thelarius.

Jack and Sylvie hid their surprise behind cool masks of composure, slowly getting used to the fact that _she_ was apparently here to stay. And they'd receive no warning of _her_ sudden commentary—or the secrets it held.

"What do you know about that voice?" Jack asked.

"Ah…" Serach smiled. "So you have heard _her_ calls. I was right then in my assumption that you picked up _her_ fragment. _Her_ heart. That foolish apprentice ran off with such a valuable piece, unaware that with the treasure he held. He could've blackmailed every prideful Elementalist in the north with it. How he was even able to take such a guarded thing is beyond me. I assume he had help."

Her, Sylvie thought. She'd had her suspicions, but now she knew, without a shred of doubt, that the voice they and Rior heard were one and the same. _The Heartstone. It's definitely the Heartstone._ Sylvie resisted the urge to hold it, to cover its glow, despite her knowledge that Serach couldn't see it behind the shelter of her robes. _But I thought they couldn't hold people. What exactly are we dealing with? Surely, not a practitioner. Not an ordinary one at least._

"But," Serach continued, "again, that is a discussion for another time. I wonder if you've told Miss Sirx about that ringing voice in your head? I can't imagine she'd be too pleased about it." He glanced at Sylvie in a demeaning way, searching her face for any signs of surprise. But to his shock—and disappointment—he found none. "So you do know. And… you actually believe him? Are you mad as well?"

"Fragment?" Sylvie asked, feigning ignorance. She ignored his taunts, in favor of trying to get him to speak.

Serach waved her off. "Nothing you need concern yourself with. From your words, I can safely assume that you've seen Rior, yes? Answer my initial question and perhaps I'll let you live long enough to see the glory of the Eastern Branch restored."

"Rior is dead," Sylvie said bluntly.

Serach fell silent.

For a nervous moment, they thought he'd shout in outrage—or worse, attack—but the expected assault never came, and they just stood there in deep, encompassing silence. Above them, the echoing sound of shoes scraping against stone could be heard, shattering it easily. Easier than they expected.

"I have killed many…" Serach said tentatively, his voice a hushed hiss, "for uttering lesser lies."

It wasn't a warning. It was a blatant threat.

One that Sylvie had no doubt he'd make good on. But she was surprised to hear no edge of arrogance in his voice. Only cold fact. Said so confidently that it could only be hailed as truth. His voice almost had a sing-song cadence to it. As if he enjoyed threatening practitioners, and did so regularly.

"Believe what you want," Jack said. "But we've told you what we know and if we're done talking, then I'd like to get on with my own plan… ensuring yours doesn't work."

I shall aid you in your plight.

Your help isn't welcome, Jack thought, but was reassured nonetheless.

Serach laughed. Cold and biting and highly amused. "You talk big. But who's going to stop me in this grand scheme of yours? You? Sylvie?" He looked at a point behind them. Where the soft pulses of magic exposed another. "Or you?"

Ethil stepped from the shadows.

Her hands clutched tightly onto the worn sides of her grimoire. A nervous spell tittered on the tip of her tongue, as she mumbled a self-assurance under her breath. She was shaking. But that did little to deter her, mustering more courage with each step, she stopped just behind Jack and Sylvie. Her right hand extended. As if to hit them. But she simply placed her palm on each of their shoulders, sending a burst of adrenaline through their veins.

"I'm here to help," Ethil said resolutely. She was still sketchy on the details, but she didn't doubt her resolve. "I won't accept anyone telling me otherwise."

They merely grinned in response.

Serach clapped, amused even more by her arrival. "What a heartfelt reunion. But perhaps you'll regret saying those words."

In a moment's breath, Jack and Sylvie crouched, prepared to pounce. Swift and sure pawns of war. As they were chosen to be. They shared a glance, their hands lighting blue with power, but before they could strike, Serach raised a hand in pause. The action was so abrupt and so assured that they stilled.

They were right to.

"Ah!" Serach's voice held careless warning. "I wouldn't move if I were you. I can blow this place up at any moment."

Serach produced an old tome.

As tattered as it was frightening, and when he opened it, ancient words spilled forth from the pages. Maledictions of an age old spell. Voices of the hissing dead convened into one guttural sound. Unnerving in its own right.

Serach's hand shone the same rusty hue as the mark on the wall, and they stumbled when the ground slipped beneath their feet. The walls abruptly shook with an urgency that made their blood boil. Far stronger than what Jack felt before. Somewhere above them, furniture tumbled over stone. As practitioners shrieked in alarm. There was a loud crash over their heads, shaking the ceiling and making the veins along the walls pulse with sudden protective insistence.

And then Serach closed the tome.

Tremors stopped. Stone settled. Their hearts resumed their beat. All in the quickness of a moment and an age.

"Did you like the letter?" Serach suddenly asked, uncaring for their mental states. As he gestured with his chin toward the engraving on the wall. "It was written by the creator of this spell. A man infatuated with a woman—always a woman—not his, of course. Still, he became obsessed with her death. I thought it only proper to engrave his words by the mark he spent his life creating. One he used to return to her side. And one I will use to return the Drowned Tower to mine."

Maurice! she hissed. **He shall harm the Zenith no longer.**

And this time, Sylvie and Jack couldn't mask their surprise. They both jumped back in alarm, Serach's gaze settling over them and carefully assessing their shock. As if he knew what was going on, despite not being able to hear *her* himself.

"Is *she* speaking now?" Serach asked Jack, not waiting for his answer and instead giving Sylvie his undivided attention. As though she'd suddenly become brilliant in the span of an instant. "Don't tell me… do you hear *her*? How? You're a Conjurer, yes? Did you drink a tonic—no, impossible. Where would you have gotten it from? That means you can simply—*hear*!"

Sylvie fell silent, carefully contemplating his words. Her lack of response was hardly noticeable. Serach spoke enough for both of them. All the while laughing manically, realizing something they had yet to.

He knows about the voice, Jack thought. *He believes in its exist-ence. Yet, he can't hear it. Why?*

He has no part of me, *she* answered vaguely, **he cannot have a part.**

And why not? Jack mentally asked, his qualms about speaking to the voice long forgotten. *Just what are you? No. Who are you?*

She didn't speak, disappearing somewhere in the silence of his mind. As *she* always did when he wanted a response. He'd long tired of it.

"Oh, how fascinating!" Serach exclaimed, unknowingly providing Jack with an answer. "That a Conjurer can hear what only Elementalists may. But can you see the darkness? I doubt it. Only those that have consumed the crystal may. Well, no matter. As long as you can hear, then that's more than enough. Of whom are you the descendant of, I wonder. Surely, not Maurice. I've had quite enough of the Drakone family. Though I am curious how exactly the Sirx lineage has managed to elude the Zenith Council for so long."

"What are you prattling on about?" Jack snapped.

"The descendants of the First Zenith, of course!" he shouted with glee. "Ferus Terria has strived, believing only the descendants of Maurice remain. Giving them power and credit where none is due, simply because they have no comparable contender. But it seems that..." Serach glanced meaningfully at Sylvie, "is no longer the case."

"Sylvie?" Jack spared her a glance. Her eyes were as wide as his, disbelief shining clearly in both of their gazes. "And what brought you to that conclusion?"

"There is no other," Serach said simply.

"Me?" Sylvie questioned, slow and incredulous. She pointed hesitantly to herself. Sylvie had no reason to believe him. But he sounded so sure and so excited that she couldn't help but consider the thought. If only for a moment. "You're joking."

"If only."

"Then you're mistaken."

"I rarely am when it comes to such matters."

"Oh, for the love of—" the flames in Jack's hands sparked with renewed vigor, as he pinned Serach with a glare, "—we don't have time for this! Let's get this over with, you disoriented fossil. I have better things to do than guess ancestry with you."

"So quick is your temper." Serach clicked his tongue in distaste. His patience slipped as quickly as sand between his fingers. "But it clouds your mind. Do you really want to chance attacking me? This mark blows away all it's written on. Human, animal, edifice. No matter their power and no matter their build. They will all crumble. These marks have been clawed along every level of every tower. Most are guarded by *her* darkness, reflexively attacking all those foolish enough to come near. But more importantly, they've been etched into *this* tower. This tower that holds the enchantment spells of every other. What will happen, I wonder, if I were to destroy them?"

"You're mad," Jack spat. "You'd use ancient magic for this? You'd rather watch the Drowned Tower be swept away under the Zexin abyss than see it strive without you?"

"Strive?" Serach scoffed, madly laughing. As if he'd made

the grandest of jokes. "Hardly. But that isn't a discussion I'd like to delve into. It seems we've reached a consensus—we both tire of this conversation. Allow me to finish it with one more question then. You claim Rior is dead. Does that mean the stone still lies with you?"

They shared a glance, a silent agreement passing between them. Ethil narrowed her eyes at them both—still so close to their secrets—the answers would be forced from them soon enough. Be it by Serach, by the Assembly, or even by the Zenith Council. None held the promise of less pain. They couldn't hold onto them forever.

"No answer?" Serach asked, peering curiously at them. "Are you protecting *her*? Only death awaits those that do."

Your sorry threats will bring you only ill tidings, scum of Maurice. For I have found what I seek and I no longer need aid from the hands that hold the powers of traitors long dead.

Serach laughed out loud at their continued silence. It was an unpleasant sound. Then, almost as an afterthought, Serach mumbled a few words and swung his hand in a lazy arc. The mark beat with urgency. As a threatening smirk graced the corners of his lips. His fingers played with the spine of the tome, prepared to open it, should they decide to move.

"I believe this goes without saying, but I do need that stone."

You will die first.

For once, Jack and Sylvie agreed.

They raised their hands and a shower of flames leapt from their fingertips. Serach rushed to the side to avoid it, procuring two tubes from his robes and throwing them to the ground, as he slammed into the floor. A cloud of toxins rose from the liquid.

Jack was quick to summon wind just strong enough to disperse the fumes. But it was still too late.

Serach held a dagger to Reed's neck, and Sylvie recoiled, her hands dropping just the slightest bit. An indication that she wasn't going to risk Reed's life, but was still prepared to roast him should he try to slit the blade across his throat.

Jack had no such qualms.

With a wave of his hand, ice sprayed in an outward arc, spreading just fast enough to crawl up and trap Serach's legs in solid ice. Four inches thick.

Jack's magic was wilder than Sylvie remembered. She didn't miss the brief moment when his red gaze widened at the swiftness of his scattering magic. As if he no longer knew his own limits. Still, his powers weren't quick enough to stop Serach's instinctual retaliation.

Sylvie watched in abject horror, as the blade split the expanse of Reed's neck. Blood rushed forward, and suddenly, without warning, Reed was awake. Blue eyes snapped open. Confusion followed by surprise flashed across them, before he registered pain. So much pain. His hands clawed upward. If he was simply trying to feel the extent of the wound or half-heartedly stop its bleeding, Sylvie didn't know. Reed didn't either, evident only by the bewildered widening of his eyes. As he gurgled something unintelligible through his lips. But his words were lost when they twisted over his teeth in a silent scream.

Reed slid downward, hitting the floor head first. His blood dripped a copper puddle that stained his robes, before sliding along the cracks age brought over stone. Through it all, Reed's eyes remained open. Even as the light left his gaze.

And then there was only silence.

Ethil covered her mouth, muffling a scream. But it wasn't enough to mask her sobs. Duward's memory was still too fresh and too clear. She couldn't handle another death. But neither of her companions turned to comfort her. Not that she expected them to. They simply looked on in shocked stillness.

Jack's hands fell to his side.

He swallowed the sudden dry lump in his throat. He chanced a glance at Sylvie, whose legs were shaking in distress, and for a moment, he wondered how she hadn't fallen yet. Her mouth opened and closed. Twice, it happened. Then she inhaled and when he thought she'd don that serious mask she wore during patrols, her lip trembled.

"Reed," she whispered, fumbling over his name.

There was no answer.

And Sylvie screeched.

She called for him with blood-curdling shouts, repeated so quickly that Jack could hardly make them out. As she blindly ran forward. Jack caught her robes and yanked her back. His glare was harsher than usual, wholly unforgiving of her recklessness. As he treated this like any other faceless death. Because that's exactly what it was. Just another death. Casualties were standard on the frontlines—it didn't matter who they were—loss wasn't cause to lose all sense of rationality.

"It's dangerous!" Jack reproached, shoving his sympathy down his throat. It didn't work. The expression that marred her face almost made him lose the final iota of control he held.

Almost.

Sylvie elbowed him in the stomach, but he was a statue of lean muscle and iron grips. Solid and unrelenting. She couldn't even hope to escape his grasp. Not easily. And certainly not in her current state. But that didn't stop her from trying when Serach panted and turned as best he could on his side. His legs were rendered immobile—already a light shade of purple from the sudden freezing of his blood. Still, he firmly grasped the hilt of his dagger, and with an enraged cry, stabbed Reed twice in the stomach. All in a vain attempt to uncurl the coil of anger inside of him.

"Stop!" Sylvie sobbed.

Fire sparked around her. Only to be doused by a wave of wind and frost, courtesy of Jack, who, for once, was far more composed. Too composed.

With his sound mind, he easily countered all of her desperate attempts at escape. He kept a firm handle over his emotions, hiding them beneath the mask of seriousness he and his fellow chosen apprentices donned only during the worst of situations. The same mask he saw crumble from Sylvie's eyes. The same one he couldn't afford to lose while she was like this.

They couldn't both be clouded by desperation and wild abandon. No matter how much he wished to lose himself in it.

He was no fool.

"Please," Sylvie said. Quieter. Weaker. As she half-heartedly tried to escape his grasp. "Please stop. Let me go."

Sylvie's cries only made Serach plunge the blade in with more vigor. Jack whispered something to her, but it was lost to the blood and the ringing in her ears. The ice continued to climb its way up Serach's legs, slower now. As if Jack's magic had a will of its own—perhaps it did, perhaps the voice in his head controlled it—intent on making Serach suffer a slow, cold death.

But it wasn't enough. Nothing was. As Sylvie watched him stab Reed again. She tried to lift her hands. To use her flames, to burn him, and stop this madness. The sparks of heat licked at her fingertips. But they trembled with regret and rage. And when she finally calmed enough to force them into obedience, Jack's own hand went up. Steady, anchoring, and just past her own.

He produced flames in her place.

Angry, angry flames.

Serach screamed in agony when the fire licked away the ice, not stopping until it burnt his flesh. But he didn't let go of the dagger, continuing his work like a madman possessed by devotion. Then, in a moment too quick to register, the blade was struck from his burnt hands. By a small figure with familiar brown locks and deep eyes.

Myrrh stood there, using Serach as a human shield against Jack's magic until he found the sense to stop. She let out a low, vicious noise and shoved Serach to the floor, watching mercilessly as he tried to scramble away, shakily mumbling the incantation of a healing spell too low to hear.

Jack hid his surprise behind a tight lipped line, disregarding Myrrh for the moment and opting instead to carefully let Sylvie go. She hobbled forward, falling to her knees by Reed's side, and grasping for his face. Distantly, Jack noted that he'd accidentally singed the tips of his hair. As Sylvie murmured a string of ruined sentences too wracked by sobs for him to comprehend. But her apologetic tone was clear enough for him to guess her words.

"Reed," Sylvie cried, not noticing or simply not caring about his blood that now stained her fingers. As she shook him, trying to rouse him from his slumber. To no avail. An expected outcome.

Ethil was by Sylvie's side in an instant, placing glowing blue hands upon her shoulders and forcing her to relax under her grip. Ethil whispered soft comforts in her ears, all the while squeezing her own eyes shut in frightened disgust. Tight enough that flecks of white clouded her vision.

Jack watched them for a moment, then said, "It's you."

"It's me," Myrrh echoed, gazing morosely down at Reed's still form. Only when she looked up, did she momentarily forget her sorrow, sudden terror taking its place. As Jack was starting to become accustomed to whenever someone saw the darkness that wallowed within his eyes.

Jack saw a question forming on the edge of her tongue, her mouth opening and closing, unsure how to word it. He didn't give her a chance to figure it out. Jack turned to Sylvie, who, to his surprise, stared unwaveringly at him. Tears stained her cheeks, more threatened to spill from her eyes, and in her gaze—behind the grief and panic—he saw rage.

Pure and thicker than blood.

"We're going to do everything we can to get him away from here," Jack assured, but his voice came out rougher than he intended. He tilted his head toward Reed, the corners of his mouth scrunched downwards into a frown that he hoped showed compassion and not pity. "So don't lose yourself. Not yet. There will be time to grieve. *Later.*"

And though Jack's eyes were blacker than Sylvie had ever seen—the wisps swallowing so much there was nothing left of crimson—she believed him. Power rolled off of him in waves, reminding her of Rior just before he was enveloped in black. But unlike Rior, Jack was in complete control of himself.

So, she nodded.

Jack had yet to give her reason to do otherwise.

"I'll hold you to that," Sylvie croaked.

Jack didn't waste time with further talk. He didn't even bother to nod in acknowledgement or question Myrrh about her sudden appearance. Jack simply turned on his heel and grasped the barely clinging robes covering Serach's back, before throwing him across the room with a sudden burst of strength he knew would make his muscles ache later. He watched, unsympathetic, as Serach clumsily healed his burns. His focus funneled to the slow, but sure mending of muscle and the soft whitening of charred skin. Healers were always the most troublesome. Jack's face twisted into something between overwhelmingly furious and morbidly fascinated.

The former ruled. As it always did.

"Don't waste your energy," Jack said, deathly still.

His muscles were wound with tension. The vein along his temple throbbed, as a growl escaped his throat. Low and guttural. His head lowered like a wild animal prepared to strike — more Amorph than Elementalist.

"You're going to die," Jack told him with the air of a seer able to prophesize the future. Calm and sure. "It's written on your face."

"Will you be the one to kill me?" Serach laughed. It was interrupted by an ill-timed cough. Blood flecked over his lips.

Jack ignored it, feeling no sympathy for his pain. He only stepped closer. His entire form burst into flame.

"I'll take that as a yes." Serach laughed again. Humorless and full of self-deprecation. As he gripped his pounding head, his already receding hairline was half-singed and mostly gone. Blood decorated his teeth and he spat it on the ground by Jack's feet. The splotch reflected fire. Hot, angry fire.

"Die, prideless Elder."

Jack stretched his hand without flourish. And Serach reacted. It was now or death. The latter wasn't an option. Not unless he took the rest of the Drowned Tower with him.

Serach reached into his robes and procured a vial filled with amber liquid. He downed the tonic, as Jack set him aflame. Serach resisted the urge to cry out in pain. The liquid trickled down his throat in a pace too slow to bear. He was so focused on the fire that he could hardly taste it. Hardly register when some of it fell over his neck and evaporated into steam. Hardly felt the crystal lodge itself in his throat and clear his lungs.

An endless second passed. Then two. Three more.

Jack didn't cease—he didn't plan to—though Serach was sure his skin had melted off his bones long ago. Despite this, he was still conscious. Still alive. He didn't know how. He didn't even know remaining conscious for something so excruciating was possible.

Then time stopped.

A moment of pure understanding dawned upon him, and a promise of madness followed.

Serach's entire body numbed. Cooling off, despite Jack's unrelenting flames. He felt the *Orivellea* crystal he'd swallowed begin to move. Like a parasite, it crawled from his throat and crept upward, breaking and mending his insides as it did. The crystal entrenched itself on the side of his burnt head. Where his magic circuit lay. It pulsed with sudden ferocity. And then what he thought he knew of the world became a thing of the past. As terrified voices screamed and cried and finally convened into one singular entity. Darkness encircled him, clouding his vision until he saw a long line of wisps surrounding everyone—though they were mostly centered around Jack and Sylvie—and he smiled in understanding.

"I see now," he said, his voice was the epitome of insanity.

Jack's eyes widened, surprised to hear him speak. Something coherent no less. He dropped his hands to look at him.

Serach was burnt to the bone.

A walking puddle of red. Blistered flesh clung to his sinew. Barely. And though his eyes had melted long ago, Serach twisted his neck, as if he could still see.

That was when Jack saw it. Dark tendrils crawled upward along his skin, slowly encasing him in black. It healed everything it touched. Jack watched Serach's eyes slowly remake themselves from nothing, and he stumbled back in terror.

"Jack!" Sylvie yelled, already knowing what was coming. But her voice was lost to the ringing in his ears. Jack didn't move. Not even when she ran to him and yanked him backward.

Kill him! she suddenly ordered, startling them both. A burst of power spread forth from Jack's fingers, itching to be released. *Kill him now!*

When Serach's eyes widened, Jack knew he heard the threat.

Serach let out an ear piercing laugh. It grated on their ears. Shrill and raspy all at once. Jack's temper flared at the sound. But when he raised his hands to silence him once more—hopefully for good—Serach's gaze made him stop.

In the brief instant before he was covered by a faceless mask, Serach's eyes had reflected his own.

Deep and red.

***

The Institute is shaking. Columbus balanced himself on the stairs that led deeper into the older sections of the Assembly's Tower. *Why does it keep shaking?*

It had been for some time now.

Only stopping for the briefest of moments, before it began again. Each tremor worse than the last. He was afraid that the roof might collapse and trap them deep beyond the reach of ordinary magic. Behind him, his students gasped in shock, lurching dangerously forward before grasping each other in fear of falling. Some took to sitting instead. They settled themselves over the steps, not trusting their own two feet against the Tower's sudden instability. Smart.

A face full of stone was terribly unpleasant.

They yelled things that were lost to the bang of toppled furniture and the thoughts whirring inside his mind.

They were scared. Columbus didn't blame them. He was, too. Though he was far more adept at hiding it.

Columbus continued down the juddering staircase, peeking through the hall of each platform he passed to check if any practitioners roamed about. But the halls were void of company. The silence that stretched beyond their group unnerved him. Still, he admonished his nervously chattering students, hushing and forcing them into some sort of order with only a look and a careless tilt of his wrist. They easily obeyed. Quick and without question. Jittery little things. More obedient than most of his apprentices—and just as quick to defy.

"Quiet your steps," he said, his voice came out gentler than he liked, unable to fully order them to do his bidding. Not when they lacked proper training. Not when they were here simply because he had no other choice but to bring them.

Columbus stopped to touch a blue vein along the wall. Soon, the cracks in the stone would give way to engravings. The scant torches would be replaced by light from magic so raw it made even his skin crawl with fright. They were close.

"Where are we going?" a girl with too bright eyes asked.

Columbus watched them dim as soon as the words left his mouth, "To find the one responsible for this. Or perhaps whom I suspect is more accurate." Though there wasn't much difference.

She sputtered, stepping back in sudden alarm and almost tripping over the stairs. She would have, had half a dozen helping hands not shot out to aid her. Nevertheless, Columbus could see courage in her eyes. In all of their eyes. Faith that swelled and waned in the span of a moment. It was only a matter of time before those feelings burst, unable to withstand the heart pounding pressure of hesitance and doubt.

Columbus wondered if cowardice would emerge the victor.

"Can we do this?" she asked. "I mean... should you really have brought us? You didn't need to. You can still go upstairs and find a few of the primary apprentices to take with you."

Columbus couldn't.

He didn't have that kind of time to waste. But he didn't tell her that. Instead, he watched as the others nodded in agreement. More than he expected would. While the rest stared on in disdain, trying to silence her with their glares alone. A fruitless attempt. Silencing someone took skill. A certain mien they didn't have. He vaguely recognized the ones that tried though, and he knew why they were so bent on proving themselves to him. They were older practitioners, well past the age of requirement. Yet they continued to study under someone from the Assembly. They were tossed from Master to Master every year—the unluckier ones, every month—while the rest of their peers went off to find different areas of expertise.

It must've been disheartening. But some just weren't as adept as others. That was fact. Just as the chances of being chosen after the age of requirement were rare. And to become a practitioner of respectable rank, despite all odds, even more so. They tried though—were still trying—and Columbus couldn't fault them for that. They knew all too well what it was to try and to fail.

This endeavor frightened them the most.

"Are you scared?" Columbus asked. They turned their heads away in shame. A collection of mixed whispers answered him. "Then you're free to leave," he offered, startling them back into attention. "Or rather… I encourage it."

They glanced at each other for assurance, but not a single one moved.

Columbus smiled.

"May the Zenith guide us then."

They smiled back. A warm atmosphere settled like the infant dawn of a crisp summer morning around them. Like all dawns, however, it lasted only to be swept away by the frigid chill of the Tower shaking once again. Stone rumbled with a vengeance.

They held onto each other in fright. Amidst the sudden madness, a practitioner stepped back to flee. The fear of being trapped was clearly too much. Another quickly followed. Then, without warning, the ceiling cracked. A block of granite fell from its place above them, completely crushing their bodies, starting with their heads. As if the Institute itself found the traitors and quite literally squashed them, before their notions of cowardice spread.

It only served to make the rest scream.

Blood coated the floor, and as another crack tore across the ceiling, Columbus didn't bother checking if they could be healed.

The way forward was blocked.

"Down!" Columbus yelled, urgently pushing them down the flight of stairs. The Amorphs transformed in fright, turning into small rodents less easily crushed. But Columbus didn't have time to envy them, as he repeated, "Go down!"

And they did.

They ran, as if Thelarius Merve, himself, was punishing them for crimes they had no knowledge of committing. Some tripped, those that stopped to help died with them. And it was only when they reached the next platform that led to the opening of a new floor, did they find respite. They turned into the hall, not stopping until they were a good distance away from the flight of stairs, all too quickly falling in on itself. They heard when the tumbling finally ceased. It stopped a few floors down. Columbus could guess where. Right above the older sectors of the Tower.

Where magic was strong and the walls were stronger.

But the rumbling didn't cease. The Tower still shook. Even faster now. And Columbus couldn't escape the feeling that these quakes should have been the least of his worries. Something was wrong. Terribly wrong.

What's happening? he wondered, dazedly looking over the trembling practitioners he had left, barely able to count them without a rush of relief tainting his thoughts with each additional number. *Four. Five. Six—six of them left.*

He'd started with eleven.

Some were shocked into silence. But most bawled, mumbling something his ears didn't deem necessary enough to register.

Ridiculous. This was ridiculous.

And he'd had enough.

Columbus suddenly stood, panting and tense, but unafraid. Magic, pale blue and bright, encircled his hands. As he lifted them to cast a healing spell over those that remained, giving them energy and enveloping them in warmth. He was a Healer. It was his job to hope for those who had none. To support those that couldn't support themselves. But more than that, he was part of the Assembly. The official Arch Poten of an entire Institute of practitioners. And he had a job to do.

In that moment, he made a promise to himself.

Them, at least, he would save.

25

Serach was encompassed in dark, magic resistant tendrils.

They stretched across half of his body, leaving the other a burnt mess that, from experience, Jack knew shouldn't be moving. Somewhere in the distance, Ethil whispered encouragements to herself as she dragged Reed's corpse away from the fight. Closer, a dark voice repeated words of death and power in his mind. And in a place beyond sense and knowledge, was Myrrh, who had disappeared once again into the stillness of the Tower—doing what he could only hope was something productive—as she left them to fend for themselves.

Sylvie was nearer.

Jack was astonished by how easily she could narrow his focus. He heard her gasps, saw the quiver of her lip, and the pain etched along the lines of her face, as she abruptly stepped in front of him to shield him from a large, black appendage. Entirely too claw-like to be human. It stretched out, encasing Serach's arm to extend its reach. Enough to turn him into something a little less mortal.

The claw pierced a hole through her side. It pulled out just as quickly. And torrents of blood gushed over raw skin. Warm and red. So much red. It fell at an alarming rate. Swiftly and without pause. But she didn't let the wound deter her. Not yet.

Serach moved backward.

A step just beyond their reach, tucked safely between two protruding veins of raw magic, trying to grasp for a shred of control over his body. He ran his hands over the length of his face, slowly being enveloped in even more black. It inched its way over his form, swift and demanding.

And Sylvie tore him from it.

With desperate hands, her fingers clawed their way around the little left of his human arm like a vise. Magic spread from her fingertips, burning away the soft ounces of muscles and sinew that remained after Jack's own flaming torture, burning away the darkness Jack had thought resistant to magic. And without remorse, she threw him at her feet. Her eyes raged with madness. Angry fury that if left unchecked would consume her — it was already consuming her — and she kicked him as hard as her wound would allow, bruising his face, bruising her foot.

A shot of pain ran up her leg, more blood spilled from her side, and it *hurt*. But not more than the satisfaction she felt when she looked upon his beaten face, half enveloped in black.

"You're not going to disappear," she said lowly, seething in her wrath. Flames erupted around her, flaring along with her temper. "I won't allow you to escape into the darkness that *thing* has to offer. You're going to stay right here and answer for your crimes."

Despite her fury and despite her will, blood still poured from the hole in her side. Sheer will kept her standing, but no more. Sylvie staggered sideways, dizzy and trying to blink away the uncertainty of her surroundings.

Serach took the chance to fumble back, folding his chin to his chest, as his arms swept circles above him in maddened frenzy. He wept in confused agony. He screamed profanities and spoke words too quick to register, losing himself in an ongoing battle between whatever mentalities resided inside of him.

Jack saw a crystal throb incessantly on his head, and his eyes widened at the grotesque sight. *An Orive crystal,* Jack realized. The trench it made along his skull was deep, but not unfamiliar, and he touched his own head in silent shock.

A gasp shook him from his thoughts.

His attention was recaptured by Sylvie, who fell to the floor, coughing blood. She tried to balance herself on wobbly knees. Jack braced himself for a cry, a groan of pain, even a gut wrenching sob. But Sylvie—with all her panting and her sweating and a hole as large as her head speared into her—had the audacity to laugh. A dry and utterly resigned laugh that made her tip in on herself.

And he lost it.

Jack crossed the distance between them in two short strides. He cupped her chin with a thumb and forefinger, bringing her gaze up to his own to skewer her with the fiercest glare he could muster. It wasn't much. Jack opened his mouth to say something cutting, but when her eyes fluttered close in obvious exhaustion, he swallowed the words whole.

"Jack," she whispered, falling against him. No longer able to hold her own weight. Her breaths were little more than gasps against his skin. "Get away from here."

"I'm taking you with me," he said. The uncertainty of desperation crept into his voice, before he smothered it with a rough cough and sheer will. Jack had seen death in all of its forms. He'd seen men burn from a distance, women fade against a deliberate blade, and children die at his feet. He was responsible for more than a few. Quietly stood by for even more. And he knew enough to know that Sylvie saw little and heard less.

I'm not going to lose it, Jack assured himself. As he saw Serach straighten, gaining some iota of control over his monstrous body. And Jack's eyes threatened to bulge from their sockets. *I won't. I can't.*

But her blood kept spilling and he didn't know how much she had left to give. Jack didn't dare turn his head to see how far Ethil was. Not when Serach was a few strides away—and coming closer. Not when the adrenaline in his system was wearing off, giving way to exhaustion. And certainly not when he felt the dregs of his own magic slowly begin to fail him.

He'd exhausted his magic circuit.

To overuse it would kill him.

But Jack didn't dare call upon the voice in his head and, for once, it obliged, completely disappearing from his mind. As if now that Serach could hear, speaking had suddenly become more frightening. Still, he felt remnants of its power throbbing in his veins, making his blood burn. Vestiges that faded quicker than the swift hammer in his chest. He tried to hold onto it—shorter exhales, less movement, anything—to keep the power within. But as Serach took another step forward, his gaze wilful, his steps alert, and his chuckles as lucid as manic fanaticism allowed, the magic Jack didn't have no longer mattered.

Only what remained.

He left Sylvie on the ground, ignoring her weak protests. As he closed the distance between him and Serach. Far enough for her to be safe from his magic, but close enough for him to help should she need it.

Sylvie futilely tried to stand, to force her limbs to move. But blood spilled forth and a torrent of invective *Yövin* followed. Both were heavy on her tongue. Serach laughed at her state, mumbling something too low for her slowing senses. She didn't know which was more frightening—Serach's apparent clarity or the darkness trying to take him over.

"Jack," she whispered.

Again, he ignored her.

Jack grinned. A grim smile. As a spiral of fire encircled him without his knowledge. It was his preferred element, the one that never failed him, and the one that never failed to respond to danger. His magic was like a sentient being. It blurred the air around him and spilled forth. Stirring without order. Jack didn't question if this was *her* doing or his own subconscious. But he didn't dwell on it.

Serach walked along, holding the walls for balance. His blood splayed across the engraved enchantments, slipping into the careful dips of each letter and tainting them crimson. More dribb-led down the walls, painting it, as if in homage to a more heinous sacrifice.

Jack unleashed a tower of flames.

Only for Serach to shield himself with the darkness around his arm, smiling all the while. A slimy smile that made Jack's insides crawl. Despite his magic, Serach didn't stop. He continu-ed to trudge onwards and Jack's hands trembled. Not in fright, but in rage. And anticipation.

He tried water next. Ice. Then wind.

They disappeared just as quickly. His eyes unintentionally drifted to Sylvie.

How did she do it? he thought, clenching his fists. *Was it becau-se of the Heartstone?* He didn't know. But there was no time to grab it. Jack scowled, it was dark enough to send lesser men running with their tails between their legs.

He tried again.

Fire and water in rapid succession.

Serach actually laughed at him this time.

"Filan vahs!" he cursed, finding no way around this. His fin-gers itched, every instinct in his body screaming at him to find a weapon. But there were no weapons nearby for him to use. Not even an errant stone. A part of him hoped for one, what with the Tower's continuous tremors, but he didn't allow himself to dwell on the disappointment, extinguishing it as quickly as Serach did his flames. There was only one option left.

Jack surged backward, diving for Sylvie and grasping for the pulsing stone beneath her robes. But as his fingers wrapped des-perately around it, a voice whispered to him. Loud, frantic, and utterly irrepressible.

Stand up, came the sudden order. ***Stand up and finish him!***

Jack almost snapped, about to yell at *her* to leave him be. He already knew what he needed to do. Reminders were wholly un-necessary. But as he looked up, he found Serach grinning that same slimy smile and the words died in his throat.

The ancient tome was tucked safely in Serach's hands. And without a moment's hesitation, Serach opened it. Blood stained the pages—he didn't know whose—but it didn't matter. The ancient words spilled forth all the same. A flood of voices all muttering the same violent words

Serach joined them.

The entire Institute shook, stone rumbled, and the Zexin Sea trembled at the sudden disturbance, creating ripples Jack could actually hear. Water sloshed dangerously against the walls.

"Jack," Sylvie called urgently. "What's happening?"

Her voice commanded his attention for all of a moment, as she tried to sit up. He stopped her, holding a hand to her wound to quell the bleeding. His other held on tightly to the Heartstone, unable to tear it away from her. From them both.

"Jack," Sylvie called once more. A soft whisper against the mayhem unfurling around them. "What's happening?"

He didn't speak.

It's going to collapse! Jack shouted the answer in his mind. Afraid that if he said it out loud, it might suddenly ring true. He wasn't prepared for that. He wouldn't accept it—not yet. But he searched for an escape route all the same, panic clouding his features in a way that told Sylvie all she needed to know. Dust and small rocks fell from the walls, slipping around them like rain. *The Tower is going to fall and we're going to get caught in it! You're injured, and I can't fight some magic resistant, half-dead cretin and help you at the same time. I can't shift into some convenient fish to swim us to Eriam either. I can barely swim in the Zexin Sea on my own!*

An older section of the wall suddenly caved in.

The old enchantments gave way to the newer, sinister magic coursing through the Tower. And somewhere behind him, Ethil screamed. Jack turned in time to see her drag Reed away by his under-arms.

"Get away!" Jack yelled, eyes hysterical and pleading with

her to listen. "Now, Ethil! Leave him!"

"But..." the protest died in her throat when she saw the panic in his gaze. His eyes were wide and nervous in a way she'd never seen before. As he tried to silently order her to warn the others. To call for help. But most importantly, to listen to him and get away from here. Far, far away. Ethil hesitated, looking down at Reed—his eyes closed and his breaths gone—utterly asleep to the world with no more chance of waking. Could she really just leave him here? Alone in this place he had no recollection of coming to? Reed didn't deserve this. No one did.

"Reed," Sylvie called, choking back a sob.

"We can't," Jack denied fiercely, not meeting her stare. He was focused solely on the gaping wound that disfigured her side. It was *still* bleeding. "Ethil can't."

"But you can."

He looked at her then, severe and entirely uncompromising. As he bit back a torrent of vindictive *Íarre*. She was insane.

Ethil watched as a silent conversation passed between them in that look, and in the end, Sylvie conceded. Her mouth fell still. Ethil didn't know if she yielded because she believed Jack was right or if the effects of her injury finally caught up to her. But from the way Jack's eyes widened, as he began shaking and screaming her name, Ethil didn't want to know.

She dropped Reed, wincing when he fell a little too harshly. Her strength was waning. Ethil mumbled apologies in the form of prayers, before running off into the crumbling stairs for help. She didn't care from who. Anyone would do.

Jack hardly noticed her leave.

"Please tell me this is a joke, Sylvie," he muttered frantically, but she wasn't reacting. He ripped his sleeves to try and clog the wound. His hands were stained red. The metallic scent was so strong he could taste copper on his tongue. Jack fumbled for her pulse. It was a slow thrum beneath his fingertips. So weak that he almost missed it. But it was steady and it was there and it relieved him all the same.

"At least try to stay with me," he said dryly.

As if on cue, she convulsed. Her eyes shot open. Wide and diluted from shock. Sylvie gasped for breath. Her chest rose at a pace quick enough to make him jump back in surprise. But he gathered himself just as quickly and did his best to ease her. Sylvie coughed, opening her mouth to say something. Jack was quick to silence her with a reprimanding glare.

"I wasn't serious," he murmured, before saying louder, "Just take it easy! And for Silas' sake… stay still!"

Through the bleariness of her surroundings, she was able to give him one last glassy look, before her eyes closed once more.

Above them, rock cracked ominously. Jack looked up to find large splits in the ceiling. They grew longer and deeper with each passing second.

Serach's entire body was now alight with magic. Deadly and beautiful—more dazzling than a bomb was allowed to be. Serach was enveloped in the same rusty hue as the marks on the walls, and Jack watched, rooted to the spot in vivid fascination. As the color tainted the rest of the room. Blue turned red. Before it was corrupted by deep brown.

Razor sharp tendrils shot out from Serach's form, thrusting around the room with deadly sloppiness. Jack barely had time to dodge as one almost stabbed his arm. He cursed his own inability to parry. Another stroke came rushing down. Then two more. But this time, he wasn't so fortunate. They pierced his shoulder in rapid succession, going straight through bone. He saw more than felt the claws exit. A steady stream of blood followed.

Jack folded in on himself, forehead against the ground. As his face contorted in pain. He tried, but failed to muffle his screams. Good god, it hurt. His fingers were still wrapped desperately around the Heartstone—he didn't dare let it go—the sting of his nails against his palm distracted him from the injury on his shoulder. Barely.

Serach was screaming now.

A cry of pain and defiance. He crumpled into a small ball, the light still shining blindingly around him. Jack hardly noticed. Too busy dealing with his own wounds.

"I won't let you control me," Serach shouted, gripping his head tightly. As if to hold onto what was left of his humanity. "I refuse to submit to a nefarious voice enamored over a man long gone."

Serach cried out, his senses suddenly heightening. It made the pain all the more intense. A burning jolt that flared through his veins. Hotter than any heat—conjured or otherwise.

You believe offering sacrifices without offering yourself is enough? she said, speaking once more. A soft ring in their ears, stemming from an invisible place around them. *Your goals will not be realized, scum of Maurice.*

Jack had no time to feel surprised. He felt tightness grip his arm, strong enough to bruise. Jack found the same darkness encompassing Serach inching its way up from the Heartstone to clutch all too gleefully at his skin. Jack's hand burst into flame out of instinct, dangerously close to Sylvie's face. And he quickly doused the fire as she startled into wakefulness, reflexively gripping his arm with strength he didn't know she still had. All in an effort to get him away from her.

Her hands were hot, and Jack saw remnants of conjured embers burning what was left of his sleeve.

He didn't think she noticed.

Jack watched dazedly, as she touched the darkness wrapped around him. It receded obediently, only to rush up and choke her. *This happened before,* he realized. And with a bright hand, he touched the skin of her neck without pause, watching as the tendrils drew away. They receded more effectively this time. Back into the confines of the stone where they belonged. As if they were scared of magic. *What's happening? Just what is this thing?*

A crack sliced through the air.

Jack looked up in apprehension.

And then there was an explosion. So massive that the entire Assembly Tower shook. More stone fell. The veins around them shone brighter than ever before. As they were suddenly forced into overdrive. Forced to protect them from the remnants of an unknown blast.

Just then, the ancient tome suddenly stopped its erratic whispers. The air was still, shattered only by Serach's continuous screams. The marks carved along the walls emitted heat, and Jack's gaze fell upon the letter engraved between the ancient enchantments, realization dawning upon him. It was as sudden and swift as the next explosion that followed.

It rang deafeningly in his ears.

Much closer than the last. Too close for comfort.

It's going to burst, Jack realized, conjuring enough water to force Sylvie into wakefulness once again. She blinked twice and wheezed. Jack quickly adjusted her to lean against his uninjured shoulder. He kept his hand pressed to her wound. Her breaths were little more than ragged gasps against his skin. But he was no better. Only desperation and sheer will kept him—kept them both—upright.

Sylvie mumbled half a sentence, but it was lost to Serach's unholy screams behind them. Jack didn't dare look at the Elder now. There was no time. So long as he remained preoccupied, then that was enough for him.

They needed to leave. Now.

"I can't die here," he repeated to himself. Over and over. A chant of self-assurance. Anything to distract him from the jolts of pain that kept erupting from his shoulder.

They walked past Reed's still form. Jack spared him a glance, muttering a rushed prayer under his breath. That was all he had to offer.

A large stone abruptly fell from its place above and crushed Reed's legs. As if Jack needed further reason to leave him. He flinched when the sound of crunching bones sliced through air, sharper than any knife. Sylvie gurgled something unintelligible from under him and he felt her hot tears slide down his skin.

Jack turned both of their heads away.

He forced his feet forward. It wasn't hard. The disgust he felt for the puddle of blood pooling at their feet helped. Sylvie's own steps followed. Barely. He was walking for both of them.

They scarcely made it two steps, before a blast from behind propelled them forward. It shot them halfway down the hall. Jack fell right over his wound, crying out when muscles and sinew tore.

"*Vaklas,*" Jack cursed, holding his torn shoulder and gritting his teeth to keep from yelling any more than he already had.

Screaming made his head spin. And his arm wasn't quite numb enough to handle any more abuse.

He sorely wished he hadn't sent Ethil away.

Silas' flaming balls! What did I do to deserve this?

Jack looked behind him when Serach's angry screams began to fade, worried that the crazy codger might be after them again. His eyes widened in surprise when he found Serach consumed by darkness and encased in a brilliant sheen of familiar crystal. It swallowed his form whole, drowning out the last of his threats. As he finally lost to the demon within.

Wallow here with your pride, seethe in your impatience, and come back when you learn respect.

And then Serach was gone.

A large Orivellea crystal sat in his place.

His sudden disappearance brought Jack back to reality. The Drowned Tower was still crumbling. He couldn't stay here. As if to further prove his point, the tower shook again. Errant pieces of rock fell unnoticeably over his back. While an incredibly large one narrowly missed his skull.

It's the little things, Jack supposed, staring distractedly at the stone. It could've easily killed him. Half an inch to the left and he would've died. Really died.

Jack shivered, ripping his gaze away and trying to make sense of what was around him instead. The wall behind them had burst inward from the last explosion, allowing water to flood in at an alarming rate. He heard explosions coming from a far-off place both above and below them. If the granite didn't kill them, then the water undoubtedly would. He had no time to sit around, complain over a torn shoulder, and ponder over his own demise.

Jack blinked repeatedly, forcing his blurred vision away. It didn't work. He couldn't wait for it to. Jack gathered Sylvie as best he could in his arms and dragged them both away. She was barely conscious. She'd lost too much blood. So had he.

Still, Jack dragged her.

"I'm going to get us away from here," he promised, his grip tightening around her. She didn't react, and he didn't try to make her. She stared unseeingly at the flight of stairs before them. "Far, far away. You and me, Syl. We're not dying here. We aren't."

But they moved slowly. Excruciatingly so.

Water swept across their feet, and for a moment, he wished he could sink into it. Jack shook his head, uncaring for the way it made the world spin around him. He'd never allow himself such spineless thoughts. But as they finally neared the steps, Jack's eyes widened and he laughed in humorless amusement. He couldn't stop the wry tilt of his lips or the upward quirk of his brow. The First Zenith, the Creator—or whoever it was watching over them—clearly hated his guts.

The stairs had caved in.

Oh, there were a few.

… *Six, seven, eight,* he counted morosely. Eight steps that led upward, while the rest were crushed under never-ending piles of broken rock. The steps leading downward remained intact, but water continued to spill from the open wall down the hall and he had no intention of moving further from the Zexin Sea's surface. Into a place he knew would flood long before this one.

I don't even know what's down there.

Jack laughed again. If the stairs were blocked, where had Ethil gone? Was she able to leave before they fell or had she been crushed? He didn't know. One thing, however, was certain.

Help wouldn't be coming.

Jack didn't register falling against the wall. Only that he was standing one moment, and the next he simply wasn't. His legs refused to cooperate and his arm had gone completely numb. That was never a good sign.

I can't move.

The water made him shiver, so he summoned fire… he tried to. A spark barely escaped him. He was exhausted. He was losing blood. She was losing blood. They were both dying. And he could hardly find the strength for his usual acidic asides.

"Sylvie," he breathed, sparing her a glance.

She leaned heavily against him, passed out once again. Blood pooled around them—whose? He couldn't find it in himself to care. It was diluted by seawater, painting the first few inches of water about them darker than the rest.

Jack flashed her a careless grin, uncaring for her lack of response. "Surviving everything but the roof. How stupid is that? Can you believe we're actually the best the Drowned Tower has to offer?"

And then he saw it.

The soft pulse of the Heartstone under Sylvie's robes.

His eyes widened at the sight. He thought of *her*. Of the power *she* had to offer. He didn't like it, but it was their only option. Their situation certainly couldn't afford hesitation.

"Are you there?" Jack asked his stomach, his voice hopeful. He knew *she* was all around him. But he liked talking to his stomach. It gave him a point to focus on and gave *her* a place in his world, making *her* seem realer—and it made him feel like less of a loon. Which was always an added bonus.

"I need your help."

Silence answered him.

He waited for one anticlimactic moment. Two. Then three.

Nothing happened. Nothing fucking happened.

Jack didn't cry. He never would. Not for something like this. But he might as well have. His body was sore and mental exhaustion hung over him. Disappointment over something as impossible as this was an entirely new kind of low. One he swore he'd never hit. His fingers brushed absentmindedly against the stone around Sylvie's neck. He watched it thrum against his fingertips. Even stronger than the beat of his heart.

Jack's face twisted into a sinister smirk, before he threw his head back and gave a short bark of laughter. No humor to be found. Just pure self-deprecation.

What did he think would happen? That he'd gain inhumane power just because he asked? That he'd be able to escape with his limbs intact and both of their lives saved? Some deals could only exist in dreams, where reality was flawed and desire ran deep. Useless fantasies. He had better things to do than play with the monsters inside.

How stupid, he thought bitterly, *a complete waste of t—*

Jack wheezed, doubling over and gasping for air.

Gnashing his teeth, he clawed at his neck. As an unknown force knocked the wind from his lungs. His entire body erupted in waves of pain. Jack screamed, crying out in wild abandon when he felt something tear its way out of his chest. Hot and heavy. A mass of thorns and sweltering heat.

He sensed the darkness then.

Its tendrils were coiled around one of his lungs, over and under his intestines, up his esophagus, and wrapped firmly around his heart. Dangerous. Literally constricting in its efficiency. It crawled upward, blackening his skin. But Sylvie wasn't awake to peel it back, and he gasped in horror when the lullaby he'd come to dread filled his ears once more.

"Get away from me!" Jack yelled.

You wanted my help, she said simply. *I've come to give it.*

He wanted to get away from here. Not be taken over. He'd rather die than end up like Serach or Rior.

"I'm not handing over my body!" Jack snarled, furiously glaring at the wisps of darkness that spun across his vision.

I do not need it, she said, ever gracious. *Nor do I want it. You can hear me. That is enough. Destiny will bring me where I need to go, so long as I remain in the hands of the First Zenith.*

"This again?" Jack spat. "Don't mention things you don't want to elaborate."

The descendant of Silas Drayr lies beside you.

Jack's eyes widened. He looked down at Sylvie. Unconscious and dying.

"Impossible," he said lowly. "You're lying! If she's a descendant then why woul—you *need* her!" Jack sputtered, trying to find the words. "You said so yourself! If you need her then why choke her?"

A reaction against those with inborn circuits. Ingrained into me by none other than the traitor, Maurice.

He coughed, choking on his own spit in surprise. Maurice—Healer of the Frail, Champion of the Hopeless, Defender of the Just—a traitor? Absurd. Jack thought *she*'d been referring to Healers in general when speaking of Maurice, but that clearly wasn't the case. Jack didn't ask *her* to explain herself though.

There would be time for that later.

He touched the side of his head in preference.

Natural circuits, he thought, running his fingers along the Orive crystal embedded in his skull. Planted when he was born. An amplifier for his magic. A secret of all Elementalists—and the reason why deserters were all treated so brutally. When the first Elementalist deserted, they caught and tortured him. Something they had to do to all the others, so as to avoid suspicion.

"You know then..." Jack muttered, carefully choosing his words. "That Elementalists are purposefully given more."

Know? she laughed. A bitter thing. *Whose power do you think lies inside the Orivellea?*

Jack trembled at the revelation.

That snake sealed Thelarius away, she said angrily. A deep and burning anger, simmering in years of unspent fury. Ready to be unleashed at a moment's notice. *He locked me in Aethilium greviya and used my parts to create more. More, more, more.*

"More what?"

Silence.

"Why are you helping me?" he asked instead, trying to grasp *her* words. They seemed preposterous. But if someone had told him before today that the Drowned Tower would crumble overnight, then he would've laughed at them. Anything was possible with *her* in the picture. "You can already do so much on your own."

Hosts wither. Nothing takes men faster to death's side than greed.

"I don't understand." Jack shook his head, exasperated with it all. "Why stick to me? Why grant me power? Why give me answers? I'm no descendant of the First Zenith." That much, he was sure of.

There must only be one, she said vaguely. *One that holds the power of the heart.*

"One?" he asked, confused.

When *she* didn't answer, Jack searched the hazy corners of his mind, going through *her* words. As he looked upon the raging waters still pouring inside. He tried not to focus on his breathing or pain of his shoulder. And soon enough, the first trickles of realization dawned upon him.

"One," he repeated. This time with clarity.

Jack didn't trust *her*. He knew it. *She* knew it. They disregarded it. This relationship—if it could be considered one—was built on a misguided sense of vengeance and the will to live.

Nothing more. But perhaps that was enough. For now.

He laughed. Not the sarcastic laughter he gave his enemies or the amused chuckles he usually let loose. Just honest, happy relief. Everything had a price. But was that really all she wanted? Was this the reason why she sought him out? Why she sought all Elementalists out? How goddamn laughable.

"You could've taken it long ago," he said, smiling. To actually ask him—he didn't know if *she* had good manners or if *she* was just amusing herself, but he liked it. Straightforward and fair. He couldn't fault that. "I'm surprised you even offered me anything to begin with. If this was originally yours, then you should've taken it back years ago. I've never wanted something as wearisome as power."

What then, do you seek?

Jack smiled, delirious from the lack of blood.

"Life."

A woman appeared before him then. Beautiful enough to make him question his sanity. She had light gray eyes and hair that couldn't seem to decide if it was solid or smoke. Wisps of black surrounded her. Each had a mouth that sang her eternal lullaby. They rose from her feet, giving her the aura of an ethereal being. The sight should've been divine. Worthy of poems and myth. But Jack was no artist. The singing darkness only elicited an irrational sense of terror from deep inside of him.

She smiled, reaching out to trace his cheek. A featherlike prod that glided like water over his skin. Despite her jagged fingernails, Jack could hardly feel her touch. Her eyes sparked with familiar, broken warmth, and in that moment, he knew that she wasn't seeing him for who he was. But then the moment passed, and the gleeful cloud over her eyes lifted along with it. Her smile was still in place, but all traces of heat left her gaze.

Thelarius has taught me that man, despite his capabilities, cannot accomplish anything alone. So, one. I shall leave you one.

"What?" Jack asked, once again stumped by her words. *What is she talking about? Didn't she mean to take—*

You shall need it for the trials to come, she went on, interrupting his thoughts. *To protect the descendant of Silas, to protect yourself, and to change your world.*

"How kind of you," Jack found himself muttering in disdain. His previous train of thought left him, as she finished her speech. Was she reading his mind again? The only ones he'd ever said those words to were Sylvie and Tiv.

Use it wisely. Use it well.

"Why?" he asked.

The blood that fell from his wound was slower now. He had no more to give. If he was already running out, he didn't even want to think about Sylvie. Was she even breathing? He couldn't hear her.

His senses narrowed to the woman before him. Could she really pull him from the clutches of death? They were near already. So near. He could feel numbness spreading.

"I told you, I don't want your power."

Because you remind me of him, she whispered, *consider yourself fortunate.*

And he felt pain once again. Accompanied by the sudden, strong pump of his heart. He belatedly noticed Sylvie's eyes shoot open. She was screaming, clutching her head, her tears flowing freely down her cheeks. As she cried for reprieve from the sudden attack. Jack's voice joined hers, unable to muffle the agony.

Their blood burned.

And *she* continued to smile.

26

In the stillness of night, darkness reigned.

The stars were shadowed by the drear, as the moon ducked behind a cloud. The downpour did nothing to alleviate the stress upon her vision.

It seemed even their celestial guardians had grown tired of seeing them, tired of seeing their world and the continuous blood that fell upon their lands. Filled with uncivilized denizens living in yesterday. But she didn't mind. For she'd tamed the beast called darkness long ago. During her time, when the world was far bloodier a place. When spoiled children didn't run about complaining about the slightest fault in their luxury.

She'd conquered what others only dreamed of.

The wind was a far more pressing concern. Coupled with thunder and rain, it drenched her red robes. Water blackened just as much as blood. It might as well have been. For she reeked of it. Wet soil shared the same metallic scent.

And it was all over her boots.

She sat atop a large mountain, waiting for the storm to pass and allow her passage. The lands were too dangerous for her to recklessly cross in the midst of a hurricane. She didn't want to be a victim of stupidity and loose footing. Instead, she passed her time looking at the tall figure in the distance.

Pernelia's statue.

It glinted proudly amidst the storm, easily surviving nature's carnage. Just as it had done for centuries before and would continue to for the centuries to come. An unwavering protector of the

Institute's impervious Eastern Branch. The Drowned Tower was a stern box of black inside the even blacker waters, and she wished—not for the first time—that it had a more soulful hue. Surely, there was an enchantment of sorts that could keep it undimmed under the Zexin Abyss. Give it a brighter hue.

Garish yellow, perhaps, she mused with a quiet chuckle.

Her mindless thoughts reminded her of a time when she'd gaze out her window, purposely focusing on the same sights in an attempt to tire her eyes, so she could get to bed.

But this wasn't her home.

She wasn't enveloped by the torpid comfort a lit room and a warm bed had to offer. And though she didn't want to be here— a part of her still urged her to come. To do this herself. Instead of handing the job off to one of the many grunts under her supervision. How easy it would've been to do so, but she wasn't the sort to leave such pressing problems in the hands of an underling.

It wasn't all bad—perhaps if she'd be forced to extend her stay—but for the moment, it was tolerable. At least she'd be able to conclude business of a more personal nature.

If nothing else, she thought, *I'll be able to see him.*

Still, it was late. It was cold. And she knew enough about sleep to know there was none to be had tonight.

The Drowned Tower was still, as it sat under the capricious waves of the Zexin Sea. As if nothing was wrong.

She could only hope.

But she was quickly proven wrong when Pernelia's statue emitted a bright light. The Zexin Sea erupted, shaking Eriam's lands. Waves forced themselves upon the shores, moving further than she'd ever seen. They twisted the outer trees that lined Tearwood. She heard cries—whether they came from Eriam or the Institute, she couldn't tell.

A ripple emerged from beneath the water. Loudly followed by another flash of light.

And it all came crumbling down.

***

The skies remained undisturbed by the sudden explosion, still soaking her to the bone and still buffeting everything that stood between them and the already flooded ground. The waves of the Zexin Sea roared dangerously amidst the gloom, as if warning others away. Many heeded it. The practitioners she saw exhaustedly sweeping away from the restless waters only proved it.

Some were pulled back in, too fatigued or too panicked to properly save themselves. By the time she made her way down the slippery cliffs, Eriam's shores were beyond reprieve.

The practitioners lucky enough to swim away from the Drowned Tower were inconsolable, barely able to answer any of her questions. Just what was happening? Was this Serach's doing? His apprentice? How many had escaped? But those she asked were either in shock or just as clueless. And she didn't have the time to find someone that wasn't. A young girl ran past her, shoving her way straight into the arms of her older brother—one of the patrollers, she guessed, watching a dozen of them appear from where she came, surprise plain on their faces.

They were quick to gather themselves, healing who they could and shouting for missing loves ones.

Only subconsciously aware that they were too late.

A number of practitioners had already fled the area in fright. She doubted they'd return any time soon. From the corner of her eye, she saw a woman weeping, as she stood over a man's body. His lips were blue from the cold. And the Healer that had finally arrived took one look at his cold form, shook his head, then took off again. Quick as a whistle. It only made the woman cry harder. A man shouted behind her, running into the water and calling desperately for someone that could no longer hear him.

Are all eastern practitioners so mouthy? she thought.

But, mockery aside, she had to resist the urge to do the same. This wasn't the time for breakdowns. Besides, her Demar Spell was still active, so she knew better than anyone that who she sought was still alive and breathing.

For now, that was enough. She watched in mild interest as the screaming man was suddenly grabbed by the shoulders, dragged reluctantly to a safer distance, and then promptly told to shut up. He didn't. As expected. But she was surprised to see the patroller who'd taken him knock him unconscious without a second thought. She had to give their quick thinking credit.

The patrollers were just as devastated, but at least they kept some form of order. Still, it wasn't enough to warrant any voiced praise. Not from her at least.

"It seems," she murmured, speaking to the devastated Tower, "that the time has finally come for me to make my move."

She stepped forward.

"*Vanera nahn dasen*," she said in fluent *Íarre*. And with a snap of her fingers, dozens of Peose suddenly emerged from Tearwood's protective line of trees. Giant frogs stepped from the mist, sidestepping frightened practitioners and coming to a stop before her. Their veins pulsed a soft blue under the blinding rain. Their gazes were hollow and unsettling.

Unruffled by the sodding weather.

"Call my legion," she commanded, "we've much to do."

The frogs cried out in unison. A high-pitched wail that made those around them wince. Before they dispersed, jumping hundreds of feet into the air only to disappear over the Eirinne Mountains that the east boasted so highly about. She turned, ignoring the practitioners' strangled gasps of surprise.

"My name is Cheryll Dace," she introduced.

Her words were met with shocked silence. Not even a whisper of gossip. Perhaps they were still too dazed from their ordeal—this sudden turn of events was simply an extra dash of salt to a still bleeding wound. They couldn't gape forever though. Cheryll wouldn't have it.

"Everyone sit down and be still," she commanded, voice slicing through the heavy rain. "I can't watch over all of you. Nor do I plan to. So, *please...*" she emphasized, shooting them all a meaningful glance. The threat behind her gaze was more intense than anything they'd ever seen. "Cooperate."

They still didn't answer. And when Cheryll turned away, they realized that she didn't care if they did. So long as they obeyed.

A small, red bird suddenly shot out from Tearwood, flapping tiny wings toward her. There was a flash of light. Then wings extended into arms, a beak flattened into a mouth, and the bird was now a man, grinning from ear to ear with a smile bright enough to blind. He bowed in greeting. His flaming red locks were matted to his head, yet were still stark in the rain.

Enchantment, Cheryll mused, smirking at the thought. It was impossible for hair to remain so undimmed by the world around it—especially from the current somberness of their surroundings. But there he was. Red and grinning and *red*. She hated it.

"Redmond," she said, keeping her dislike far from sight.

She knew him well. For his skill and his servile personality. He was the sycophantic sort that she never got on well with. Always currying favor and never knowing when to stop doing so. It was unspoken knowledge that once childish features matured, everyone learned at least one charm to replace their puppy eyes—at least she thought it was. Now, she wasn't so sure.

Redmond was in that awkward stage where his face no longer held the appeal it once did, yet he still used it to get what he wanted. It was enough to make even the nicest of people gag.

Cheryll Dace wasn't the politest of company.

"So you were here," Cheryll said disinterestedly. "Why?"

He didn't seem offended by her lack of greeting or the coldness in her tone. "You told me I could go wherever I pleased, so long as I stayed near another one of your Hunters."

"So you chose the Drowned Tower," Cheryll finished, looking out at the sea. The waters slowly stilled, returning to its calm before this sudden tragedy. Why he chose such a dreary place was beyond her. He had strange taste.

She'd never willingly return here, and had been adamant against sending Jack, but there were some things she couldn't argue with Leonas. Jack's studies were one of many.

It was an Elementalist's duty to train their fellow Elementalist. Especially their kin. Or so he always insisted. Mule.

"What happened here?" Cheryll asked.

Redmond frowned, shaking his head, as he said, "Nothing more than the rest I'm afraid. I've been stranded out here in Tearwood. Left to take care of the Peose. Your primary apprentice may know more."

As if on cue, she appeared.

Myrrh stumbled out of the water, the fading remnants of scales on her arms and legs. But what caught Cheryll's eye was the face of another peeking out from behind her small frame. The nameless practitioner had a full head of curls darkened by the rain. The slender limbs wrapped around Myrrh told Cheryll that it was a woman, but nothing more. Her eyes were closed, shut peacefully from the disaster circling around them.

"You're late," Cheryll stated, intense and reprimanding all at once. "What were you doing?"

"I went to see Elder Serach," Myrrh answered, struggling under the extra weight of another on her back. Redmond sneered at her, his arms were crossed like stone, fully unwilling to offer his assistance.

"And the girl?"

"Ethil Mane. I picked her up before the Institute exploded. She's a Healer."

"I told you not to interfere," Cheryll muttered, glaring at her in a way that reminded Myrrh all too much of Jack. But the moment passed, and Cheryll hid her glare behind a careful mask of equanimity and looked onward. Away from her. Away from everyone. Her eyes searched the waters, trying to find someone beneath the waves. "And Serach? Rior? What happened to them? Did you find the stone?"

"Serach was dying before I left. Sylvie Sirx and Jacques Dace were finishing him," Myrrh reported, carefully looking at her to gauge her reaction. Cheryll's mask didn't crumble. It didn't even falter. As utterly infallible as she remembered. "Sylvie had the stone."

"Sylvie Sirx," Cheryll whispered, the familiar features of a proud advisor coming to the forefront of her mind. Was there any relation? It was likely. The apprentices of Arch Potens were usually practitioners from well-off families, if not blood. Cheryll vaguely recalled reading about her in one of Columbus' letters. The dolt had even bothered to send a rather detailed drawing. She didn't bother confirming her thoughts though, she'd find out soon enough. Jack was still alive. Her active Demar Spell was proof of that. And if Sylvie wasn't with him, then she doubted the name would hold any more significance.

Serach must've been deep inside the Institute. Escape was next to impossible. The chances of both of them making it out on their own were slim. If only she had a tracking spell on Sylvie as well.

"Rior…" Myrrh paused, as if searching for the words. Her face scrunched up in sudden disgust. "Rior died at their hands. He was searching for the Heartstone as well, but was eventually taken over by the darkness within. I assume he drank the same tonic Serach did. Though I doubt he did it out of desperation. He was already losing it by the time he reached Sylvie. He had…" Myrrh trailed off, frowning at the thought of his skill. She'd seen him quite a few times during her years in the Diamond Alps. He was good. Better than most naturally brought up in the Institute. "He had talent. The fact that Serach kept him was a waste. We could've incorporated him into our ranks."

"I tried," Cheryll said honestly, before shrugging. There was no use dwelling on what could've been. The stings of regret were plenty. She didn't have time to ponder over all of them. "Serach refused."

"Why?"

"Some Masters want to see their apprentices do good, but never better than them."

The silence that proceeded her words was tangible. Jealousy

was powerful. It was ugly. And yet, it reared its head whenever the chance presented itself. As if the world didn't have enough of it already.

The north overflowed with it.

Filled with petty small-minded thieves who couldn't see past their own lives, simply not caring about the truth. That their games of power affected far more than their own greed. They didn't realize that the land they so ardently adored would crumble long before the appointment of a new head. It would break in their hands. Their careless hands. The Drowned Tower was just the beginning. Soon, even the Nebbin would be caught in their affairs.

And what then?

Cheryll didn't want to find out. Instead, she regarded Myrrh in quiet contemplation, watching as she shifted Ethil on her back. Careful not to hurt her.

"Do what you will with her, Myrrh," Cheryll ordered, entirely uninterested with her baggage. But if Myrrh found Ethil important enough to save, despite her wishes to leave the situation well enough alone, than she'd have to take responsibility. Cheryll certainly wouldn't. She already had so many under her command. "You're to fly back to the Diamond Alps and wait for further instruction."

Myrrh opened her mouth to protest, but Cheryll was quick to turn her back on her. Only vaguely aware of the smug smirk that stretched across Redmond's face. Cheryll walked along the stretch of bridge that once led to the Drowned Tower's entrance, carefully testing the stone before stepping. The bridge was mostly gone, eaten by the Zexin abyss. But as she looked into the watery depths, she saw something glowing.

A soft light in the darkness. It illuminated dozens of drowned bodies and damaged furniture, but it covered something as well. A bright sheen stood between the lights' center and the waves. Cheryll squinted, trying to get a better look.

There's someone inside.

She bent to dip her hands into the frothy waves. The light

brightened with each passing second, getting bigger and bigger.

No, she realized, *it's not getting bigger. It's coming closer.*

Before she could step away, a shining crystal broke the water's surface, floating precariously above the rocking sea. From behind her, she heard the startled gasps of the scant practitioners brave enough to follow her this far. Cheryll ignored them, opting instead to glare in open disdain at the one inside the shell.

It was Serach.

Saved, ironically, by the darkness he angered.

He slept peacefully within, his body half-consumed by black. What was left of his humanity was mostly burned, yet there were also fresh patches of skin, as if hastily healed. It was a disturbing sight. But Cheryll could guess well enough who was responsible for his current state—Jack. Leonas had the same tendency to burn others beyond all recognition.

But where was he? He couldn't be dead. Her active Demar spell said otherwise. It was an aged thing, almost two decades old, though it was far better than most. Cheryll had spent an absurd amount of time honing the spell and though it was difficult to cast, no one could deny its potency.

Cheryll openly sighed, she'd have to find him later.

Once things calmed down. For now, she needed to deal with this eyesore.

"Trapped in crystal and fast asleep," Cheryll said, smirking in venomous glee. Just what did he do to end up in such a state? How much did he push *her*? "Do you think this will spare you? You betrayed the Council. I need to cut out your tongue."

Cheryll turned, motioning to Redmond to call for one of the leftover Peose. She needed to melt the Orive. Serach could suffer a little more burning. She doubted he'd mind. He deserved it for what he put this branch through. Cheryll smiled at the thought of putting him in his place. But her smile fell when she heard startled screams erupt from the shore.

A black mass crept upward, settling over the sand.

"What is that thing?" one of the practitioners cried. They stepped closer. As it emitted a soft gray light.

Cheryll's eyes widened.

"Get away!" she yelled, running toward them. They looked at her in stunned surprise, before gathering themselves and scrambling off as far as they could.

But the light died down.

And after one more soft pulse, the darkness slipped inward, receding into itself to show two practitioners lying in an ungainly heap surrounded by water and blood. Even from where she stood, she could see that they each had wounds that must've been either gaping or fatal at one point. Perhaps both. But now they were sealed shut. A grotesque scar remained in their place.

Cauterization scars.

They weren't moving. Cheryll assumed the worst. But as she finally slowed to a stop before them, the faces that greeted her struck her with a sense of vivid familiarity that made her falter. Their breaths were slow but deep. And though pain seemed to have been permanently etched onto their faces, their wounds were mostly, if not completely, healed.

"Luck favors you," she muttered, surprised by the sudden gentleness of her tone. "Pray the First Zenith does as well."

She kneeled before them, brushing dark hair from both of their faces. So as to get a clearer view of their pale skin. Their flesh was cold beneath her fingertips and getting colder under the rain. But Cheryll could do little to help them. Besides, they looked well enough. As well as two practitioners that just escaped the Zexin abyss could look.

Cheryll preferred their quiet breaths over the jittery practitioners around her. She had no doubt that they'd survive this. It was nothing more than a gut feeling. But she trusted her instincts. They told her that they'd successfully escaped death's clutches. At least for today. So, instead of calling for a Healer, her fingers danced along the closed points of their eyes. Cheryll pulled their eyelids up one by one to look at the color of the irises beneath.

Red and orange.

She knew of only two practitioners with eyes like those in the Drowned Tower, and she exhaled a sigh of relief she hadn't known she'd been holding. Behind them, the skies finally gave way for brightness. Shafts of heat burst through the heavens.

White and searing.

Ending the night with dawn's first light.

27

Tiv didn't know what happened.

One moment, he was running down the Drowned Tower's halls, evading crumbling stone and shouting at the practitioners he passed to leave and find a safe place to hide, then the next he was simply—*not*.

He awoke to a sharp kick to the head. His immediate reaction was to shout at the uncouth bastard courageous enough to actually boot him awake, but it was quickly replaced by surprise. And a flash of confusion. Tiv had expected to find himself in bed, or buried under his weight in rubble, or even floating aimlessly in the Zexin Sea on a sorry piece of timber. The one thing he hadn't expected was to find himself trapped in a cramped prison wagon with his hands and feet bound.

The wagon smelt of sweat, vomit, and piss. A putrid stench. And the white spots in his vision told him that his health clearly wasn't at its best. Where was he? What was he doing here? Before he could voice his questions, a harsh whisper sliced through air. Then another.

So, there are two of them.

They called his name. But he couldn't see their faces. Tiv tried to all the same, squinting in an attempt to force his eyes to adjust to the darkness faster. It didn't work. But he didn't give in. And when his resolve paid off, he was greeted by faces first.

Pom, Khale, Olivia, Roval, and a few other nameless practitioners he didn't recognize. Most were passed out, while the few that weren't stifled sobs of fear. Next, came his surroundings. A number of armed guards encircled them. The armor they wore had been polished to a shine. Little good it did them, as they got dirtier with each step.

It's morning, Tiv realized, confused by the thick shade. He was used to life without the horizon, but he wasn't in the Tower. That was obvious enough. *Where's the sun?*

Tiv squinted again. He found the sky's brightness swallowed by dark gray clouds, reflecting against a seemingly endless stretch of wetland. Mud caked the floor and sullied the air, accompanying the loud sounds of their caravan with even louder squelches.

They were passing through a swamp. Tiv knew of only one bog near the Eirinne Mountains—the Surbug Mire.

Where were they going? Who were these people? And why were his comrades just sitting there allowing this?

"Tiv," Pom whispered, eyes darting around in suspicion. He leaned forward just as the wagon's wheel dipped into an unstable patch of mud, making his head hit the wagon's floor. And he let out a string of curses loud enough to scare away a flock of nearby birds.

"Hey," one of the guards admonished, poking Pom's back with the tip of his bow. It was worn, but sturdy. Tiv didn't trust the confident way in which he held it. "Quiet down in there."

Pom made a swipe for him, but the guard simply jutted his bow harsher into his spine until he cried out in pain.

"One word…" he threatened. "One more word and I'll give you something to whine about."

Tiv was about to yell, to transform, to hurt them, and make them feel pain far beyond imagine. But the kick he received gave him pause. Tiv turned to face Khale with a fierce glare that would have made lesser men tremble. What ticked him off more was that the bastard didn't seem to mind that he probably bruised his shin, as he said nothing in response, merely tilted his head toward the armed guards in a meaningful way.

Tiv scrutinized their captors.

Stilling, when he noticed their eyes. Their irises were varying shades of brown. One even had green. Those weren't the colors of any practitioner. They were Nebbin.

Why are we surrounded by Nebbin? And why did these idiots just allow themselves to be taken away?

But then he saw another man walk up, his smile was all kinds of patient and placating. He placed two fingers on the edge of the man's weapon and lowered it from Pom's back. He flashed the man another easy smile. His eyes disappeared in mirth as he did so. But Tiv saw a brief flash of orange just before they did.

What's a Conjurer doing with them? Is he a deserter?

"Easy," the Conjurer said. Low and frightening. "Leave the kids alone. We don't want the merchandise ruined now, do we?"

"He's right," another spoke up. His eyes were chatoyant and blue, glowing in the darkness. A Healer. "Loosen up, Gabin." The Healer shoved a flask in his face, forcefully tipping its orifice near his mouth. "Everyone works better when they're intoxicated."

"Damn Healers shouldn't be saying stupid shit like that!" Gabin shouted, pushing him away. "Drink too much and they'll escape behind our backs. He'll kill us if we let them escape. I'm not ready for death."

"Write a will then," the Healer said easily. As if it were that simple.

The Conjurer laughed. He flashed them another easy smile. Amused by an inside joke that he didn't bother explaining to the rest. "Wills are for the living, you dunce."

Another Nebbin joined in, placing a hand on the hilt of his sword and bowing it forward in habit. "Does he really still have that kind of power?" he asked, tilting his head for effect. "There are rumors, you know? Rumors of their failing fortunes."

"Those aren't just rumors," the Healer said with a careless shrug of his shoulders, decidedly uninterested. "The Lafertti clan are poorer than street urchins. They've long sold what little they had left. But wealth has always dwindled easily. Power, not so much. And that's what the boss wants. Their influence."

The Conjurer scoffed. "I'd settle for their wealth instead. I can't continue doing this without proper payment. I don't care how long they've been buying from us. Our service means gold."

As they settled into a heated back-and-forth about their trade, Tiv glanced at the guards around them. There were more than a few Conjurers and Healers thrown into the mix of Nebbin. And Tiv had to consciously keep himself from shuddering when he looked up to find an Amorph in the form of a large spider, carefully watching over them. They were completely surrounded. It was no wonder the others hadn't tried to escape.

It was too dangerous.

Tiv didn't doubt that some of them could make it out—himself, included—but what of the others? Most were fast asleep in what he hoped wasn't forced slumber. But the small puddle of blood by one of their heads told him otherwise. It tainted the air with the scent of copper and rust. As the wagon continued to dip forward and shake, making the blood creep over their robes. Tiv watched in morbid fascination as a drop trailed over his leg.

None of the Healers made a move to help their fallen comrade, and one look at the weeping one by his side told him that they were forced not to. She was a child. No more than ten years of age. Yet she stifled her sobs, swallowing down pain and fright. She nursed her hand. As a young Amorph boy tried in vain to comfort her. There was a hole right through her palm and one of her fingers were gone. Both wounds bled out at an alarming rate, the strips of cloth she'd used to quell the bleeding were already sopping wet with blood. She shivered, despite the humidity of the bog.

She'd die soon.

Tiv wouldn't allow it. He had to do something. But, what?

He lifted a hand, hesitantly placing it over her head. Tiv had never been good with children, always handling them with deliberate distance. They were too fragile. Too pure. Too everything. But he needed to do this—for his sake—because he could do little else. And when she tried to choke out a smile for him, even he felt a little better.

"They're slavers," Pom suddenly whispered, eyeing the guards around them warily. As the Amorph above them crept to the far side of the wagon. Khale subtly covered Pom's smaller form, allowing him a brief minute to speak. "They took a lot of us during the confusion. Even pulled some of us from the Zexin Sea. You were drowning. They saved you. Me, too."

Well, I'm not going to thank them, Tiv thought bitterly.

"Overconfident loons," Khale muttered. "Can't believe they had the balls ta kidnap a cartful of practitioners, and lacked the heart ta at least leave the brats behind."

"Well, we can't exactly do the same," Pom said begrudginly. "We can't just leave all these people behind, and we have no idea how good these deserters are."

"We have to do something," Tiv urged.

Tiv let out a strangled cry when he felt pain blossom from his side. One of the guards had spotted them. The hilt of one of his many daggers dug uncomfortably into Tiv's lower back. The blow was hard enough to make him gasp. That would definitely leave a mark. And Tiv's patience was finally at its end. With a sudden flash of light backing him, he transformed into a raven, and with the litheness of years, nicked one of the man's daggers from its hilt.

Only to transform back to stab him in the throat. The man gurgled on his own blood, eyes looking at his own wildly, before the light left them. It was enough to get the rest of the guards moving. Along with the captured practitioners.

From the corner of his eye, Tiv saw those still conscious transform into deadly creatures and engage the men closest to the wagon. Pom was the first to get a blow in, shifting into a bird to claw the eyes out of the man that had prodded him earlier with his bow. While some—the younger ones no doubt—turned into insects or smaller fowl, fleeing into the distance.

Tiv cursed, though he didn't blame them. They'd never seen battle. Let alone, participated in one. But that didn't stop his insides from burning with rage at the sudden abandonment.

Khale was still inside the wagon, grappling with the spider that had suddenly grown a hundred times its size. His red head was pushed face-first into the iron bars. Twice. Before he finally realized that he couldn't do this without his powers. So, allowing his reflexes to take control, Khale shifted into a large bear. His teeth sunk into one of the arachnid's legs.

It screeched deafeningly.

Their fight startled the rest of the practitioners into wakefulness. Their sudden panic forced the wagon to swivel and tip over. But Olivia was finally up and, despite her confusion, she wasted no time picking the lock of the wagon's door, allowing the others a chance to escape. The children ran out first, vaulting through the door with fear in their eyes and in their shouts. The older ones were next. Followed by the fiercely battling Amorphs.

They tumbled out, struggling on the ground, as they charged each other again. Blood spilled from the wagon's side. Remnants from those unlucky enough to have stayed a minute too long.

Blasts of fire and water suddenly surrounded them, decimating their surroundings. The Conjurers amongst them had finally joined the fray. Tiv watched in abject horror as the young girl he saw ran in a frantic circle, burning alive. He quickly transformed into a large hound, pinning the Conjurer responsible to the ground and tearing out his throat.

An arrow promptly pierced one of his legs, forcing him to whimper away from the man. But it was too late. The Conjurer was dead. And when Tiv returned to his usual form, blood coated every inch of his mouth. It tasted of copper and memories, dragging him back to the times when he first started patrolling the Eirinne Mountains with Jack. But he wasn't fighting for his home now. He wasn't fighting for his partner or even for his life. Right now, Tiv fought simply because he was angry.

Nothing more.

Tiv hardly registered the sting of a dagger tearing through the ligaments of his shoulder. He merely turned sharply and glared at the Nebbin responsible. The man backed away in sudden fright. He didn't get very far. A dagger as sharp as frost stuck out from behind his throat, glinting triumphantly in the gloom. It was pulled out just as quickly and the man fell forward to reveal Pom, who had a look of utter fury on his face.

"The wind hasn't picked up. No ice either," Pom said with gritted teeth. Tiv knew the implication behind his words. They didn't have a full variety of Conjurers. "Some of the kids ran far. Olivia's healing those that didn't." Pom looked him in the eye, tightening his hold over his gory blade. "There aren't many."

The implication of that was clear as well. Just how many of them had died? And how many decided to turn tail and run? Where would they go?

This was the Surbug Mire.

A famous dump site for the dead in the past. Falling into a trench and never crawling out was a likely occurrence.

Tiv growled in frustration, running his hands through his hair in exasperation. "What about the slavers?"

"Either dead or gone," a foreign voice interrupted. They turned to see Khale bounding up to them, he was covered head to toe in blood. As he fumbled with a spider fang two times the size of his head. "Well, most of them."

"What?"

Khale snorted and tilted his head off to the side where a man tried to quietly scurry away without their knowledge. A pitiful attempt. His leg was twisted in an impossible angle and he left a long, noticeable trail in the mud. Though Tiv still gave him points for trying.

"He looks talkative," Khale said, tickled.

Without a second thought, Tiv grabbed the man by his hair. One look in his eyes told him that he wasn't a practitioner. That made things easier.

"Who do you work for?" Tiv whispered, tightening his grip. Tears streamed down the man's face and he mumbled something incoherent. Tiv didn't have the patience to decipher it. "I didn't catch that," Tiv said, dangerously low. "I'll give you one more chance. Who do you work for?"

"No, please," the nameless man begged, sobbing and failing to get away. "Please let me go. We were just hired by the Lafertti clan to capture you. Please, please, please. I don't want to die."

"Who are they?" Tiv asked. "And how did they find out about the Drowned Tower so quickly?"

"It's barely been a day," Pom said, joining him. He played with a dagger, tapping the sharper edges of it against the man's neck. It wasn't his—he didn't know where his had gone, but he had a feeling it was a thousand leagues under the Zexin Sea by now—though it served as a suitable replacement. "Did they have a part in this?"

"I don't know!" he cried. His eyes warily followed the trail Pom traced along his collar. He flinched when the dagger drew blood. "I don't know the details! We get told to do something and we do it. No questions asked."

"Sounds familiar," Pom snickered, grinning evilly down at him. "But you must know something."

"I don't!"

"How about this?" Tiv began. "You tell me what you know and I make Pom here go away. Say a little more, then I'll even consider releasing you."

"Really?" he stuttered.

"Really."

Pom shot Tiv a fierce glare, but he ignored it. The man agreed all too eagerly. And Tiv tilted his head, a silent order for Pom to scram. The smaller Amorph wasn't happy. But he pocketed the dagger and left without further complaint. Though he kept his eyes trained on the Nebbin as he did.

Khale was quick to follow, indifferent to their affairs. While he fiddled with his spider fang triumphantly.

"The Lafetti clan is a faction of Healers in the Weeping Grove," the Nebbin said, calmer now that Pom was gone.

"Healers?" Tiv's eyes narrowed in suspicion. "What does the Western Branch have to do with this?"

"I don't know," he repeated, screaming when Tiv's grip tightened. "I swear! They hire us. We deliver. And that's it! That's all I know!"

Tiv glared, staring at him for a moment longer than necessary and assessing the honesty behind his gaze. He was desperate enough to spit out anything right now. "Then..." Tiv muttered. "You've outlived your usefulness, haven't you?"

The man screamed, pleading, as Tiv tilted his neck to an almost impossible degree. But then he abruptly stopped. His fingers faltered and he hesitated. Not because of the flood of emotions that normally came with the act itself—he'd killed too many to be bothered by such nonsense now—but because of the young boy a distance away. His eyes were trained on him.

Roval, Tiv recalled. The boy that forcefully calmed his nerves during his sedition in the Drowned Tower. The same one that tried to soothe the girl that had burned to death. Why wasn't he with the rest?

Before Tiv could call out to him, someone grasped his injured shoulder, and he cried out in shock. His entire body trembled from the sudden jolt of pain. Tiv turned, barely noticing the chatty Nebbin break free from his clutches. Only to die from an arrow shot with perfect precision through the back of his skull. The surprise was still etched clearly on his face when he fell. Along with the faint traces of a smile from his momentary triumph.

The newcomers surrounded Tiv, eyeing him as he stumbled from his wounds, the pain only now catching up to him. There were four of them. All Nebbin. Though they didn't don the same polished armor as the ones before. They wore simple green and brown tunics. Light enough to move in and sturdy enough to last. Their weapons, however, were just as worn. If not more so.

They'd seen many battles. Regardless, Tiv could still get away. He knew he could. He just needed to morph into something small enough.

But he stilled once again when he heard a pained cry. Tiv turned to find Roval, raised from the ground by his collar, as he tried in vain to keep the two men holding him away. The others were quick to take advantage of Tiv's sudden distraction, pinning him with their weapons before he could transform.

"Hold it, Amorph!" the one holding Roval ordered. He brought a knife up to the boy's neck in a very Pom-like fashion. "Shift and the boy dies."

Tiv was still tempted to do so.

He couldn't let himself be captured.

Where are those two? Tiv thought, cross.

They must've heard Roval's scream. If he could just buy some time, then perhaps they'd be able to help. But the Nebbin surrounding him must've seen the determined look in his eyes and the callous decision behind them because one slammed the hilt of his broad sword down on Tiv's head.

The last coherent thing he saw was Roval struggling against his captor. And though he willed his body to move towards him, it was no longer under his command.

Tiv fell to the ground. Barely able to give the blurred faces that hovered over him a proper glare. But the muddled fury in his eyes said it all. He'd get his vengeance. Whether that was now or decades away didn't matter.

It was a promise.

28

Grief was a monster with beady eyes and sharp teeth.

A figment that shoved sorrow in Sylvie's face, etching its claws deep enough to hit bone, yet leaving no marks in its wake. When Sylvie tried to reach out and touch it, it evaporated into thin air. Only for her to find it on the floor, peeking at her through the floorboards of her subconscious.

Right now, however, Sylvie stared grief in the face. An ugly little thing with no arms—all the better—at least she knew no one would be there to catch her when she spiraled into oblivion.

This was her mind. Yet she didn't reign. Perhaps she wasn't focused enough. Too much had happened. Her home was taken before her eyes, and here she stood in a sea of unending darkness. No horizon. Only nothingness.

Ferrus Terria was filled with victims, sufferers, and the forgotten. Why weren't they inside the gloom with her? No one was truly alone. So long as they lived. Literally speaking, they'd never be free from company.

But here she was. Alone.

No. That monster was there, staring at her.

A demon? Sylvie played with the thought before shaking her head. *Just a figment.*

Because she was alive—of that, she was certain.

She didn't know how she knew. It was just a feeling. And when knowledge and reason failed, all she had left were her instincts. She trusted them well enough. If she didn't, then panic would surely settle. Her inner voice would shout out, crying for help.

And she'd lose her composure.

That couldn't happen. She wouldn't allow it.

But Sylvie didn't know where she was. Nor the trivial details concerning her arrival. Just darkness. It stretched as far as the eye could see—and then some.

Magic is beautiful, Sylve thought absent mindedly. *Absolutely amazing.* The wonders of it were second to none. There was so much left to discover. But in the quiet stillness of the shadows, Sylvie couldn't find it in herself to further compliment its greatness. Because, despite her baseless assurance of her survival, her mind continued to reel with senseless thoughts. Ones she knew wouldn't help ease her.

Sylvie thought of home.

Her memories. The smiles. The laughs. Its destruction. And the stinging pain that made her blood boil. There was nothing here to distract her from dreary recollections.

Then I'll make one, Sylvie decided. She chanced using her powers, but her fingers refused to spark with the familiar warmth that always had the ability to calm her frazzled nerves.

A practitioner that couldn't use magic. How laughable.

Reed would have a field day.

Sylvie stopped her thoughts. Reed. Her partner. She'd digressed but a moment and now she was sad again. How ridiculous. Memories were such a cruel, stabbing thing. They were good for a time, but just when life got a little rough they made her feel inexplicably lonely. A sadness beyond reason that crept into her heart, made its home, and never left. She'd accepted her situation, the curse that came with being born a practitioner of any merit, long ago, but sometimes it was still so surreal.

Loss, however, was even more so.

The more Sylvie tried to forget, the more she remembered. Her mind remembered what her heart never failed to recall.

Sylvie wasn't foolish enough to expect happiness. She didn't deserve something like that. Not when she'd killed so many in the name of the Institute.

Still, staring loss in the mirror was anything but pleasant.

Sylvie looked around, but she couldn't find the little monster anymore. She gave up, opting instead to just peer at the nothingness above her. Sylvie missed the stone walls of the Drowned Tower. At least it had lines she could focus on. The Tower had always been dark, but it wasn't like the pitch black currently trapping her. Never-ending darkness was its own kind of hell.

Perhaps this is oblivion, Sylvie mused, but she quickly dismissed the thought. *Of course it isn't.*

She was alive. She'd confirmed this. She wasn't so grief stricken as to further wound herself with foolish thoughts of her own demise. Instead, Sylvie thought of other things. More worthwhile things. Anything to pass the time. Because time passed strangely in the dark. She could track it by the rise and fall of her chest, by the endless steps she took forward, but then it evaporates, slipping past her fingertips like water. Seconds turned into minutes, and minutes into nothing.

Sylvie occasionally spoke. A soft whisper that hardly pierced the stillness, but it was loud enough to alert anyone nearby of her presence. But she had the sinking fear that if she kept talking, a monster would come to quiet her. And so she was always quick to lapse back into silence.

So, to pass the time, she thought of Reed and his niceties, his awkward attempts at small talk and his shy grins. Myrrh, who talked big for such a small girl. Master Cephas, and the nights he'd force her to spend in the archives. Ethil, who was still able to hold her head up high and do her job, despite her losses. Tiv, and his contradictions that left him with a strange set of morals she'd never understand. But he did his job. And for a practitioner, that was more than enough.

Jack, Sylvie closed her eyes, imagining his form. The pale skin, protruding veins, and cocky smirk. A walking corpse without the outward rot. *Conceited, hot-blooded, and too smart for his own good.* He knew how to press all of her buttons. And did so every chance he got. *Where is he?*

She was just with him.

"I hope you didn't die, too," Sylvie breathed out. Her mind drifted to Reed without her consent. "You told me that you'd sooner kill me yourself than die for my sake. I hate liars."

Just then, she saw something shining.

A stone.

Clear, small, and being tossed.

Up and down. Up and down. Up and down.

It was pitched high into the air then caught a moment before it could be swallowed up by the shadows. She knew of only one person who had the ability to blend so well into the darkness.

He usually talked more.

"Are you here to haunt me?" Sylvie asked, watching the figure step out. The darkness moved back, as if making way for him. It was an eerily familiar sight. She recalled the time she sat in her favored Research Archive, and the one she'd least expected to see had shown himself. "Leave me alone. We've spent too much time in the last two days together as it is. I'm tired of this extended farewell. If you're a ghost, then stay in the past. If you aren't, then go back to where you belong. This is my darkness."

She stared pointedly at him.

"You're not welcome here, Jack."

Jack remained there, standing stock still, his lips curling up just enough to show teeth.

"So, you've figured out that this darkness is your own," Jack said, carelessly shrugging. His movements were so real. "I'd expect nothing less from you. But," he tapped his temple, "I'm in here. If you want me to leave, think it, and I'll be gone."

Sylvie concentrated, but a minute later, and there he was.

Still and grinning.

"Maybe you want me here as a distraction," Jack guessed. He looked around, clearly unimpressed. "Not even Thelarius knows how boring it is in here. Your mind is so drab. But at least I come with my own mini Heartstone." Jack tossed the stone up once more for emphasis. "How cool is that?"

"I hope it chokes you."

"A ray of sunshine, aren't you?" Jack scoffed, shaking his head. "It's not my fault your ugly right now."

She gaped.

Jack smirked. That cocky smirk he donned whenever he was amused. As he gestured to his stomach. "You've got a big wound here, Syl. It must hurt. Don't you feel it?"

She didn't dare look down.

Instead, Sylvie crossed her arms and closed her eyes. She wanted a distraction. Not a figment of her lonely mind. But a real, live distraction she could focus on. Anything would do. Anything to get her imagination to leave her alone and stop playing cruel tricks on her. She wouldn't beg for one, but she mentally swore that she'd be eternally grateful.

"Don't ignore me," Jack whispered. Closer now.

A distraction. Anything was fine. Someone grant her this one wish. The First Zenith, a Master, an Elder, a Hunter. Anyone.

"You'd think I'd be appreciated more after saving your life, oh, I don't know, half a dozen times?"

She'd repay them tenfold.

"Ah…" Jack added almost as an afterthought. "But you were practically begging for death that final time. *'Oh, it hurts! Leave me alone, please! Oh, please make it stop!'*" Jack mimicked, his shoulders shaking from laughter.

"Hey," he went on, "do you really think you're alive?"

Sylvie opened her eyes.

Before her was no longer the willowy practitioner she'd somehow come to respect. It was that tiny monster. Now twelve times bigger with razor sharp teeth a hair's breadth away from her face. Ready to eat her. Ready to swallow her whole. Ready to digest her in that stomach where only dark thoughts awaited.

And she… snapped.

No.

She'd be damned if she allowed herself to go down without a fight. The monster inched closer. Sylvie would've moved, had her body not frozen for reasons beyond comprehension. Her eyes narrowed, her face twisting into something frightening.

She'd had enough. If she was forced to remain in darkness with this—thing, then it had to know who was in control. This was her mind. No one else's.

"Man, you're a handful."

The monster suddenly ceased its advance.

Sylvie's eyes widened. She reluctantly drew her gaze away from the creature and looked up, around, even below her. No one. But she knew that voice. The monster had just assumed its owner after all.

"Jack?" she chanced calling him.

No response.

Sylvie looked back at the monster. It was steadily shrinking. As her thoughts drifted away from the Drowned Tower, from her friends, from her life under the Zexin Sea. Sylvie focused on nothing, but that voice. She could still hear it echo in her ears. A loud ring. Clear as a bell.

Forget the stone. Forget that abomination. Forget everything. But the will to live.

She recalled the feeling of desperation she felt just before she passed out, of utter hopelessness at the sight of the cracking roof when her eyes closed, of the searing pain she felt before sleeping, and finally, the relief of that voice finding her in the darkness.

"If you don't wake up soon, I'll really get angry," the voice said. A remark so undeniably… Jack. She couldn't help but grin. "What then? I've got things to do, Sylvie. The world won't disappear if you ignore it. Reed won't come back, no matter how long you wait. Change needs to come. Change always comes. Wake up. I told you that I wouldn't let you die. I told myself that I'd survive long enough to make it back to the Diamond Alps. I'm no liar, Syl. Don't make me one."

Jack was scolding her, she knew. Regardless, Sylvie closed her eyes in content at the sound of his voice. It was real. Proof of another. Proof that she was alive.

She reveled in it. Lost herself in it.

What a pleasant distraction from the mess before her.

29

When Sylvie opened her eyes, finally free from the hazy chains of her subconscious, she blinked twice in silent surprise. Not quite sure what she was seeing. Moonlight streamed in from a half-open window, its curtains curiously thrown to the floor. A draft breeze and chirping crickets accompanied the light, adding life to a room where there was none. The room was nothing short of shabby. It looked as if it hadn't seen guests in decades. Dust lined every surface. Frightening cracks stood out along the wooden walls. And an improperly wound clock torpidly ticked away the time. As though counting the seconds until the walls gave in to age. Sylvie lay in the middle of it all, on a bed with clean sheets, yet still smelt of storage.

An outsider invading a world long abandoned by humanity. She didn't belong here. It was a picturesque sight, better fit for a painting than for her eyes.

Sylvie didn't know if her mind was still recoiling from her strange dream, as it faded into the neglected corners of her subconscious, but she didn't bother voicing her doubts. She felt too lethargic for that, as if she'd been sleeping for a long, long time. Though that couldn't be right. It just couldn't. But as she looked down at her stomach in sudden remembrance of a wound she vaguely remembered receiving, she found little more than a grotesque scar in its place. A pink thing. Ugly and protruding.

Sylvie winced when she recalled the stinging pain she felt coursing through her veins before she succumbed to forced slumber. She remembered it feeling like a living nightmare. Made up of seconds that lasted lifetimes. It was no wonder she passed out soon after.

Her hands instinctively wrapped around the Heartstone and she was surprised to find that it remained untouched beneath her clothes, despite her obvious change in attire. Someone had changed her—or she didn't remember doing it herself. Unlikely.

Where am I?

This certainly wasn't her room. Or any room in the Drowned Tower for that matter. The builders were against timber. Afraid that it would crumble more effectively with age.

Sylvie chanced standing, cursing herself when she wobbled and found that she needed to drag her hands against the dust-covered walls just to keep herself from falling. But it was better than staying in bed, waiting for people she didn't know to return. Were they enemies or allies? The latter was likely, seeing as how she wore no evidence of lasting injuries. But if worst came to worst, she wanted to be up and about—and fully prepared to burn this place down.

She heard the sound of a door opening and closing in the next room, followed by two pairs of soft footsteps. Their words rang clear, despite the walls separating them. It reminded her of the Institute. Lumber, however, burned better than granite. And her hands sparked with familiar heat, small and flickering. Her magic seemed to be at odds with the rest of her body. Not yet awake.

Had she exhausted her magic circuit?

When she heard a stream of venomous *Íarre*, the light in her hands died. As relief washed over her. Sylvie cracked the door as much as her curiosity allowed, peeking through the warm light to see a woman taking a drag from a long pipe. Its wooden body was flanked by polished silver, and from the intricate design along its edges, it was terribly expensive. The woman smoking it had dark hair and a proud nose, her eyes spoke of malice even as her mouth quirked up into a highly amused grin.

She looks like Jack, Sylvie realized, flinching when eyes as black as death turned to her as if sensing her eavesdropping.

"Come out," she said, exhaling a cloud of smoke and ignoring the way Jack coughed. He muttered curses under his breath. "We're all friends here."

Before she could, a hurried body immediately appeared in her vision and forced the door wide open. Jack stood before her, eyes brimming with obvious relief. As though he hadn't expected her to be up and about so soon. From the way his eyes subtly scrutinized her side, she realized that he hadn't.

He looked no worse for wear, donning robes two sizes too large and patched so many times, she found six different shades of blue on him. But what surprised her the most was the quick twist of his lips, as he brooded over something that was apparently her fault.

"What?" Sylvie asked, lifting her eyebrows in question.

"It's been six days, Syl," he said, gripping the side of the door so tightly, his knuckles had gone completely white. "Do you have any idea how worried I was?"

Her eyes widened at the revelation.

"Six days?" she asked, stupefied. Then added, "Well, don't blame me for not waking up."

Jack ignored her completely and continued his rant of petty frustration. "I've been trapped in this tiny cottage, forced to do nothing for hours on end. Watching the days go by without any news about anything. Then that voice in m—our head suddenly disappears, telling me to wait for you to wake. Flanes, no! Do you have any idea what it's like to sit around for something I don't know will come with," Jack pointed accusingly at the smirking woman behind him, "her?"

Instead of taking offense, the woman laughed heartily. Her eyes shone with obvious amusement. "He says that now, but he was gladder than anyone else when he awoke to find me by his side. Isn't that right, Jack?"

He huffed and turned away.

"Oh, don't be shy," she said, smirking. "I haven't seen you in so long. And here I thought your attitude had bettered since last we saw each other. But I see that you're still trying to escape as soon as the chance presents itself."

"A thing to be grateful for. Someone has to carry on your legacy of unparalleled stubbornness."

"Lest, what?" she asked, letting out a short bark of laughter. "Lest others forget it? Forget me? You give yourself far too much credit. My name won't fade anytime soon, and you're certainly in no position to make it."

"At least your ego still seems to be intact, mother."

Sylvie's turned with a start, getting a better look at the woman speaking. She was tall, obvious even when seated. Lines of stress creased her brow, but did little to take away from the natural beauty of her overall appearance. Or the practiced elegance of her movements. There was a deadly calm behind her gaze. Sylvie saw it clearly, as Jack's mother assessed her in turn. Her eyes roved over her in silent judgment of her worth—quick and clever, taking all of her in within the span of a moment—as if she was used to evaluating, laughing, and then dismissing practitioners by the dozen.

Sylvie didn't doubt it.

Cheryll Hallan was famed across Ferus Terria for her skill as both a Hunter Captain and a researcher. Her renown only increased when she married into the Dace family.

"Sylvie Sirx, I presume?" Cheryll asked, though she already knew the answer. "My son has been terribly worried about you. Look," she pointed at Jack's dark scowl with a look of utter pleasure, "he looks like his father with that hideously concerned face. Both hide behind their petty frustrations like armor. But it's the mouth that gives them away." Cheryll brought the pipe back up, as if to gesture to her own lips. "Their mouths are *so* expressive."

Sylvie merely stared at her, swallowing her surprise.

She couldn't find it in herself to be amused at her blatant teasing of Jack—someone she could never quite ruffle without getting at le-ast a few ego-wounding remarks in return—she was too stunned by her mere presence. Why was someone of such high rank here? Sylvie had expected another Elder to deal with the problem. Not someone under the direct command of the Vanguard Circle.

"You're a Hunter Captain, aren't you?" Sylvie asked, bemused by the sudden turn of events. Just what had happened while she was sleeping? Cheryll surely couldn't have made it all the way to the Drowned Tower in a mere six days. It was impossible. Even for the most talented of Amorphs. "When did the Diamond Alps learn about Serach?"

"As soon as he moved," Cheryll answered, shrugging without a care. "I've never liked him. He smiled too much and worried too little. Leonas should've rid the world of him long ago. As I suggested when we first realized his horrid scheme. Still, it gave me reason to come out here, so I suppose I'll forgive him. Just this once."

Sylvie's hands shook with sudden fury, her lips curving up into a snarl. As she clenched her fists to try and control the urge to scream and shout at the woman before her. Jack's family or not, a Hunter was still a Hunter. Sylvie didn't know what she was capable of when provoked. "If you knew, then why didn't you stop him before he came to the Drowned Tower?"

"To figure out the reason behind his actions, of course," Cheryll said, exaggerating her voice, as if it should've been obvious. It was. But Sylvie's mind was too muddled to form any sort of coherent connection. She'd just escaped her own nightmare only to wake in an entirely different kind. It didn't help that Cheryll wasn't the sort that gave someone time to adjust. "Motive is important, despite however petty his turned out to be. You'd do well to remember that. Perhaps you'd benefit from lessons in the Diamond Alps under your father, Miss Sirx."

"The Hunters could've helped!" Sylvie reasoned, ignoring her jab. She could see where Jack got his tongue, assuming his father didn't have a more scathing one. "We saw one in Tearwood. I'm sure there were more lurking—*somewhere*!"

"Hunters keep their ears to the ground and wait for orders

in silence," Cheryll said with finality, before sighing in irritation. As if she'd had this conversation dozens of times already. From the way Jack rolled his eyes at her answers, perhaps she had. He wasn't one to let things go so easily. "As any good spy should. My primary apprentice is highly skilled in that regard. Yet I hear she intervened to assist you. You must be important, indeed, to make her act."

"Hardly," Jack spoke then. His gaze hard and unforgiving. "Myrrh showed up for a moment only to disappear the next."

"She saved more lives than you know," Cheryll said, vague.

"Wait." Sylvie turned to Jack, her eyes widening in surprise. "Did you say, Myrrh? Myrrh is your primary apprentice?" That couldn't be true. But what reason did she have to lie? Sylvie recounted her time spent with Myrrh and the hazy events of that long night.

The pieces clicked together like clockwork in her mind. The outlandish number of Peose in Tearwood, their form—Myrrh's favored one—and how she suddenly appeared to stop Serach. Myrrh valued freedom and open space, spending all of her free time studying under different Masters just to be given the privilege of leaving the Tower. Or was that just an excuse, so she could wander about?

It made sense.

But Sylvie refused to believe their words. She wouldn't believe them until she saw Myrrh with her own eyes and asked her face-to-face. Sylvie refused to blindly hail things as truth—not now and never again. Everything she thought she knew was crumbling into pieces around her. Just like the Drowned Tower.

"Yes," Cheryll said, smiling. "And a splendid one at that. At least until a few nights ago. I've sent her back to the Diamond Alps for the disobedience. She took that pesky little girl with her. Ethil, I believe she was called. Why she saved her is a question for the ages."

Sylvie's eyes widened even more because apparently that was possible. She stared unwaveringly at Cheryll, trying to find a hint that she was lying, or at the very least, joking.

She wasn't.

"And what were your Hunters waiting for exactly?" Jack asked, bringing them back to the topic at hand.

"Are you hard of hearing now, Jack?" Cheryll mocked, intent on riling him. "Motive. They were waiting to realize Serach's motives. I've already answered that."

"Who do you take me for?" Jack sneered. "I'm not one of those witless fools you and father like to spend your days frolicking with. Don't lie to my face. It's insulting."

Cheryll suddenly turned to look pointedly at them. Her glare was sharp and demanding all at once, it demanded compliance, telling them not to push her. But then her eyes softened, settling over their maddened faces, before briefly drifting down to Sylvie's collar.

"For the Heartstone," she said. Honestly this time. Her voice softer. "They were waiting for it to make an appearance. It's a treasure of the Diamond Alps after all."

Sylvie unconsciously gripped the Heartstone. Was this really the cause of all this?

"Take it then," she said resolutely, tearing it from her neck and letting it dangle in the air between them. It was bright and beating. Darkness stirred within. Though the voice they associated with it was gone—faded into silence. "I don't want it."

"Neither do I," Cheryll said plainly.

"Then why go through all this trouble for it? Why wait until the very last moment to…" Sylvie abruptly cut herself off, cursing her own mind in every language she knew, as she suddenly remembered something of utmost importance. "The Drowned Tower…" she began again, swallowing the lump in her throat. "What happened to the Drowned Tower? The last time I saw—"

It was crumbling, Sylvie thought. Unable to say the words.

"It's gone," Cheryll told her, not sparing her feelings. That served little purpose. "Obliterated. Destroyed. Nothing more than piles of rubble under the sea. A shame, really. All that knowledge gone to waste."

"No," Sylvie denied, furiously shaking her head. As if that would make her statement more clear. "You're lying."

"Why would I?" she asked, offended. As she jutted her chin toward a nearby window. "Go on. See for yourself. Pernelia's statue is gone. One of the Institutes have fallen. Which one will be next, I wonder?"

Sylvie glared at her, before making a move toward the window. Only for Jack to grab her by the elbow and yank her back with enough strength to stagger even the largest of men. But Sylvie had prepared for it. He was always jerking her back during situations like this. As if he wanted to spare her from a world she'd long been knee-deep in, but this time, she wouldn't have it. Sylvie whirled around, pinning him with the most ferocious glare she could muster. It wasn't much. And the tears that clung to her eyes did her no favors.

"You'll regret it," he warned.

"It's my decision to regret."

Sylvie shrugged his hand away. He let it fall willingly.

She walked to the nearest window, realizing for the first time that they were along the eastern borders. On the Eirinne Mountains. The house they were settled in was above a deep chasm, built between two rocky cliffs, unscalable by most. The surrounding area was filled with trees and angled ground that even skilled climbers would be hesitant to trek. Just how did they get here? Did Cheryll transform and bring them?

The thought left her, as she looked upon the Zexin Sea. Her eyes trailed over the Drowned Tower's ruined bridge where a number of practitioners scurried about. *Hunters,* she realized, seeing the Peose from Tearwood trail behind them like lost dogs. There were residents from Thyme amongst them, curious about the damage. Her eyes lingered over them for a moment longer, before finally settling upon the raging waves.

Pernelia's statue was nowhere to be seen.

Only lingering remnants of furniture remained, floating about without use. Sylvie could scarcely make out the tunnels of rock below the surface, before her vision was distorted by the restless waters.

"Reed!" Sylvie suddenly shouted, turning to face them. Her vision was blurrier than she remembered. And she felt something wet and hot trail down her cheeks. "Master Cephas, Tiv, all the rest. Did they make it out?"

"Many did," Jack said, "supposedly."

"Many died, too," Cheryll said. "Though we aren't certain who or how many. It was a long night. As you already know. But my legion is currently chasing after those that were fortunate enough to escape." She immediately held her hands up in placation as soon as the words left her mouth, already knowing what they were thinking. "They don't have orders to kill them. Those found will simply be relocated to a camp on Eriam until we find a way to rebuild the Tower. Those that run further will be brought to the Red Veld."

"As refugees," Jack said, seeing red. "Return them here!"

"I only have so many Hunters to spare. They can't watch over such a large number of practitioners."

"The southern plains are awful! You know that. Everyone does. The Red Veld might be a citadel, but even buildings can be sieged by poverty. Even if only a scant dozen were brought to the south that would still be too many for such a poor Institute."

"What would you have me do?" Cheryll asked. "Bring them to the Alps? The Grove? They'll be turned away at the door. The Veld is riddled with strife, but they'll be accepted."

"Barely!"

"It's useless to rant and rave and cause people misery," she reprimanded. "This is the way the world works. This is the way I work. If you're unhappy with my decisions, then stop complaining and do something about it."

Jack's fists clenched, and in that moment, Sylvie saw where he got his motivation.

"Is that an invitation?" he asked quietly. "Because when I go to the Diamond Alps. I'll make sure you regret those words."

Cheryll shook her head in a mixture of disappointment and exasperation. As if she were speaking to a child. In a way, she still was. This was an old topic—one they'd discussed at length many times before—one he still didn't seem to understand.

"You're always looking up, Jack. Take your time. Search the ground. There's always a mess of missed opportunities below."

Jack kept his silence, drilling holes into the ground with his eyes. He saw no opportunities before him.

Sylvie coughed, quietly interrupting. It was enough to startle them both into attention. "How did we make it out?"

Jack visibly flinched.

"That sweet thing around your neck knows. It holds the answers to possibly everything," Cheryll muttered, standing. Already tired of these recurring topics. "I'll remain here to salvage what's left of the Drowned Tower. That stone seems to behave around you, so I'll leave it in your care for now. You're going to the Alps anyway, it'll save me the burden of an extra trip. Show the stone to Leonas."

"What does he want with it?" Jack asked.

"Go see for yourself. The two of you are going, aren't you?"

Their eyes met, a silent look of contemplation passing between them, before it was snuffed by mutual agreement.

"We're going," Sylvie was the one to say.

"Good." Cheryll nodded briefly. "You'll have to travel past the Yovakine Plains, cross the Wymeran River, and then find passage through Curran. You should be able to find a guide amongst the Healers in the Weeping Grove. You two have a long trip ahead. Pack lightly."

"You're not taking us?" Jack asked in disbelief.

Cheryll smiled. A knowing smile that Sylvie had seen on her son's face far too often during their brief friendship. It was the smile of someone about to pass on a troublesome burden—and they knew it.

"The Diamond Alps is currently undergoing a shift in power.

The Zenith Council has finally decided to hold a Summit. A new leader will be appointed soon."

"And of course, father's a leading contender," Jack finished dryly. "That has little to do with me."

"No," Sylvie cut in, understanding dawning upon her. "It's me."

"You catch on quickly," Cheryll practically sung, smiling from ear to ear. Too fox-like to be considered genuine. "With Columbus Cephas presumed dead, the duties of Arch Poten fall upon his primary apprentice."

"Then all the more reason to go with you," Jack said, opening his mouth to argue more, before suddenly clamping it shut when he saw the large smile stretching over her lips. It unnerved him in ways only the most frightening of foes could.

"Weren't you concerned about the Veld, Jack? This is your chance, you know? Your chance to help all those practitioners my legion will undoubtedly bring to them."

Jack's eyes narrowed in suspicion. "What are you planning?"

"If those puppets in the north value anything, its tradition," Cheryll explained, all too happily. "The Summit can't begin without every Arch Poten present. As it so happens, I've been having trouble coercing the Southern Branch's representative to our side. Politics are always influenced by miniscule changes after all. It is… difficult to please everyone. But who better than a son, in the confidence of another Arch Poten," Cheryll looked meaningfully at each of them, "to convince her to cast her vote to his father?"

"You're joking," Jack scoffed. Did he actually hear that right? She wanted him to travel to the south just to sway the opinion of someone he could care less about? Absurd. He was more interested in seeing to the welfare of his homeless comrades than running off to do her bidding.

"I'll go," Sylvie suddenly said, and Cheryll's smile widened. As Jack turned to her, his disbelief plain for everyone to see. "I want to go. I'll even cross the Wymeran River, rather than find an Amorph in the Yovakine Plains. Let's do it your way."

Cheryll nodded in approval. "That's what I like to hear."

"Why?" Jack asked, stunned.

"Because," Sylvie shrugged, "Silas' and Maruice's Institutes must have archives, right? I'm sure there must be something about the Heartstone there."

Silas, Jack thought. *She's his descendant. But she doesn't know that, does she? What's driving her then?* He found his answer, as he looked upon her determined face. And he couldn't help but smile in momentary triumph.

"Do you really want to leave this place?" he asked.

Sylvie stared at him—a thousand unspoken words passing between them—before she finally nodded. It was nothing more than a small tilt of her head, but it was firm, and it was more than enough.

And Jack laughed.

"I see you two are close," Cheryll muttered, reminding them of her presence. She grinned when a burning flood of embarrassment crossed their cheeks and stained their ears. They turned away, suddenly self-conscious. "Since we're all in agreement, allow me to explain whose confidence you need to win."

They faced her once more, all traces of playfulness gone, as they fell into step before her. Only the serious gazes of two skilled practitioners remained. Cheryll grinned, visibly pleased by how much Jack had grown since she'd last seen him.

"Vidal Verne," she began, "renowned underworld auctioneer and husband to the current Arch Poten, Monet Verne, previously, Monet Thareen. To most, Vidal is in a class entirely his own. To me, he's nothing more than an eccentric, overgrown child with too much power and too much time. And like all in his grade, his family is an influential one. His wife's, even more so. The Verne and Thareen families have controlled the Yovakine Plains and the Red Veld, respectively, since the times when maps still warned of dragons. Together, they control a large portion of the south."

"Those are big families," Sylvie muttered. "Will we really be able to just request an audience?"

"Of course," Cheryll said confidently. "The best cartels know the importance of keeping up appearances. Mention your family names enough times and you should have no problem acquiring anything you wish. Though I suggest focusing on winning over Vidal. Once you do, he'll go about convincing Monet."

"Why not just go straight to her?" Jack asked. "Running off to her husband seems… tedious."

"Monet is…" Cheryll paused, trying to find the words, "priggish, so to speak."

"Then why would she agree to marry someone with ties to the underworld?" Sylvie asked, skeptic.

"I'm vague on the details. He's a peculiar man. But I'm sure you'll understand once you make it there."

"That's reassuring," Jack said sardonically. "And when do you expect us to leave exactly?"

"When day breaks," Cheryll said. The order was clear. "I can take you to the base of the mountain, but no further. Pack lightly, don't talk about yourselves, and avoid attention. The far corners of Ferus Terria aren't as forgiving as the east."

Without another word, Cheryll stood to her full height. She was tall enough to dwarf a number of men and women alike. She patted their heads in momentary fondness, contradicting the steely persona she'd exuded mere moments before.

Her eyes apologized to them in place of her tongue, speaking volumes of the danger she'd be putting them through. Cheryll's hand lingered over Jack's hair, as she took a moment to recollect herself. Then, all too soon, her hands fell.

She flashed them an ambiguous smile, before carefully leaving the room. The door closed noisily behind her, shutting them in with the weight of a burden they had yet to fully realize.

But they would. Soon. Whether they accepted it or not.

The enticing lullaby that suddenly permeated the air was definite proof of that.

30

Dawn found them together.

Depraved of both sleep and joy, they watched the sun slowly rise into wakefulness with nothing but new lines around their eyes. The light gray blurs of early morning crept over the waking sea. As torpid as anything ought to be at such an ungodly hour. It stopped just before reaching the shore, not yet ready to stir the denizens of Eriam. And though it was beautiful and breathtaking and warmer than fire, it was the grimmest morning they'd ever seen. Which said much, considering they'd once watched first light stretch across battlegrounds littered with blood not yet blackened by age. But this was different.

There was something melancholic about looking out at the Zexin Sea and not finding Pernelia's proud statue glinting against the sun. But with each passing second, that was the reality they were forced to face—the same one that kept them up all night— as they thought of what they lost, sharing grief like fine wine. Trapped by how a grave could feel so close to home.

They lost much, yet gained little in return. Jack would get the freedom he'd always wanted. But Sylvie wasn't so fortunate. She looked at the world Jack was so fond of, her eyes flashing in something like grief. It didn't quite feel like grief though. Sorrow, perhaps? No. That was an inadequate description.

It felt like burning. A dull ache that bothered her more than the sharpest of pains. An unnamable thing. Unworthy of word. Indescribable through song.

Just the empty realization of no home to return to.

Sylvie stared at the mountain ranges. They spanned miles, hiding the Drowned Tower like a secret from the rest of the world. She never wanted to leave. Never thought she'd be forced to. But she didn't think Reed would die before her either. He was a good, kind soul that deserved more than what he'd received. He deserved life and happiness and warmth. Far more than she. She, who had actively fought and carried out the bidding of her superior's like a missionary spreading words of faith.

Except her trail was covered in ignorance and blood, of sleep plagued by nightmares, and of smiles at the expense of another's own. Anything to protect the quiet box of comfort she lived in. She'd give her life if it meant Reed could have another chance at his. The world, however, was never so simple.

What a shame.

Sylvie touched the Heartstone around her collar. Not for the first time, she thought that maybe picking it up hadn't been the brightest idea. Reed had warned her. He said she'd be cursed for it. Was this it? Losing her home, losing those she loved—was that the curse? Or was there more to come?

She didn't think she could handle anymore.

But she couldn't turn back now. She'd see this through to the end. Because that was better than the alternative. She didn't want to run away and hide inside an Institute buried in on itself. Where only more ignorance awaited her. She could only trudge onward and seek the answers for herself.

With fire banked beneath her skin and careful consideration of what was to come, she wondered if leaving would really be so easy. Yes, they had a Hunter Captain at their backs and her name as Arch Poten, but she'd always seen it as an act of desertion. To cross the border into the unknown with permission to do so sounded absurd to her ears.

Sylvie squeezed her arms just to remind herself that this was real. Jack, on the other hand, was far more optimistic about their upcoming expedition. His excitement to leave this place still remained, despite the Tower's destruction. He'd wanted to leave this place for so long that nothing could truly dampen that desire. Not even a night of hell.

"Look," Jack suddenly said, hiding his grief behind an easy grin and a shrug. He made it look so easy. Jack spread his arms, showing her the world. "From here you can see everything."

He was right. Of course he was. He'd simply stated the obvious. But Sylvie knew him well enough by now to know that he only said it to break the silence. The sunrise signaled what was to come, but they had yet to talk about anything of true import since Cheryll's abrupt departure the night before. Perhaps now was the time. Yesterday was lost to grieving.

When Sylvie opened her mouth to respond, she found that her train of thought wasn't the only thing clearer. "Your mother will be here soon."

"Don't remind me."

"Aren't you excited to leave this place?" she asked, instantly regretting the bitterness in her tone. "You can finally change your world."

"That's just it," Jack muttered, looking off into the distance. For a moment, his eyes reflected her own. Exhausted. Sad. So, so sad. Then the moment passed, and he was looking back at her with his usual confidence plastered over him like armor.

"Have I ever told you why I was brought here?" he suddenly asked. Sylvie shook her head. "Well, where should I begin? I'm sure you know that children of higher ranked families are always sent off to other Institutes to study, right? I assume you were sent here as well, weren't you?"

"I wasn't," Sylvie said. "But my brother was. He was sent to the Weeping Grove. I, on the other hand, was born here. My father left me in the care of Master Cephas when he was officially declared an adviser to the Council. But that was years ago. Near the time my mother died."

"Hmm…" Jack hummed, then shook his head. "Funny how

we're only talking about this now."

"We didn't exactly have the luxury of time on our hands. We still don't."

"Fair enough," he agreed easily. "Well, when I was a child, it was decided that I'd be sent off to another Institute to further my studies. They considered sending me to the Grove. It's where most Elementalists go. Problem was, even at seven, I kept trying to escape the Institute. The Diamond Alps was so big to me back then. It was almost too easy. My parents were always fed up with me. So they—well, my father actually—thought it funny to bring me here. The Drowned Tower. Known for its confined structure. Needless to say, I hated it."

"I remember," she said. Jack looked at her curiously. "When they brought you here, I mean. Master Cephas always grumbled about you. And before I knew it, Reed and I were clambering from our beds to see what all the fuss was about. When we found you, you were being sent to the Iniquities Chamber!"

"Can you believe those fools?" Jack covered his face with his hands, exasperated by the memory. "They sent me, a kid that just got there, to the Iniquities Chamber. People used to be *tortured* in there."

"I think they were trying to scare you."

"It didn't work. I loved that place."

"Obviously."

"Tiv and I used to run down there for fun." His eyes flashed, as the memory played in his mind. He could almost hear his high, squeaky voice. Small, but loud enough to echo across the halls. And the rest of the world disappeared—if only for an instant. "We'd go inside those broken cells and practice our magic in secret. Tiv would morph into rats sometimes, then have me find him. It was so easy. He used to be so bad at it. Oh, and those chains along the walls? We'd climb them to see who could reach the top first. Tiv always won."

"Well, Tiv's an Amorph."

"And that, in itself, was cheating. I tried to tell him. He denied it, of course. Still does."

Sylvie laughed, easily forgetting about the things they'd lost in the face of finer memories. The pictures painted themselves vividly in her mind. And though Jack may have been happy to leave, it didn't mean he'd grieve any less.

He'd lost a partner as well.

They had no clues about Tiv's whereabouts. He was either long gone, or as well as. And though Jack hid his affliction better than most, she saw the way his eyes turned away from her. The small downward tilt of his lips, as he smoothed his wrinkled brow by quirking it—finding that relatively more discreet than running his thumb over the skin. In that moment of mutual pause, Sylvie could clearly imagine him as a young boy, sprinting down the halls of the Assembly's Tower. While Reed and her dawdled in the archives. Both wasting time away. As if it was an infinite thing. Perhaps it was. Back then.

It felt so long ago. It *was* long ago.

The world was different now, and they both knew it.

"I have something to tell you," Jack muttered grimly. So low she could hardly hear. "It's about our escape."

And just like that, the atmosphere that settled around them vanished. She turned to face him, once again noticing the dark wiisps in his eyes. The Hearstone felt like lead against her collar. She grasped it, half-expecting that voice to speak out again. Thankfully, *she* didn't. The last they'd heard from *her* was the night before, when *she* decided to remind them of her presence with *her* usual lullaby. As if they'd forget. They'd been thoroughly silenced after that. *She* didn't bother speaking to them, seemingly satisfied about their upcoming travels. Perhaps they worked in *her* favor. No. Of course they did.

"What?" Sylvie asked, realizing that he was waiting for her to prompt him. But she wasn't entirely sure she wanted to know what he had to say. The hesitant lilt in her voice was clear.

But he told her all the same. Because this didn't just involve him. Keeping her in the dark with matters regarding them both could very well get them killed.

"I…" he stopped, looked down, breathed. This was harder than he'd expected, but he wouldn't back down. It was better to say it all at once. "I have an Orive crystal in my head. All Elementalists do. They're placed during birth. It enhances our magic circuits. It's kind of like… one of those good fortune traditions."

Silence.

"Pardon?" Sylvie asked, dumbfounded.

He would've laughed had the topic been a different one. But Jack didn't give her a chance to properly take in his words, laying all of his secrets bare one after another. They'd be easier to digest that way—or so he believed. "You're a descendant of Silas as well, apparently." Jack tapped his temple, watching Sylvie's eyes get wider with each passing second. "*She* told me. Apparently, that's the reason you can hear her. Only Elementalists should be able to since we have Orive crystals in our heads. *Her* power fuels them by the way, and only those she personally takes as hosts can see those dark tendrils. Though Serach was able to make a potion that allowed him to hear what we could. It forcefully made him a host as well. I'm a bit vague on the details."

Sylvie stared at him like he'd grown a second head.

"And one final thing," he said, holding up a finger. "I only have one element. It was the price *she* took from me to save us. No, that's not exactly true. It's more like the price she took to save *me*. Because I doubt *she*'d let you die so easily. You're—"

She clamped his mouth shut with her hands. Her mouth was twisted into the darkest, most unattractive scowl he'd ever seen.

"If this is a joke, Jack. It is a very *poor* attempt at humor."

Jack wasn't deterred by her disbelief, carefully drawing away from her with all the dangerous ease of someone who hated to be silenced. His lip curled venomously.

"Believe what you will, Syl. But I don't lie."

Sylvie knew that. She did. But his words were absurd. Outlandish. Decidedly unbelievable. He couldn't be telling the truth.

"Do you really expect me to believe I'm a descendant of the Great Conjurer Silas Drayr? Really? And that you somehow have an Orive crystal in your head? That—"

She stopped. The words died in her throat when Jack parted his hair to show her the edge of a crystal peeking out beneath his locks. Blue veins pulsed with intensity beside it, but they were far less pronounced than Serach's had been. Far, far less than the Peose they'd encountered in Tearwood. And Sylvie finally realized where the veins along the side of his forehead stemmed from. They always stood out, unnaturally so, but Sylvie never considered the reason why they did.

Sylvie jumped, stepping away from him in sudden, belated shock. The action was so goat-like, Jack couldn't stop the laugh that escaped him. It was a loud bark. Hoarse and startled out of him, as surprising as her step away. But the thought of her reflexive need to place distance between them had it dying just as quickly.

"Don't tell me you're scared," he taunted. Though his words held an undertone of something else beaneath them. Something that she couldn't put her finger on. "I'm not like those Peose in Tearwood, Syl. I won't hurt you. Not unless you try something that is."

Sylvie stilled, realizing what that unidentifiable tinge was. Because even Jack, with his seemingly infinite self-confidence, had his insecurities. Sylvie knew they existed. Everyone had a few. She just never thought he'd actually make them known to her of his own accord. Sylvie thought that she'd have to wring his weaknesses from him, wrestle them out until he reluctantly conceded.

In a way, this situation did the work for her. And she hated it. The thought of someone laying themselves bare before her out of sheer necessity made her stomach churn in discomfort.

Had their situation really come so far?

She already knew the answer.

Sylvie looked him in the eye, reclaiming her lost step, and said, "We aren't defined by our powers, Jack."

He smirked at that. The corner was turned a little softer than usual. Less feral. Less bitter. And she smiled in return.

Forgive me, Reed, she thought, thinking about their likeness. *But I think I'm going to enjoy change a little more.*

"I can't believe you're not more surprised," Jack abruptly said, breathing a sigh of relief. He crossed his fingers and pillowed them behind his head. "I spent so much time wondering how to break the news to you, yet you barely dwell on the fact that you're a descendant of the First Zenith! The First Zenith, Syl! It's not something to just skim over!"

She hesitated, not wanting to tell him that she didn't actually believe it. It was too farfetched. Too unexpected. Too everything. She needed something more concrete than his words. From the way his eyebrows rose in contemplation of his own declaration, she knew that he didn't fully believe it either. It was a ridiculous notion.

Even if it was true, it meant little to her.

She didn't know what to do with such a title. Knew less about the sorry sods foolish enough to believe it. And regarding skill, it made no difference. She still wasn't the best Conjurer, nor did she hope to be. If anything, it was an unnecessary weight on her shoulders. One she'd be better off without. One others would be better off not knowing. If fate had something in store for her, then the only good her lineage served was in her curses—at least she knew who to blame.

"I'm more interested in that last thing you mentioned," she told him, subtly shifting the subject. "One element. What do you mean by one element?"

"It's exactly as it sounds. Look." Jack's hand settled on the railing before them. It froze quickly, cracking as frost spread over aged wood. She lifted a finger, carefully running it over his magic. Ice was beautiful. The way it scattered and encased. The way smoke rose, making her shiver involuntarily. The way it sparkled in the light.

His palm shone once again. More ice crept out. Then again. Three more times. Until he groaned and ran his hands through his hair, thoroughly infuriated.

"I swear I tried to burn that."

"Maybe you're just not using it correctly?" she offered.

The scowl he gave her then could crack glass. His voice reached a plane beyond dour. "I'm only going to say this once. I know how to use my magic, Syl. When I say I can't use it—I can't."

The plainness of his words dawned on her like the rising sun before them. Quicker, however. As if he'd thrown a pail of freshly chilled water over her head.

"Wait, so you're," her eyes widened in disbelief, before the shock was lost to laughter, "you're a Conjurer!"

His expression mimicked her own, humorless though it was. As she doubled over, holding her stomach.

"How can you find this funny?"

"How can you not?"

"For the love of—"

"Jack," Sylvie emphasized, pointedly looking at him. As if he should know the kind of banal nonsense running in her mind. "You *despise* Conjurers."

He did. For the most part. They were just so… subordinate in comparison. "I do not," he lied, and his own personal principle backfired on him then. "Perhaps a little."

She laughed again. But he'd had enough.

"We should go," Jack interrupted her fit. "Mother's fuse is a short one."

Sylvie turned, all traces of amusement dying on her lips. Swifter than he expected it would. He didn't know if he should have been glad or guilty by her reaction.

"Will she place a Demar Spell on us?" she asked.

Jack shuddered at the question. Old pain haunted his gaze. "She wanted to put one on you, but I convinced her otherwise. It's... problematic. You should thank me."

"Problematic?"

Jack lifted his robes, showing her his ankles. The ancient words wrapped around them weren't the same black marks she'd become accustomed to—perhaps even grown fond of. Jack's had an almost arctic hue, blending with his skin. She quirked a brow when she found newer words beneath. The trader's tongue.

Upon closer inspection, she found the entire spell slightly raised. She'd seen something similar before, but never with magic imbued inside of them. And certainly never on a human. Just how many magical modifications did he have?

"They're brands," he said. Even his smirk had disappeared. "Permanent and highly effective. Mother put them on me, before I came to the east."

There was old anger in his voice, buried beneath years of carefully crafted composure. She let it be, knowing from past experience when to step away and when to draw near in their turn. But this was neither. This was simply ground Sylvie didn't dare tread. It was past her right to. They were personal affairs—ones she didn't want to get too heavily involved in.

So long as they didn't affect him too negatively, then she'd let them pass with nothing more than a nod of her head.

Jack dropped his robes. And she knew then that she'd made the right decision. Because the moment of almost tangible tension passed, as if it had never been there to begin with, and then he was smirking again. That unbelievably infuriating smirk from the Zexin abyss. It felt like an age had passed since she'd gotten a proper look at it. Since she'd seen it grace his lips so often.

And suddenly, she felt tired. So very tired. It washed over her. Addled her mind and staggered everything else. But the time for sleep had passed. They needed to leave. They had things to do. Places to be. The world wouldn't stop for them and the sun certainly wouldn't cease its ascent. Time trudged onward, despite their dispositions. Always slipping past, unnoticed by the rest of the world. It would escape them, too, if they weren't careful.

With impeccable timing, they heard a knock on the door.

Three loud rasps in rapid succession. Cheryll was there.

It was time to go.

"Are you ready?" Jack asked, holding out a hand. "Not that you have a choice."

Sylvie brushed it away.

"It's my life," she said decisively, sidestepping him. "I'll do it with my own power. If I accepted help from others, it wouldn't matter, right?"

His smirk widened then, becoming a full-blown grin that she would've missed had she not lurched to a halt as it happened. It was an enthralling sight to behold—Jack's features morphing into one she'd never seen before. Cheryll was right. His mouth was an expressive little thing. Jack was impressed and satisfied and entirely too smug than any one person should've been allowed to be with themselves. It was as if he'd accomplished a great feat. Or fulfilled a personal goal. Perhaps he had. His expression said he did. While his tongue said nothing.

Jack opted for pushing her out of the door instead. Out of the cottage. Out of her previous life.

And into the world that awaited them.

It was a bright, terrifying place. Sylvie flinched, unused to the sun's intensity. The Heartstone, however, shined vivaciously in its light.

Cheryll watched them, her eyes impatient and wearier than they remembered. It was clear that she hadn't slept either. They could only guess the sort of things that kept her up at night. A small, winged creature was wrapped around Cheryll's arm, its tail extended down toward her legs. A reptile equal parts graceful and never before seen. It looked like a creature from stories and song. But the blue veins around its body told them otherwise.

"My personal Peose," Cheryll said affectionately. "He'll fly you down."

They should feel honored, Sylvie supposed, as she touched the creature's great wings. A chimera. Crafted from a bearded lizard, an eagle, and an animal she didn't know. Just another product of research. The Diamond Alps was a frightening place, indeed. But it wasn't enough to deter her.

Not yet.

No more words passed between them. Cheryll's eyes lost some of their edge, encouragement taking its place. As she allowed them another moment, tilting her head obligingly to the view at their backs in a silent, but clear gesture. One last look at what they were about to leave behind.

But they shook their heads in a joint, seemingly planned motion. Together, they turned toward the stretch of land beyond the Eirinne Mountains, quietly regarding the weight of the job thrust upon them. Despite their joyful reminiscence, despite their amicable conversation, only one thing remained in their hearts, scarring their memories of this place. As it always would.

Because there would always be reasons to laugh. That was simple. The rest wasn't so easily dismissed. Death wasn't easily forgiven. Grudges weren't easily forgotten.

This was Ferus Terria.

There were no judges here, only the wicked.

And they were furious.

Acknowledgements

This novel owes its creation to a number of helpful and incredibly patient associates, who have put their life-blood into formatting this once awful mess because heaven knows I had no idea what I was doing.

First and foremost, my brother, Gabriel, the greatest source of my procrastination. Thank you for listening to all of my nonsense. To Bunny, who I promised to include here on a whim for keeping me occupied during endless nights of sleeplessness and for being a wonderfully, perfect food buddy. Double yay for always playing along with my impulses.

To my artist, Fabian, for bringing my awfully drawn ideas to life. I lucked out finding you. Here's to both our dreams coming true. Finally, to Helen, who I've only known by another name. I raise my glass to you and your stories. They inspired me to write, and for that, I'm eternally grateful. May they continue to urge aspiring authors to do the same.

The magical land of Ferus Terria has many influences, some not as alive as the rest, but still geniuses in their own inanimate right. Recognition of all seems impossible, else I'll even be thanking the creator of that one tune I mistakenly kept on repeat during the composition of the final chapters of this novel. There's always too much thanks to give and never enough words to do so. Just know that I adore you all, and I appreciate the support.